Praise for

OUTLAW

"Sullivan has created a fine adventure-thriller hero in Monarch, who fits perfectly into the Ludlum or Vince Flynn mode. The action and the surprises are nonstop. Readers will demand the next one in the series, pronto."
—*Booklist*

"Thriller fans fond of high-stakes rescue scenarios will be more than satisfied." —*Publishers Weekly*

ROGUE

"A true juggernaut of a thriller, pure adrenaline in print. With the creation of Robin Monarch, Sullivan has crafted a Jason Bourne for the new millennium."
—James Rollins, *New York Times* bestselling author of *The Devil Colony*

"This lightning-fast read brings to mind Robert Ludlum and *Mission: Impossible*—and will definitely appeal to adrenaline junkies." —*Booklist*

"Fast-moving and well-written! *Rogue* reminded me of the Bourne books and movies, only it's much, much better." —James Patterson

"A loud, brawny festival of action."
—*Publishers Weekly*

OUTLAW

Mark Sullivan

St. Martin's Paperbacks

This is a work of fiction. All of the characters, organizations, and events portrayed in this novel are either products of the author's imagination or are used fictitiously.

OUTLAW

Copyright © 2013 by Mark Sullivan.
Excerpt from *Thief* copyright © 2014 by Mark Sullivan.

All rights reserved.

For information address St. Martin's Press, 175 Fifth Avenue, New York, NY 10010.

ISBN: 978-1-250-04829-5

Printed in the United States of America

St. Martin's Press hardcover edition / October 2013
St. Martin's Paperbacks edition / September 2014

St. Martin's Paperbacks are published by St. Martin's Press, 175 Fifth Avenue, New York, NY 10010.

10   9   8   7   6   5   4   3   2   1

For Joe and Josephine

PROLOGUE

A BREWING TYPHOON

IN A PRIVATE DINING room above an alley on the crowded peninsula of Kowloon, the Moon Dragon spooned rare tea leaves into a fired clay pot while using his peripheral vision to examine his visitor for any sign of worry.

"You are sure that everything has been taken care of, Mr. Farley?" he asked in English as he raised the glass kettle exactly six inches above the pot and poured boiling water into it.

A British expatriate in his mid-forties, Farley exuded a competent air when he replied, "Precisely as you requested, Mr. Long."

"I trust so," Long replied, and sat back to let the tea steep.

Long Chan-Juan was in his early fifties, and in robust health. He wore a finely tailored Hermès blue suit, starched white shirt, Parisian silk tie, hand-sewn shoes, and a rare Cartier watch, a gift from his wife. On his right hand was a gold signet ring that depicted a crescent moon and a winged lizard, an iconic representation of his name, which meant Moon Dragon in Cantonese.

The Moon Dragon fingered the ring, said, "All records of the transactions destroyed?"

"Of course, sir," Farley said. "But then again, I always work with the utmost discretion."

Long leaned forward, and with precise and graceful gestures poured the fresh brew from the clay pot into Farley's cup.

"A present for you then, Mr. Farley," the Moon Dragon said. "I just received it from the mainland. A very rare *pu'er*. One thousand dollars an ounce."

Farley looked on as Long poured a cup for himself and raised it toward the Brit. "To the future: may it be long and profitable."

The Brit bobbed his chin, raised his own cup, and said, "Very, very long and very, very profitable, Mr. Long."

The Moon Dragon smiled, sniffed, and took a sip of the tea, enjoying the pungent first pass aroma and taste. Farley took two longer sips, closed his eyes in pleasure.

Long set his cup on the table, studying his visitor again. When Farley opened his eyes, he said, "It pleases you?"

"Brilliant, sir," Farley said almost breathlessly. "That is the most exquisite tea I believe I've ever been fortunate enough to taste."

"It gets more subtle with the second and third infusions," the Moon Dragon replied. "Truly remarkable. And it's yours. The entire ounce."

Farley looked pleased, and said, "Very kind and thoughtful of you."

"The least I could do given the circumstances," said Long, bowing.

Farley drank the rest of the tea, then exclaimed, "Brilliant, Mr. Long, but I have another appointment to—"

The Brit stopped, blinked, and then coughed. He blinked again, slower this time, and the teacup slipped from his hand and fell to the bamboo floor.

Frightened now, Farley looked to the Moon Dragon, tried to speak, but couldn't. He rocked forward on his elbows, and his head swung slightly as he began to fight for air.

"I'm sorry, Mr. Farley," Long said, rising from his chair. "There was dried poison on your cup. My friends and allies like to keep things tidy, no loose ends that might come back to haunt us."

The Moon Dragon stood there, watching the Brit, fascinated by the spasms and tics the poison was causing. "You were a competent errand boy. You simply knew too much and would suspect our involvement in the events of the coming days. You should have foreseen that we could not chance your betrayal. I'm sure you understand now."

Farley's eyes rolled up in his head and he attempted to swallow his tongue before crashing to the floor beside his teacup.

"A few more moments," Long said to Farley as he quivered in the throes of death. "Then you meet your ancestors. May you embrace them with great joy."

He went to an intercom on the wall and pushed a button. Moments later, a Mongolian man who was almost as wide as he was tall entered the room, said, "Yes, Moon Dragon?"

Long said, "Strip him, Tuul. Take him toward Macau tonight, weight, and dump him. The sea and the sharks will do the rest."

NIGHT AND CLOUDS TOOK jagged bites of the fiery horizon until there was only blackness beyond the aluminum halo cast by the *Niamey,* a 380-foot custom oil tanker cruising at six knots in the deep, deserted waters of the South China Sea, bound for the Dung Quat refinery on the Vietnamese coast north of Ho Chi Minh City.

On a balcony below the tanker's bridge, Agnes Lawton stood at the railing feeling the wind and the storm coming amid sweltering heat. She had just watched the end of day near the equator, hoping to see the legendary green flash said to appear at the moment where day meets night in the tropics. She had hoped the flash would be a positive omen, but she had not seen it, and she wondered what would become of her.

In her late fifties, attractive, a sharp intellect, a commanding personality, Agnes Lawton nevertheless feared that her current task might exceed her capacities. She hung her head and began to pray. Before she could finish her prayer, however, she heard the bulkhead door creak, and then a male voice said, "The others have asked that we adjourn for the evening."

Turning to face her assistant, she said, "The election is in nine days. Tell them to come out on deck, get some air, and we'll go at it again."

"They're exhausted," Reynolds protested. "You're exhausted. Sleep does wonders for people's dispositions."

Agnes Lawton thought to argue, but then ceded the point. "I'd at least like a word with them before we retire."

Fifteen minutes later, belowdeck, she paused in her impromptu speech, gathering her thoughts, her attention roaming over the worn faces of the two men, a Chinese and an Indian, who sat across from her looking as if they each carried an enormous weight.

"Both of you know that your countries seem to be at risk as much as mine," Agnes Lawton went on. "We can't lose sight of that fact."

Both men nodded gravely, rose, and reached out to shake her hand, and then they left with aides trailing them out the door.

Gathering up her papers, she glanced at her assistant, who smiled and clapped silently. "Just the right tone, I think," he said.

"I hope so. If these things came to pass . . . well, I can't even imagine what the world would look like."

Her aide bowed his head slightly. "Shall I have a snack delivered to your cabin?"

"I'm not hungry," she said, snapping shut her brief-case and going out into the narrow hallway. Two men in plainclothes carrying Heckler & Koch submachine guns guarded a hatchway door at the far end. The taller of the men opened the hatch.

Before Agnes Lawton stepped inside, she said, "Wake me at five, Steve."

"Yes, ma'am," the taller guard said. "Sleep well."

She watched him shut the door after her. Then she threw the lock, undressed, and lay on the bunk in the darkness. She had heard a storm might be brewing and as she fell into sleep Agnes Lawton asked God for a peaceful night.

Three decks above Agnes Lawton's stateroom, inside the oil tanker's bridge, Jim O'Hara, the captain, was working at a computer, plotting his course. Suddenly, horrible, off-key singing came over the shortwave radio bolted to the ceiling above the helmsman.

O'Hara cringed at the voice, screeching like a wounded cat with no hint of melody, and in a language he did not recognize. The singer sawed on a few more bars until the irritated captain walked over, reached up, and twisted down the volume. He glanced at the man at the helm.

"You understand any of that, Manu?" he asked. "You're from these parts, right?"

The helmsman nodded, "He sings in Indonesian, Captain. He's saying all Malays like to have sex with dogs. Giving and receiving."

"Sounds like a hit to me," chuckled a deep male voice behind O'Hara.

The captain looked over at a beefy American carrying a pistol in an exposed shoulder holster. Beside him was a considerably smaller Chinese man carrying a shotgun, and an Indian who had a pistol in a side holster and looked ready to doze.

"You can go below and sleep," Captain O'Hara said to the Indian. "Supposed to get weather later, but we're right on course." He glanced at the radar screen beside the helmsman. "Nearest vessel is two miles away. Looks like a fishing boat."

The American nodded and said, "Go ahead. I'll take first . . ."

His voice trailed off as he caught a shadow becoming movement out the window. And then, floating out of the night into the aluminum glow, four men appeared dangling from parachutes. They wore black head to toe, and utility vests adorned with grenades, knives, and spare clips. AK-47s dangled at their waists, held level by three-point slings.

"We got company," the American yelled, going for his gun.

The captain snatched up the shortwave microphone. He turned up the sound on the receiver. The man was still screeching his obscene songs.

The captain triggered the mic, and tried to shout over him, "Mayday! Mayday! This is the *Niamey*. Position . . ."

O'Hara glanced at the GPS readout over the helm. But before he could spit out the longitude and latitude coordinates, the helmsman dove for the floor behind the American, the Chinese, and the Indian, who were heading toward the door, shouting into their own radios, demanding reinforcements topside.

A fifth attacker floated by the bridge at less than ten feet. He had the butt of a Kalashnikov rifle slammed into his hip and sprayed bullets at them. The American was hit in the back. So were the Chinese and Indian. The captain grabbed for the shotgun, intending to provide cover for the men coming from below.

O'Hara never had the chance.

He heard an explosion and then nothing ever again.

The helmsman lowered the pistol he'd taken from the body of the dead American. He dug in his pocket for his own radio and said in dialect, "Tell him to stop singing. Bridge is clear. Deck controlled. I'm disabling SHIPLOC."

Agnes Lawton heard the rattle of gunfire even though her room was two decks below the bridge. She'd been drowsily preparing to sleep, but now, wide awake, she threw on a jogging suit.

A sharp rap came at the door followed by a guard, saying, "Mrs. Lawton?"

She opened the door. The guard said, "We're under attack."

Agnes Lawton's hand went to her throat. "By who?"

"Unclear. They have forces aboard. Parachuted in. They've jammed our communications. We've lost some people topside, but are moving reinforcements into position."

"Have you—?"

Shooting from a deck above cut her off.

Going stony, the guard said, "Do not under any circumstance open this door to anyone but me."

He yanked the hatch door shut before she could reply, leaving her to fight a sense of growing terror. She cursed the insane secrecy surrounding her mission and her decision not to bring a satellite phone with her.

Throwing the deadbolt on the hatch door, Agnes Lawton looked to her laptop, open and glowing on the bunk. She tried to call up the Internet, but got no connection. She stared at the wireless icon. It had shown strong reception not ten minutes—

An explosion roared in the hallway on the other side of the stateroom door. If Lawton had not been seated, she would have been thrown off her feet. The force of it pulsed through the door, leaving her shaken and disoriented.

How was this possible? No one knew she was there. Well, a handful of people, but they were more invested in this meeting than she was, or the Chinese, or the Indian.

The hallway went silent, revealing the ringing in her ears. A man's voice barked orders in an unknown language. If this man was calling the shots, then her bodyguards were—

She looked around wildly, spotting the fire extinguisher and a small ax in a compartment recessed into the near wall. A key slid into the door lock.

She grabbed the ax, lifted it, and then drove the blade into her computer again and again, splintering the case, the screen, and the hard drive.

Behind her, a man's gravelly voice said in thick English, "Drop it."

She froze, clutching the ax as if it were a very unstable ladder.

"Drop it, or I shoot you, make mess," he commanded, in a strange accent.

Agnes Lawton set the ax on the bed amid the destruction of her computer. No matter what calamity she had faced in her long and remarkable life, she'd never given up. Not once. And she wasn't about to start. She threw back her shoulders, and turned to face her captor.

Wearing a hood, he was sweating and breathing hard as he glared at her over the barrel of a shouldered machine gun. He wore green cotton pants, black high-top sneakers, and a sleeveless shirt. He had ropey, hard muscles, tribal tattoos, and deep reddish brown skin, as if stained by the juice of darker berries.

But it was his eyes that held most of Agnes Lawton's attention. Wide, glassy, fervent, and quivering, they were dominated by irises as black as night. Whatever his cause, he was a fanatic. She knew it in an instant and almost showed fear.

"Turn around," he snarled. "Hands behind."

He took a step toward her.

Agnes Lawton glared right back at the gunman. "Do you know who I am? Do you know what a nightmare you're about bring down around you?"

He was blindingly fast, sweeping the butt of the gun down, forward, and up so quickly she had no time to react. The gunstock caught her flush under the chin and drove her back and onto the floor.

Dazed, Agnes Lawton felt him grab her arms and haul her to her feet.

He spun her around and cinched her wrists behind her back.

"Don't you know who I am?" she protested.

He hauled her to her feet saying, "We know you. You in prophecy, yes?"

Then he reached in his pocket and pulled out a matchbook. He tossed it in the corner, and lifted the hood with his thumb, exposing a bearded chin. He spit out something ghastly red. It flew through the air and splatted against the wall.

PART I

A THIEF, A SCOUNDREL,
A PROPHET, AND A KING

1

THE PILOT OF MARINE One curled the helicopter around the Washington Monument and hovered to a soft landing on the south lawn of the White House.

Inside the blue and gold chopper, a big athletic man with smooth features yawned and unbuckled his seat belt. In the navy blue suit, starched white shirt, and silver tie, he could have been anyone from a visiting foreign dignitary to a favored political donor.

"Are you ready?" asked Dr. Willis Hopkins, a shorter, older man wearing black-framed glasses and a tweed jacket that made him look more like a math professor than the current director of the Central Intelligence Agency.

"As ready as you can be for this sort of thing," the bigger man replied. The side door opened and the staircase lowered. He followed Dr. Hopkins off the helicopter.

By all rights, he should have been exhausted; in the previous seven hours, he'd traveled by F-16 from his home in Patagonia to Andrews Air Force Base in Maryland. But the fifteen-minute ride in Marine One had left him feeling completely awake, as if he were hyper-caffeinated. He'd rarely felt this alert before. Then again, he'd never received a personal summons from the President of the United States before.

Two armed U.S. Marines stood at the base of the staircase as he exited into a crisp fall night, feeling and hearing the blades slowing above him. Waiting on the lawn was a blonde in a dark-blue business suit, pearl necklace, and black pumps. She looked harried and her breath smelled of mint trying to mask cigarette smoke.

"Well done, Dr. Hopkins," she said. "The President's very pleased you could find and get him here on such short notice."

"The least I could do, given the circumstances, Cynthia," Dr. Hopkins said.

She turned to the other man, regarding him with great curiosity, as if studying some exotic specimen. He could almost hear her thinking: late thirties, six-two, two-ten, olive patina to his skin, a face that seemed drawn from many races and ethnicities, a man who could blend in almost anywhere.

"The infamous Robin Monarch," she said.

Dr. Hopkins pushed his glasses up the bridge of his nose, saying, "Robin, meet Cynthia Blayless, White House chief of staff."

She reached out. Monarch shook her hand, found it

clammy, but said, "A great pleasure, Ms. Blayless. Dr. Hopkins said you needed some help."

"We do," she said, gesturing toward the White House. "Several people are waiting for you inside. They'll explain."

As they walked toward the Rose Garden, Blayless said, "Your reputation precedes you, Mr. Monarch. Your resolution of the Green Fields affair last year was quite impressive."

"I had a lot of help. Look, Ms. Blayless, I'm honored, but I don't work for the agency anymore. I have no real obligation to—"

"The President knows all that. We all know that," Blayless said impatiently. "And we're glad you've at least come to hear our proposal. I think you'll find it quite rewarding."

Monarch was torn. Over the past four years he'd become profoundly distrustful of government officials, any government official, and he tried to avoid them at all costs. For the past nine months, he'd been living a solitary life on a remote estancia in Patagonia. He had intended to stay there indefinitely until Dr. Hopkins called him.

Two armed Marines stood at the far end of the colonnade in front of a pair of French doors. Blayless opened them and stepped inside.

Monarch was rarely intimidated, but he felt off balance stepping into the Oval Office. At a sweeping glance, he realized the President was not in the room. But he recognized the four people gathered under the watchful gaze of Abraham Lincoln, whose portrait hung over the fireplace.

The long, wiry man with the enormous head standing behind the sofa was Kenneth Vaught, the current Vice President, and the nominee of his party in the upcoming general election. On the sofa in front of Vaught perched Elise Peck, the national security advisor, a fair-skinned redhead with a dancer's posture.

Across the coffee table from Peck, Richard "Ricky" Jameson, the florid-faced Louisiana-born secretary of Homeland Security, tapped a packet of Equal into a teacup. Beside Jameson, Admiral Philip Shipman, current chairman of the Joint Chiefs of Staff, studied the contents of an open manila file.

By the time Monarch had taken two steps, these four were scrutinizing him with sober, calculating expressions that made him want to crack a joke of some sort. He resisted the temptation.

"This is Robin Monarch," Chief of Staff Blayless said. "Dr. Hopkins and the President thought it a good idea for him to be present at this meeting."

"What's this all about?" demanded National Security Advisor Peck. "Who is he?"

Blayless and Hopkins hesitated.

Monarch cleared his throat and said, "I'm a thief."

2

THE FOUR REACTED WITH expressions that ranged from indignation to outrage.

"A thief?" said Admiral Shipman, looking at Monarch closely now.

"And a scoundrel, and excellent at both, I understand," interrupted the unmistakable tenor voice of President Robert Sand.

President Sand was exiting his private office to Monarch's left. A short, but highly photogenic man with bouncy dark hair, Sand wore a windbreaker with the presidential seal, exercise pants, and running shoes. He strode across the room, reached for Monarch's hand, and said, "Thank you for coming, Robin. I know it was a long trip on short notice."

Monarch shook the President's hand. He'd seen Sand thousands of times on television over the almost eight years Sand had been in office, but only now, in person, did Monarch see the complete fatigue in the President's eyes, sense the great burdens he'd carried and more than a tinge of regret.

Sand was from Oklahoma, a reformer who had not managed to change much in his eight years in his office. Here it was, the beginning of the President's final days of his second term, the lamest of lame ducks, a leader who could already feel the reins of power slipping from his hands.

Sand's administration had been consumed by two wars and a struggling economy. In Monarch's opinion, the President had never really had the chance to fulfill his promise to voters to work for the good of the country rather than—

A second man exited the President's private office. In his late fifties, and looking grave and shaken, he wore khakis, a navy sweater, and an open-collar white shirt. Monarch had no idea who he was, but the rest of the room sure did.

"Bill?" said National Security Advisor Peck, puzzled.

Vice President Vaught's response was harsher. "What are you doing here?" he demanded, looking to the President. "Are you kidding? What is this?"

Sand cut him off, said, "You'll understand in a minute, Ken." He looked back to Monarch, and said, "Our nation has lost something of utmost value, Robin, and I need you to retrieve it for us."

"Okay," Monarch said, taking in the surprise on the faces of everyone but Bill, whoever he was. "What did you lose and where did you lose it?"

The President hesitated and glanced at Chief of Staff Blayless, who said, "Perhaps we'd better do this in the Situation Room."

Sand nodded.

But Homeland Security director Jameson grimaced and glanced at his watch, "Mr. President, I've got a meeting with the transition teams in five hours and I haven't had a wink of sleep."

"Then get someone else to attend the meeting, Ricky Lee," Sand said, moving toward the door.

"Wait!" Vice President Vaught shouted, and gestured toward the man Monarch didn't recognize. "You're taking someone from the other side to the Situation Room?"

The stranger glared at Vaught, said, "My role in Senator Burkhardt's campaign officially ended an hour ago."

"You were fired?"

"I resigned."

"So everybody downstairs," the President said.

Five minutes later, the same group gathered around the conference table in the White House Situation Room. At Sand's insistence, Bill sat to the President's left, and Monarch to his right while enduring the hostile glances of everyone present except Dr. Hopkins. The CIA director stood next to a large screen at the opposite end of the room. A still photograph of an oil tanker appeared on the screen.

"This is the *Niamey*," the CIA director began. "She's a U.S.-owned, Liberian-registered custom tanker carrying two hundred thousand barrels of light crude from drilling platforms off southern Indonesia to the oil refinery at Dung Quat, north of Ho Chi Minh City."

The screen shifted to a satellite image of a gigantic tropical storm. "This typhoon is now covering the area where the tanker was last heard from, approximately three hundred and thirty miles southeast of Vietnam, inside a vast stretch of the South China Sea, and bound by Thailand, Malaysia, Borneo, Singapore, and Sumatra."

"Big-time pirate waters," Monarch said.

The CIA director coughed, said, "Yes, well. A little over twenty-three hours ago, the tanker's SHIPLOC GPS tracking signal stopped broadcasting. Several moments before that happened, the *Niamey*'s captain sent this shortwave transmission."

The Situation Room filled with a screeching song in Indonesian, and barely audible over it the harried voice of Captain O'Hara crying: "*Mayday. Mayday. This is the* Niamey. *We are—*"

The rattle of automatic gunfire cut the captain off in a cry of agony that bowed Monarch's head.

"We've got the ship's last-known coordinates according to SHIPLOC, just before that typhoon hit," Dr. Hopkins said. "We lost satellite imagery at almost the same time."

"How long ago was that?" Monarch asked.

"Twelve hours ago. It's a huge, slow-moving storm."

Monarch looked at Sand. "Let me get this straight, Mr. President. You want me to what, find this tanker and steal it back?"

"Sort of," Sand said.

Monarch gestured toward the screen. "With all due respect, sir, whoever seized the ship has probably pumped off the oil and is scuttling her in deep water by now. Even with a typhoon raging."

"He's right," National Security Advisor Peck said. "This sort of thing happens all the time. Why are *we* interested, Mr. President?"

Sand looked irritated and snapped, "We're interested because of the people who were aboard that tanker when it was attacked and seized."

Homeland Security secretary Jameson and Vice President Vaught sat forward in their chairs, studying Sand until the President answered the unasked question: "Lin Hao Fung, the foreign minister of the People's Republic of China."

"Fung?" the national security advisor cried, bewildered.

"And Tarrant Wali, India's foreign minister," Dr. Hopkins added.

The President cleared his throat. "And Secretary of State Agnes Lawton."

3

A LOUD NOISE AND a lurching sensation helped Agnes Lawton to slowly regain consciousness. The U.S. Secretary of State was aware first of the smell of brine and feces. Then she felt the oppressive heat and humidity, and that she was lying on something very hard and damp. Soon she keyed in on the sound of water lapping against wood and the whine of mosquitoes.

Secretary Lawton's head ached. Realizing that she was gagged and blindfolded, and that her wrists were bound in front of her, she vaguely recalled that the hijackers had injected her with something. The last thing she clearly remembered was seeing her guards dead in the passage before it all had gone black and blank.

How long ago was that? A day? Two? What about Josh Reynolds? Was her aide dead? Or was he here with her? And where were Fung and Wadi?

She moved her leg. She felt something heavy around

her right ankle, and a general sogginess around her hips—someone had put her in a diaper. She was instantly fully alert and furious. How dare they, whoever they were! How dare they!

Secretary Lawton fought for control, trying to convince herself that her moment-to-moment comfort was unimportant. Surviving was what mattered. Seeing her husband and the children and the grandchildren again was what mattered. Bringing the men who'd kidnapped her to justice was all that mattered.

No sooner had she had that thought than she heard the scuffing of shoes coming closer, and closer. He stopped right next to her, stinking of sweat and something ranker. He untied her gag and her blindfold. Agnes Lawton worked her jaw and blinked blurrily, remembering that she was wearing contact lenses and had no idea how long they had been in. They were good for a week, weren't they?

Secretary Lawton blinked again and her vision partially cleared. The light was dim and she was belowdeck in some kind of boat. Crouching over her, holding a plastic jug was the same man who'd dragged her from her cabin. He was still wearing his hood, but the tribal tattoos around his biceps were unmistakable.

"Water?" he asked.

She shook her head, said, "I wish to use the toilet. I will not lie here in a diaper."

Inside the hood, she saw his eyes narrow to slits, but then he gestured with his chin toward a bucket a few feet from her. "Go ahead. Take off."

Seeing he meant to humiliate her, she said, "When you're gone."

His eyes widened angrily. "You have other things you do now. Drink water. Get strength. You need it."

The secretary felt soaked to the skin from the heat and the humidity and realized he was right. She was going to need all the water she could get. She took the bottle in her bound hands, and looked dubiously into the neck.

"Boil," he grunted.

Secretary Lawton hesitated, but then drank greedily. At that moment she'd never tasted anything so good in her life.

When she was done, she set the jug down and asked, "Who are you?"

"Captain Ramelan," he replied, flashing his eyes. "Ramelan means 'one who is prophesized.' The wife of serpent on moon say I am prophecy."

Secretary Lawton stared at him, sensing that same fanatical air about him she remembered from the *Niamey*. Get him talking, she thought. The more she knew, the better. "What do you believe you are prophesized to do, Captain Ramelan?"

He lifted the bottom of his hood, revealing teeth stained blood red, and spit again. "Change world."

Before she could ask how, he gagged her again. She struggled. He put a knee into her back and tied the blindfold on. But then he undid the leg iron around her ankle, and pulled her harshly to her feet. The Secretary of State felt wobbly and weak, but managed to stand upright, gasping, wanting to know where she was going, and why.

Holding her by the nape of her jogging suit jacket,

Ramelan maneuvered Agnes Lawton forward and kept her on her feet when she stumbled against ribs in the boat's hull. Then she felt herself lifted by many hands, and immediately saw light behind her blindfold, felt an ocean breeze and heard the cawing of birds. The air smelled of wood smoke and frying fish. She realized she was ravenously hungry just before she was jerked along and down a ramp of some kind.

The secretary hit ground, felt dizzy, and almost slipped because it was slick. Hands dragged her on and through the blindfold she saw the light wane. The wood smoke was gone, replaced by moldering vegetation, jungle, and mud. Vines tore at her hands and face. Ooze sucked at her jogging shoes. And everywhere she heard a symphony of birds crying and singing, monkey's howling, and insects whining. They stopped. A creaking noise. She was pushed forward into near darkness and thicker heat. Hands grabbed her shoulders, turned her, and pressed her down.

"Sit," Ramelan commanded.

Secretary Lawton sat down on a crude chair. The blindfold came off, but the gag stayed knotted in her mouth. Facing her was a simple cell phone mounted on a tripod and connected to a laptop computer. A barechested man in a white hood stood behind it.

Agnes Lawton turned her head left and right, and saw the Chinese and Indian foreign ministers sitting to either side of her, wrists bound, gags intact. Both men were filthy. Wadi had a nasty gash above his left eye. Fung looked dazed, as if he still did not believe their predicament. How bad did she look?

A hand came over her shoulder holding a newspaper. "Hold," Ramelan ordered.

The Secretary of State hesitated, but then realized that fighting right now was useless. She took the newspaper with the fingers of her bound hands. Her captor said something in a language she didn't recognize. The hooded man behind the camera, turned on a brilliant light, and aimed it at them.

Secretary Lawton refused to cower from the light. She knew what Ramelan was up to and she decided to take advantage of it. She stared at the camera, knowing that she was being filmed and praying to God that she appeared strong and defiant.

But then behind her, Captain Ramelan began to speak harshly in English, and the fiery resolve she felt inside was replaced by the first inklings of terror.

4

"AGNES?" VICE PRESIDENT VAUGHT said, stunned, looking over at Bill, who had that thousand-yard stare. "My God, man, I'm sorry. I never—"

"Wait, that's not possible," National Security Advisor Peck complained to Bill. "She's in Tahiti, taking R and R before she starts her round of farewell visits."

Bill shook his head, looking completely lost. Monarch put it together then, recognizing him from an article on Washington, D.C., power couples he'd seen in *Time* magazine. Bill Lawton was the Secretary of State's husband, a high-dollar lobbyist and lawyer, who appeared on CNN commenting on politics from time to time. The Lawtons were like James Carville and Mary Matalan, from opposite ends of the political spectrum, but madly in love and devoted to each other.

President Sand went grave, said, "Tahiti was a cover story. Agnes requested the secret meeting months ago.

She thought it important that she have frank, off-the-record discussions with the Chinese and the Indians in advance of our elections. They have become our two biggest trading partners after all, and geopolitical power-houses, and she wanted to reassure them about conti-nuity in U.S. trade and foreign policy regardless of how the election turns out."

Before anyone could comment on that, Sand went on, "But as we got closer to the meeting, the agenda changed drastically. Willis?"

The CIA director adjusted his glasses and said, "For the past seven weeks, we—the NSA and my agency—have been picking up background chatter that sug-gested threats to—"

"Threats? Wait," National Security Advisor Peck said. "I heard nothing about—"

"Hear the man out, Elise," the President ordered.

Peck stiffened, but nodded.

Dr. Hopkins said, "The raw intelligence we first picked up indicated a coup plot unfolding in India. We informed their government, only to discover that India's intelligence network had uncovered evidence of a pos-sible rebellion in the Chinese provinces along China's southwestern border with India. Then the Chinese in-formed us that they were picking up the possibility that a group might attempt to disrupt the election."

"What election?" Vice President Vaught demanded.

"Our election," President Sand said.

"And you didn't think to tell me?"

Sand shot back, "You're not president yet, Ken. And

according to the polling numbers you still might not be after the vote. So, no, we didn't think to tell you."

Vaught hardened. "Don't you think *your* numbers have something to do with that? They're eating me alive out there, calling me 'More of you.'"

"My deepest apologies," the President said wryly.

Looking confused, Lawton said, "What exactly was the threat to the election? Didn't you think to have Senator Burkhardt briefed?"

"We didn't brief the senator for the same reason we didn't inform the Vice President: The intelligence was unclear," Dr. Hopkins replied firmly. "Some of it suggested that a terrorist group might try to disrupt the vote through some kind of attack. But perhaps more important, because the time frame on all three fronts— the U.S., China, and India—was similar, it felt, well, coordinated."

The Vice President said, "What are you suggesting, that there's some plot out there to take over the world?"

"How about a plot to radically upset the world?" Dr. Hopkins retorted. "Think about it: If you destabilized three of the world's superpowers, you've made the planet more dangerous, more susceptible to upheaval of every kind."

"What makes you think the three are connected?" Monarch asked.

"The coup, the rebellion, and the disruption of our election were to take place within days of each other, all before the end of this month, with our election coming first. Armed with that information, Agnes felt it was imperative and urgent that she meet with the Indians and the Chinese to discuss these matters."

"I agreed," the President said. "And so did the Indians and the Chinese."

The CIA director said, "The day before yesterday a helicopter dropped Agnes on that ship along with six bodyguards, all veteran Diplomatic Security Service agents. The Chinese and the Indians came with similar bodyguards."

"Must have been a big force that attacked them," Admiral Shipman said.

Monarch agreed, said, "Was there a real-time satellite watch on the ship?"

The President hesitated, and then said, "No."

"Why not?" Admiral Shipman demanded. "That should have been protocol."

"It *is* protocol," Sand replied. "Agnes and I and the Chinese and the Indians decided to waive the protocol in order not to draw undue attention."

Bill Lawton had been slowly steaming, and now he barked, "With all due respect, Mr. President, waiving the protocol has put my wife in jeopardy. I hold *you* responsible."

The President looked as if he'd been punched in the gut. "I hold myself responsible, but I promise you, Bill, we'll get her." He turned, ashen-faced, and looked at Monarch, said, "Which is where you come in, Robin."

"A thief?" Admiral Shipman grumbled in disbelief. "You're going to give the job of finding and rescuing the Secretary of State to a criminal?"

"He's not a criminal," Dr. Hopkins said. "He's more like an outlaw, but for the greater good."

Monarch almost smiled. He kind of liked the sound of that.

Vice President Vaught snarled, "Jesus H. Christ, whatever you call him, it's—"

Admiral Shipman cut him off, "Mr. President, we can have SEAL Team Six on the ground in twenty hours. You want pros in there, not some hack."

"I agree," said the Secretary of State's husband.

"Monarch did eight years with a Joint Special Operations Command unit of elite forces, including SEALs," Dr. Hopkins shot back. "He spent seven years running an elite SOG team for us at the CIA. For God's sake, who do you think stole the Iraqi War plan before we invaded? Who do you think destroyed the Green Fields device?"

Monarch was not particularly proud of either of those feats, but it was interesting to see the President's inner circle reappraising him.

"Which is why I brought Mr. Monarch in. This situation has to be handled quietly and delicately," Sand said.

"You're damn straight it does," said Vice President Vaught. "This gets out, the election *will be* disrupted and my campaign *will be* done!"

"Nice of you to think about Agnes first, Ken," the President said.

Bill Lawton turned his attention toward Monarch. "You think you can find my wife, rescue her?" He hesitated. "If she's alive?"

Monarch returned his gaze. "I can try, sir."

National Security Advisor Peck's jaw jutted forward as she looked from Monarch to the President. "If he doesn't work for us in an official capacity . . ."

President Sand caught her drift. "We're hiring him on a onetime basis."

"And we're paying him?" she asked archly.

"Yes."

"How much?" General Shipman demanded.

The President turned to me. "What's it going to take?"

Monarch thought about that, said, "You pay expenses for me and a team of my choosing, no more than four. If we find and return the secretary, the U.S. government pays one point five million dollars to each member of my team, and ten million to me. Maximum fifteen million."

The President thought about that a moment, said, "Done."

"Mr. President!" General Shipman protested.

"I said done!" Sand roared, ending discussion before turning back to Monarch. "What do you need?"

Monarch looked to Dr. Hopkins. "Start positioning and training satellites on the entire South China Sea. We've got to find that tanker as soon as the typhoon moves on. Have someone analyze tide charts and the tanker's specs and create the limits of the search area, one based on the *Niamey* still running her engines, and another with her set adrift. And I'll need Gloria Barnett in theater, ASAP. Tatupu, Chavez, and Fowler to follow."

Barnett had been Monarch's operations "runner" at the CIA. She was a genius at logistics, procurement, and raw intelligence analysis. John Tatupu had served in the U.S. Army Rangers with Monarch and on his team at the CIA. Chanel Chavez was the best sniper he knew. Abbott Fowler had been with Delta Force and, on an ad hoc basis, the CIA.

"That all?" the President asked.

"I also need the fastest jet you've got," Monarch replied.

"There's an F-22 at Langley air base," the CIA director said. "I'll arrange to have it fly you to Clark in the Philippines. Barnett will organize any other transport you might need over there."

Monarch looked to the chairman of the Joint Chiefs of Staff who had not stopped scowling. "Admiral, I could use your support as well."

Displeased, Admiral Shipman nevertheless said, "In what way?"

"Move two full SEAL teams to the region," Monarch said. "If we find Secretary Lawton, we'll need them sooner than later."

Shipman softened somewhat. "I can arrange that."

"We're done then?" the President asked, looking to his chief of staff.

"Yes, Mr. President," said Cynthia Blayless, who'd been largely quiet during the entire briefing. "I'll have a draft of our agreement with Mr. Monarch in ten minutes for your signature."

"Just one more thing, sir," Dr. Hopkins said. "The Chinese and the Indians have each requested that one of their top agents be allowed to help in whatever efforts we may mount to rescue Secretary Lawton and the others."

Monarch shook his head. "I work alone or with hand-chosen people."

"The Chinese and the Indians are fully cooperating with us," Dr. Hopkins said. "They know we're better equipped to mount a rescue, but they've made the demand to save face, or at least sharing face if that makes sense."

Monarch made to protest, but the President cut him off saying, "How important is the money to you?"

Monarch hesitated, and then said, "Very."

"Then you'll take the Chinese and Indian agents."

Monarch saw the futility in arguing further, and nodded.

"Mr. Monarch," said Bill Lawton, who looked like a man clinging to his last bit of hope. "Please find my wife. She's a wonderful person, the love of my . . ."

The Secretary of State's husband choked and could not go on.

5

ABOUT TWENTY MINUTES AFTER Monarch boarded Marine One and flew off toward Langley Air Force Base, a black Buick town car exited the White House grounds through the southwest entrance. The car rolled purposefully through the nearly deserted predawn streets of the nation's capital, crossing the Roosevelt Bridge into Arlington, Virginia.

The Buick went east and then south before driving into Prince William Forest Park, close to where the park abuts the Marine Corps training base at Quantico. At the top of a deserted rise in the road immediately north of the base, the car pulled over and dimmed the headlights. The driver let the tires roll until the front fender of the Buick reached a specific mile marker and turned into an old bridle path just beyond.

The driver lit a cigarette. There were enough trees behind the car to completely shield it from view. Ahead through the forest a mile or so stood a jungle of satellite dishes, the ultra-secure communications hub for the Marine base and FBI academy. There were so many radio waves pulsing in the area that it was a notorious dead zone for cellular traffic. Even the listeners at the National Security Agency would get nothing here.

The driver rolled down the window, flicked out the cigarette, and then went to the glove compartment for a rarely used but very powerful satellite phone that he quickly connected to a laptop computer and used to bring up Skype.

The driver waited until the network icon blinked indicating an Internet link had been established, then punched in the number of a prepaid cell phone. It rang three times before a man said in a slight southern drawl, "How can I be of service to you?

"We have a problem," the driver replied.

"You mean a challenge, don't you?" the man countered.

"The beach man threw a wild card," the driver insisted. "He brought in a mercenary, former CIA spook and Special Forces operator. He's also a thief. Evidently a very good one. I think our friend to the east needs to know."

After several moments, the man said, "Yes. I'll call him."

"I can do it."

"Let's not overly complicate things," he replied and hung up.

6

LONG CHAN-JUAN WAS OBSESSIVE about his personal security. He knew who he was, and what he represented to scores of other power-hungry men throughout Asia. Any way he looked at it, even with the extreme measures he took, the Moon Dragon was a target.

In response, Long had equipped his house with cameras around the exterior and an ultra-sophisticated alarm system that featured motion and pressure sensors. He kept a minimum of three guards patrolling outside at all times. And just the month before, he bought a two-hundred-and-fifty-thousand-dollar, bulletproof Mercedes S-Guard sedan.

Ideally, Tuul wanted the Moon Dragon to make the transition between the Mercedes and his home through the garage. But the garage was being retrofitted as well, equipped with bombproof walls and doors. The construction forced Long to enter the house from the driveway and through the front door, where he was exposed for a time to the road. Tuul liked to use three men to search the area for snipers and such before allowing Long to exit the vehicle.

That's where the Moon Dragon was that autumn evening, in the backseat of the bulletproof Mercedes, waiting for the all clear, and listening intently to the languid voice and cadence of his anonymous friend with the southern accent.

"So y'all got a response coming," he said. "Our mutual friend thought you ought to know."

"Better to know a thief is about than not to know," the Moon Dragon said.

"That one of those Chinese sayings?" his friend asked and chuckled.

"It should be," Long said, and then sobered.

"Any case, that's what you're dealing with," his friend said. "He's supposed to be good, real good."

"Suggestions?"

"Your hemisphere, your call. Say, how's that grandson of yours?"

"Very well," the Moon Dragon said, perking up. "Yours?"

"Hell, kid's running so fast his granddad can't even think of catching him."

"The story of youth."

"Right, well, I won't keep you. You go on home and see your grandkid, and call me when you think the time is right. I'll be waiting."

The phone went dead. Long looked at it a moment, and then opened the back of the cell, pulled the chip, and then tore out the entire electronic assembly. As he did, he thought, a thief?

The Moon Dragon didn't like thieves. In his line of work, he needed them every now and then. But he'd learned the hard way that you couldn't trust them. They really had no honor. They'd turn on you if given the chance. Every time.

But what could a mere thief do to someone like me, and my allies? He almost laughed at the absurdity of the idea.

Long, however, had not gotten to his precariously high station in life by being overly confident. Thieves could be sneaky, conniving, and very resourceful. That this Robin Monarch was an experienced and innovative government operator on top of being a first-class thief gnawed at him even after Tuul came to the back passenger door of the bulletproof Mercedes and opened it.

"We're good, boss," the bodyguard said.

The Moon Dragon nodded, got out, and walked toward the front door of his grand villa high on the side of Hong Kong Island's Victoria Peak. Long opened the front door. Deep inside his house, he heard his wife, Madame Long, bark, "Anna!"

Small feet pattered. The Moon Dragon caught a glimpse of a tiny Filipina woman in a gray and white uniform dart from the kitchen toward the living room at the far end of the entry hall. Long stopped to sift through the stack of mail on a table in the hallway.

"Madame?" he heard the maid, Anna, say.

"You missed dust on the chair there, girl," Madame Long said coldly.

"I address this at once," the maid replied timidly.

"See that you do," her employer replied, and paused. "By the way, I know the law entitles you to the day off on Sundays, but I demand that you respect the curfew Mr. Long and I have set for you. You were late the other night."

"Just a few minutes past nine, Madame," Anna said.

"Twenty minutes and you were drunk and had the smell of a man on you."

The Moon Dragon frowned, set the mail down and walked down the hall until he could see into the ornate living area. His wife, tall and big boned for a Chinese woman, had pale porcelain skin from a lifetime spent hiding from the sun. Wearing embroidered slippers, black Chanel pants, a chic black housecoat, and an eight-hundred-year-old jade piece at her throat, Madame Long towered over the tiny maid, whose head was bowed.

"You think I did not have you followed?" Madame Long asked, not noticing her husband watching and seeming to enjoy her maid's discomfort. "You think I don't know you go to the Poseidon Club in Wan Chai on Sunday afternoons? And that you drink whiskey and give your body to the first man who strikes your fancy?"

Anna said nothing, but her cheeks burned with shame.

"Let that be a lesson if you wish to continue to be employed in this house."

Anna bowed, almost trembling. "Yes, Madame."

The maid backed out of the room, bowing, and then bowed even deeper when she spotted the Moon Dragon. In her early thirties, but looking old beyond her years,

Anna had large brown eyes and a cleft palate that she often hid with her left hand.

When she'd gone, Long entered the room, saying, "My mother once told me that if you treat people like dogs long enough, they bite."

Madame Long shot her husband a wicked glance, then hissed, "Public drunkenness? Random sex with strangers? I think even your mother would treat her like the disfigured dog that she is."

The Moon Dragon knew better than to take the argument with his wife much further. In the world outside their home he was the owner of several successful legitimate businesses, and the ultra-secretive leader of Shing-Tun, Hong Kong and southern China's most powerful triad, an organized crime organization with influence all over Southeast Asia. But here at home his wife had absolute control. He held his hands up in surrender.

Madame Long bowed in satisfaction, and then looked at him curiously. "Your business acquaintance the other day. Did the book get it right?"

Long bobbed his head. "Mr. Farley did indeed go on a long voyage."

Madame Long hugged herself, said, "The book rarely lies."

As he often did when mulling a decision, the Moon Dragon crossed to the drapes, opened them, and looked out. The view was panoramic and stunning.

A jungle of corporate neon signs glowed far below him in Wan Chai and Causeway Bay. Ferries, ships, and Chinese junks crisscrossed Victoria Harbor, looking like fireflies. Beyond was Kowloon, the densest population center on earth, where the city lights gathered and glittered like a massive constellation of stars.

Long had been born and raised in Kowloon, much tougher and more Chinese than Hong Kong Island, with its lingering British influence. He thought of how far he'd come, how ruthless he'd been to survive, much less prosper. But hadn't he prospered? Hadn't he become more powerful, more influential with each passing year?

But the course on which the Moon Dragon had recently embarked was on a whole different scale from anything he'd ever been involved with before. It frightened him and he was not a man easily frightened. Within days chaos would be sown throughout the world, and China's central government would be weakened, distracted, and then needy. At that point, they'd open the door wide to his plans and he'd have all the power and money he'd ever dreamed of. All of Asia would lay at his feet.

But if something went wrong . . . if this thief . . .

Looking out his window, the triad leader was no longer drawn to what was bright and neon about Hong Kong. He was staring at the inky darkness of the harbor, wondering about its depths.

Madame Long came up beside her husband. "You are troubled?"

The Moon Dragon hesitated. He rarely told his wife about his life outside their home. It was better she not know particulars. She understood he led a secretive life, probably suspected certain things, but she had no idea of its magnitude and dimensions. Madame Long also seemed to be more accurate in her predictions when he kept things vague and shadowed.

"I am entering a difficult period," he announced.

Madame Long gazed at him, touched his arm. "And you wish to know what tomorrow might hold?"

Long bowed his head, said, "I do."

His wife nodded, and walked away from the window. Long followed her into their personal quarters, past their bedroom, and into an anteroom with white walls, a pale bamboo floor, and a hexagonal window that faced east toward the dawn. The room was bare except for the shell of an ancient sea turtle suspended on its back in a cradle carved from camphor wood that sat on a pedestal dead center of the room.

Madame Long stopped before the sea turtle shell as if in the presence of some greater power. Seven centuries before, sixty-four squares had been carved into the sea turtle's under-armor. In each square there was a hexagram, a stack of six horizontal lines. Some lines were whole. Others were broken. None of the hexagrams was exactly alike.

From a silk pouch set in a carved depression dead center of the turtle's belly, Madame Long drew three gold coins. Like the turtle shell, the coins were treasured gifts from her late mother, who had received them from her great-grandmother, and so on back ten generations.

The Moon Dragon's wife cast the three coins across the turtle's belly, read the heads and tails. There were two tails and one head thrown. She assigned three points for each heads, and two points for each tails, therefore seven. Transfixed by the process now, Long used a pencil to note the number 7 on a piece of paper. His wife tossed the coins five more times. He stacked the results in ascending order first to last.

7

6

9

7

7

7

Madame Long took the pencil and paper from him, and beside each number created a line, broken if the number was odd, whole if the number was even. The six and the nine were the numbers of change, so she drew lines that were their opposite. Six turned broken and nine became whole.

— —

— —

———

— —

— —

— —

Madame Long studied the top three lines—broken, broken, whole—as if they were one unit.

"The 'Chen' trigram rules," she said with great satisfaction. "Chen reflects the arousing of great forces, like typhoons brewing."

A thrill passed through the Moon Dragon. The I Ching, or Book of Changes, was one of the oldest prophetic texts in the world. His wife was arguably one of its greatest interpreters. Madame Long had spent her entire life studying the I Ching. Her ancestors had been devotees of the text for as long as the turtle shell had been in their family.

And now she was telling him that he had done the equivalent of raising a typhoon, one of nature's most powerful forces! That was true, wasn't it? There was a terrible typhoon ripping across the South China Sea at this very moment.

Madame Long tapped her fingernail on the three bottom lines, all of which were broken. She said, " 'K'un' trigram. It mirrors the receptive forces of nature and the earth."

Long nodded, feeling grounded in his actions. "And the whole hexagram?"

On the turtle shell, Madame Long found the hexagram that combined "Chen" over "K'un." She let her fingers run over the carving as if she were reading braille.

"Hexagram sixteen," she said, smiling. " 'Yu,' enthusiasm."

"Yes?" he said, wanting her to interpret.

Madame Long said, "The I Ching says that 'enthusiasm' is the greatest force a leader can promote when faced with a monumental task."

Long blinked, trying to find direction in that pronouncement.

His wife saw his confusion, put her hand on his forearm, and beamed at him, saying, "Don't you understand your great good fortune, husband? In the words of the Book of Changes, 'Enthusiasm enables kings to set armies marching.' "

A king, he thought. Armies marching.

He smiled, thanked his wife for her remarkable gift, and then kissed her on the forehead. "Lo-lo?"

"Asleep," Madame Long replied. "He had a long day."

"I'll look in on him," the Moon Dragon said.

He wove through the villa, ignoring Hong Kong's skyline and the fine antiques, rugs, and silk wall tapestries that filled his home. A king, he was thinking. Armies marching. The I Ching does see all!

Fortified, Long slowly opened a door at the far end of the villa. Inside, on a low bed, a six-year-old boy lay asleep, sucking his thumb. The Moon Dragon's heart thawed several degrees as he watched and listened to the boy's gentle breathing. His grandson, Lo-Lo, was the future. Lo-Lo was everything.

I will be a king of men, Long thought, and someday you will be, too.

He shut the door softly, thrilled at the idea, feeling the power of twenty typhoons welling inside him. Then he remembered the thief, Robin Monarch, and understood how best to deal with him. The Moon Dragon would go to his office and act the warrior king, deceive his enemies, and launch yet another army into the war.

PART II

THE SOUTH CHINA SEA

7

MONARCH ROUSED AT THE sound of metal striking on metal. His eyes fluttered open, vaguely aware of the oxygen mask across his mouth and the flight suit, helmet, and visor he wore. He saw the glow in front of him coming from the control panel of the F-22 Stealth fighter, and heard a clank again, though this time it sounded like something metal had connected, seated, and locked.

He groggily looked up through the canopy and saw the hulking outline of an aerial tanker above them and understood. It was a long way to the Philippines even in a jet that boasts a cruising speed of eleven hundred miles an hour. For a second he wondered at the magnitude of what he had to do to earn the President's money. Even though there did not seem to be a deadline or a demand from the hijackers, he could sense that it was going to take an all-out effort to find the Secretary of State and rescue her.

Just keep focused on what the money could do, he told himself. Just remember who the money is for.

Her name was Sister Rachel Diego del Mar. A doctor and missionary, she ran an orphanage for street children outside Buenos Aires. She also ran a clinic in the Villa Miserie, the worst slum in the city, which is where she had saved Monarch's young life in so many ways.

Monarch's parents—an Argentine con-artist mother and an American cat burglar father—were murdered, gunned down by policemen after they'd swindled a distant relative of the Peron family. The Perons' brutal retaliation had left Robin an orphan at thirteen, hiding from the police and forced to scavenge in the *ano,* the garbage pit for the Village of Misery. Monarch was eventually taken in by a street gang called La Fraternidad de Ladrones, the Brotherhood of Thieves. Four years later, he was stabbed in a knife fight with the leader of the gang, and rushed to Sister Rachel's clinic with chest wounds and a collapsed lung.

Sister Rachel operated on him in the clinic, and tended to him while he recuperated. During those months, she'd turned his head around, changed him, and made him want to be something more than just a street thug. She was the one who suggested he join the U.S. military as a way to employ his unorthodox skills and to put Buenos Aires, the street gang, and the slums far behind him.

Monarch had never forgotten what Sister Rachel had done for him and what she continued to do for orphaned street children. In the past couple of years,

since he'd quit the CIA and started taking on assignments from the highest bidder, he'd started giving her
money, lots of it, enough to expand and improve housing at the orphanage and to build new classrooms. If he
found and rescued Secretary Lawton, her work would
reap the lion's share of the reward.

"Rogue?"

While serving in Special Forces, Monarch had
picked up the handle "Rogue."

"Rogue, do you copy?"

He startled awake, realizing that he'd dozed off
again, and that it wasn't the pilot's voice coming to him
over the headset he wore. It was a woman.

"Gloria?" he said.

A pause, then Gloria Barnett sighed and said, "There
you are, Robin. Sorry to disturb your beauty sleep,
but I wanted to give you a chance to wake up and orient yourself before you landed. For the record, you've
just flown 8,600 miles in less than eight hours and
you lost a day a few miles back. While you've been
sleeping, the oil tanker, the *Niamey*, was spotted run
up on shoals along the west coast of Borneo. I've
made arrangements for a helicopter to take you there.
And Dr. Hopkins just messaged me that there's been
another development. He'll brief us after you're on the
ground."

"Us?" he asked, shaking his head to clear the cob-
webs. "Where *are* you?"

"At Clark," she said. "Hopkins found me vacationing
at a spa near Chiang Mai in Thailand, and flew me over
about five hours ago."

"Sorry we had to interrupt the mud baths," Monarch said.

"I was actually having some energy work done, but it doesn't matter. See you very soon."

Before he could reply, the stealth jet began to drop through thick storm clouds over the island of Luzon. After a few minutes of turbulence, they broke through and he could make out the lights of Angeles City and then runways, several of them.

"We landing on cargo strips?" Monarch asked.

"Negative," the pilot replied. "Philippine Air Force controlled."

As they landed, Monarch looked out the canopy at what used to be Clark U.S. Air Force Base. It was now a busy international airport, free-trade zone, and home to the PAF. He was glad that the lights on the military runway dimmed almost the moment they'd slowed to a taxi. No use attracting any more attention than they had to.

They taxied into a dark hangar. The engines died. The hangar doors slid shut behind them. Lights went on. To his surprise, when the cockpit bonnet rose, Monarch smelled not spent jet fuel, but the tropics: the rain, the soil, and decaying leaves, so different from Argentina, where it had been spring, and a world away from late October in Washington, D.C.

Monarch immediately began to sweat in the flight suit, and he grimaced as he starting climbing out of the cockpit. He was fit from months spent hiking and skiing in the Andes, but his legs felt stiff from all the recent flying. He patted the pilot on his helmet as he passed, and said, "Appreciate the lift."

"What, no tip?"

"Sorry, they don't let me travel with my wallet," Monarch replied, smiling as he climbed down the ladder. Off to one side he spotted a Filipino Air Force officer watching him with open displeasure. Monarch waved. The officer did not return the gesture.

Climbing off the last rung of the ladder, he heard the click and shuffle of approaching footsteps and turned to see Gloria Barnett, a tall, thin crane of a woman, early forties, with a wild shock of red hair. Wearing a black rain slicker, she hurried toward him, lugging a canvas beach bag. A pair of reading glasses swung from a chain around her neck. As usual, she looked more like a harried librarian than the best spec ops runner he'd ever known.

Monarch hugged her as he might a dear sister, and then said, "Tats and Chavez?"

"Our sweet Samoan was getting his mother moved into an assisted living facility in San Diego, but should be on his way by now. Chavez put me off at first because her sister, Regina, just got diagnosed with breast cancer, but she caved when I explained her fee. She's catching a cargo flight to Pearl Harbor out of San Antonio."

"That sucks about Regina," Monarch said.

"It does," Barnett agreed. "She's only twenty-five. And Fowler's heading to Pearl from Anchorage."

"Anything about an Indian or Chinese agent?"

She nodded. "They're delayed by the storm a couple of hours." She glanced toward the Filipino officer, and then murmured: "Hopkins wants to talk to us in private."

The Filipino seemed to know Barnett was talking about him and scowled even deeper. Barnett turned and walked back the way she'd come with Monarch following and muttering, "What's with him?"

"General Garcia is ticked off because we've been making all sorts of demands of the Filipinos, namely of him, but we've given him very little information in return."

"Has to be that way sometimes," Monarch said as she opened a door and then entered an office.

"I know," Barnett said and waited for the door to close before reaching into her canvas bag and pulling out two brand-new iPads, an iPhone with a shockproof and waterproof case, two backup batteries, and two small Bluetooth devices. She kept one iPad and one earpiece/microphone for herself and handed the rest to him.

"You always make it feel like Christmas, Gloria," Monarch said.

She winked at him, said, "Great duty-free at the Bangkok airport. I figured we'd need excellent communications for this all to work, given the size of the search area."

Barnett had turned from him by then, and was typing on her iPad. A moment later, Monarch heard the director of the CIA say, "Do you have him there, Barnett?"

"I do, sir," she said and turned the screen toward Monarch. Dr. Hopkins was staring into the screen over a secure connection, looking very tired.

"Robin, we've got a ransom demand, a deadline, and

a responsible party," the CIA director said. "Hold on a second. We'll run it for you."

A second later the screen jumped to an mpeg video that showed Secretary of State Agnes Lawton, and the foreign ministers of China and India, bound, gagged, and sitting in a glaring light on crude bamboo chairs in some kind of a hut. A copy of the previous day's *South China Morning Post* was visible in Secretary Lawton's hands. On the wall behind her was a banner with a seal that read "S.O.P" and below it the words "Sons of Prophecy" in English and in Arabic.

Below the banner and in back of the diplomats stood a wiry guy in a white shirt, pants, and hood. He was aiming a Kalashnikov rifle at the hostages. Fung and Wadi looked shaken, filthy, and exhausted. But Agnes Lawton stared straight into the glaring light, blinking and pausing, blinking and pausing with an expression that struck Monarch as rich with defiance.

The hooded man spoke, saying, "Sons of Prophecy release prisoners when paid five hundred million dollars by each country, and release political prisoners each country.

"Ransom be paid and prisoners release by Sunday, November 4, seven P.M. Eastern Standard Time. Failure results in prisoners lose head. You try find, rescue them they lose heads."

The screen went blank, and then was filled again with Dr. Hopkins's face.

The CIA director said, "Analysts here, at Homeland, and at NSA say they've never heard of this Sons of Prophecy group before this video was sent to the

White House press secretary about two hours ago," he
said.

Monarch thought about that, said, "You'll contact us
if you get anything more?"

"The second we get it," the CIA director promised.
"Where now?"

"The *Niamey*," Monarch said. "Gloria's already arranged a ride for me."

"What about the Chinese and the Indians?"

"Delayed by the storm," Monarch replied. "And I'm
not waiting for them."

You could tell that was not what Dr. Hopkins wanted
to hear, but he nodded.

The screen went blank. Monarch said, "Where's this
helicopter?"

"Repair facility about six miles from here," Barnett
said. "Don't worry. I talked to the pilot. It was routine
stuff and she just passed flight inspection. A Bell similar to the Jayhawks the Coast Guard uses. Very stable
platform."

"Range?"

"Thousand miles fully fueled," she said. "And you're
only going south of the Spratly Islands."

"Heard the Spratlys are lovely this time of year,"
Monarch said, as she headed toward the door on the
other side of the room.

Barnett opened the door, revealing a rain-spattered
parking lot, and said, "Except when they get hit by typhoons."

"You are a glass half-empty kind of gal, aren't you?"

"Someone in the crew has to be."

They climbed into a Land Rover, with Barnett driving. She fired up the truck, put on the headlights, and started to back out. That Filipino Air Force general was standing outside under an eave, watching them go with cold eyes.

"I don't like that guy," Monarch said.

"His ego's just a little bruised," she said. "He'll get over it."

But Monarch watched him until they'd almost passed out of sight, and saw the general raising a cell phone to his ear.

8

THE MOON DRAGON LISTENED to his cell phone, heard the Filipino general say, "They're heading for the gate in a white Land Rover. My men are right outside. You should have visual soon."

"Excellent, General Garcia. You'll get the bonus we discussed for putting this together on such short notice. Call the next number on the list to confirm," the Moon Dragon said, and clicked the phone shut. He handed it to Tuul, who promptly put it under his heel and destroyed it.

Long Chan-Juan stood up, feeling energized, and began pacing in the offices of his import-export business in an old factory building deep in the heart of Kowloon. He threw the shutters open and leaned out the window. It was a full two hours before dawn and the streets below him were already alive with the shouting of mongers on their way to the fish market, and old men sweeping the sidewalks, and a crew of bakers smoking out in the back of their shop across the street, joking with several drunks walking home after a long-lost night.

The Moon Dragon loved Kowloon, the brilliant colors, the intoxicating aromas, the teeming enterprise, and most of all the sheer density of humanity. When he leaned out his window like this, Long could not help remembering a childhood of poverty and misery, when leaning out the window of the single room where his six-person family lived meant looking down on fantasy and unattainable dreams. The triad leader remembered his promise to himself that he would never go hungry when he was a man, that he would steal every dream and fantasy in the streets of Kowloon for his own.

And now look at me, he thought. I am the dragon king in his lofty lair, ruler of the dark side of Kowloon, Hong Kong, and southern China as far north as Shanghai. And within days, the dragon king will grow more powerful than he's ever been, fly higher than he's ever been, and spout more flames than he ever has. The mainland will be—

"Boss," Tuul called, interrupting his thoughts. "You got a call. And the Filipinos are up on camera."

The Moon Dragon pulled his head inside and went quickly to his desk, taking the cell as he passed the Mongolian.

"Yes?" he said, looking on the laptop computer, seeing a night scene with palm trees drooping in the rain outside the gates of the Philippine Air Force City.

"Just wanted y'all to know that someone spotted the

tanker," his southern friend said. "She's lying in Vietnamese waters south of Spratly Island."

That had to be where Monarch was going. Of course
it was; the ship was the scene of the crime.

"That's useful to know," Long said. "Thank you."

"Anytime," his friend said and clicked off.

On the laptop screen, a white Land Rover rolled to
the inside of the gate. Long could only make out the
silhouette of a man and woman in the front seat. Their
documents were checked and the gate rose. The Land
Rover turned right, heading north.

Accompanied by the sound of motorcycle engines,
the camera swung in behind the Land Rover, about one
hundred yards back.

The Moon Dragon allowed himself a small smile,
and said to his bodyguard: "General Garcia has served
his purpose. See that he's paid before the sun rises."

Tuul nodded, and got out his own cell phone.

The triad leader's attention, meanwhile, stayed fixed
on the computer screen and the taillights of the Land
Rover.

Good-bye, thief, the Moon Dragon thought, then
opened his mouth wide and howled silently out at the
screen as if he were breathing fire.

9

"YOU EATEN?" BARNETT ASKED when she pulled out of the main gate and headed north. She'd seen the group of men on motorcycles across the street, but it was a common-enough sight in Southeast Asia, even at this dismal hour.

"Nothing yet," he replied.

When flying long distances Monarch tried to drink water often, but ate little. The practice helped him reset his circadian rhythms as quickly as possible.

"There's food in the pack behind you," she offered. "And water, several passports, and a waterproof watch/location transmitter. It will let me track you in real time if we somehow lose other comm. The lower button right side of the watch sends an S.O.S. message. There's also a Glock 19 in .40 caliber with fifty rounds already in the helicopter. Sorry, I just couldn't come by an H&K .45 on such short notice."

Pity, Monarch thought. He liked the knockdown

power of a .45 and the feel of the H&K USP, but said, "You're still the best, Gloria. Anyone ever tell you that?"

"Yes, and quite often," Barnett replied, still pleased at the praise. "Oh, did I tell you two other ships in the region were attacked within a forty-eight-hour window around the *Niamey* hijack?"

Monarch reached over the seat, found the sack with the food, said, "No."

"Looks like a cluster attack," Barnett said.

Monarch got out dried meat, a bottle of water, and a Ziploc bag filled with dried mango slices, said, "Cluster?"

"That's evidently been the MO for pirates operating in the South China Sea the past few years," she explained. "They'll target several ships in a two- or three-day time frame. They board, steal, and leave. And then they'll lay low, engaging in very little activity for two to three weeks after."

"Any hostages taken from those ships?" Monarch asked.

"Not that I know of," she admitted. "But they were boarded by heavily armed men who extorted money from the crews, took electronics equipment, and left."

"So what, you're saying this might be a crime of opportunity?" Monarch asked. "That it was sheer coincidence that these pirates boarded the *Niamey* and got the secretary and the foreign ministers?"

"Possible," Barnett replied. "Let's say they are pirates. They board the ship, and realize who is on it, and then decide to kidnap them for ransom. Maybe this whole Sons of Prophecy group is something they made up."

Monarch did not reply, but looked out the window

through the pouring rain and gusting wind. The old Clark air base, much of which was destroyed during the volcanic explosion of Mount Pinatubo in 1991, still dramatically influenced the area. The street they traveled was wide, well-tended, military straight, and ran off through modest bungalows set back from the road.

"You have GPS coordinates for the tanker?" he asked at last.

"Close enough that you'll be able to spot it from the air," she replied.

"Any reports of oil in the water around the tanker?"

Barnett looked surprised at the question. "I don't know."

"Who spotted it?"

"French ship. Said it was all lit up and appeared abandoned."

"How'd we find out?"

"The French contacted the tanker's owner, Deep Horizon or something, and they contacted the State Department, trying to find out who has control of the islands closest to the shoals so they could start arranging for salvage."

"Who controls the islands?"

"Vietnam, I believe," she replied. "But at least five countries claim some ownership of the Spratlys. They form a loose archipelago of—"

Strong headlight beams appeared behind them suddenly. They came close, slashed through the truck cab. Monarch looked over his shoulder, temporarily blinded by three beams, including one that started cutting to the pickup's right-hand side.

"Tap your brakes, then accelerate," Monarch ordered.

Barnett did so without hesitation, and in the moment the red brake lights were illuminated, Monarch saw that the headlights belonged to three different motorcycles, including the one cutting to his right. It barely missed clipping the truck's rear fender. It was so close that Monarch saw the driver in a poncho, and the man riding behind him, carrying a sawed-off shotgun.

"Gun!" Monarch shouted.

He saw the headlight gaining ground up the right side of the truck, and ducked a second before the right rear passenger-side window exploded.

Glass shards and shot sprayed through the cabin, hitting Barnett about the back and side of her head. She jerked the wheel hard right and they skidded across wet leaves and almost flipped. But Barnett, cut and bleeding from tiny shards of glass, somehow managed to counter steer and right the pickup.

"Weapon?" Monarch shouted at her.

"They're in the helicopter!" Barnett cried, eyes on the road.

The whipsawing of the truck after the shot had caused the motorcycles to fall back several yards, but now Monarch heard the high whine of their engines revving and saw the headlights closing on them once more.

"Weave," he said.

Barnett began cutting back and forth across the slick road in a lazy slalom motion. The motorcycles kept trying to dodge forward, but her action kept them back.

Monarch crouched down, said, "Straight now, faster, and prepare to brake hard."

Barnett who had trickles of blood down her neck

nevertheless nodded, crouched, and sped the Land Rover straight down the center of the road. The motorcycle and gunman who'd shot out the back window sped forward again. Monarch watched them coming in the side-view mirror, and cried, "Now!"

The Rover went into a skid. He flung open the passenger door. The motorcycle's front tire hit it almost square, causing it to twist violently. The driver and the gunman were bucked and hurled through the air. The motorcycle crashed and spun wildly behind them. A second motorcycle hit it dead on, and the two men on it were thrown head over handlebars at fifty miles an hour.

The third motorcycle did not relent, just sped up behind them. A burst of automatic weapons fire turned the rear window into a cloudy spider's web and left chunks of windshield on the hood. Miraculously, neither he nor Barnett were hit.

Monarch saw the last motorcycle headlamp dart toward Barnett's side and without thinking he threw himself over into the backseat, shouting, "Lower the rear driver's side window."

He landed on his hands and knees in the backseat, head down, but aware of the rear window going down. Hearing the motorcycle accelerate up the left side of the truck, he yelled, "Brake, then throw the wheel quick to the left and then right!"

Just as motorcycle came abreast of the open rear window, Barnett did just that. The instant Monarch felt the vehicle brake and dodge left he thrust his upper body out through the open window, his hands reaching out into the pouring rain.

His rib cage collided with the window frame, but he ignored the pain. The motorcycle was moving slightly past him toward Barnett, now no more than a foot away. The gunman on the back of the motorcycle had his shotgun up and was trying to aim. Monarch snagged him by his shirt collar, jerking him completely off the motorcycle.

Barnett took this as her cue to swing the wheel back right. Monarch's ribs hit the window frame a second time and he let the shooter go. In the split second before his back and head smashed off the asphalt the gunman triggered the shotgun. The stray fire hit the driver in the back. The motorcycle swerved off the road and crashed into a banyan tree.

Monarch pulled himself back in through the window, wincing at the pain in his ribs. He felt the Land Rover slow, and heard Barnett say shakily, "When did you take the car as weapon course?"

As he gingerly palpated his ribs, he said, "Couple of years ago, in my spare time."

"Should we turn back, see if any of them are alive?" she asked.

"And get into it with the Philippine police?" Monarch said. "No way. We get to that helicopter."

"But someone knew we were here, and ordered the attack," Barnett insisted.

"I'm guessing that was your friend, General Garcia," Monarch said. "Question is was he working for himself or someone else?"

"I'll pay him a visit after I drop you off," Barnett said.

Monarch nodded, his mind running in several directions, trying to develop a list of everyone who would have known he had just flown in. The list included everyone who'd been present inside the White House Situation Room and the various unnamed officials involved in sending the Indian and Chinese agents. There was also the possibility that General Garcia was linked to the Sons of Prophecy.

Before he could gauge that likelihood, Barnett flipped on her blinker, and took a right into a narrow lane. Monarch glimpsed a sign that said something about aviation before they disappeared into thick sopping vegetation that hung down over the vehicle like so many dripping rags.

They emerged into a clearing that featured a hangar much smaller than the one they'd left. A big red Bell construction helicopter sat on a pad in front of the hangar.

"Winch on board?" Monarch asked.

"Pulled for repair, sorry," she replied, reaching into her purse for something to mop up the trickles of blood in her hair.

A man appeared in the open doors to the hangar.

"That the pilot?"

"Nice guy," she said, pressing bunched tissue to the biggest cut. "From New Zealand. Ever notice they're all nice down there?"

"Must be the clean living and lack of natural predators," Monarch said, grabbing the pack. "Go talk to Garcia, and let me know."

"Robin?" she said as he climbed out.

Monarch looked back in at her.

"Stay safe," she said.

"Always," he replied. "Well, almost always."

10

THE MOON DRAGON GLARED at the computer screen in his office in Kowloon, seeing the headlight of the motorcycle shining on the skinned trunk of the banyan tree it had just crashed into, leaving only the sounds of someone moaning.

The idiots! They'd had the Americans unarmed and they still couldn't finish!

He wanted to pick up the screen and hurl it against the wall. Instead he tried to keep his emotions in check by pacing again, going through his part in the plan, step by step, trying to figure out if the thief's escape jeopardized any of it both short and long term. After several minutes, he tried to convince himself that even if the Americans did know the *Niamey*'s location, Robin Monarch was looking for three needles in the vast haystack of Southeast Asia. It was an impossible task.

The Moon Dragon glanced at a calendar on the wall. Less than six days until the polls opened in the U.S. Less than five days until the deadline on the lives of the diplomats. Could they be found in that time? Could the thief do it?

Feeling a moment of anxiety, Long considered calling one of his allies, but then quickly discarded the notion. He was fully capable of keeping up his end of the bargain, and his friends had their own issues and roles to tend to if this was all going to work. Besides, in less than a day, the situation would be much different, with far less attention being paid to Southeast Asia.

Still, with Monarch heading to the abandoned oil tanker, the triad leader wondered whether to push the timetable ahead a few hours, or to try to eliminate the thief again. He stopped his pacing to look once again out the window, weighing his options, watching as the sky over Kowloon lightened toward dawn, and the noises of the streets began to gather, and the air turned aromatic with the scents of jasmine and ginger tea brewing in the pot of a street vendor below.

Both, he decided at last. I'll do both.

Turning back to Tuul, he said, "Use our influence with the Vietnamese military. Let them know that a foreign national, an American spy, will soon invade Vietnamese airspace and try to board a stranded oil tanker south of the Spratly Islands."

"Straight away, boss," Tuul promised.

"Before you do, I need face time with the pirate."

The Mongolian nodded, went back to the computer, plugged a headset into it, and started giving commands on the keyboard. As he did, Long sketched schemes in his mind and calculated their effects at multiple levels and distances, as if he were over in Macau, playing mahjong at a dozen different tables.

Five minutes later, with full light coming on outside, Long believed he knew how best to act. He considered calling his wife and asking her to consult the Book of Changes, to make his vision of the future certain. But then Tuul said, "He's on."

Coming around the desk to see the computer screen, Long was greeted with the sweaty, wild-eyed visage of Ramelan looking back at him.

"Captain," the triad leader said, bowing his head, and addressing the crazy pirate as he had requested the first time they met.

Ramelan's eyes darted about before he bobbed his head deferentially.

"How are your guests?" the Moon Dragon asked.

A smile broke out on the pirate's face, revealing those betel-stained teeth. "Hot, sick, and tired of life."

"That's good," the triad leader said. "But their boat's been found, run aground up the west coast of Borneo. I thought we agreed to set her adrift with her anchors trailing."

"Big storm, can't control," Ramelan said, the smile gone. "Tell me of future."

Inside the Moon Dragon sighed. But knowing how the man could become erratic at a moment's notice, he said soothingly, "As I've told you, Captain, you *were* prophesized long ago, you are no doubt a Son of Prophecy."

Ramelan, an Indonesian, had come to the triad leader's attention several years before. The pirate worked the Java and South China Seas, boasting eight high-speed boats, sixty skilled men, a large cache of weapons, and a reputation for total viciousness in pursuit of plunder. He also suffered from the lingering effects of a syphilis infection that went undiagnosed for nearly eighteen months, leaving the captain more than a bit mad and prone to grand delusions about himself. Long figured this out about Ramelan early on, and had been using it to his advantage ever since.

"Look at the name your mother gave you," the triad leader went on. 'One who is prophesized.' Your actions *are* changing the world."

The smile evaporated, and there was an edge to Ramelan's voice when he said, "But world no know. Ramelan watch Internet."

"Perhaps *you* are a prophet," the Moon Dragon replied, acting astonished. "You're already ahead of me, Captain. It *is* time the world knows about your great deed. Make a new video and send it to our friend in Kuala Lumpur. He'll take the Web site live, and show the world what you've done, the blow you've struck for freedom."

The pirate beamed, wiped the back of his greasy hand across his mouth, and said, "I do that. I start now."

"Nothing would make me happier," the Moon Dragon said, then he cut the connection and looked at Tuul. "Now, let's deal with the Vietnamese."

11

MONARCH HAD PROGRAMMED THE time zones into his iPhone's clock, determined to keep close track of the deadline the Sons of Prophecy had given. He had exactly one hundred twenty hours and fifteen minutes to find and rescue the Secretary of—

"Twenty minutes out," the helicopter pilot said, tapping the GPS readout.

Monarch glanced at the New Zealander. He was good. They'd flown through some terrible weather at the beginning, but he'd handled it like a pro. Monarch wondered whether the Kiwi would take a couple of thousand dollars extra to delay his return to Luzon, make the Chinese and Indian agents even later than they would have been, maybe long enough that he'd already have gone through the stranded oil tanker and moved on. The President had ordered him to work with them, but what could you do when there was a typhoon screwing up transport all over Southeast Asia?

In the end Monarch decided it wouldn't matter. By the time the pilot made the round trip, he'd have had at least five hours on the tanker, maybe more.

Daylight built, revealing a sea churned gray-blue by the passing storm. Here and there he spotted small-uninhabited tropical islands, and then a bigger chunk of land before them to the south.

"Spratly Islands?" Monarch asked.

The pilot nodded and gave them a wide berth. Forty minutes later, the sun had risen well above the eastern horizon, revealing shallow water turbid with silt the passing typhoon had stirred up from the shoals. Monarch was the first to notice the glint of the sun off the *Niamey*'s wheelhouse.

The oil tanker was much as she'd been described. It had run up on a wide sandbar, and was listing hard to starboard. They circled her. There was no oil sheen visible on the water, which meant the oil had been pumped off, or a miracle had occurred and no oil had leaked during the grounding. The decks were deserted, but Monarch could clearly see the shattered glass of the bridge windows and the bullet holes that pocked the metal housing.

"Can you land for me?" Monarch asked.

The New Zealander shook his head. "Best I can do is hover over the roof of the wheelhouse. You'll have to jump the last few feet."

Monarch didn't like that option, but he nodded. He removed the earphones and unsnapped the harness, feeling the bruised ribs again. He snapped the Glock into the shoulder holster and grabbed the rubberized dry bag containing the supplies Barnett had gathered for him. Monarch got the dry bag on his back as the pilot circled the wheelhouse a second time, and then pulled on a pair of leather work gloves.

Holding tight to the door release, Monarch watched out the front window as the pilot brought them expertly in over the tilted bridge of the oil tanker. Satellite dishes and antennas jutted from the wheelhouse roof.

The pilot said, "This is as close as I can get, mate."

Monarch yanked the handle, slid the door back. Stepping out on the strut, he looked for an opening between the communications gear and jumped. He landed hard, and immediately lost his footing on the steep, slick surface.

He crashed to his belly and even as the helicopter pulled away began to slide down the roof of the wheelhouse toward a seventy-foot drop to the sea. Monarch's hands slashed out, trying to first grab hold of the housing for the navigation system, and then the satellite antenna. But both of them were out of reach.

As he slid over the edge, Monarch felt his boots go out into the air, followed by his knees, hips, and chest before he finally caught a heavy gauge whip antenna with his gloved right hand. It bent and he went over the side, his grip sliding down it. He threw up his left hand, and got better hold of the whip. His slide was halted and he dangled above the water. It looked far too shallow to drop into from that height.

Panting, he craned his head around. He saw that the

side window of the wheelhouse was below him, about three feet away, and completely blown out by gunfire. Kicking his feet and praying that the antenna would not snap, he got himself swinging, and then kicked hard with his entire body and let go. He snagged the window frame, arched sideways and got a foot up. With one last effort he pulled his torso over into the wheelhouse and then slid down the wall, sweat pouring off his head. The helicopter was now just a buzzing noise in the distance.

Monarch smelled the rancid blood before he noticed it smeared all over the floor of the bridge. He looked to his right along the tilted wall. Three bodies, all male, were piled against each other, and beginning to bloat.

He looked left and saw empty rifle cartridges lying on the floor. He went and picked them up—7.62 mm. An AK-47 had been used to kill the three men. For a moment, Monarch considered what that might mean. The AK was the standard weapon in this part of the world, and easily accessible to anyone with enough money.

Monarch shuffled forward as if in some kind of fun house, with one foot angled on the wall and the other angled on the floor, making his way toward what appeared to be a gangway to the lower decks. It took him a moment to figure out his balance on the steep spiral staircase, but then he dropped quickly to the next lower level.

He reached a landing where a closed door with a porthole window led out onto a balcony below the bridge. Monarch peered through the window at the balcony and deck below. Before he could take another step, he felt the crown of a gun barrel pressed to the back of his head.

12

SHACKLED AT THE ANKLES, chained to the thick plywood wall of a thatched-roofed hut, and feeling grimier than she'd been in her entire life, Agnes Lawton stared at the closed door to the shack, listening to the alien world beyond it. She heard the clucking of guinea fowl, the baying of dogs, and in the distance the muted arguments of men. She smelled coffee and frying fish and moaned with thirst and hunger.

Her blindfold and gag lay on the floor beside her. Though her wrists were bound in front of her, she'd managed to tear off the diaper the evening before, and now had to urinate badly. Worse, her exposed skin was puffy and itched from the bugs that had attacked her incessantly from sundown on.

She'd survived the horrid conditions by focusing on her family. They had to know by now. What were they thinking? Feeling? She thought of her husband Bill. As unlikely as it had seemed to some, it had been love at first sight. Bill had always been her biggest cheerleader, her rock from the moment they'd met. This must be tearing him apart. Then she thought back to an argument they'd had a couple of months ago, how she'd handled it, and felt guilty.

"It's the job," she'd insisted. "You knew what it would be like when I accepted the President's nomination."

"I didn't expect you to be on the go for eight solid years," he'd snapped.

"There are things I don't like about your job, but I accept them."

"Like what?" he asked, arms crossed.

"Some of the people your firm represents, their causes," she said.

"I didn't know I needed you to vet every contract the firm gets," he said, acting insulted. "And by the way? Their causes gave us a comfortable life when you were still teaching at Georgetown for nothing."

He'd turned and left in a rage.

They'd made up later, of course, but sitting there in the brutal heat, Secretary Lawton had to admit that a lot of the things Bill had said were true. She'd been absent a lot the last twenty-five years, ever since entering politics. She'd never made much money either. Without him, without the firm, they'd have lived a far more difficult existence.

She thought of her sons, Ethan and Timothy, and wondered whether her absence had been a grind on them. Bill and a succession of excellent nannies had raised them. Her boys were now fine men, and good fathers, blessed with wonderful wives and healthy young children. But do I know them as much as I could?

Forced to confront her life, Agnes Lawton's family seemed . . .

She didn't know how to put it, a feeling more than anything, as if she'd lost her way. Suddenly, desperately, the Secretary of State wished she had spent more time with her husband at every stage of their marriage. She wished she'd spent more time with her children and grandchildren at every stage of their lives.

Those wishes weighed on Secretary Lawton as dawn came and went. It had been light for quite a while now, but no one had come to give them food or water or to let them use a latrine. Indeed, no one had come in at all since the night before. With every minute, the sun outside grew more intense, the air inside the hut more sweltering, and her discomfort more acute. To get her mind off the regrets and the heat, she looked around. The Chinese foreign minister was about eight feet to her left. Fung was dozing, his chin down on his chest. The Indian diplomat was eight feet to her right. Wadi appeared feverish, and though the light in the hut was dim, she thought the gash on his forehead might be infected and festering.

"How do you feel?" she asked.

"Better than I will without a head," the Indian replied sarcastically.

"You need medical attention, my friend, and they wouldn't dare kill us."

"Tell that to our esteemed host," Wadi said, and laughed wearily and then sadly. "Agnes, I have tried since a boy to live according to the concept of karma, that what goes around comes around, and that good deeds will yield future good fortune."

"I've always felt you were honest in our talks," Secretary Lawton said. "A frank and reliable ally."

"Yes, and what good has it done me?" the Indian demanded angrily. "I try to act on behalf of my country, to protect it, and I end up in a jungle hut held by some lunatic who thinks he's prophesized and wants to behead me for reasons I have not even begun to fathom. Did I tell you my youngest daughter is getting married next month? Who will give her away if . . . ?"

The Secretary of State sensed his growing despair, but her mind seized on something else he'd said. Despite the hunger and the thirst, despite itching head to toe, feeling filthy, and desperately having to pee, her agile mind seized on it and all sorts of questions began to fire off in her brain.

"I'm sure you'll be right there with her," she said. "But I don't understand what the Sons of Prophecy want, either."

"I take a man at his word," said Fung, who'd woken up and looked at them with drooping, rheumy eyes. "Ramelan wants money and the release of political prisoners, just like he said."

"He can't believe he'd get either, can he?" Secretary Lawton replied skeptically. "He's got to know that our governments won't pay or release anyone in this kind of situation."

"You are trying to rationalize a madman," said the Indian diplomat.

"Unless he's not really crazy," she countered. "Unless there's some ulterior motive to all this."

The Chinese foreign minister shrugged. "I'm listening, but I think all you'll tell me is fantasy. Unless you know facts that I don't."

The Secretary of State did not respond. Instead, she reviewed the "facts" as she knew them. Intelligence provided and shared by the three nations had suggested a coordinated effort between forces trying to overthrow the Indian government, cause a rebellion in northern China, and disrupt the U.S. presidential election. That's why they'd all decided to meet together on the tanker in secret.

No, wait, that wasn't quite true. Secretary Lawton remembered that she'd requested the meeting several months before, telling Fung and Wadi that it would be a good thing to sit down one last time in private, without all the pomp and circumstance of a formal visit, and really try to establish common ground between the countries before the next administration took power. She pondered that, and came to a suspicion. But before she could voice it, she heard footsteps coming.

Locks unsnapped. The door flew open. Captain Ramelan entered, wearing his hood, and his eyes looking possessed. "You come now. Talk your countries. Tell them meet demands."

Agnes Lawton stiffened. "I am not saying a thing in your favor."

"Yes?" Ramelan growled. "Is so?"

He walked over and kicked her high on the outside of her left leg. The blow was shocking and the pain intense. But the Secretary of State took the hit and gritted her teeth, refusing to show fear or call retreat in any way.

"You tell!" he shouted.

"I will not!" Secretary Lawton shouted back at her captor. "You won't feed or give us water. You won't even allow us to use a toilet! So, no, Captain, I will not talk to my country on your behalf!"

For a second, she thought sure he was going to snap and beat her, or kill her right on the spot. But then he smiled, "So, I give you eat, drink, take you piss, maybe shit, and you talk. Yes?"

Agnes Lawton glanced left and right at her fellow captives, especially the Indian foreign minister.

"And clean out Mr. Wadi's wound and get him medicines," she said. "Antibiotics. He needs cream and pills."

Ramelan started to laugh. "Where you are? We clean cut. The rest—God's will. Allah's will."

She didn't like it, but when she looked around at Fung and Wadi, she found them nodding. Taking their approval, she pondered her suspicion again, and decided it would be wise to relay her thinking to Washington in the only way she could.

"You have a deal, Captain," she said. "I'll talk to your camera."

13

"ONE MOVE, YOU DIE," a woman said in a firm voice, and pushed on the gun slightly, causing Monarch's head to bob forward.

Somehow she'd slipped up behind him in a confined space on a metal surface. How was that possible?

A second gunman appeared in the hatch window, looking in at him from a balcony, and aiming a Glock 17 pistol.

"Hands at back of your head," the woman snapped

"You said one move and I die," Monarch replied, studying the man through the hatch window. With skin the color of ox blood he had a burly torso fitted inside a blue T-shirt, and his eyes were as dark as his wavy hair.

"Hands!" she barked, and Monarch caught a reflection of her silhouette in the window glass. She was big, big enough that he decided it was smart to raise his hands behind his head. He never felt her hand or arm as she reached for his holster. He didn't even feel a tug when she removed the H&K. To Monarch's way of thinking, she was suddenly a very, very dangerous adversary.

"Take two steps back. Drop to your knees," she said.

Monarch retreated two steps and was preparing to squat when her companion left the window to open the door. He saw his chance. Dipping his chest forward as if struggling to kneel, he mule-kicked back at the woman. His boot hit the soft flesh of her abdomen and he heard her make a sound between a cough and a grunt.

Knowing that he'd blown the air right out of her, he spun low and sprang. She was bent over, disbelief written all over her face, but trying to raise the two guns. The blade of Monarch's left hand struck her on a nerve center on the inside of the right wrist, causing her grip to sag and a gun—his gun—to clatter to the floor. At the same time, Monarch's right hand swung in a counterclockwise motion hooking her left elbow as he stepped into her blind spot. His left hand reached over and around the back of her neck. He hooked his thumb in her shirt collar, and then went to his knees twisting and pulling both of his hands inward and down. The motion spun her and left her in a backward arch, her left arm barred and her neck throttled. Her gun fell into his lap. It had all taken less than two seconds.

In the next instant, her companion pushed open the door. He found Monarch using her as a shield and aiming her weapon at him. The red laser dot was already locked between the man's eyes.

"Don't," the man said, moved his hands slowly to his sides, and dropped his gun.

Monarch pushed the woman forward until he had his own gun pinned beneath his boot. It was only then that he looked down at her. As he'd thought, she was big and athletic. She had exotic features, which were very attractive, especially the almond shape of her eyes and the luxuriousness of her jet-black hair. He inspected her gun. It was a QSZ-92. Monarch glanced at her companion a second time, and then at his weapon. He understood all now.

In disgust, Monarch pushed her away from him toward her partner. She got up, stumbled, caught herself, and turned to look back at him.

"I'm insulted," Monarch told them, "truly insulted that you told my government that you were going to meet me at Clark, and that we'd all fly down together. Instead, you fuck me over, fly in early, and then hold a gun to my head. Is that any way to treat an ally?"

The Indian's shoulders relaxed and he almost smiled. But the beautiful Chinese woman's scowl only deepened. She spat her words at him, "Did you think we were going to be dictated to by an American, told when and how we could look for *our* foreign ministers?"

"That was the deal as I understood it," Monarch said.

"You understood wrong," she snapped. "We do not need you."

"Uh, I'm the one with the guns," Monarch said. He made a show of looking at the weapon in his hand. "This one's yours, I believe."

She struggled for a moment, and then sputtered, "*You* deceived *us*. You came here from Philippines by yourself. *You* didn't wait for *us*."

"Now *you're* splitting hairs," Monarch scolded. "If you want to get your foreign minister back, you'd better be listening to me, and following my lead." He looked at the Indian. "Am I right?"

The other man glanced at the woman, gave Monarch a grudging shrug, said, "I'm okay. As long as you're not a world-class asshole about it."

"Me, a world-class asshole?" Monarch replied, acting even more insulted. "Never. Okay, rarely." He looked at the woman. "If I return your weapon, do you promise not to try to shoot me?"

She regarded him bitterly for a long beat, but then nodded. He dropped the clip, ejected the live round in the chamber, and tossed it to her. She caught it, holstered it, looking furious for having been disarmed.

"Names?" Monarch asked. "Affiliations?"

"Why?" the Chinese woman said, brushing back her hair, revealing a light scar that traveled a several inches down the left side of her head.

Monarch noticed it, said, "I check on people before I reveal state secrets."

She thought about that, said, "Song Le. Chinese Ministry of State Security."

Monarch gave her a look of open reappraisal. The MSS was China's all-powerful intelligence agency, with operators working domestically and abroad. MSS agents engaged in all manner of tradecraft, including counterintelligence, spy recruitment, the stealing of technological secrets, and the repression of internal dissent. That this woman would be the one agent sent by the MSS to help recover the Chinese foreign minister spoke volumes.

He looked to the Indian, who said, "Bashir Rhana. NIA. You can call me Bash."

India's NIA or National Investigative Agency was formed in 2008 after the Mumbai bombings in order to combat terror in India and abroad. Monarch had never worked with any of its investigators or operators before.

"Experience in hostage rescue?" Monarch asked.

Bash nodded. "Extensively with the British SAS and the Gurkhas. But my expertise is investigation in delicate circumstances."

"Mine too," Monarch said, looking back to Song Le. "You work counterrevolutionary or counterterror for MSS?"

Song Le remained expressionless, said, "Expect that I am capable of anything. What about you? Who do you work for? What is your name?"

"My name's Monarch," he replied. "I work for myself."

"So," the MSS agent said, her brows narrowing. "The U.S. sends a mercenary?"

"Of a sort," he agreed.

"What sort?" she pressed.

Monarch spoke to her in Mandarin, said, "The thieving kind."

Monarch did not wait for Song Le to reply, but instead looked to Bash, and said, "We split up. We look for evidence, the blatant stuff for now. Each of us handles our country's quarters. I'll call for an evidence team to come in—"

"Already done that," the Indian said, cutting him off. "My people are en route and they're Scotland Yard trained."

"Perfect," said Monarch; he reholstered his pistol, glanced at Song Le, who still appeared pissed off, and then headed belowdeck.

Over the course of an hour, Monarch moved through the tanker, looking everywhere, trying to reconstruct what must have happened the night of the hijacking. The blown-out windows on the bridge made him realize that the ship had been attacked from the air, and possibly the sea, which meant the hijackers, the Sons of Prophecy, were not your run-of-the-mill pirates or terrorists. They were skilled, brazen, and well equipped, which meant they were well financed.

In a lower hallway, Monarch found bullet holes and residue from a flash bang grenade. The stench was horrendous. Four U.S. Diplomatic Secret Service agents were dead in the hall and decaying in the equatorial heat. Blowflies were already gathering.

Monarch took off his shirt, held it over his mouth, climbed over the bodies into the stateroom. He saw a woman's business clothes still hanging in the closet, saw the ax, the destroyed computer, and knew for certain that this was where Secretary of State Lawton had been taken.

Monarch had run renditions—government-sanctioned

kidnappings—in the past. Abductions in general were almost always screwed-up affairs in his opinion, and this one looked no different. If the Sons of Prophecy had come in search of the highly classified intelligence that had to have been on Secretary Lawton's computer hard drive, they hadn't gotten it.

He'd never met the Secretary of State, but the deed impressed him. When grenades are going off and your bodyguards are dying right outside your door you have to be one tough, committed individual to throw out all thoughts of self-preservation and act on the country's behalf. He looked around again, noticed a dried, red substance plastered to the wall. He crouched to look at it, saw bits of nut and stained leaves, as if someone had spit it there.

He heard a cough before Song Le stepped into the cabin, said archly, "Have you found anything of importance?"

Monarch pointed to the stuff spit on the wall, said, "Betel nut chewer in the bunch that grabbed Secretary Lawton."

"You don't know that."

"You think the Secretary of State chews betel nut?" he asked, standing.

"No," she replied. "But it could have been there before."

He shook his head. "The other walls are spotless. This is in plain sight, and was spit there arrogantly."

"Pirates chew betel nut," the Chinese agent said. "But so do a great number of people in at least ten countries in Southeast Asia."

"Even in some parts of India," Bash said, joining them.

"I don't care where he came from," Monarch said, gesturing at it. "Whoever spit it, left his DNA, which I want."

Song Le shrugged as if to say, "Whatever."

"You find anything?" Monarch asked the Indian agent.

"The petroleum is still on board."

"All of it?" Monarch asked, surprised.

Bash nodded. "I lit up the gauges and checked the log report when they took on the crude. The volumes match."

That struck Monarch as extremely odd. There were millions of dollars worth of crude belowdeck. If you're a pirate, you target the tanker for the oil, having no idea that the foreign secretaries of three different countries are on board. After you manage to overpower at least ten trained, well-armed bodyguards and take the secretaries hostage, why leave the oil?

There was a huge logistical issue with pirating that much oil, of course, but it still struck Monarch as questionable that men after five hundred million dollars would leave a potential fifteen-million-dollar haul behind.

"Is Secretary Lawton a smoker?" Song Le asked, breaking Monarch's train of thought.

"What's that?"

The Chinese agent gestured behind him on the floor. He turned and saw a matchbook there, just under the bunk. With his gloved hands he picked it up. The cover read, "Apocalypse Now Bar. Saigon."

There was such a place?

Monarch flipped it over, saw a printed phone number and address: 2C Thi Sach St., Ho Chi Minh City, Vietnam. He opened the matchbook and saw figures written in ballpoint pen that he did not recognize.

"Read Vietnamese?" he asked Song Le and Bash.

The Chinese agent said, "Enough."

He handed it to her. She studied it a second, said, "It's actually Indonesian. It says, 'October 31, eleven P.M. Here.'"

"Tonight at eleven P.M.?" he asked.

"Today is October 31."

"That'll work," Bash said.

"Question is where is 'here'?" Monarch asked.

"Isn't it obvious?" Song Le sniffed. "Here is this bar."

It was very strange that this matchbook would have been dropped in the stateroom, especially with a date, a time, and a location, though there were signs of struggle. Maybe one of the kidnappers—

A clanking noise sounded somewhere higher in the ship. Monarch went for his gun, said, "Sounds like we've got company."

They were in a narrow, confined space. Defending narrow, confined spaces made you vulnerable to grenades and other close-quarter explosives.

The Indian and Chinese agents seemed to share the same misgivings, because they hurried after him down the hall past the rotting corpses, and climbed up the gangways. Monarch reached a door a deck below the oil tanker's bridge. He looked out the porthole window and saw nothing. He eased open the compartment door, stepped out, and looked around, still seeing nothing. Song Le and Bash followed.

Monarch spotted the first man when he rounded the front of the bridge. He was down on the main deck, armed with a pistol, and wearing an officer's uniform: dark pants, pale blue blouse, and peaked hat. He was bending down to pick up a bullet casing off the deck. Then Monarch noticed ten or more men dressed much like the officer, moving awkwardly right to left on the tilted deck. All carried AK-47s.

One soldier caught sight of Monarch first, and then the Chinese and Indian agents. He raised an alarm. Suddenly ten automatic weapons were pointed their way, and the officer was screaming at them to drop their weapons in Vietnamese.

14

LONG CHAN-JUAN PACED IN front of the windows of his villa high on the Peak, watching a tropical cyclone lash Hong Kong, his mind chewing on the news that Monarch and the Chinese and Indian agents were being flown to Ho Chi Minh City to be interrogated. But how long could the Vietnamese hold them?

Despite the Moon Dragon's fervent belief in the I Ching's power to guide him, he was prone to second-guessing the universe. What if his wife had interpreted the hexagram wrong the other day? The fact that this thief had appeared during a time of cyclones compounded the triad leader's unease.

Though he told no one, not even his wife, Long hated typhoons and cyclones, pathologically feared their wrath and unpredictability. He hated them, but could rarely take his eyes off them. A storm had surrounded his father's death, hadn't it? And what about his father-in-law? And his son? He, too—

"Grandfather!" Lo-Lo cried in a woeful voice, trudging into the room.

The Moon Dragon's eyes left the storm, left his fears, and found his grandson. He smiled. It was always so. Lo-Lo was the future, the future of it all. The triad leader did not need a prophetic text to tell him that. As far as he was concerned, everything about his grandson was a stack of perfect trigrams, a ringing prophecy that spoke of his family's rising power.

"I want to go out to the zoo," Lo-Lo pouted. "But it's raining."

"I can see that," Long said.

"And grandmother says I can't use the Internet, and can't watch television until Mr. Woo gets here," he grumbled, referring to his tutor.

"I can't imagine," Long said.

Lo-Lo crawled onto the sofa beside him and rested his head against his grandfather's shoulder, said, "Tell me a story. About my father."

The triad leader felt a sharp pain in his heart. Even now, six years later. He looked down at his grandson and saw his dead son in grandson's eyes, in his nose, and along the line of his jaw.

"Your father was big and strong and smart," Long began. "He could do anything he set his mind to, and so can you."

"That's not a story," the boy said in mild protest.

"No," the triad chief said, smiling. "I suppose it's not."

He leaned over and picked a bell off a coffee table. He rang it with a crisp flick of his wrist. In moments, the sound of the bell was replaced by the slap of the Filipina maid's shoes running into the room.

"Yes, Mr. Long," Anna said, giving her employer a half bow.

"Bring us some tea," the Moon Dragon said.

"And some cookies?" Lo-Lo asked.

Anna smiled, and then covered her cleft palate with her hand. Long studied the maid a moment. It was necessary of course that Lo-Lo interacted with Anna, but his wife did not like that her grandson and the Filipina woman seemed to share a bond of sorts.

"The girl's disfigured and inferior," Madame Long had said more than once. "She should not have such influence on a boy destined to take over your businesses."

The Moon Dragon could not argue with his wife's logic. But what were they to do? They needed a maid, didn't they? His wife needed help with the boy, didn't she? And the cleft palate? How could the poor woman help that?

"Please, Grandfather?" Lo-Lo said.

Long hesitated, but then nodded. "Bring a plate of cookies."

Anna bowed and hurried off.

"Tell me about when he was seven like me," Lo-Lo said. "My father."

That request caught the triad leader off guard. He flashed on the image of an old Chinese junk and felt upset. The Moon Dragon had not planned on telling his grandson this particular story for many years, but the boy had asked, and he felt compelled to answer.

"When your father was seven, he was very brave," Long said, feeling his throat constricting. "He had to be."

The crime lord told his grandson that his great-grandfather, Madame Long's father, was a merchant mariner, who retired, bought an old Chinese junk, and restored it. When Lo-Lo's father was seven he went out sailing with his grandfather.

"A storm like this one came up out of nowhere," Long said gesturing at the wind and the rain. "It turned the boat over, capsized it. Your great-grandfather, your father, and two crewmen were thrown into the sea. The only one we found alive was your father. He was clinging to the bottom of the boat."

Lo-Lo's eyes were wide. "He *was* brave."

"And so are you," the Moon Dragon insisted. "When your parents died in the accident, you lived, Lo-Lo. You were only a baby, but you were brave and strong, just like your father."

Lo-Lo beamed. "What was *she* like? My mother?"

Long hesitated several beats before admitting, "I never met her."

"What? That's—" Lo-Lo began, before hearing the slap of the maid's feet returning with a tea tray and a plate of cookies.

Anna set the tray down and Long's grandson instantly forgot about his dead mother and began devouring the treats. That was as it should be, the Moon Dragon thought. The dead are only memories. Cookies are a big part of a little boy's life.

He went to the window, looked out into the storm, his thoughts once again returning to the thief. Despite the fact that Monarch was on his way to a Vietnamese military prison, he felt deep unease. He wanted to get his wife to throw the coins and divine what the Book of Changes sensed quivering in the universe now. But Madame Long was out shopping. He would have to make certain decisions on his own.

The Moon Dragon's ever-roaming mind began to tick through the ruthless actions about to be set in motion in the coming days. He decided it wise to move up the timetable on his responsibilities yet again, to ratchet up the pressure on his enemies, and create chaos and opportunity everywhere around them.

To that end, the triad leader went to his office, shut the door, locked it, and used another disposable phone to dial a number on a list he kept in a drawer.

His southern friend picked up, said, "How can I be of service to you?"

"I'm having the second video sent wide earlier than planned."

There was a long silence on the other end, as if the man were considering all the ramifications of that, then he said, "Then I guess it's time things got going back my way and beyond. That what you're saying?"

"Move it up a day," Long said, shivering at the sheer audacity of their next series of moves. "Give them the all go."

"In for a quarter, in for a dollar, I always say," his friend replied in a good-natured tone. "You watch now. This here is gonna stir up a shit storm of epic proportions."

15

NINE HUNDRED MILES TO the south, Monarch glared at the Vietnamese Army captain who watched him with sardonic amusement from behind mirrored aviator sunglasses. They were inside an open-door Soviet-era military helicopter that was chugging along over open water toward the coast of Vietnam.

The officer had a jump seat. Monarch, Bash, and Song Le sat on the hard steel floor, buffeted by the hot wind coming in the doorway. Their right wrists were handcuffed to metal loops in the helicopter hull. Their guns had been taken. So had their phones, credit cards, and passports.

"Captain Su," Bash said. "I am asking you again to have your superiors contact our governments. We've given you the phone numbers, and I'm telling you that you are costing us precious time."

The officer's amusement turned to a barely controlled

snarl. "You tell why you are on ship aground in Vietnamese waters with many people dead on board and you carrying guns, and no Vietnam visa, and maybe then we call numbers. And what you losing time for anyway?"

"We are not free to tell you that," Monarch said with a groan. "We've been through this."

Indeed, after they'd made the decision not to engage the Vietnamese Army in an open gun battle, they'd surrendered and been questioned at length on board the *Niamey* and again back on Spratly Island. The discussions had all gone the same way. He was asking, but they weren't talking. In the end, the captain informed them that they would be brought to Ho Chi Minh City, the former Saigon, and hadn't said much since.

Monarch looked at Song Le and said, "You try."

The Chinese MSS agent began speaking to Captain Su in Vietnamese. Monarch didn't speak a word, but he got the gist of it. The officer remained unbowed. Monarch looked out the door, saw that they were no longer over the ocean, but flying above a vast marsh that soon gave way to denser jungle and then to brilliantly green rice paddies.

He had never been to Vietnam, and they were flying only two hundred feet in the air, giving him a full vista view. He could see the bent backs and conical hats of people working in the paddies, and every so often small, ornate buildings in the fields that he took to be tombs. Within twenty minutes these fields gave way to denser settlements that abutted the insanity of Ho Chi Minh City. Monarch saw French colonial–era architecture, modern shopping malls, and the sort of sprawling, sham-

bling, dingy developments that are widespread throughout the Third World.

But in the former Saigon, he witnessed the surging
energy of a city coming alive. It was everywhere below
him, especially in the streets where millions of motor
scooters sped along in massive weaving packs of mayhem. Monarch had never seen anything quite like it.

They landed in front of a military barracks near the
airport, where they were transferred into a transport truck
and driven through the streets, swept up in the growling,
beeping din of the scooter wars. Some scooters had only
a single rider, evidence of the growing middle class in
Vietnam. Others supported entire families—mom, dad,
the kids hanging off the back, a baby balanced on the
front handlebars. One fellow was somehow balancing a
three-tier wedding cake on the seat behind him.

Then, at a stoplight, three, young, filthy, and ragged
children came to the back of the truck, hands out, begging the soldiers for money. One, a girl, had a bruised
scab on her forehead, as if she'd been struck recently.
One of the soldiers jabbed at the children with the butt
of his rifle, and they fled. Monarch flashed on his days as
a street urchin in the slums of Buenos Aires. He thought
of Sister Rachel, working tirelessly on behalf of children
just like those kids, castaways as he'd been.

With this delay he wondered if he had a chance of
getting the fifteen-million-dollar reward. What was the
probability of one or even three talented operators lo-
cating exactly where, in all of Southeast Asia, the Sons
of Prophecy were holding the diplomats?

Monarch knew the odds of success were abysmally

low, but then again, it wasn't his job to consider the long odds. It was his job to keep moving, to keep digging until—

The truck brakes squealed, tearing Monarch from his thoughts. He heard a gate whine and they lurched forward again, passing inside a high wall topped with razor wire.

"Where are we?" Monarch asked Captain Su.

"TC-two," the Vietnamese officer said, amused again. "Military Intelligence. They take care of spies like you."

Armed soldiers met them, watched their transfer on a loading dock.

"You will be separated," Captain Su informed them. "Then you will talk."

Monarch felt like slapping the man silly, but figured it would only result in the butt of one of the rifles being slammed against the back of his head. He couldn't afford a concussion. He had to be on his game even if he was in handcuffs and under armed guard. The opportunity to escape could come at any moment. He knew his wristwatch had to still be transmitting his location via GPS, and hoped that Gloria Barnett was coming to his rescue.

As he was led inside the TC2 building, Monarch's thoughts swung toward Agnes Lawton. Were the Vietnamese behind the hijacking? Was that why they were getting zero cooperation? It would be different if Agnes Lawton's kidnapping were not a state secret. Monarch knew there were political benefits to staying quiet about the attack on the *Niamey* for as long as possible, especially for Vice President Vaught's campaign. From his perspective, however, Secretary Lawton's right to safety overrode the political benefits. He thought President Sand owed it to his Secretary of State to alert the entire world that she was missing. Then again, he wasn't president.

Following the Vietnamese soldiers deeper into the military intelligence building, Monarch suddenly wished he hadn't accepted the mission. He'd left the CIA because he was sick of being part of someone else's hidden agenda. He was beginning to sense that was going on here as well.

Monarch was halted in front of a steel door with a small square window in it about head high. He knew what was coming, and as one of the soldiers fumbled with the lock, he closed his eyes and began breathing deep to prepare himself. He'd endured long stretches of confinement and even torture before, and it took a very specific mind-set to survive it.

The room smelled of piss, and was bare except for a cot with a thin mattress, a reeking toilet, and a stained sink. One soldier trained his gun on Monarch from the door. The other told him to sit on the cot and hold out his arms so the handcuffs could be removed. Monarch saw the glimmer of a chance. He almost allowed his instincts to take over, to use the handcuffs as a weapon, stun the guy removing the restraints, and drive him back against the soldier with the gun. But that kind of move was low odds. He might overpower the two guards, or he might get shot. Since the latter seemed more likely, he kept his hands to himself when the soldiers took the handcuffs, and backed out of the cell.

He lay down on the cot, shut his eyes, and sighed: "Home sweet home."

16

PRESIDENT SAND ROUSED AT the hand shaking his shoulder. He opened his eyes, saw the digital clock on the table next to his bed, and knew this would not be a good thing. The times he'd been awakened like this in the past eight years had all turned out to be the result of tragic events.

"Mr. President?" a voice whispered.

He twisted his head, surprised to find Cynthia Blayless, his chief of staff, looking down at him and appearing shaken. That startled him fully awake. Ordinarily, his personal assistant came to wake him in times of trouble. This was a first for Blayless.

The President nodded, slipped from his bed so as not to wake the First Lady, took a robe and followed his chief of staff into the hallway.

"What—?" he began after shutting the bedroom door.

"The Sons of Prophecy have gone public, sir," Blayless said. "The story's out, and all hell's starting to break loose."

Sand closed his eyes for a moment, feeling the weight on his shoulders grow tenfold. He'd known it was coming, of course, but had somehow irrationally hoped this Monarch character would manage to find and rescue Lawton before . . .

The President opened his eyes. That pipe dream was over. He had to accept the cold hard facts now, deal with them, and accept every bit of the blame.

"How did the story get out?" he asked.

"They put up a Web site, Mr. President, and there's another video."

"Agnes?"

"She's alive, thank God, and looks better than the other two," his chief of staff said. "I've taken the liberty of assembling a crisis team, mostly the people who were in the Situation Room the night after Agnes was taken, and FBI director Riggs."

It made sense. Sand nodded without comment, went to his closet and dressed in the warm-up outfit he wore to work out in the White House gym. By the time he reached the Oval Office there were seven of his top people waiting, including Vice President Vaught, Homeland Security director Jameson, CIA director Hopkins, Admiral Shipman, and National Security Advisor Peck.

FBI director Fred Riggs, a stocky ginger-haired man with a no-nonsense style, was there as well. Riggs and the other aides were all looking at a television screen that showed the home page of www.sonsofprophecy

.info. In the middle of the Web page was an imbedded YouTube clip.

"Let's see it," the President said, and watched as the clip came alive.

The hooded gunman was there in back of the diplomats again. Agnes Lawton was dead center of the streaming video, flanked by Fung and Wadi. All three looked much worse than they had in the ransom video the day before. The Indian foreign minister was sporting a bandage around his head. The Chinese foreign minister seemed dazed and having trouble staying awake. But the U.S. Secretary of State appeared unbowed and unbroken.

Then Agnes Lawton began to speak. "The men holding us, the Sons of Prophecy, have made it clear that they mean to kill us if the five hundred million dollars per country is not delivered and all political prisoners released. We call on President Sand and the leaders of India and China to have mercy on us, and cede to their demands."

The video died, leaving Secretary Lawton with her eyes closed.

Sand wanted to close his eyes, too, but he couldn't, and so he looked around at his advisors.

Vice President Vaught raised both hands in surrender. "Don't look at me."

The chairman of the Joint Chiefs of Staff craned his head around before saying, "Sir, my very real and personal feelings about Agnes aside, I have to advise against meeting any of their demands."

"I agree," said National Security Advisor Peck. "To

do so would project weakness at a time when the country can ill afford—"

A knock and the door to the reception area outside the Oval Office opened. A duty staffer, a young woman in her twenties, bobbed her head.

"I'm desperately sorry to interrupt, Mr. President, but Mr. Lawton is here, quite anxious, and would like to speak with you."

Sand hesitated, but then said, "Show him in, Betty."

The Secretary of State's husband came in a few moments later, skin ashen, cheeks unshaven, and his suit so wrinkled he'd probably slept in it.

"Are you going to meet their demands?" he asked.

"Bill," the President said, going straight to the man, and looking him right in the eye. "I assure you once again that we're doing everything in our—"

Lawton got angry. "I completely disagree with you, Bob. You are *not* doing everything you can to find my wife. If you were, you wouldn't have hired a thief to find her. If you were doing everything you could, you would have three hundred FBI agents already on the ground in the countries around the waters where she was kidnapped. If you were doing everything you could, you'd be moving a fleet of warships into the region and informing those countries that you are going to pick one at random and start lobbing in Tomahawk missiles, and then you're going to pick another country and lob them in, until someone talks and my wife, my Agnes, is released!"

There was a stunned silence in the room.

Sand couldn't remember the last time someone had

challenged him so openly. But he kept his composure and said softly: "You know I can't start throwing missiles around at innocent people, Bill." He took his eyes off the man, looked at FBI director Riggs. "But I will send the FBI agents, and muster as much political and diplomatic pressure as I can."

"And their demands?"

"I can't meet them," the President replied. "I won't meet them."

"You're saying you'll let her die?" Lawton demanded, tears welling.

"I'm saying nothing of the sort, Bill," Sand replied firmly. "I'm saying we have four and a half days, and we're going to use them."

Lawton's lower lip trembled. He wiped at the tears with the sleeve of his suit coat. "I . . . I don't know what I'd do without her."

The President put his hand on Lawton's upper arm, said, "I don't know what I'd do without her. The nation doesn't know what it would do without her."

There were murmurs of support from the others in the room.

Lawton bobbed his head, humbled, and said, "I'm sorry about . . . before."

Sand patted his arm again, and said sincerely, "I can't imagine the strain you're under." Then he turned to his advisors. "What do we know about the Web site? Where it came from? Who's behind it?"

"It surfaced about ninety minutes ago, Mr. President," said Riggs, gesturing at the Sons of Prophecy Web site on the television screen. "I've got a team at

Quantico tracking it. We should know more by the end of the day."

Sand looked at his chief of staff. "Cynthia, I want updates every hour. I'll need help drafting a statement. And alert the media that I will make that statement and take questions at eight A.M. eastern."

"That's just great!" the Vice President said in disgust. "Just go right ahead and preempt the millions of dollars in media buys we've got going in the morning news hours. Damn it, this'll screw me with the women's vote."

The President did not like Vaught much, but he felt for him, knew the kinds of pressure the man was under with only six days until an election and the feeling that it was all slipping away.

"I'll do it at noon, Ken," Sand said. "Does that work?"

The Vice President looked around, nodded, said, "That will help."

The President looked back to FBI director Riggs. "Get your men in the field as soon as possible."

Riggs nodded. "I'll move most of the Honolulu office there this morning."

"All right then," Sand said. "I'll leave you to it."

It was the President's way of saying: *Everyone get out of here. I'm going to get hit hard with this and I need some space and time to think.*

One by one his tops aides and then Lawton left the Oval Office until there was only Cynthia Blayless and Dr. Hopkins, who said, "Mr. President? A moment alone, sir?"

Sand felt irritated. People were always trying to get a moment alone with him and it almost always was some kind of power play. But the CIA director had never gone that route before, so he looked at his chief of staff and said, "Give us five minutes?"

Blayless gave a sharp look Hopkins's way, then nodded, and left the Oval Office by another door.

President Sand said, "Have you heard from Monarch?"

"Not since he was flying to the oil tanker," the CIA director said. "But this has nothing to do with Monarch. It's Secretary Lawton."

"Yes."

"Did you see the way she was blinking?"

Sand looked puzzled. "No."

"She was blinking in Morse code," he said. "Take another look at the video, you'll see it."

"What's she saying?"

Dr. Hopkins told him, and the President felt an even greater weight come down on his shoulders. It felt as if the floor below him was going to collapse. He shook his head and shifted his shoulders at the burden of it before saying, "Then God help me, God help Agnes, and God help the entire nation."

17

IN THE HOLDING CELL deep inside the Vietnamese TC2 complex, Monarch had fallen into a deep, dark sleep that eventually gave way to vivid dreams featuring the street kids he'd seen at the back of the transport truck. The children were running from him. No matter how hard he tried to close the gap, they kept getting farther away. And with every step there were more of them, ragged, hungry, and soon crowding the street until—

The bar on the cell door was thrown, waking him. He looked around groggily, realizing the door was going to open. He checked his watch, wondering how much time he'd already lost and saw he'd been asleep roughly two and a half hours.

The door swung open. Standing in the doorway was an older man wearing the uniform and bars of a Vietnamese Army general. He said crisply, "We see there has been a terrible mistake made, Mr. Monarch. You are free to leave."

"Good," Monarch asked, sitting up, and then standing, his ribs aching. "You are?"

"Major General Han," he replied. "Head of military intelligence in Saigon."

"Nice to meet you, General. Sorry to meet under such circumstances. I suggest you have a serious talk with Captain Su. The man's an idiot."

"This is well known," the senior officer replied, gesturing toward the hallway. "That's why he was sent to Spratly Island. We thought he could do little damage there."

"Who is he, the son of some heavyweight?"

The officer's lips tightened. "Captain Su is my son-in-law."

"Ouch," Monarch said.

"In his defense, he was following orders from his superior, a colonel who can be an utter jackass," General Han's lips tightened further. "In any case, we know of Secretary Lawton's situation. It is all over the Internet and the news."

Monarch wondered how that had happened. "Did my government make contact with you?"

"Shortly after we learned that Secretary Lawton and the foreign ministers had been taken hostage," the general replied. "How may we help? Do you need to return to the tanker?"

"No, I'm good. Where are the other agents?"

"They are being fed," General Han said, gesturing toward the hallway. "May I make the same offer to you?"

Monarch left the cell with no look back. His mind was already in motion, trying to figure out how best to use the congenial General Han, who led him to a commissary where several Vietnamese officers were eating. They watched him enter, some with great curiosity, others with open disdain.

There was a television screen on one wall blaring CNN. Bash and Song Le sat at a table off to one side, watching the coverage, and eating greedily from steaming bowls of *pho,* a Vietnamese soup dish. Bash nodded to him. Song Le completely ignored him. It had been hours since Monarch had eaten, and when they set a bowl before him, he set to it ravenously, one eye on the news.

He quickly learned that a video of Agnes Lawton and the foreign ministers had been uploaded to You-Tube around one A.M. EST. In the hours since, the clip had gone viral, and the Sons of Prophecy Web site had immediately started trending.

Reporters had the White House under siege, demanding answers. So were journalists in India and in Beijing. The Asian and European financial markets had reacted swiftly to news of the kidnapping, plunging as shaken investors sold stocks and moved to gold. Wall Street was looking at similar turmoil in the trading day to come.

Then CNN aired the chilling video. He watched closely as Agnes Lawton spoke, caught something odd, and then realized she was blinking in ones and twos. It was subtle, but it was there. From that point forward, Monarch ignored whatever she was saying. He didn't care. He was reading code. The four words she blinked came as a shock and then he saw the logic behind them, and thought she was probably right. The Secretary of State was one shrewd lady. There was no doubt about that.

The video died and the news anchors began talking about the effect the kidnapping might have on the U.S. presidential elections. Every single one of the pundits portrayed the event as a disaster for Vice President Vaught's campaign for all sorts of reasons.

Monarch didn't pay attention to any of that blather either. Instead, he ate and monitored the Chinese and Indian agents, trying to determine if either of them had picked up on the fact that Secretary Lawton had been using Morse code. If they saw it, they weren't letting on.

"Have you been in contact with your governments?" he asked.

They shook their heads.

"We're going to need three secure lines so we can do that," Monarch told General Han. "We need to know the latest intelligence."

The Vietnamese general quickly made it happen. A few minutes later, Monarch was on an encrypted Skype hookup with Dr. Hopkins in Washington, D.C.

"Did you see her blinking?" Monarch asked.

"I thought I was the only one," he said. "If the press figures that out, it might be the straw that breaks the camel's back. As you might imagine, it's a clusterfuck already. Journalists and Congress are accusing the President of everything you can think of, from malfeasance to gross incompetence."

"Are you looking into it? What she's saying?"

"It would be criminal not to," Dr. Hopkins snapped. "I've informed the President, what he does with it is his call. And if you haven't seen it yet, Sand dispatched two hundred FBI agents to the region. SEAL Team Six is being fully mobilized as well."

Monarch replied, "I think it's a good idea."

"Sands had to appear to be doing something," Hopkins said in a rare moment of cynicism. "In the meantime, NSA's got filters going on 'Sons of Prophecy.' There was literally nothing until news of the hijacking got out, now it's everywhere, so many searches, so many texts and tweets, that they're having a helluva time trying to figure out what's real and what's not. Totally viral."

"You locate the server hosting their Web site?" Monarch asked.

"There are dozens of them," the CIA director said. "Clones, and more of them springing up every hour."

"Where was the video uploaded to YouTube?"

"At an Internet café in Kuala Lumpur."

"Same café as the first?"

"Different. Opposite sides of the city."

"Barnett?"

"She's heading to Kuala Lumpur to dig. The rest of your team will join her there. Or do you want them to divert to Ho Chi Minh City?"

Monarch considered that, replied, "I don't know how long I'm staying. It could easily be a coincidence that the *Niamey* was pushed into Vietnamese waters, and the hijackers are now somewhere far away. I'll let you know."

By the time Song Le and Bash had finished speaking to their people, it was pushing nine P.M. They, too, had little to report. Other than the video, and the Web site—mostly hate and vitriol directed at the developed world and a promise to restore God to prominence on Earth—it was as if the Sons of Prophecy had appeared out of thin air.

"Have you ever heard of them, General?" Bash, the Indian agent asked.

"Never before this," General Han replied.

"Are there pirates in Vietnam?" Song Le asked.

"There are pirates everywhere in the South China Sea."

"Doesn't answer the question," Song Le replied.

She had an abrasive style, Monarch decided. Too bad. Smoothness was always the better approach.

"Of course there are pirates in Vietnam," the general snapped. "But if you are asking whether any of them are sophisticated enough and brave enough to take three of the world's top diplomats hostage, I'd tell you not one chance."

"Why?" Bash asked.

General Han said, "Why would Vietnamese pirates be interested in the release of Chinese, Indian, and American political prisoners?"

"Maybe it's a cover," Song Le offered.

"A possibility," said Bash. "Maybe all they really want is the money."

"Maybe, but they are not *Vietnamese* pirates," the general insisted. "All those armed bodyguards killed in the takeover? That's does not say pirate to me. That says a trained military force, crazies or mercenaries."

Monarch thought that the general was as smart as his son-in-law was stupid. A trained force made sense to him, too. But what kind? Some zealot organization trained in the camps of the Middle East? Or a crew for hire?

"What do you know about the Apocalypse Now Bar?" Bash asked.

General Han frowned, but then replied, "A place for expatriates to celebrate Francis Ford Coppola when he was creatively insane. Why?"

Monarch smiled. The general was growing on him. "Criminals?"

"We suspect drug dealing, prostitution. Beyond that—" He shrugged.

"Could you give us directions?" Bash asked.

"You think this is linked to the Apocalypse Now Bar?" the general asked incredulously.

"We found a matchbook from that bar in Secretary Lawton's cabin on the oil tanker," Monarch said. "There was writing in Vietnamese that suggested a meeting at that bar tonight at eleven."

"Where is this matchbook?"

"Your son-in-law took it," Monarch replied. "Along with our passports, money, and weapons."

The vein on the side of General Han's head began to pulse, as if he were contemplating a stroke. "The idiot wrote nothing of these things in his report."

18

EARLIER IN THE EVENING, after a short ceremony, the Xanadu Casino and Hotel on Macau opened its doors for the first time. It could have easily been a disaster. The skies were overcast and dreary there by the sea. And it was the middle of the week. But to the delight of the Moon Dragon, who was a silent investor in the casino, his wife had been right again in her interpretation of the I Ching. Throngs of customers had lined up two hours early, bulled their way inside when the doors swung open, and quickly created a happy din punctuated by the bells of slot machines and the cries of croupiers.

Wearing a tuxedo, Long Chan-Juan mingled with local political dignitaries and casino executives on a balcony mezzanine above the baccarat section of the gaming floor. He was drinking fine champagne, and watching as thousands of gamblers and the merely curious moved through the opulent facility, which was designed as if it were the interior of Xanadu, the mountain summer palace of the Emperor Kublai Khan.

The walls of the vast casino were covered in trompe l'oeil murals that depicted ancient tapestry hangings, bird cages, and huge palace windows and flower-laden verandahs that overlooked misty, steep mountains, shimmering lakes, and the rumor of distant waterfalls. Pagoda-shaped chandeliers hung over the central gaming floor, which though more than two hundred meters long and half again wide, was packed now and giving off a noise that sounded to the Moon Dragon like the steady crash of coins.

Look at them, the triad leader thought, happily scanning the massive crowd. This kind of scene would not have been possible twenty, thirty years ago. Back then Macau was a seedy backwater of the gaming world. Now, it was quickly becoming the biggest gambling center on the planet, most of it driven by the exploding middle and upper classes of mainland China.

Asians, and especially the Chinese, love to gamble. It was in their nature to seek the odds, try to predict the future, and win. Casino-type gambling, however, was illegal on the mainland, so the moneyed masses, millions upon millions of them, traveled to Macau every year. And now they'll come to the incomparable Xanadu.

"There you are," Madame Long said, breaking his thoughts. "You must come back to the party."

The Moon Dragon almost argued, but then paid for the drink, and followed her back to the opening celebration, barely aware of her prattling on until they were back at the rail of the balcony, overlooking the gaming room. She shook his elbow.

"You're not listening," his wife said. "I asked if you are happy?"

"With?"

"With?" she replied in disbelief before gesturing at the huge crowd below. "Why this of course."

The triad leader thought and said, "I am satisfied. For the evening."

"What more could you ever do than this?" she demanded, looking around at the fabulous dimensions of the casino.

"Nothing here," Long replied, not wanting to elaborate. "Xanadu is perfect, thanks in no small way to your expertise with the Book of Changes."

Madame Long looked pleased, but said, "I'm going to call home, see about Lo-Lo. No telling what that fool of a girl . . ."

The Moon Dragon all but tuned her out. Giving her a smile of vague acknowledgment, he turned back toward the gaming floor. There was much to do, so much more to do. If the status quo could be shaken, chaos would soon follow. That was just the nature of things. Long believed that fervently. He also believed that chaos gave the clearheaded man, the planning man, the chance to forge into the void and reap fortunes, possibly even an empire that the great Khan might have—

"Boss," Tuul said.

Long startled, and frowned when he saw his bodyguard, who looked completely out of place. Instead of a tux, Tuul wore a loud orange Hawaiian shirt and dark wraparound sunglasses.

"I told you to wait downstairs," the Moon Dragon said, displeased.

The Mongolian bobbed his head, proffered a disposable cell phone, whispered, "No disrespect, but you have an urgent phone call from Saigon."

Long's expression soured further, but he took the phone and walked away from the balcony railing toward a buffet table laden with food. "Yes?"

"They've been freed," a male voice said.

"Freed!" the triad leader hissed. "I told you twelve hours minimum."

"They have an ally who outranks me," the man replied. "A general. But I have pictures of them and I know where they're going and when."

The Moon Dragon said, "The Apocalypse Now Bar around eleven tonight."

There was a stunned silence on the other end of the line until his man in Vietnam said, "How did you—?"

"It doesn't matter," Long said impatiently. "I hope you can provide perimeter security for them."

Another pause. "The general I spoke of. He is personally running perimeter security for the three agents."

"Then you'll just have to deal with the general, won't you?"

"How?"

"Be creative, and there'll be more money in it for you," the triad leader snapped. "And send me pictures of them."

He punched the end button and almost out of habit

handed the phone back to Tuul so he could take it somewhere and destroy it. Instead he tucked the cell in his pocket, and said, "Book us on the ten P.M. helicopter to Hong Kong. Call our people in Saigon and tell them their assignment has changed. They should go with cameras *and* weapons. And I want a real-time Web hookup."

Tuul left without another word.

The phone in the Moon Dragon's pocket buzzed three times, and he soon had three grainy, ill-shot photos to study. The first was of a burly Indian man eating soup. The second, blurrier, was of a woman that he guessed was Chinese, though it was hard to be sure from the angle. The third man was shown clearly, however, a big, ruggedly built man of indeterminate origin.

That had to be Monarch. Long studied the picture, and felt a rush. This was better than he'd ever imagined. Almost as an afterthought, he'd told Captain Ramelan to drop the matchbook as a way of putting investigators on a false trail heading in exactly the wrong direction. The idea was that if the matchbook was found in time—and this had most certainly happened—the false clue might bring whoever had discovered it within range of cameras so that the Moon Dragon might clearly see the face of his pursuers.

But now he had a chance to get his pursuers in the range of his gunmen. Best of all? He'd get to watch the action as it unfolded.

"Tuul said we are leaving," Madame Long said in an accusatory tone.

"Ten P.M. helicopter," the Moon Dragon said.

"I bought this dress at Chanel," his wife complained. "It's couture. You can't expect me to wear it for just a few hours."

Long managed not to show his annoyance. "The dress does look astonishing on you. But I'm sure it and you have been noted many times tonight already. Look at the thousands of people down there. I've seen so many eyes looking your way it's like you're a star. And the worst thing that can happen to a star is overexposure."

She threw him a skeptical look, and then hardened. "You owe me for this, something big."

"Just put it in the box with all the other IOUs," he replied blithely. "In the meantime, we're going home. Now."

He endured his wife's silent wrath on the short helicopter ride back to Hong Kong, the drive to their villa high on the flank of Victoria Peak, and the wait for Tuul to clear them to enter the house. The Moon Dragon looked in on his sleeping grandson, ignored Madame Long's scolding of Anna the maid for some perceived domestic flaw, and then locked himself in his home office.

It was five minutes to eleven in Hong Kong, and an hour ahead of Saigon.

To kill time, Long surfed the Web, reading about the mounting turmoil in America. President Sand had not said a word yet, and his press secretary was refusing to explain how the Secretary of State and the foreign ministers had been taken in the first place. Reporters covering the campaign were focusing on Senator Burkhardt, who had gone on the offensive once word of Secretary Lawton's situation came out, charging that Vice President Vaught was part of an "imperial, inept presidency that cannot even protect its diplomats," and that "the country deserved better than a government cloaked in secrecy."

The U.S. markets had opened, as predicted, in utter turmoil. Wall Street was in free fall. Gold's value had shot up nearly thirty percent. This greatly pleased the Moon Dragon. He had bought thousands of gold coins in the prior few months. He would sell them the following Monday, the day before the U.S. elections, when fear of political and economic upheaval would be at its highest.

After the market roundup, the coverage cut to a story about the two hundred FBI agents on their way to the region. The piece also quoted officials in Malaysia, Vietnam, and Indonesia pledging to help find the hostages. It concluded, saying, "All eyes are now on Southeast Asia as the hunt for the missing diplomats gets under way in earnest."

Two hundred FBI agents? All eyes on Southeast Asia?

The Moon Dragon decided he wasn't worried in either case. He knew that by the time the FBI got on the ground and mobilized, the world's attention would have shifted far away from the South China Sea. The police? Long had moles in every major law enforcement agency in the region. He'd know their plans and actions at every turn. Wasn't that the case in Vietnam? Obviously.

At eleven forty-three, the triad leader at last tore his attention away from the news. He signed into a Web site registered to a shell company created by his ally in Kuala Lumpur. The screen blinked, split into six different segments before the feeds went live.

Dance music suddenly pounded in the triad leader's ears and six views of the Apocalypse Now Bar appeared on his computer screen. Two feeds showed the nightclub's front exterior. One scanned the line of patrons waiting to clear security, and another focused on the sidewalks and street traffic.

Long also had four different views of the club's interior, including a crowded dance floor, pool tables, and a lounge area out back. From the angles, he suspected that the men wore the fiber optic cameras attached to ball caps, or tucked behind their ears.

The men with the cameras had no idea who he was. They had never heard his voice before. They never would again. But they would follow his orders without question. They had been well paid to do so.

The Indian showed up by taxi at ten minutes to eleven with the Chinese agent trailing. But where was Monarch?

"Let them all get inside," the Moon Dragon said. "We've got a third still to—"

Long's words froze in his mouth because he had gotten his first really good look at the Chinese agent. For a moment he did not trust his vision, or his memory. Then she turned in semi profile and the triad leader knew for certain he was looking at Song Le.

In his gut, the Moon Dragon felt strange, and then

fearful, as if he were about to be exposed. Fate had dealt him a wild card he could not have anticipated in a hundred years. How was this possible? What were the odds of her being assigned to the case? What were the possible ramifications of her presence?

Before the Moon Dragon could begin to formulate theories, his attention jumped to another feed. Monarch was there moving through the lounge. The thief must have come in through a service entrance. He walked right by one of the cameramen. Seeing the Chinese agent come into the nightclub on an adjacent feed, he thought of his wife and turned as bitterly sharp as an icicle.

Hello thief, the Moon Dragon thought. Hello Song Le. And good-bye.

19

THE PULSING TECHNO MUSIC made Monarch wince the instant he stepped through the rear service door of the Apocalypse Now Bar. At a glance, he took in a terrace covered with a green plastic roof. There were perhaps twenty people sitting at various tables, couples, foursomes, the odd guy nursing a beer and looking hungrily at one of the small groups of trolling women.

Monarch saw the flash of the strobe light coming from the main club, and wondered if they'd have been better off chasing down some other angle than the matchbook. After all, how can you spot someone when you have no idea what he looks like, and strobe lights are on?

Still, he moved into a long room that held a crowded dance floor to his left and a bar and poolroom to his right. Monarch hated places like Apocalypse Now. Crowded. Smoky. Saturated with booze. Reeking of lust and desperation. He scanned the crowd, aware of the Glock at the small of his back, and trying to believe that this was a productive avenue of investigation, rather than some wild-goose chase. Then again, someone, probably one of the hijackers, dropped the matchbook during the course of Secretary Lawton's capture and abduction. Based on the writing in the matchbook, Monarch believed he was looking for a Vietnamese, who had a meeting scheduled here four or five minutes from now. He might already be inside the nightclub.

Monarch squinted when the strobe lights went on again and picked up something odd. The loner on a stool along the wall to his left—a gangsta wannabe with the black wife-beater tee, the tattoos, and the buff build—was wearing a clip-on LED light. The light wasn't on. But it was there attached to the brow of the loner's L.A. Lakers hat, which he wore low, shading his eyes.

Monarch used such lights to move about at night from time to time. But something about the LED lamp did not fit the vibe of the Apocalypse Now Bar. He spotted Song Le coming down a staircase opposite him. She was wearing a Bluetooth device in her ear. So was Bash. So was Monarch.

"Anything?" he said.

The Chinese agent looked disgusted, shook her head, said, "I don't know what I'm looking for."

"Join the club," said Bash, who was over in the poolroom, leaning against the back wall, nursing a beer.

Monarch decided that he liked the Indian. He had a steady confidence and seemed bemused by life. Most of the men Monarch had known who'd thrived in the

high-stakes world of special ops without deep psycho-
logical problems were like Bash, always aware of the
cosmic joke. John Tatupu, a Samoan-American Monarch had worked with for years, had the identical dis-
position and—

Monarch spotted another man in the poolroom
wearing one of those clip-on LED headlamps. This guy
seemed interested in Bash. Muscular, with the thick
features of central Asia, he wore a white tunic shirt,
and carried a pool stick in absurdly huge hands.

Monarch studied his clip-on lamp. Unless this was
some sort of local fad, it seemed strange that men would
be wearing the headlamps in that nightclub, especially
when they were identical.

Monarch didn't want to take a chances. He said,
"Bash, be aware of the stout guy with the headlamp on
his cap to your right."

Bash nodded, glanced over at Mr. Big Hands, who
was at the pool table prepping for his shot. Monarch
scanned around, and spotted a third man wearing a clip-
on LED headlamp. This guy was up against a wall, right
angle to Song Le, who was on the staircase less than
twenty feet away.

There! LED man just looked at her.

Monarch's instincts went on full alert. "To your left
Song Le," he said. "LED lamp on the cap brim. General, how far out are your men?"

Monarch and Song Le had left General Han several
blocks from the nightclub. The Vietnamese intelligence
officer's men were ready to close ground and surround
the nightclub if Monarch called them in.

"General Han?" Monarch said again.

But there was no answer. The hair prickled on the thief's neck, made him feel suddenly vulnerable. Where was that first guy with the headlamp, the one behind him, back in the lounge? As he pivoted to look, he reached back under his shirt, found the pistol's grip.

The gangsta wannabe stood not four feet away. He had a red windbreaker draped over his right forearm. There was a stout pistol silencer sticking out from under it, aimed right at Monarch's stomach.

20

"KILL HIM!" THE MOON Dragon hissed, reveling in the stunned expression on the thief's face. "And the woman! Now!"

A waitress walked in front of Long's man, blocking Monarch just as the assassin shot. The woman was hit at point-blank range. She dumped her tray of drinks, and fell.

The thief was gone! So was Song Le!

The camera whipped around, looking for Monarch while the club's oblivious patrons danced on. The triad leader caught a glimpse of the thief. Then the camera jerked, slashed sideways, and dropped to the floor, unmoving, aimed at the strobe light.

Long was shocked when Monarch grabbed up the camera, and looked into the lens. "I don't know who you are yet," the thief growled. "But I am hunting *you* now."

The screen blurred, went blank. Shaken, the Moon

Dragon looked away to the other feeds, hearing the first shouts of alarm in the club.

"Kill them all!" he thundered.

But the Indian agent already had his gun drawn and aimed directly at one of the cameras. Suddenly the Indian buckled and dropped, revealing a second gunman rising from a shooting crouch.

At the other end of the club, one of the assassins had locked on Song Le, who was aiming elsewhere. The Moon Dragon felt zero pity for her. Quite the contrary, he was pleased that he'd get to see her die like this, up close, and yet impersonal.

The wall next to the camera exploded, throwing debris at the lens, which swung wildly away from Song Le and spiraled lower as if the man holding it had ducked in retreat. As the camera spun, the Moon Dragon thought he saw Monarch again before the lens jerkily showed the glass in the nightclub's inner door shattering, then the entryway, the stunned bouncers, and the street scene outside the club.

Long went ballistic, shouting into his microphone. "Cowards! Turn and fight or I'll have every one of you hunted down and shot!"

He looked at the other two feeds outside Apocalypse Now showing one of the assassins escaping. "Get in there," he shouted. "Finish the job. One hundred thousand dollars to the man who gets it done!"

"General Han, we've got shots fired and an armed man coming out the front door!" Monarch shouted into his Bluetooth.

Ignoring the screaming as panic built in the club, Monarch had vaulted the bleeding waitress's body, trying to get another shot at the assassin who'd been closest to Song Le, the one now making his escape.

Monarch had a clear line of fire as the man went through the shattered glass of the front door. But Song Le jumped in the way, blocking the shot.

Pushing people out of his way, Monarch ran after her. He spotted Bash on the floor between the pool tables. The Indian agent's eyes were open, but unfocused and his mouth chewed the air as if he were struggling.

The crack of a bullet passed just behind Monarch. He spotted another gunman moving behind the bar. Monarch fired and hit the assassin on the bridge of his nose.

"General Han, answer," Monarch grunted as he sprinted through the broken front door in time to see Song Le squeal out on a white Honda scooter in pursuit of three other scooters already a block ahead of her. They were racing east toward the Saigon River.

Monarch shoved his gun in the face of the closest guy sitting on a scooter. "I'll bring it back," he promised.

The owner got off, looking pissed. Monarch started the scooter, squealed out in pursuit. Even at midnight the street was crowded with dozens of scooters. He wove in and out of them, accelerating every chance he got until he spotted Song Le fifty yards ahead of him, racing toward a large rotary that led to the riverfront arterial road. He thought he spotted the three scooters she was chasing about fifty yards beyond her, already entering the rotary.

There was a small park in the middle of the round-about with vegetation low enough that Monarch could look across it. The three escaping gunmen were roughly three-quarters of the way around the rotary now with Song Le at the halfway mark.

Instead of circling counterclockwise and chasing their tail as Song Le had done, the thief went into the rotary in the opposite direction, straight into on-coming traffic.

The scooter headlights shining in his face were almost blinding. Getting low over the handlebars, he made his eyelids slits, and ignored the shouts and the horns beeping frantically as he dodged his way forward. One rider panicked, skidded, and laid his scooter down. The downed machine and rider slid down the pavement inches to Monarch's left, throwing sparks into the night. The next scooter driver cranked his handlebars too hard, lost control, and hit a cement retaining wall.

Monarch cleared one last scooter, which left him less than eighty yards behind the escaping assassins and well in front of Song Le as they left the rotary for Ton Duc Thang, the river road heading north. Monarch angled his scooter after them, twisted the throttle wide open. The bike had far more power than he expected, and he shot forward.

Monarch was closing ground now, bracing his pistol between his palm and the handlebars. When he got close, his instincts said shoot the tires out, get hold of one or more of the fleeing killers and force out some answers.

Two Vietnamese Army jeeps came flying out of a side street to his left, came across the entire road. The fleeing assassins got past the jeeps. But Monarch had to hit the brakes hard to keep from crashing into them broadside.

"Get out of the way!" he roared. "I'm working with General Han of TC-two!"

The front passenger side of the jeep flew open. Captain Su got out, training a submachine gun on Monarch.

"My father-in-law is dead," Captain Su said. "And you are under arrest for his murder."

In a rage, the Moon Dragon tore off his headset and threw it at the wall. The thief had killed three of his hired men. Luckily the others had escaped before they could be caught and interrogated. Not that they would know anything that could lead back to him. And yet this failure, coupled with the sighting of Song Le, left Long feeling as if his future were growing darker by the moment. He got a bottle of Johnnie Walker Black Label from a cabinet, poured four fingers in a tumbler, and took several deep gulps, trying to—

A knock at the door. "Are you all right?" Madame Long called.

The triad leader wanted to yank open the door and punch his wife in the nose. Instead, he opened it slowly, smiled at her, and said, "I was watching a soccer game."

Madame Long hardened. "And for this we left the party of the year?"

The Moon Dragon didn't know what to say at first,

but then replied, "I was working with the television on and I got caught up in the moment."

His wife said nothing, and walked away with her head held imperiously high.

The Moon Dragon thought to follow her, to try to salve her anger. Instead he shut the door, locked it, and returned to his drink. Long downed it and again sat at his desk. From the top drawer he drew out a pistol, a SIG Sauer .40 that he unloaded and set on a pile of envelopes.

Scrounging in the wastepaper basket, the triad leader came up with the *South China Morning Post* and spread sections of it on the desk. After pouring another drink, he set about dismantling and cleaning the gun.

The Moon Dragon was obsessive about clean guns. Dirty guns misfired and jammed. Clean guns didn't. These were lessons he'd learned working at the Hong Kong Rifle Association when he was a teenager. Over decades, gun cleaning had become a meditation for Long. The rote task allowed his mind to relax, forced him to step back, to see things from a broader perspective.

Why was Song Le, of all people, involved in this? What were the odds?

He thought about the people he knew inside the Ministry for State Security. How many agents did they employ? Thousands? So why send her? Was she that good?

The Moon Dragon dwelled on those final two questions as he completed the cleaning job and began to reassemble the weapon. But by the time he'd finished, reloaded the pistol, and returned it to the top drawer of his desk, he still had no concrete answers. And he really was in no position to make inquiries of the people he knew inside the Chinese intelligence apparatus. That was an absolute no go for the time being.

As he left his office, heading for his warm bed and cold wife, Long tried to believe that it was a coincidence, a simple twist of fate that had brought Song Le onto the scene. But deep down he feared the Chinese agent's appearance might be something more than happenstance, something preordained.

Monarch, meanwhile, was aware of the wailing of police sirens, but his focus was entirely on Captain Su's machine gun. "What are you talking about?"

"General Han is dead," Captain Su said, his voice shaking. "He was shot in the head in his car. We just left there. Put down your guns."

"Not a chance," Monarch said. "I didn't kill your father-in-law. He was alive when we left him. I was chasing assassins who attacked us inside the bar. Bashir is hit."

Song Le arrived, and halted beside Monarch, facing Captain Su. Su looked over at her and said, "Put down your gun as well. Do it or I will shoot the both of you!"

"By the time you shoot one of us, the other one will have killed you," Song Le replied calmly.

Captain Su looked uncertain.

"What is going on here?" Song Le asked Monarch.

"He wants to arrest us for General Han's murder."

"Murder?" she said, bewildered. "He was alive when we—"

Monarch cut her off, said, "What are *you* doing here, Captain? I never heard the general say he was bringing you into this."

"My superior said I could redeem myself," the captain said defensively. "I was on the perimeter, waiting for his order to move in with my men."

Song Le said, "I think *you* killed your father-in-law because he thought you were an idiot."

Outraged, Captain Su shot back, "I didn't kill him and he did not think I was an idiot."

"Yes, he did," Monarch said, thinking about the sequence of events that had unfolded that long day. "But I don't think you killed him."

"Of course not," Captain Su sputtered. "You did."

"No," Monarch said. "I think your superior did."

"Colonel Nguyen? Impossible."

"Really? Who told you to go to the tanker? Who else knew about the matchbook we found? Who else knew we were here?"

Captain Su nodded slowly, looked at Monarch with a torn expression. "But the colonel has worked with my father-in-law for years. Why would he do this?"

"Exactly what we'd like to know," Monarch said.

"I . . . I can't just arrest him."

"So arrest us," Song Le said. "And bring us to him."

21

FOUR VIETNAMESE MEDICS WERE carrying Bash out on a stretcher by the time Monarch, Song Le, and Captain Su got back to the Apocalypse Now Bar, where Colonel Nguyen was said to be overseeing the investigation.

The Indian agent appeared more alert now than he'd been after the initial shock of being shot, but in greater pain. Speckles of bright blood showed at his lips and nose.

"Lung?" Monarch asked.

"They think he nicked one," Bash said, his voice sounding like he was gargling. "Maybe collapsed it."

Monarch flashed on an image of his younger self in much the same condition. "We'll contact your government," Monarch said.

"They'll medevac you immediately," Song Le said.

"Good working with you," Monarch said, meaning it. "And don't worry. We will find your foreign minister."

"Wait," the Indian said weakly. "Where are you going?"

Monarch looked toward the nightclub. "To break this case wide open."

He waited until Bash had been loaded into an ambulance before climbing the stairs to find the lobby blocked by local police. Captain Su barked something at them and they reluctantly stood aside.

The interior of the Apocalypse Now Bar looked anemic and sad when the strobes were dead and the floodlights were fully on, revealing a general dinginess accented with corpses, spent casings, broken glass, blood, beer, and other debris left over from the gunfight. Shouting quick, sharp orders that Monarch couldn't understand at a crew of armed soldiers, Colonel Nguyen slowly strutted through the relics of mayhem, inspecting the carnage, his chest puffed out like a spurred rooster before a cockfight.

The Vietnamese military intelligence officer spotted them then, and Captain Su. He had a thin mustache that twisted with rage. He came toward them, pistol out and spitting his words. "Why aren't they in handcuffs, Captain?"

Colonel Nguyen did not wait for an answer, but stopped and brandished his pistol. Monarch wanted to snatch the gun from the man, but the colonel was just out of range and all of his soldiers were shifting the aim of their automatic weapons.

So he just stood there when the colonel shouted, "I

was right. You should have been kept in the cells. You *are* foreign spies. This story about the diplomats is some kind of cover for you to come in here and disrupt our country."

"And how were we supposed to do that?" Monarch asked calmly.

The colonel flipped the safety off and aimed his pistol between Monarch's eyes. "You started by killing General Han."

"We did not kill him," Song Le said. "But we think you did."

The military intelligence officer's eyes darted from the Chinese agent to Monarch before he laughed in caustic disbelief. "General Han was a close friend. Why would I ever kill him? This is foolish. Nonsense. Captain, take them back to TC-two where they'll be interrogated properly."

But when Colonel Nguyen glanced left, he saw that General Han's son-in-law had drawn his own pistol and was now aiming it shakily at his superior. "I can't do that, sir," Su said. "You're under arrest until we can sort this out."

Colonel Nguyen regarded his subordinate as if he were vermin, like a rat who'd just squeaked an alarm. "What you're doing is treason, Captain. Can you handle the consequences of that? Treason?"

Captain Su suddenly looked completely in over his head, and Monarch could tell he was about to cave.

Before he could, his boss made some kind of snap decision and swung his pistol over toward Captain Su, saying, "In Vietnam, Captain, the penalty for treason is—"

Two shots went off almost simultaneously. Colonel Nguyen's bullet blew through Captain Su's left thigh and left him sprawling on the floor, screaming and squirming in agony. Captain Su's shot caught his superior below the right eye, and the colonel fell like a trapdoor had opened beneath him. The soldiers in the room had their weapons up immediately, and were shouting insanely in Vietnamese.

Monarch did the smart thing, laced his fingers behind his head and went to his knees facing Colonel Nguyen's lifeless body. Song Le did the same thing.

Four of the armed soldiers rushed them. One hit Monarch with the muzzle of his rifle, opening up a small cut. The thief didn't move a muscle.

"No!" Captain Su gasped. "Let them go. Get me an ambulance, but leave them be."

The soldiers fought among themselves for a few moments before signaling Song Le and Monarch to rise. Another soldier was working on Captain Su, putting a belt high on his leg. General Han's son-in-law was panting, sweat pouring off his face.

"See?" he said. "I'm not an idiot. I saved your life, and mine."

"You did," Monarch said, crouching next to him. "But you also took away our ability to talk to your boss about why he killed your father-in-law."

"Isn't it obvious that he did it?" Captain Su said in a painful hiss. "When you brought it up, he tried to kill me."

"I think you'll find evidence that his gun was used

on the general," Monarch agreed. "But I'm more interested in why. Can I search him?"

Captain Su look uncertain, but then nodded. As the wailing of an ambulance neared, Monarch went through Colonel Nguyen's pockets, finding his ID, business cards, and a cell phone. He opened it, looked at the most recent calls. In the last two days, the Vietnamese officer had made eighteen phone calls. All were to numbers in Ho Chi Minh City.

"We need to search his home and office," Monarch said.

"I can't give you that permission," said Captain Su, as the sirens stopped wailing, replaced by the sound of doors slamming and men shouting.

"Who can?" Monarch demanded.

"I don't know," he grunted.

Song Le said quietly, "I don't care how cooperative the Vietnamese say they'll be, they're not going to let us search through the files of one of their top military intelligence officials."

The thief knew the Chinese agent was right. They'd have to wait for a Vietnamese team to go through Colonel Nguyen's office, home, computers. It could take hours, even days, and they had precious little time to waste.

As medics rushed in and began working on Captain Su's leg, Monarch stood back, understanding that there would be high-ranking police or military intelligence officers on the scene within minutes, which meant they might be detained yet again.

He looked at Song Le, and said, "I'm leaving. You coming?"

"Where are you going?" the Chinese agent said coolly.

"I don't know yet, but it beats being here when the good guys arrive."

She understood. They headed through the lounge and out through the service entrance into an alley, and moved off quickly, trying to put the nightclub well behind them.

For several minutes, they jogged in silence. Monarch still did not know what his next move was, but then something General Han said came back to him. He slowed and raised his hand to hail a cab.

"Where are we going?" Song Le asked again.

"The airport, and then Bangkok."

Her face knitted doubt. "I see nothing in this case that suggests Thailand."

"It's a question of perspective," Monarch said, as a taxi slowed.

The Chinese agent crossed her arms. "What perspective?"

"In this case, the late General Han's," Monarch said, climbing in the taxi and scooting over.

Song Le did not look happy, but she climbed in. "What about him?"

"Airport," Monarch said.

"No, airport," the driver said. "No planes until morning."

"Someone's picking us up," Monarch growled. "Take us to the airport."

The driver scowled, and tapped on the meter, saying, "You pay me cash two times go airport."

"Deal," Monarch replied.

"General Han?" Song Le said in an insistent tone as the cab started moving. "Bangkok?"

"That's right. The more I've thought about it, the more I believe the general was very smart and absolutely right. The Sons of Prophecy stuff aside, the attack on the *Niamey* reeks of a professional job, which means mercenaries. Big-time mercenaries."

"What does Bangkok have to do with big-time mercenaries?"

Monarch shot her a reproving glance. "Where else would you go to find an agent who represents them?"

"And you know this agent for mercenaries?" she asked skeptically.

"I do. We go way back."

"So why don't you call him?"

Monarch laughed. "You honestly think a mercenary agent answers his phone? It doesn't work that way at all. This kind of business is done face to face."

Song Le studied him a moment, and then said, "Why do I get the feeling that you have lived many lives on the long road to who you are now?"

"Hasn't everyone?" he said. "Haven't you?"

"You have no idea," she said, and nothing more.

22

WEARING A HEADSET BENEATH an absurdly large sunhat and large dark sunglasses, Gloria Barnett perched in the back of a hired Mercedes as it rolled into a residential neighborhood north of the Shah Amal Highway. The row houses and apartment buildings were all relatively new and beautifully maintained. A Malaysian man was scrubbing the cement walkway with soap and water in front of her destination: the B&L Internet Café, a storefront that featured a bright sign and English, Malay, and Arabic writing.

"I'll tell you, Robin, from the outside this place doesn't look like your normal terrorist hangout," she said. "Too affluent."

She was looking at her iPad now and the exhausted face of Robin Monarch. The thief shrugged, said, "It's a good cover then. But are we sure it's where the videos and the Web sites were uploaded?"

"Videos here, the Web site about seven miles on," she replied. "I'm going there next."

Monarch turned his head, as if he were looking out a window, and said, "Still no Gulfstream."

Barnett frowned as the driver parked down the block from the Internet café, and said, "It lands at eleven fifteen. He'll refuel and you're gone. You'll be in Bangkok by three P.M. at the latest."

He rubbed at his temples. "Sorry, I haven't had much sleep and I feel like I've stepped into quicksand."

"Understandable," she said. "Luckily I was around to throw you a rope."

Monarch and Song Le had arrived at the Saigon airport without exit visas, nor entry visas for that matter. As soon as he got there, he'd called Barnett, waking her from a dead sleep in her hotel room in Kuala Lumpur. She had been at work ever since.

She had started by calling Dr. Hopkins and asking for the CIA's help with the documents Monarch and Song Le needed. During the conversation she learned that the director was already dealing with Vietnamese officials irate over the murder and mayhem at the Apocalypse Now Bar. But Hopkins promised her that Monarch would get out of Vietnam if she could find him a jet to rent.

She located one online—a Gulfstream 550 due in Kuala Lumpur from Australia at 7:30 that morning. With turnaround, and a new pilot, the private jet would be in Ho Chi Minh City at 11:15.

"I appreciate it, Gloria," Monarch said. "Anything else?"

"Your documents are all set," she said. "Oh, and by the way, the Vietnamese have shared a few things with Dr. Hopkins. They've gone through Colonel Nguyen's office, home, and car. Based on a preliminary comparison between the bullet found in General Han's head and the colonel's service pistol, Nguyen was definitely the shooter."

That seemed to perk Monarch up. "But we still don't know why?"

She shook her head. "There's speculation that there was bad blood between them, but nothing concrete yet."

"No, it had to do with the kidnappings. I'm sure of it. Tell Hopkins to get Nguyen's bank accounts, phone records, and recent travel patterns in the hands of our analysts," Monarch replied.

"Hopkins has already made that request," she replied. "But given how pissed off the Vietnamese are at you, I don't know how long it's going to take."

Monarch glanced to his right again, then looked back and smiled. "There's our ride, Gulfstream right on time."

"Contact me tonight?"

"Definitely," Monarch said. "Tats and Chavez? Fowler?"

"All delayed in Honolulu," she replied. "That typhoon's hitting there. Nothing's flying for ten, maybe twelve hours."

"Nothing we can do about it," he said. "Good hunting."

"You, too."

Barnett clicked off the connection, leaned forward,

and rapped on the window separating the seats. It rolled down.

"Yes, ma'am?" said the driver, a middle-aged Malaysian man with a kind face and a bright colored fez on his bald head.

"I might be a while," she said. "Don't leave."

He looked puzzled. "But you have the Internet connection, a very good one, in your hotel, no?"

"I'm just seeing an old friend," she said before grabbing a large canvas shopping bag and climbing out.

God it was hot. Tropical hot.

Barnett slung the purse over her shoulder and crossed the street in her long, jilting gait, already suffering in the heat and humidity. Tall, pale, and with that flaming red hair, Barnett knew it would be impossible to blend in here no matter how good her disguise. So she'd played on that, adding the big floppy sunhat and the weird grandma sunglasses. They made her seem goofier than she was, and that, she'd learned, could be very helpful. Entering the B&L Internet Café, she intentionally tripped over the transom and sprawled on the floor.

A young Malaysian woman wearing a blue head scarf, a light blue blouse, and a dark blue ankle-length skirt was working the coffee counter. She rushed out, hands together in a prayer posture, bowing and crying, "Are you all right, miss?"

"I'm such a klutz," Barnett said as if it were an apology, and trying to get back on her feet.

The Malaysian woman got her elbow and helped her up. "You are hurt, miss?" she asked in a fretful voice.

"No, no," Barnett said, glancing around and seeing a rectangular room about thirty feet by twenty. By her quick count there were twenty desktop computers in the room, all Dells, with black keyboards and screens.

A Malaysian man in his twenties sat at one along the near wall. A woman older than the clerk, but dressed similarly, was working at another computer. The rest of the stations were empty. That made things a little easier.

"Do you own this lovely café?" Barnett asked, looking at the badge on the clerk's smock. "Azura?"

"No, madam," the woman said, smiling and bowing. "It is my husband's."

Barnett dug in her purse, came up with a card that she'd mocked up after arranging for Monarch's jet. It identified her by her real name as an employee of Microsoft, based in Singapore, and specializing in "Quality Research."

"Is he in?" Barnett asked. "Your husband?"

Azura bowed again. "No, madam. But he is not accepting salespeople. We have just bought all new computers."

"Perfect," Barnett replied, ad-libbing. "So they're fast?"

"Very fast. The best."

"Perfect. Perfect," Barnett said and put her hand gently on the woman's forearm. "And I'm not selling anything, so don't you worry."

Azura beamed again. "You wish to use one of our computers?"

"Yes, as a matter of fact," Barnett replied. "All of them."

The owner's wife lost her smile. "All? This is not—"

"Let me explain, Azura," Barnett said, smiling again as if they were the best of friends. "I'm in quality research at Microsoft. We're going all around the world testing things like processor, software, and Internet speed on publicly used computers that run our operating system."

"Why would you do this?" Azura asked, confused.

"To help us make better products," she said. "It will only take three or four minutes at each computer. And we'll pay you for the time and use."

"Pay us?" the owners wife said, beaming again. "Oh, yes. You can start."

Barnett put her hand on the woman's arm again, and said, "Aren't you the sweetest little thing. Thank you, Azura."

She walked to the first computer, sat down, and reached into her purse. She came up with a memory stick that she plugged into a USB port. The stick was loaded with software that did not measure the speed of anything.

FBI analysts at Quantico had studied the Sons of Prophecy videos uploaded to YouTube and the Web site, and extracted several IP addresses and electronic signatures. Everything in the videos pointed to one of the computers inside the B&L Internet Café.

Barnett wanted to know exactly which one. The first computer was a bust. So were the second, third, and fourth machines she probed. She got nothing more in the next five, but then hit the lottery on number eleven. Whoever had uploaded the Sons of Prophecy video had

done it via that specific computer two days prior at 1:20
P.M. He, or she, was signed in as "M. Ex."

She got out a second memory stick and launched a
second piece of software designed to look for other
actions taken by M. Ex on the computer. Barnett was
hoping for e-mail activity, or anything else that might
give her a clue as to the user's identity. What she got
was inconclusive. M. Ex had been online less than ten
minutes. He signed into YouTube using the same M. Ex
handle and offering the password "prophecy." He'd uploaded the video and signed out. Pulling the memory
stick, she tucked it in her pocket, and returned to the
front counter, noticing that the two other customers
were gone. She and the owner's wife were alone.

"Azura?" Barnett said. "I think that's a solid sample.
I was using your computers for almost an hour. Does
this cover it?"

Barnett laid out three times the normal rental rate,
and the Malaysian woman bobbed her head, pressed
her hands together, and bowed. "Yes, miss. Thank you,
miss."

"Can I ask you some questions before I go?" Barnett
asked. "They could be of help to me and to Bill Gates."

Azura bowed again. "Of course. Bill Gates. Of
course."

"Do you keep a log of everyone who comes in?"

She shook her head. "The law does not require it.
Why?"

"Just interested in trying to correlate computer
speed with length of use," Barnett said, but then
shrugged and went for broke. "I saw that someone used

that computer there yesterday for a very brief time, ten minutes between one and two yesterday afternoon."

The owner's wife frowned. But Barnett pressed on, saying, "The user uploaded videos at a high rate of speed, and left. Do you have any idea who that might have been? I'd love to interview him or her as part of my research. Were you working yesterday?"

Azura nodded absently, glancing at the computer Barnett had pointed out.

"Do you remember someone here for only a short period of time like that?" Barnett asked.

The Malaysian woman brought her gaze back on the tall redhead. You could see the suspicion in her attitude. It was vague, though, not pointed.

"And you wish to talk to her?" Azura asked.

"The woman?" Barnett said, feeling her heart pound. "Yes. Do you know her? Where I can find her?"

The owner's wife shook her head. "I remember her because she had her baby with her, but I'd never seen her before."

"Was she Malaysian?" Barnett asked. "Just out of curiosity."

Two teenage girls came into the café. Azura looked at them, and said, "Yes. And just out of curiosity, what are you *really* looking for?"

"A better product," Barnett said, feeling like she was pushing her luck. "You've been very helpful."

23

A YOUNG MALAYSIAN WOMAN with a baby had uploaded the files. Barnett hadn't even remotely considered that. She'd figured she was looking for some young, disaffected male zealot.

During the twenty-five-minute ride to the Lucky Moon Internet Café on the west side of Kuala Lumpur, she chewed on the ramifications of a woman, a mother no less, involved in the kidnapping of the diplomats. Why not? Fanatics come from every persuasion these days.

The driver pulled over in a neighborhood that was older than the one they'd just left, but no less spotless. Using that same exaggerated awkwardness as before, Barnett tripped entering the café where someone, perhaps a young woman with a baby, had uploaded the SOP Web pages. The owner, a congenial man named Panjang, had rushed to her side as quickly as Azura had. Barnett made the same play, and was soon granted permission to check the speed of the eighteen computers, all of which were much older than the ones she'd probed at the first café. There were six people, all young, using the computers, so it took her twice as long to find the one she sought. The fourteenth machine she checked was the one used to upload the Web pages the day before by "M. Ex."

Okay, she thought.

Barnett ran the second piece of probing software and was able to place M. Ex on the machine for nearly two hours the day before between four and six P.M. In that time the Sons of Prophecy Web files were e-mailed through a blind account in Bombay to more than twenty different hosting companies around the world. It was unclear how the hosting had been paid for, but Barnett guessed it would be from some kind of blind account as well. Still, it was something, a fingernail hold at least.

Two hours was a long time in a place like this, she thought. For several moments, Barnett considered taking the same tack she'd used with Azura, wanting to interview a customer. Then she noticed that the café's young clients had all departed, and thought of how little time was left before the scheduled execution. She needed to bull ahead.

Barnett went to the front door, closed it, and turned the open sign to closed.

"Hey misses, what is this you doing there?" Panjang cried. "We don't close until midnight!"

Barnett set the equivalent of five hundred U.S. dollars on the counter, and said, "Do you have a log of your customers?"

The owner looked confused, shook his head. "It is not—"

"I know," she said. "Look, I'm not really a researcher from Microsoft."

"No?"

"I am an American agent trying to find Secretary of State Lawton. You know she's missing, right?"

Unnerved now, Panjang said, "What is this? What kind of agent?"

"An agent who can be nice and lucrative to you, or very mean and destructive," she said, putting an edge in her voice. "Someone working with the Sons of Prophecy uploaded big files through one of your computers yesterday between four and six P.M."

"No," the owner protested. "This is good place. Legal place. Nobody does this monkey business. No one even looks at the porno very much. You make mistake."

"No mistake," Barnett said firmly. "So if you don't want me to report you to the Malaysian police for aiding and abetting terrorists, you're going to answer my questions."

Panjang hesitated, nodded fearfully. "What do you want?"

"You were here yesterday between four and six?"

"I am always here," the café owner replied. "I live up the stairs."

"Do you remember who was using that computer in the corner over there at that time? A woman? With a baby?"

She pointed at the machine where she'd picked up evidence of M. Ex.

Puzzled now, unsure of everything she'd told him, Panjang stared at the computer in question for a long moment. "No. No woman," he said finally. "No baby. I know this man. He is good man. He comes here many times. Sometimes with his daughter."

Excited, Barnett said, "You have his name? Where I can find him?"

The owner balked again, looked down at the bills on the counter.

Barnett said, "I'll triple that and no one will ever know."

Ten minutes later, Barnett climbed from the hired car for a third time. She was running on fumes, but determined to reconnoiter the address she'd been given. According to Mr. Panjang, Adiputera Mohammed, a struggling Web designer, lived and worked in the modest house across the street. Like virtually every place she'd seen in Kuala Lumpur so far, the place was well cared for. The small dirt yard had been swept recently, and the shrubs were blooming a full riot of color.

There was a steel-barred security door blocking the front door. Both were closed. The windows boasted similar bars. She looked around at other nearby homes. About half of them had the same security features. She almost turned around, telling herself to return to her hotel and sleep until it was time to pick up Tatupu, Chavez, and Fowler, and then come back in force. But then again, the clock was ticking and she was right here.

Deciding to play the Microsoft cover one last time, Barnett knocked on the door. No one answered. She rapped the door again, louder this time, and called out, "Hello?"

No answer. It was midday. Mr. Mohammed and family could be out shopping, or eating, or at the mosque, or wherever. That seals it, she thought, and started to turn. The breeze shifted ever so slightly, no longer blowing at her neck and toward the house, but from the house to her. She smelled something foul.

For a moment Barnett stood there, thinking: What would Monarch do?

Then she went around the right side of the house. The stench was stronger here, and she saw that one of the side windows was open several inches. The horrible odor was coming out that window. She held her breath, walked up to it, and as she did, she heard the buzzing of flies. Suspecting that she wasn't going to like what she was about to see, Barnett nevertheless cupped her hand to shade her eyes from the sun, and peered through the security bars and the windowpane.

She was looking into a small kitchen. A man she assumed was Adiputera Mohammed was slumped against the oven, a bullet hole through his right eye. A woman who was likely his wife was sprawled on the floor, unmoving, dried blood all around her. A girl, six or seven, was rocked back in a chair at the table, shot through the throat.

"Oh, God no," Barnett moaned when she saw the fourth victim.

The baby was slumped in a high chair with so much blood on its face that she could not tell if it was a boy or a girl.

24

IN BANGKOK, A FINE mist was falling in the ninety-degree heat, steam bath conditions scented by curried meat cooking in a tandoor. Monarch climbed from a cab on Phahurat Road. The thief's head was pounding. The wavering Bollywood music pulsing from a nearby shop wasn't helping. Neither was the cacophony echoing everywhere in the neighborhood as food mongers chanted and shopkeepers jabbered in praise of their wares amid the ringing of bicycle bells, the honking of horns, the backfiring of buses, and the chain-saw revving of motorized rickshaws called "tuk tuks."

Monarch rubbed at his temples, suspecting dehydration as the source of the headache. He should be drinking a lot more water. Song Le climbed out the other side of the taxi and paid the driver. The Chinese agent, showing the stress of the last fifteen hours as much as he was, had said little on the ride in from the airport.

He stood there a long moment, enduring the headache and trying to filter the news Barnett had just relayed to him about the murdered family in Kuala Lumpur and their apparent involvement with the Sons of Prophecy. She'd called in the crime scene anonymously, and was sitting in a car watching a hoard of Malaysian police descend on the house.

"Your mercenary agent works here?" Song Le demanded skeptically. She was craning her head around at Bangkok's Indian neighborhood.

"I actually have no idea where *he* is," Monarch said.

Song Le turned hostile. "Then what are we—"

"We're going to talk with someone who will know where to find him," Monarch replied before checking the Bangkok address he'd found on the Web on the flight over from Vietnam.

"There it is," he said, pointing to a sign that read, "Rafiq's Extraordinary Silks and Fine Fabrics."

"A fabric store?" Song Le said.

"The Rafiqs have these stores all over the world," Monarch explained. "They're also the finest forgers money can buy."

The fabric shop was an airy, high-ceilinged affair with lazy bamboo fans and row upon row of low platforms that held bolts of fabric. Chinese, Indian, and Thai men and women crowded the place. It was several seconds before Monarch spotted the man he was looking for: a short, pot-bellied Lebanese wearing glasses and a floral print silk shirt open too far down his hairy chest. He was up in an office on an elevated platform at the rear of the shop, arguing with an Indian woman about his returns policy.

"You defame me," he told the woman. "I never, never say this!"

Monarch called up to him, "Sami, give the poor woman her money back."

Sami Rafiq stiffened, and his head seemed to creep around as if he really did not want to confirm the identity of the voice. Monarch smiled at him.

That set Rafiq off. His face reddened. He waved both hands. "No, not a chance," he sputtered. "I want nothing to do with you, Monarch. Leave my establishment. Now."

Monarch climbed the stairs, his hand over his heart, saying, "Sami, I'm crushed at this greeting. I always considered us old and dear friends."

Rafiq stood there fuming a moment, then wrenched open a drawer, counted out cash, and shoved the bills at the woman. "Tell everyone Sami Rafiq is an honest man."

She glanced at Monarch and Song Le, appearing doubtful, but snatched the money and hurried down the stairs.

"Old friends?" the Lebanese forger hissed at Monarch once she'd gone. "The last time I saw you, three crazy Muslim women with machine guns attacked my store in Algiers. I was left with two bodies to deal with and it brought all sorts of heat on me, too much heat. The family decided to move me here."

"I'd heard that," Monarch said apologetically. "But this is better, right? I mean, Algiers or Bangkok? C'mon, Sami. I did you a favor."

"Yes, yes, I am happier here," Rafiq admitted, but then hardened again. "And I want to keep it that way."

"What makes you think I'm going to change that?" Monarch asked, amused.

The Lebanese shopkeeper threw him a sardonic look. "Are you kidding? Every time you show up bullets and crazy people are not far behind."

"I've got no crazy people behind me here," Monarch assured him. "At least not that I know of. Meet Song Le."

Rafiq got irritated again, but bowed, said, "Enchanted. You MSS?"

She blinked. "How did you know that?"

"Missing diplomats from the U.S. and China? Hello?" he replied, rapping his knuckles on his head. "I may run a fabric shop but I am not an imbecile."

"She knows who you really are, Sami," Monarch said.

"Oh," Rafiq said, his face lifting. "That what this is about? Papers again?"

"No," Monarch said. "I just need to find an old mutual friend. You tell me where he is, and we'll leave."

The Lebanese squinted at him, said, "What old mutual friend?"

"Archie."

Rafiq stiffened again. "What makes you think I know anything about Archie? That was ten years ago."

Monarch laughed. "C'mon, are you trying to tell me that when you were transferred here he wasn't one of the first people you contacted? If you didn't, you're not as good a businessman as I thought."

Rafiq took off his glasses, rubbed his nose. "You think he's involved?"

"No," Monarch admitted. "You?"

The forger shook his head. "Never. Archie has ethics. Odd ethics. But ethics."

"Exactly, but I figure he might know something, or have heard something. And I want to talk to him."

Rafiq hesitated again, then put his glasses back on and consulted his watch. "Happy hour starts at five on Soi Cowboy. He'll be holding court at the Old Dutch Bar, for a few hours anyway."

Late at night, a gaudy neon arch glows over the entrance to Soi Cowboy, one of the more notorious adult entertainment districts in the Thai capital. At night the narrow road is as brightly lit as the Vegas strip, and wall to wall with furtive men, sex vacationers scurrying from one go-go bar to the next while scores of young Thai girls try to tempt them with their wares.

But when he and Song Le got there around five that afternoon, the neon arch was dark. The bars and the go-gos that lined both sides of the street were just opening. The heat and humidity was stifling. Thunder rumbled in the distance. A scattering of foreign men, most of them in their late forties, early fifties, sat nursing the first, or second, or fifth drink of their day, joking with the bar girls on early duty.

"Nice friends you have," Song Le sniffed as several of the girls in front of the Rio Agogo Bar eyed her stonily. "Nice places they frequent."

"You hunt buffalo where buffalo live," Monarch said impatiently.

"What does this mean?" she said with equal impatience.

"It means that Thailand has become a place where former Special Forces guys from all over the world come to live after they're no longer on active duty," Monarch explained. "Cost of living's cheap here and most of them can live well on their pensions. If they can't, or they've got too many girlfriends to support, they go to Archie Latham."

"And Latham puts them to work?"

"More like he brokers their services," Monarch said. "He knows everyone in the special ops world. He's Aussie but went French Foreign Legion before he turned gun for hire in Afghanistan. He used to be one tough hombre, but took a round to his femur that never set right. So he does this."

Song Le shook her head. "But don't they have companies in your country that hire mercenaries?"

"Sure, but these days there are two kinds of mercenaries. You've got the guys who work for private security agencies run by former special ops commanders. Legit shops. Most of their work involves the training and deployment of guards. For the most part, the U.S.-based PSAs, the private security agencies, don't get involved in the second kind of mercenary activity, and that's where Latham enters the picture."

"I don't understand. Why are not the PSAs involved?"

"Because they've got boards of directors, civilized things like that," Monarch replied. "Second-level mercenary activities are high risk from too many angles to count, not the least of which is the real possibility of dying in great numbers."

Song Le thought about that. "So it's dirty work?"

He shrugged. "Depends on what you call dirty."

"This Latham makes a lot of money?"

"He's well-off as I understand it."

They neared the end of Soi Cowboy where it met Sukhumvit Road, and Monarch immediately heard an uproarious, infectious, familiar laugh before he saw a big good-looking shambles of a man in his late forties with longish brushed-back tawny hair and a beard going gray. Wearing sandals, khaki shorts, and a white linen shirt, Archie Latham sat at a table in front of the Old Dutch Bar looking like the actor Jeff Bridges gone up-scale beach bum.

A beautiful laughing Thai woman was seated on the mercenary agent's lap. He looked genuinely delighted by her. Latham's laughter ebbed to chuckles. He picked up a can of Singha beer, raised it to his lips, and his eyes shifted to the street, focused, and then widened.

"Well, I'll be fucked cross-eyed!" he bellowed in an Aussie accent, and started chortling. "Robin Monarch! Rafiq wasn't bullshitting me you were in town!"

"Archie," Monarch said, smiling as he crossed to him.

A big black dude with a shaved head stood up from a chair nearby.

Latham waved him off, said, "No worries, Spooner, he's an old friend. Also one of the most dangerous men in the world."

Spooner glared at Monarch, as if to say, "Uh, that's my job."

"I'm a teddy bear, really," Monarch assured Spooner.

Song Le snorted in disgust.

Latham glanced at the Chinese agent, and then at the Thai woman in his lap. "Robin, meet Yuri, my new wife."

"Again?" Monarch said.

"What can I say? I'm a hopeless romantic. We're on our honeymoon."

"Nice place for it," Song Le said wryly.

Another Thai woman came up and started nuzzling Mrs. Latham's ear. The mercenary agent was beside himself with happiness, chuckled, "Yuri and I both like the same things."

"Sorry to interrupt," Monarch said, "but we've got business to discuss."

Latham sobered, then tapped Yuri and the other girl, and said, "Give us some space there, loves. And I'd like another beer." He looked at Monarch and Song Le. "Two? Three?"

Monarch moved past Spooner, saw Latham's stainless-steel cane for the first time, and took a seat opposite its owner, said, "Sure. Beer sounds good."

Displaying broad displeasure, Song Le shook her head.

"All MSS agents so agreeable?" Latham asked good-naturedly.

"This is not a time to be agreeable," she shot back.

"Any time's a good time to be agreeable," Latham replied, grinning lazily. "Unless a course, you're having heart attack from an impacted bowel or something."

She looked at Monarch. "This is a waste of time."

"She always like this?" Latham asked.

"So far, pretty much," Monarch said.

"Lucky you, mate," the mercenary agent said, and began ignoring her. "Rafiq said you're here about the missing diplomats?"

Monarch nodded. "I was on the ship, the oil tanker they were taken off of."

"And?"

"Multiple dead DSS bodyguards. Multiple dead Chinese and Indian bodyguards."

Latham nodded. "Got to be damn good. Damn well planned."

"Which is why we're here. It looks like professionals to me."

"None that came through me if that's what you're implying," Latham said quickly and emphatically.

"I'm not implying anything," Monarch said. "Just looking for the most up-to-date information. You had any big hires lately?"

"No, it's been slow as a matter of fact," Latham said, annoyed. "Slow enough that I haven't minded taking a few vacation days and enjoying the latest honeymoon."

Yuri returned with the beer, set the cans down, looked harshly at Song Le, as if she were competition, but then left to tend to other customers.

"I may not let that one divorce me someday," Latham said, getting out a cigarette from a Seven Light package. He started laughing. "You seen this?"

He showed Monarch that on the side of the cigarette package was a picture of a man who'd had his jaw removed. "Fucking Thai health warning," Latham said. "In your face about it, aren't they?"

"Effective?" Monarch asked, cracking his beer.

"Nah," Latham said, laughed, and lit the cigarette. He took a drag, blew three perfect smoke rings, and said, "You want my take on this situation?"

"That's why I'm here," Monarch said.

"Pirates," Latham said. "Or actually, more like privateers. There's a difference, you know? There's a new breed of them about. Like nothing we've ever seen before. They've had military training, use technology, and they've got religion."

"Pirates are religious?" Song Le said.

"Muslim pirates as a matter of fact, like off Somalia," the mercenary agent replied, not looking her way. "There appears to be two, three, maybe four different crews operating. Malaysian. Indonesian. They've all got the same idea: use stolen cargos to fund holy wars. You're not hearing much about it because the shipping companies are doing everything they can to keep a lid on the fact that they can't assure the safety of cargos anymore, at least not in the South China Sea, the Java, or the Malacca Straits."

"Names? Places we can start?"

Latham thought about that, looked uncomfortable, sipped his beer, and said, "I met one of them once, back in January. Sitting right where you are now, drinking a Sprite, surrounded by his goons."

"Name?" Monarch said.

"Akrit. Akrit Mahdi."

"How did you know he was a pirate?" Song Le asked.

"I asked to check his international pirate's license, but he said he lost it at the fuckin' buccaneer's ball," Latham shot back, and broke into a throaty roar of laughter.

That went right by the Chinese agent, but Monarch grinned. Latham had not changed a bit.

"No other form of identification?" Monarch asked.

"Malaysian passport," Latham replied. "Look, Mahdi came to me, said he wanted to do a trade. Said he had a huge load of consumer electronics taken off a Dutch ship in the Java last October. Mahdi wanted to exchange the loot for weapons: AKs, grenades, shoulder mounted rockets, and .50 cals, about eight million worth."

He looked at Song Le, smiled lazily, "And like I said, his name was Mahdi, as in the Shiite Muslim messiah 'the Mahdi'? In my admittedly slow brain, I deduced he was a Muslim pirate or in with them anyway."

She was unimpressed. "And so you sold him these weapons?"

"I don't do weapons, darling. Just the people behind them."

Monarch asked, "He get the weapons?"

Latham shrugged. "He seemed keen on them. You'd have to assume so."

"Is he capable of taking on an entire DSS contingent?" Monarch asked.

Latham traded his cigarette for his beer. "If his people are armed like I think they are, yeah, he's capable."

Song Le crossed her arms. "You have any idea where we can find him?"

Latham grinned, winked at her, said, "As a matter of fact, love, I do."

Song Le was unconvinced by Latham's claim. "How?"

"He told me in a roundabout half-assed way," the mercenary agent replied. "He kept talking about this river called the Sungai Setiu in northern Malaysia, said it was the most beautiful river on earth, runs by his village, which is called Fitri, if I remember correctly."

Monarch pulled out his iPhone, called up Google Earth, and typed in the names of the river and the village. After studying the satellite picture a few seconds he said, "If those are deep channels beyond the estuary where it meets the South China Sea, and they've got the right kind of strike boats, it could be a strong base for a crew of marauding pirates. And they're in range of where the *Niamey* was taken."

Latham nodded. "Exactly what I thought when I looked at it. And I read up on that Dutch cargo being hijacked. They described it as a 'military-style assault.' So I figure Mahdi's boys do their business on open water, be quick about it, and get upriver and inland ASAP."

"Especially if they've got diplomatic hostages."

Latham got out another cigarette, smiling. "Always said you were the smart one in the bunch, Robin."

"Thanks, Archie," Monarch said. "This helps."

"Glad I could be of service to an old mate," he said, returning to his jovial self. "You full time with the CIA again?"

"Freelancer," Monarch replied.

Latham cocked his head. "You looking for representation? We could make an awful lot of legal tender you and me."

"I'm flattered, Archie," Monarch said. "But I'm fine."

"No man but a fool represents himself in an arm's-length negotiation."

"I try not to do business with friends," Monarch said, finished his beer. "But I'll keep your offer in the back of my mind."

"Another round, brother?" Latham asked.

"Next time through," Monarch promised. "We've got a deadline."

"Heard that," Latham said agreeably. "Good luck with the harpy."

Monarch fought the urge to glance at Song Le, said, "I'll need it."

"Got a number where I can reach you if I hear anything?" Latham asked.

"If you give me yours."

"Absolutely," the mercenary agent replied, and they traded numbers.

Monarch went to shake Latham's hand when they were done. But the big bear of a man grabbed his cane and used it to push himself to his feet before throwing his arms wide and saying, "After what we been through, Robin, a handshake's not enough."

"Good seeing you, too, Archie," Monarch said, hugging the mercenary agent and slapping his massive back.

"Outstanding, simply first class," Latham said, stepping back, his eyes shiny. "Always, always a pleasure." He looked at Song Le, said, "Don't you go expecting a hug now, love."

She looked like she'd chipped a tooth, said, "Afraid I'd get fleas."

Latham hesitated in wonder, and then threw back his head and roared as if it was one of the better lines he'd heard in a long time.

"See there, mate?" he said to Monarch. "I say there's more to this one than meets the eye."

25

IT WAS PITCH DARK. Not one light shone in the ghost city.

That's what the Chinese called them, massive multi-building high-rise developments built out in the middle of nowhere under orders from Beijing, and funded by the savings of the burgeoning Chinese middle class. No one worked in any of the office towers abandoned at various stages of completion. Apartments, hundreds of thousands of them, stood empty, waiting in vain for peasants who made two dollars a day to somehow leave the land and live in hundred-thousand-dollar flats.

Some of those cities were ghostlier than others. The development at Quan Baat, thirty kilometers west of the town of Bayankhongor in central Mongolia, was one such place. Abandoned by its builders when the recession hit, the majority of the soaring structures there were unfinished save their rusting ironworks, which towered above the steppe, looking like the upright skeletons of alien creatures frozen in death and clawing at the sky.

Or so it had always seemed to Bataar Zaya, who lay belly down on the eighth floor of one of those alien structures, dressed in dark heavy wool clothes, his cheek welded to the stock of a Soviet-era Dragunov SVD sniper rifle.

Zaya's thick-featured face was taking a beating from a bitter wind that whistled in the raw iron works above him and started to spit snow. But he did not turn his head from the numbing cold. Peering down through the Dragunov's infrared scope at a stretch of provincial highway that ran east to west through the ghost city, Zaya was feeling a part of destiny, as if every second of his wretched life had led up to this moment.

"You are ready, Zaya?" said a gravelly voice behind him.

Zaya, looked over his shoulder at the silhouette of a man he knew only as "Chullun," or "Stone."

"I've been ready for this since they let me out," Zaya said.

"Six years is a long time to deny a man his freedom just for speaking his mind," Stone agreed. "But such a man, bent on revenge, could let his emotions take control when he should be calm, focused, cold."

"I said I am ready, brother," Zaya insisted. "I know this is only the beginning. I know we are in the right. And millions of others will, too."

There was a brief silence, as if some final decision were being made.

"Then you, Zaya, shall strike the first blow for

freedom," Stone said at last. "You shall be the one who goes down in our history books."

Zaya was stunned. He thought of the wife who'd left him while he was in prison. He thought of the son he'd never known. Pride and humility rose up and tumbled inside him, made him tremble with gratitude. All the years, all the loss, all the heartaches, and all the impotent rage had been worth it.

His son would know of his father, of Zaya! His ex-wife would know of Zaya! The whole world would soon know of Zaya!

"Can you do this?" Stone asked. "Cast the first stone?"

"It will be an honor!" the sniper gushed at last. "What is my target?"

There was another brief silence before Stone said, "Take out the driver of the lead truck in the convoy, then start shooting his tires. If you can, get the second truck, too. We'll take care of everything else."

"A great honor!" Zaya said. "Blessings upon you, Chullun!"

Stone said nothing. His head cocked as if he were hearing something in the distance. Then Zaya picked it up, a lone howl far away to the east, a kilometer or more, from the ironworks of another tower. Other invisible men perched high in unfinished skyscrapers on both sides of the highway picked up the call, like a pack of feral dogs howling after prey. Hearing the men, thirty, maybe more, all crying this way, and then going dead silent, Zaya felt so excited he thought he might piss himself. That would not do, he thought frantically.

The first one to fight should not piss his pants in the fight.

He got up from behind the gun, took several steps to where the rough cement floor met a hundred feet of open air, and pissed off the edge. When he finished, he stepped back and looked east again.

There! Zaya thought. There it is!

Headlights were blinking out there on the cold desert plains. Soon he could make out ten sets of them, then twenty, then thirty until the line looked like a sparkling caterpillar creeping toward the ghost city. Zaya heard several sharp hissing noises behind him in the darkness. He thought he smelled a chemical odor, like paint, but then the breeze shifted and it wasn't there anymore. The headlights grew brighter, and the long caterpillar inched closer.

Zaya looked all around, wide-eyed. He wanted to remember all of it, sear the images in his memory so he would be able to recall every detail until the day he died. The first trucks entered the city. He could hear engines revving and the transmissions grinding.

"Zaya!" Stone called from somewhere in the darkness. "The driver first."

Zaya threw himself down behind the Dragunov, shaking with anticipation. Quicker than he expected, he saw the first headlights. Pulling the rifle butt tight to his shoulder, Zaya welded his cheek to the stock, made the gun a part of his bones.

His breath turned shallow. Doubt ran through his mind. Don't miss! Don't miss the first shot of the rebellion!

The first truck in the convoy appeared, and all doubt vanished. Months of training took over. Resentment born of years of punishment anchored him. And a focus wrought out of total loss seized every bit of his body and mind.

Zaya aimed at a spot on the highway roughly two hundred and twenty-five meters away, well within the Dragunov's effective range of eight hundred meters. The target truck would be coming around a slight curve, veering right, and the driver would be perfectly exposed to the infrared scope.

He flipped the safety lever, took a deep breath, and let it out slowly until the lead truck came around that little bend in the highway. The second transport vehicle's headlights revealed writing on the near flank of the lead truck: "PLA." It was a supply and transport convoy belonging to the People's Liberation Army, the Chinese war machine.

Perfect, Zaya thought bitterly. Absolutely perfect.

With both eyes open, Zaya brought the crosshairs to the center of the hood and then up the driver's side of the windshield. He thought of his son and squeezed the trigger. The shot came as a surprise, a good indicator for a long-distance marksman. A semiautomatic, the Dragunov threw little recoil and Zaya was able to watch that first tracer round strike right where he'd aimed, shattering the windshield, and hitting the driver high in the chest. The truck swerved sharply.

Zaya swung the rifle at the near front tire of the transport, and shot again. The tire ruptured and the truck lurched before going off the highway and smashing into a pile of construction debris. The sniper adjusted his position again, found the windshield of the second truck in the convoy, saw the silhouette of the driver, and killed him. That truck crashed just beyond the first.

Flares went off, climbed, and burst, revealing the bones of the ghost city and the length of the Chinese Army convoy. Automatic weapons opened up on both sides of the convoy, firing down on it.

East toward the outskirts of the ghost city a series of bombs went off, the huge detonations cutting the legs of a twenty-story iron skeleton, which seemed to scream as it fell across the highway, sealing the convoy from retreat.

In the flares' fading light, Chinese soldiers began to pour from the transports right into the deadly hail of fire raining down from all directions.

"It worked!" Zaya screamed.

He swung the crosshairs, looking for a new target, when over the rattle of gunfire, he heard Stone shout, "Zaya!"

The sniper jerked his head back, and started to look over his shoulder, only to realize that Stone was standing right next to him, so close that Zaya could see the tritium sight of his pistol pointing right at his head.

"I am sorry it had to be you," Stone yelled. "It was nothing personal."

Zaya had a moment of confusion before a blinding flash and explosion ended every thought he'd ever had of revolution.

26

A WHITE VOLVO PICKUP bearing the emblem of Delhi's Department of Public Works drove north on Ashoka Road in the center of the Indian capital. The truck slowed and pulled off on the shoulder between the Bank of India and the National Philatelic Museum. Five men dressed in white jumpsuits, rubber boots, and orange safety helmets climbed out.

At this hour in Delhi, traffic was as light as it would be the entire day. They put up flashing traffic barriers around a manhole cover on the near side of the road, and left plenty of room for cars to pass in the far lane. They were prying up the cover when a Delhi Police cruiser slowed to a stop by them.

"What are you doing there?" the officer riding shotgun asked, sounding more curious than suspicious.

The biggest of the five men said, "There's been a lot of rain the past two days, sahib, and there's been reports of the sewers backing up. Just trying to make sure the big pipe's not broke somewhere." He made a vague waving gesture to the north.

The cop behind the wheel said, "You won't have this lane closed during rush hour, will you?"

"No chance of that," the workman said. "We should be in and out in half an hour, maybe less."

"Better you than me going in that hole," the near officer said.

The workman shrugged. "We use ropes to anchor us so we don't drown."

To his relief, a jitney jammed with people, animals, and boxes came up behind the police car, and they moved on. He turned to look at the men who'd stopped their work.

"I almost shit my pants right there," one of them said.

Laughing, the others set to prying out the manhole again. They raised it, and laid it aside. The stench from the hole was nauseating and the sound of rushing water was surprisingly loud.

Two of the men, Qutub and Akbar Ali, cousins, were lean, hard types in their thirties. They pulled on heavy-duty rubber gloves with gauntlets that ran up to their elbows, turned on their headlamps, and climbed down the wrought-iron ladder into a main trunk line of the central New Delhi sewer system.

It had indeed rained a few hours before, and the water was still running higher and faster than normal in the big pipe. The cousins clung to the ladder above the flow and waited while the three other men ferried several heavy rubberized dry bags from the truck to the hole.

Two bags were handed down and each cousin managed to get one on his back before dropping into the sewer water. Two of the three other men came down with the remaining dry bags on their backs. Tall, muscular guys with thick, tight cropped beards and deep bronze skin, they had to duck their heads not to scrape their helmets on the ceiling of the pipe.

The cousins had taken to calling the bigger men Mr. One and Mr. Two. They didn't know their real names and Mr. One and Mr. Two didn't know the Alis' real identities and reputation. The four had only met the previous evening, but all of them understood the plan.

Mr. One, the workman who'd talked to the police, climbed down into the water last. He looked up at the fifth man, said, "Start the generator as soon as you can hook up."

"Twenty minutes tops," the driver promised, and then pushed the manhole cover back into place. With a clunking noise the sounds of the city died. The truck would be abandoned near a slum where it would be picked clean in a matter of hours, and covered with so many fingerprints that any they might have left by mistake would be smudged or marred beyond recognition.

The cousins watched Mr. Two pull out a smart phone wrapped in a waterproof case.

Mr. Two aimed the smart phone upstream. "Five hundred meters."

Akbar Ali led the way, pushing against the current of the rank water flowing as all water does on the subcontinent, toward the Ganges River and the sea. The older of the Ali cousins breathed through his mouth so as not to gag at the smell in the big pipe. His cousin Qutub, directly behind Akbar, slogged forward at the same pace, the way he'd done hundreds of times in the mountains of the Hindu Kush, carrying a load that would strain a donkey's back.

Bent over under the roof of the pipe, Mr. One and Mr. Two looked grimly repulsed at their circumstances, but pressed on after the Alis, bound by a common purpose that they'd all pledged to attain at any cost, even their lives. The five-hundred-meter wade took fifteen minutes. At last they reached a section of pipe roughly one hundred meters long and uninterrupted by man-hole covers or sewer grates.

"Right there should do it," said Mr. Two, gesturing at the curved slimy east wall of the pipe.

Mr. One opened his dry bag, brought out a small electronic device, turned it on.

"How does it work?" Akbar asked.

Mr. One said, "Our friend upstairs goes to the closest electrical transformer. He clips a machine called a sound pulse generator to the main line and turns it on. The pulse travels up the line and out in all directions."

He shook the device, "This is a signal receiver tuned to the frequency of the pulse."

Qutub frowned, "So that thing *hears* the electrical line?"

"Close enough," Mr. Two said.

Mr. One went to the wall and held the sensor to the cement. There were analog and digital readouts on the face of the signal receiver. But neither showed any indication of a pulsing signal. Two minutes passed, then five.

Qutub Ali said, "Are you sure this is where—?"

Mr. One turned, grinned, said, "One hundred percent sure." He shifted the face of the handheld so they could see the needle on the analog readout rising and falling.

Mr. Two stepped forward with a length of angle iron about two inches wide and three feet long. He set it horizontally and drew a chalk line along the length of it, then repeated the process two feet below where the pulse was being heard.

When he was done, he looked to the cousins, and said, "Your turn."

The cousins were already digging in their dry bags. Akbar Ali got out a drill and Qutub Ali a stout bit about twelve inches long. They locked the bit into the drill, then Akbar carried it to the right end of the top horizontal chalk line.

The carbide tip spun and then cored into the cement with a violent grating sound. A minute later Akbar felt the bit break free and he passed it back and forth several times to fully clear the hole. Sweating hard, he handed the drill to his cousin who repeated the process at the center of the upper chalk line and again at the far left end. Mr. One and Mr. Two took over to complete the process, drilling three holes equidistant on the lower line.

Akbar used a smaller drill bit to core out holes in the cement, then attached narrow brackets to the face of the pipe just below the two chalk lines. He hung those long pieces of angle iron on the bracket so the *L* faced the sewer wall.

Mr. One and Mr. Two had pulled up the hoods of their suits and were fitting gas masks to their faces. When the cousins were equally prepared, Akbar Ali retrieved a multiliter bottle marked with the letters *HF*, and featuring a skull and crossbones symbol.

Akbar Ali poured a generous amount of hydrofluoric acid all along the lower piece of angle iron and into the three holes. Almost immediately, the cement and metal began to throw off toxic fumes and curls of smoke as the acid started to eat. HF doesn't react with plastic, but will melt cement and would eventually eat through the iron, too.

The four men watched the acid work, adding more fluid when the chemical reaction seemed to slow. Thirty-five minutes after they began, there were ragged hollow cuts in the form of a rectangle split in two.

Akbar got out a plastic jug filled with fine white granules. He poured small mounds of dry Spilfyter acid neutralizer into the slots before the acid could cut to water level. When he was satisfied that the reaction had died, he looked at Mr. One and Mr. Two. The bigger men stepped forward with short-handled sledgehammers, and struck at the inside of the rectangle. Much of the cement around the edges was friable due to the caustic chemical reaction, and pieces and then chunks began to break away.

Once they had opened a hole large enough to shine a light through, they saw what they were hoping for, a gap of roughly three feet between the sewer pipe and a second cement wall. By the time they'd expanded the passage big enough for any of them to fit through, it was nearly four A.M.

"We've got two hours and ten minutes to get this done," said Mr. Two, who was shining his headlamp into the gaping hole in the sewer wall, revealing electrical conduit about fourteen inches in diameter. "Whatever you do, try to avoid contact with that little nasty sister-fucker."

It took the Ali cousins and Mr. One and Mr. Two a good forty minutes to shimmy sideways down that narrow gap between the two walls. Mindful of the electrical trunk line, which could hit them with thousands of volts, they moved carefully until, at last, they saw faint light ahead.

All four men switched off their headlamps, and groped their way toward that dim light, reaching a widening in the passage where the trunk line passed through a large control box. Opposite the box was a steel hatch door that was padlocked on the other side.

Wordlessly, Mr. One removed the last items in his dry bag: a pocket torch and a roll of thick metal ribbon. He snipped off lengths of the ribbon and handed them to Mr. Two, who fitted the strips around the hinges on the hatch door. The four men again donned gas masks.

At 4:32 A.M., Mr. One lit the torch and licked at the ribbons of magnesium, which ignited with blinding intensity and a hissing focused flame that neatly sliced through the metal hinges. Mr. Two slid his gloved fingers beneath a flange on the back of the door, gave it a pop with his shoulder. The hatch creaked and sagged open, unhinged, held up only by the hasp and lock, and Mr. Two's powerful fingers.

The Ali cousins squirmed and jumped out through the hatch, falling several feet and landing on loose stone beside steel tracks in a high-ceilinged tunnel. Mr. One came next, and got his shoulder under the hatch door so his partner might exit. Together they pressed the door back into its frame. At a glance, except for the scorching in places, nothing looked amiss.

It was 4:46 A.M. In one hour and fourteen minutes the third rail would go live, and the trains of the New Delhi Metro system would begin to run. The four men wanted to be out of the train tunnel by ten past five. They had twenty-five minutes to complete their mission. They began to jog north.

Rounding a long slow curve a few minutes later, they came upon one of the metro trains sitting idle, and dark. Akbar Ali and Mr. One went up the right side of the train. Qutub Ali and Mr. Two went left. Both teams slowed to a creep as they approached the lead car, which was sixty-yards shy of Patek Chowk Metro Station, one of several subway stops that serve the Indian Parliament and hundreds of thousands of government workers.

The Ali cousins lay down and rolled under the nose of the train, careful to avoid the third rail even if it was supposedly dead. Mr. One and Mr. Two handed them packages with dull silver wrapping paper that closely imitated the color of the underside of the carriage. Using thin wire, they strapped the two packages in place, and rolled back out.

After everything they'd gone through to get here, it seemed anticlimactic. Silently, Mr. Two pointed back down the tunnel toward the hatch in the subway wall. They split again, and started back into the tunnel, the Ali cousins leading on both sides.

Neither of the Alis had noticed that their larger companions still had those short-handled sledgehammers. Without warning, Mr. One hit Akbar Ali at the base of the neck, a crushing blow that severed his spine. When Qutub Ali heard the noise, he started to squat to look under the train car. Even better, Mr. Two thought and smashed Qutub's exposed neck.

They dragged the bodies under the car and behind train wheels where they wouldn't be noticed. They positioned the corpses side by side, feet facing the front of the train, and their shoulders touching the third rail. To make sure the bodies would travel with the train once it began to move, they ran picture wire from their ankles to the underside of the carriage. While Mr. Two spray-painted something low on the subway tunnel wall, his companion stayed under the train to unzip Akbar's jumpsuit and push a smaller version of the shiny package inside. It was 5:05 A.M.

"Five minutes to spare," Mr. Two whispered as they turned to escape.

"Clockwork," Mr. One said, bumping knuckles with him. "Precision clockwork."

27

MONARCH LOOKED OUT THE windshield of the floatplane. The moon, a quarter off full, was brilliant in the equatorial night sky. It made the water off the coast of northern Malaysia look like polished steel.

"Can you put us down without running lights?" Monarch asked.

The pilot nodded, told them to hold on, throttled back, and they began to drop. As they did, Monarch felt the iPhone Gloria Barnett had given him buzz. He pulled it out, and saw her there on the FaceTime app, looking very tired.

"The Sons of Prophecy posted another video," she said.

"Hold on," he said. He motioned to Song Le, who sat in the hold behind him, and then switched on the speakerphone. "Lawton and the foreign ministers again?"

"Not this time," Barnett replied. "It shows a sophisticated ambush attack on a Chinese Army convoy in one of those empty cities in central Mongolia about six hours ago. The video ends with the words "Sons of Prophecy, the revolution begins.""

This development surprised Monarch, and broke Song Le's normal stolid expression.

"Takes a lot of brass to go up against the PLA on their own turf," he said.

"And a lot of men and a lot of weapons," Barnett agreed. "There are fifty PLA soldiers confirmed dead."

"Fifty?" Song Le cried in disbelief. "I must call my superiors."

She pulled out a satellite phone.

They were no more than six hundred feet above the water now and angling toward a landing.

He put the attack in China out of his mind for the moment, said to Barnett, "Any luck on getting us a better look at the village?"

"As a matter of fact," she said. "I found nautical charts that show the estuary and the river channels off it, which I'll send over in a minute. And Dr. Hopkins just transmitted a higher resolution satellite image of the area taken about three hours ago. There appear to be almost one hundred people living in and around that estuary. Most of them are students attending a regional boarding school. You'll want to avoid it."

"Thanks. Any chance you pinpointed Mahdi?"

"No," she replied. "Though as you'll see from the satellite photos, there's a compound of sorts on the north end of the village. I'd focus there."

"The others?"

"They get in around one P.M."

"What about that family that was killed?"

"So far, not much. But I'm operating under a journalism cover. I can ask questions. Doesn't mean they'll answer, but I can ask."

"You figure out where the video was uploaded this time?"

"Still working on it."

"Be careful," Monarch said, and hung up.

Song Le, meanwhile, was talking rapidly in Mandarin behind him. Before he could concentrate enough to listen closely, the plane skipped twice off the swells, and then skimmed and slowed to a stop. He looked at the GPS app on the iPhone. They were roughly two miles offshore of the Sungai River estuary.

"You got five minutes," the pilot said.

Monarch freed himself from the copilot's harness. He went into the hold to find that Song Le had ended her conversation and was already moving the raft toward the open side door. He climbed out on one of the pontoons. The air was warm and still, and the sea was calm, almost glassy. He pulled the raft out, unfolded it, and triggered the pressurized CO_2 tanks to inflate it.

Song Le tossed oars and packs into the raft, and then climbed out. They clambered into the inflatable and were rowing away when the plane's engines coughed to life, and their ride lifted off.

"What are your people saying?" he asked from the back of the raft.

Song Le said, "Every military base in the country

has been put on the highest alert. And they've identified one of the dead terrorists. A known dissident and
anarchist named Zaya, who was released from prison
in Mongolia about a year ago and then disappeared."

"Nothing else?"

"Not yet," Song Le said. "They've got investigators
heading to the ghost city, but there's no reliable electricity there and a snowstorm is going on."

"Changes how we have to think of them, the SOP I
mean. Really expands their reach and their brazenness."

"Makes you wonder how big they really are."

"And how they stayed under the radar for so long."

They began to row in earnest. Song Le was strong
and together they made good time. After they'd covered a half-mile, navigating with a handheld GPS programmed with the coordinates of the mouth of the
estuary, Monarch said, "So tell me the long road you
took into the Ministry of State Security."

For several long moments he thought the Chinese
agent had not heard him or was simply refusing to di-
vulge anything personal.

But at last, Song Le said, "People from the party re-
cruited me because I was an athlete and good at lan-
guages. I was in army intelligence before I transferred
to MSS."

"Really? What was your sport? Ping-Pong?"

She looked over her shoulder and said, "Heptathlon,
dickhead."

Monarch couldn't help but smile. Maybe Latham
was right. There was more to her than met the eye.

"Sorry," he said. "You go to the Olympics?"

"Close enough."

"How long have you been at MSS?"

"Seven years," Song Le said and rowed harder. "Six in the field."

"Boyfriend?"

"No."

"Husband?"

Hesitation. "He died before I became a field agent. So did . . . my baby."

Monarch instantly felt differently about her, felt her humanity for the first time since she'd stuck her gun against his head aboard the *Niamey*.

"That's tough, I'm sorry," he said, and meant it. "How'd it happen?"

"A tragic accident," Song Le said, and left it at that.

"So what, you decided fieldwork was a better fit after they were gone?"

"A strange thing about tragedies," she replied, rowing harder. "After surviving them you are often offered another path in life. I was and I took it."

Song Le didn't seem interested in talking anymore, so Monarch pulled against the current, reminding himself that Secretary Lawton and the other diplomats now had less than sixty-five hours to live. He stared ahead at the shoreline. Was this where he'd find her? Was this guy Mahdi in with the Sons of Prophecy? How was he connected to the uprising in Mongolia?

He began to suspect that there had to be some centralized authority, some mastermind or masterminds who were choreographing events within some larger plan, and for some larger purpose. A plot to destabilize the world? Wasn't that what Hopkins said the NSA had heard rumor of in the weeks before the diplomats were taken? As he rowed, he tried to remember exactly what was said in the White House Situation Room. Evidence of an armed uprising in China? Well, there it was, clearly. And a coup in India? Could that be coming—?

The sound of waves crashing ahead broke Monarch from his thoughts. Scudding clouds crossed the moon, throwing the sea and the land ahead deeper into the shadows. Glancing at the GPS on his iPhone, he realized the current had taken them south of the estuary mouth by at least two hundred yards.

He leaned into the paddle, and turned the raft north. Together he and Song Le stroked without stop until a swell took them toward the estuary. Just shy of the freshwater, another wave threw them sideways up onto a sandbar.

Monarch and Song Le dragged the raft across the sandbar to the river. The channel mouth was not very wide, no more than thirty feet, and relatively shallow. The tide had to influence navigation here, Monarch decided. A deep-hulled boat wouldn't make it through at certain times of the day.

It was steamy hot once they left the beach and set off into a long, lakelike estuary. Bugs swarmed all around them. Frogs and night animals cried in the marshes, which stank of salt and decay. Paddling quietly southwest, they passed the smaller of two islands. Another forty yards and he swung them into a deep, wide channel that broke west into a narrower arm toward the village of Fikri.

"Stop!" Song Le hissed.

Monarch stilled his paddle, straining to hear above the buzzing whine of the insects and the steady thrum of frogs. Then it came to him, the sound of drunken laughter from the west bank up ahead. He eased the raft to shore, felt it bump against a half-submerged tree trunk lying on its side. Song Le slipped over into the brackish water, found her way up onto the mucky bank, and secured the raft to the root end of the downed tree. Monarch was impressed; she'd made almost no noise doing any of it.

Checking the pistol in his shoulder holster, Monarch climbed forward and out of the raft. He could now make out a fire flickering far downriver.

"You lead," he told the Chinese agent.

Song Le moved like a cat, passing through stands of reed and mangrove with no more than a rustle. Monarch was gifted at this sort of thing, but she was better at it.

"You would have made a good thief," he whispered in her ear when she slowed and stopped to listen.

"Never," she whispered back, parting the foliage in front of her.

Monarch looked through, seeing the six boats for the first time. Two were cigarette-style, meant for fast ocean travel; they bobbed in the channel. The others boats were shorter, deep-hulled, painted dark, and pulled up on a beach of sorts, their massive twin outboard engines tilted up out of the water. The beach itself was deserted but for a single man holding a bottle of some kind. He crouched beside a fire, singing, talking, and laughing to himself.

"Pirates' den," Monarch whispered. "Or their marina anyway. Wait a few minutes, then distract him without having him raise an alarm."

"How?"

"I don't know. Use your feminine charms."

Monarch moved before Song Le could reply, slipping counterclockwise through a jungle thicket until he was no more than thirty yards from the drunken sentry. He'd been standing there less than a minute when Song Le stepped from the marsh grass into the fire's glow.

He smiled. Topless and holding her gun and shoulder holster wrapped in her shirt, the Chinese agent walked seductively toward the drunk. The pirate seemed to catch movement out of the corner of his eye, started to struggle to his feet, going for his rifle, and then saw her clearly. His eyes glazed over as if he were witnessing a dream come true.

Song Le said something softly to the man in Malay. He set the bottle down and took two uncertain steps toward her, leaving his back to Monarch, who moved quickly up behind him and put the muzzle of the Glock to his neck.

The pirate stiffened, and looked wild-eyed when Monarch slid the muzzle around the side of his head until it rested between the man's eyes, which were wild with fear. "Well done," he said as Song Le put her bra and shirt on.

"Men are predicable," she said curtly.

"You had my attention," Monarch said.

She ignored him and spoke rapidly to the pirate in Malay. Monarch heard "Akrit Mahdi," but understood nothing else. At first the man looked at her defiantly, but that quickly vanished, leaving him horrified and nodding.

"What did you tell him?"

"I said that I was a sorceress, and that I would cut off his scrotum if he did not show us where we could find Mahdi," she replied.

"Sorceress?"

"The Malaysians are as superstitious as the Chinese."

"Good to know," Monarch said, reappraising her yet again.

Song Le drew her gun, said something else in Malay, and the man turned and led them past the boats into the darkness. The Chinese agent kept prodding the pirate forward. Monarch brought up the rear as they cut off the bank of the estuary onto a trail that led west through high grasses and reeds.

The soil underfoot was muddy, indicating they were on a well-traveled route. Monarch wondered whether the man hoped to encounter his allies, or if it was simply the quickest way to Mahdi's place, or both. In any case, they met no one along a path that crossed rice fields and wound through a small banana grove. It was 3:15 A.M. when Monarch first made out a gathering of buildings ahead, all dark, the village of Fikri.

A dog barked halfheartedly. Monarch heard the lowing of cattle before Song Le pulled up short on a mound of dirt on a rise above the village. She still had her gun to the pirate's head, and whispered to him. He replied for several moments. The Chinese agent nodded and then hit the man hard behind the ear with the butt of her pistol. He collapsed at her feet.

"He says Mahdi lives there," she whispered, gesturing to the compound on the other side of the village. "The wall is topped with broken glass. Three guards, and an attack dog sleep in the compound. Mahdi's a polygamist, three wives. He sleeps with them in turn."

"Akrit," Monarch said. "You mad man."

But his mind was already dealing with the challenges. A wall with glass on top was not a problem; he'd dealt with that scenario many times. The three guards were tougher. The dog was tougher still. And which wife was Mahdi sleeping with tonight? There was no way to know.

The smell of rotting fish caught his nose, and spurred a possible solution to one or more of his challenges. "Wait here," he told Song Le, and slipped off, using his nose to guide him toward a dump of sorts not far off.

When he returned he was carrying a burlap bag that reeked of fish. In his mind he'd already dealt with two of the obstacles.

"What's that for?" Song Le asked.

"Help with the dog," he said.

With a gun in his right hand, bag of rotting fish in his left, Monarch slipped toward the village with Song Le right behind him. He made out a structure that he pegged as that regional boarding school Barnett had described and gave it a wide berth. He didn't want any teenage kid to wake up, see them, and sound an alarm.

He stopped diagonally across the street and well down the block from the compound where Mahdi lived. The moon had come out once again and he was able to better see the wall, and the suggestion of the glass shards.

There was a wooden gate in the barrier about thirty yards to their right. Unless alerted, Monarch reasoned the guards would all be gathered there, on the other side of the gate, sleeping on mats, under mosquito netting.

He whispered his improvised plan to Song Le, who for once did not question every aspect of it. She simply nodded.

He checked the wind, felt it blowing across his right cheek, and then dashed in a long circle downwind and away from Mahdi's compound until he reached denser cover and stopped. Song Le was right there. He'd never heard her moving behind him.

Monarch turned panther then, went deep inside himself, made every gesture fluid as he pushed aside brush and climbed over downed logs, hyperaware of a dog's ability to hear and smell. But he heard no barks, no snarls, and no panting when at last they reached the west end of the compound. Satisfied with their stealth, he reached inside the burlap bag and removed a fish.

Monarch cut a slit in the fish's belly, then he went in the pack Barnett had put together and found the medical kit, and a vial of oxycontin painkillers. He shook six into the slit fish belly, pushed them in deep enough to disappear, and then lobbed the fish up and over the wall, hearing it splat in the dirt. Then he hustled through the vegetation crowding the compound until he reached the north wall and a tree with branches that hung six or seven feet above it. He stopped, listening.

"What—?" the Chinese agent began.

"Shhhh," Monarch said, trying to hear.

A full minute passed and then Monarch heard the chomping of jaws and teeth and grunts of pleasure.

"Dogs can't resist ripe garbage," Monarch whispered to Song Le. "Like bears. He'll have a nasty stomach in the morning, but wake up essentially fine."

The feast went on another two minutes. Five minutes of excruciating silence followed before he heard an insistent whine that rolled into a panting moan.

"Here we go," Monarch whispered, figuring the dog would be too sick and too drugged to raise much of an alarm for the near future.

He tossed the empty burlap bag up onto the wall. When he turned to shinny up the tree, Song Le had beaten him to it. She climbed like a squirrel, caught the first stout branch, and went hand over hand out it until she was directly above the burlap bag. She dropped the six feet. Her shoes touched the wall for an instant, crunching the glass shards beneath the burlap, and then rebounded into another leap that dropped her into the compound.

She landed with a soft sound. Impressed yet again by her physical skills, Monarch climbed after her, and repeated much the same move, dropping onto the wall, and bounced off it into a forward dive. He reached for the ground with his right thumb curled under and toward his chest, causing his arm to form a curve. The blade of his hand touched first and Monarch tensed, which threw the momentum of his entire body forward in a roll that brought him to his feet.

Song Le was already moving, circling well away from the inert form of the now snoring dog, heading toward the front of the compound. Monarch followed, seeing four structures built in traditional Malay style: up on low stilts with steeply pitched thatch roofs, carved plank-wood walls and multiple windows with shutters. He figured the largest and closest one had to be the main house. The three smaller huts set to the left had to be the wives' sleeping quarters.

They padded past the main house. A baby began to cry. Song Le froze.

Children, Monarch thought. He hated it when kids were in the line of fire. He hated everything about it.

A woman hushed the baby in the closest hut. The baby squalled once more, then made contented sighs, beginning to feed at its mother's breast.

"We're good," Monarch whispered.

Song Le had not moved a muscle but now she nodded and slipped to the corner of the main house and crouched there. Monarch eased up behind her, standing so they could both scan the shadows. She poked him in the knee and pointed immediately to their right. About fifteen feet away a man slept on a cot beneath a mosquito net. Monarch looked toward the gate and spotted the forms of two other cots, one set to either side of the exit.

Monarch gestured at her and then at the closest guard. Song Le uncoiled and slithered toward the sleeping man without pause. He padded toward the sleeping guards at the gate, catching the barest sound of a struggle before it died. He glanced over to see Song Le gagging the un- conscious guard and binding him with zip ties.

Monarch did much the same with the first gate guard, clamping a hand over the man's mouth and nose, and using his cleverly trained fingers to find the carotid artery and a bundle of nerves below the ear. He dug into it. The guard went rigid, and then collapsed back.

It took Monarch seconds to gag him and get his hands and legs bound. When he withdrew from the mosquito net, Song Le was already sneaking up beside the third sleeping guard.

Monarch came from the opposite side. The Chinese agent got there first, and started to lift the mosquito net when the guard startled awake and shouted out in alarm. Monarch sprang not to help Song Le, but back toward the three huts even as he heard the Chinese agent's pistol hit the man's skull and silence him.

But the baby was crying again, and voices of confusion mumbled inside the huts. From the middle structure he caught the softly barking voice of a man. Monarch circled to the side, eased up under an open window toward the front of the hut and waited, hearing nothing for several beats, and then the creak of the door of the hut closest to the main house, back where the baby had been crying.

Monarch peeked around the side of the middle hut, and saw the silhouette of a woman walk a few steps before calling out something in Malay. The door to the middle hut opened, but no one replied and no one came out.

A gun barrel poked Monarch from the open window, and he heard a man hiss harshly at him in Malay. Monarch understood and dropped his pistol. The man climbed out the window while still keeping the gun muzzle tight to the back of Monarch's head—a professional's move.

The gunman prodded Monarch to his feet, and used him as cover, pushing him forward out into the yard. The man called out something in Malay just before the woman screamed and the baby began to cry.

A generator coughed to life behind the huts. Three bare bulbs lit, revealing Song Le behind the mother, arm around her throat, pistol pressed to her head.

The Chinese agent shouted at the gunman in Malay. He barked back something and flipped off the safety on the gun he held at Monarch's head. Song Le put the muzzle of her pistol to the baby's temple.

"Not a good idea," Monarch said.

"English? American?" the gunman demanded.

"I speak English. Akrit Mahdi?"

A hesitation. "Tell bitch put my son down."

"Is your son a Son of Prophecy?" Song Le demanded.

"Put down or this one die," Mahdi said, jabbing Monarch at the base of his neck as if the gun barrel were a spear.

"I don't care if he dies," the Chinese agent replied. "But if you do kill him, I promise your baby dies and then your wife and then you."

Mahdi's wife must have understood some of it because she began to cringe and to whimper and to plead with the pirate. After several long moments the gun came away from Monarch's neck. He looked over, seeing a small, tough, wiry man, shirtless, with skin the color of tobacco juice.

Mahdi held the AK-47 at his side, but remained defiant. "What you want from me, man?" he demanded.

"Secretary of State Lawton," Monarch said, glancing beyond the man at his pistol back there on the ground.

"And Minister Fung," Song Le said.

Mahdi looked back and forth between the two of them, first in confusion, then grinning incredulously, showing teeth stained red from chewing betel nut.

"Oh, yeah, they right here!" he cackled. "I keep them here in my huts with whole world looking for them. You think I that tough?"

28

MONARCH ALMOST BELIEVED THE Malaysian pirate's claim to know nothing about the kidnapping of the diplomats, but he kept looking at Mahdi's red teeth and remembering the betel nut spit on the wall of Secretary Lawton's cabin aboard the *Niamey*.

"How many men do you have under arms?" Monarch demanded.

Mahdi's smile ebbed, but he said nothing.

"Answer him," Song Le snapped, moving the gun on his baby's face.

"Depends on size of fish I trying to catch," the pirate replied.

"You mean like a freighter versus an oil tanker?"

"Oil tanker?" Mahdi said. "That out of my league. We work small and fast. Only got seven boats, but they fast."

"You out the day the typhoon hit?"

"Only crazy man goes out on typhoon sea. And I am no crazy man."

"But you are a pirate," Monarch said.

"That a crime?" Mahdi asked.

Monarch almost smiled.

"I have many mouths to fill," Mahdi said and shrugged.

Monarch recalled the eight-million-dollar weapons deal Archie Latham said Mahdi had been trying to set up. "You Muslim?"

The pirate sobered. "So?"

"Radical Muslim?"

He found that amusing. "I am money Muslim."

"For Jihad?"

"For Mahdi."

Monarch studied him, believing him. "Okay, so you fry small fish. Know anyone working the South China Sea with the guts to take on three of the biggest fish on earth?"

"You mean, like a pirate or terrorist or something?"

"Any of above."

Mahdi thought on that, almost shook his head, but then got a far away look in his eye. "Yeah, maybe that one. He wild enough."

"Tell us," Song Le said.

"He Indonesian," Mahdi said. "He makes one big attack, not many small. He steal tankers, palm oil. Things like that. Works for big syndicate."

"Name?" Monarch asked.

"I don't know his real name and I never see him, just hear of him, but he call himself 'Ramelan'," Mahdi said. "It mean 'Prophecy' in Indonesian."

It certainly fit. But was Ramelan real?

"Where can we find him?" Song Le asked.

The Malaysian pirate turned his lips down at the corners. "He work the deep waters east and north here. Big shipping lanes. Like I say, out of Mahdi's league."

"You said he works for a big syndicate?" Monarch asked. "Ramelan?"

The question clearly made Mahdi nervous. "Just the rumor I hear."

Monarch's thieving mind came back around to the weapons Latham said Mahdi had been trying to buy and he saw a possibility. "So where are the guns, grenades, and rockets you were trying to buy back in January?"

That question clearly upended the Malaysian pirate. "Not me," he said finally. "You got the wrong guy."

"That's not true," Song Le said. "We have eyewitnesses all over South China Sea say you were looking for weapons back in January."

That wasn't exactly the case, but Monarch admired her instincts.

Mahdi hesitated again. "Okay, I try to buy, but I never get guns."

"So you're sitting on the electronics you stole?" Monarch asked.

Mahdi smiled again. "No, I move these things a long time ago."

"Through the syndicate?" Monarch asked. "Ramelan's syndicate?"

The smile evaporated. "No, I no know—"

"You do," Monarch said. "Who bought the electronics and the guns from you?"

Mahdi's eyes shifted as if he were looking for something he'd just misplaced. "I don't remember—"

"I can tell you it's a tragic thing to lose a son," Song Le said, abruptly yanking the baby from his mother's arms. The woman began to scream and cry and babble at her husband in Malay.

Looking torn, Mahdi pleaded with Monarch, "I can't tell you. He kill me. He kill all of us. He very, very dangerous man."

"We are very, very dangerous people," Monarch growled. "Take your pick: the gun that's going to kill your son right now, or the ones that might later."

The Chinese agent cocked the hammer on her pistol.

Mahdi's wife went down on her knees, begging Song Le for mercy.

"I'll tell you," Mahdi cried finally. "Just give my son back to my wife."

Her face still stony, Song Lee handed the baby back to its mother.

"He kill you," Mahdi promised. "You never get to that man."

"We'll take our chances," Monarch said. "Name?"

"I just say you are dead man now," Mahdi said.

"Name?"

The pirate finally broke, said, "Tengku. He live in KL, up one of those silver towers. You cannot—"

Men were suddenly shouting outside the compound, coming closer. Mahdi's head went up. They pounded at the gate and yelled in Maylay.

"They've found the one guarding the boats," Song Le translated.

Gunshots now. They were trying to shoot open the gate.

Mahdi started to raise his own weapon. But Monarch was too fast. He flung out his hand, grabbed the barrel and twisted it over and past his head. The spiral action pinched the pirate's fingers, and broke his grip. Monarch ripped the gun away and then chopped back at Mahdi with the butt of the gun, hitting him in the solar plexus. The pirate groaned and pitched back onto the ground.

Song Le was already in motion, leaving the astonished mother holding the crying baby, and sprinting back the way they'd come in. Monarch grabbed his pistol and ran to the back of the huts, saw the generator, and put two bullets into it. The lights died. He took off after the Chinese agent.

"How do we get over the wall?" she gasped when he pulled up beside her.

"I don't . . ."

Song Le tripped, and stumbled. Monarch barely managed to avoid the wet depression in the compound floor and grabbed her by the elbow to prevent a fall. He skidded to a halt, still holding her elbow.

"What?" she said, shaking free.

"There's another way out of here," Monarch said, turning around, running quickly back to confirm his suspicions.

Hearing more shots, he saw to his satisfaction that the depression was more of a ditch that drained water. It ran toward the southeast corner of the compound. Monarch didn't bother to follow the ditch, but took off toward that corner, finding a large metal grate where the ditch met the wall.

He squatted, pulled, and felt it budge only slightly. The front gate slammed open. Mahdi was shouting now.

"Help," Monarch said.

Song Le got opposite him, wrapped her fingers in the grate, said, "One, two, three."

Monarch drove straight up from his heels, feeling the grate move two inches, and then four. When it was free of the drain hole, they heaved it aside.

"Ladies first," Monarch said.

He followed her into the hole, crawled under the wall through muddy water and trash, and then pushed himself to his feet.

Song Le called, "Here."

Monarch ran toward her voice, and then saw her moving through the trees south of the compound and the village where people were shouting and more dogs were barking. But there were no more—

Machine-gun fire erupted behind them from back near the compound wall. Tracers zipped by Monarch, who started dodging and weaving as best he could in the low light. Dawn was coming soon, a blessing and a curse.

Song Le had an uncanny sense of direction, almost equal to Monarch's. She led them in a fast circuit of the village, finding that rise they'd crossed earlier, and then the path that led back through the banana grove, across the fields to the high grass and reeds that bordered the slough.

Dogs started baying no more than three, four hundred yards behind them. Men were with the dogs, calling to each other, spreading out, flanking as they came toward the estuary, and daylight grew brighter by the minute.

They broke out of the reeds onto that beach where they'd suckered and subdued the drunken pirate not two hours before. Song Le raced into the water, swam, and pulled herself up into the closest cigarette boat. By the time Monarch got himself over the gunnel, she'd moved under the dashboard, a flashlight in her mouth, hands up, fiddling with wires.

The shouting was getting closer. So were the dogs. It was almost broad daylight and Monarch hefted Mahdi's AK-47, and turned as the cigarette boat's onboard engines roared to life. Monarch put three rounds in the controls of the second cigarette boat and four more into the gas tanks. Song Le cut the mooring line, scrambled back to the wheel.

"Take us slow past the other boats," Monarch yelled.

Song Le threw the boat in gear. The bow turned on the inky water, and she pressed the throttle just enough to take them down the middle of the channel toward the four Zodiac inflatables pulled up on the bank. As they motored past, Monarch put three rounds though the side of each raft, and two more bullets in their outboards motors.

Six boats? Mahdi said he had seven.

Men appeared on the beach far behind them and opened fire.

"Go to our raft!" Monarch ordered, pivoting and returning fire at the beach where more and more pirates were emerging from the jungle.

Song Le accelerated two hundred yards down the channel, backed off the throttle, and they slid neatly beside the raft they'd paddled in on. Monarch reached over, snagged the rope hanging off the back of the raft. He tied it solidly to the stern of the cigarette boat.

"Slow at first," Monarch said. "You don't want to tear out the cleat."

"But the raft's tied to that submerged tree," Song Le said.

"Exactly," Monarch said.

She still looked confused, but threw the prop in gear. The rope lost slack, strained and for a moment Monarch thought it would snap. But then the downed tree slid off the bank, following the raft as the cigarette boat slowly sped up. Song Le swung them wide into the main estuary. Machine guns opened up, raking the side of their boat.

Monarch spotted a third cigarette boat speeding at them down another side channel about eighty yards away. "Go!" he yelled. "Give it everything!"

The Chinese agent hammered the throttle forward. The boat's bow rose like a dolphin surfacing and for a second Monarch thought the awkward weight and drag of the tree would be too much and they'd stand on end and flip.

But then Song Le trimmed the prop, and the tree trunk dragging behind the raft settled and submerged. The bow lowered, and they sped on toward the mouth of the estuary. The other cigarette boat shot out of that back channel unencumbered by dead weight and immediately started closing the gap.

Monarch could make out the driver. It was Mahdi.

Three men lay forward on the hull. They opened fire again.

Bullets smacked into stern of their boat, blew up the raft and skipped off the water all around them. Monarch fired four times with the Glock, and then looked over his shoulder at that sandbar where the river met the sea. The sandbar looked bigger than he remembered it. Low tide.

"Deepest part of the channel!" he yelled.

Mahdi's boat was no more than sixty yards back now and gaining ground. The pirate at the wheel was grinning maniacally, sure that he was going to catch the people who'd held a pistol to his son's head.

Thirty-feet past the sandbar, they struck the first on-coming swell. Monarch cut the line tied to the deflated raft and the log. Freed of dead weight, their cigarette boat launched through the air, and smashed down on the next wave of the coming sea.

Behind them the raft twisted in the chaotic eddy there at the confluence of freshwater and salt. Mahdi headed straight at it, sure that he could go right up and over the top of it.

"Do it," Monarch muttered.

Mahdi's hull hit the submerged tree trunk going sixty miles an hour. The impact flipped his boat on its nose, hurling the pirate and his men through the air. For a moment the vessel seemed to slide on end before hitting a wave, cartwheeling twice, and coming to rest capsized, the busted hull visible in the rising sun.

Monarch stood in the stern watching the water for movement. Just before they passed out of range, he thought he'd seen someone surface back there in the water, but couldn't be sure. Part of him hoped he hadn't widowed the baby's mother. The other part of him hoped Mahdi would be incapacitated enough not to warn the mysterious Tengku.

Song Le turned them south, and eased off on the speed after several miles, saying, "Where now?"

"Like the man said, Kuala Lumpur."

"We've only got a tank and a half. It's nowhere near enough."

"Keep heading south," Monarch said, and got out the iPhone. He punched in Barnett's number. To his surprise, she answered on the first ring.

"Don't you sleep?" he asked.

"Not much when I'm working. You?"

"Not enough," he admitted.

"The Sons of Prophecy have struck again," she said.

"China?" Monarch asked.

"New Delhi. A bomb went off in a subway station that serves the Indian Parliament. Eight people are confirmed dead, twenty wounded. They're counting themselves lucky."

"How's that?"

"The bomb detonated minutes after the Metro system opened. An hour later, there could have been hundreds of victims."

"And the Sons of Prophecy are taking credit?"

"On the Web site," she confirmed.

Monarch flashed again on the NSA intelligence regarding an attack or coup attempt in India. "What's India's response been?"

"Outrage, of course," she said. "And given what happened in Mongolia, their military is on high alert as well, and they've beefed up security all around their parliament. The prime minister is going to give a press conference in about an hour. Evidently a woman who works in his office is one of the dead."

Monarch absorbed that, but put it aside. He'd think about the strategic value of bombing a subway station near the Indian Parliament later. At the moment, he needed Barnett's remarkable logistical skills.

He said, "Well, in this small corner of the Sons of Prophecy conspiracy, we need another ride. Preferably winged."

"You're demanding, Robin, anybody ever tell you that?"

"You."

"Smart woman, me. Anything I can tell Dr. Hopkins while I try to track you down another float plane?"

As Song Le piloted them due south paralleling the Malaysian coastline about six hundred yards out, Monarch gave Barnett a thumbnail sketch of all that had occurred inside the pirate's compound, including the single name of the fence who took the pirated electronics gear and weapons.

There was a long pause, then Barnett snapped: "Spell that?"

"Not sure exactly. Either T-e-n-g-k-u or T-e-n-k-u."

"It's Tengku," she said firmly. "Ketu Tengku."

"How do you know that?"

"Because while you've been glamorously blowing up pirate ships, I've been slogging my way through on-line Malaysian public records. Ketu Tengku is part owner of two of the three buildings that house the Internet cafés the SOP have used to upload their videos."

"That seems thin," Monarch said.

"Maybe," she replied tartly. "But add to that the fact that Mr. Tengku also owns the house where that young family was murdered. He's their landlord."

29

WITH THE TELEVISION BLARING the BBC's coverage of the bombing in New Delhi, the Moon Dragon went to the shuttered windows of his import-export business and flung them wide open. Long wanted his throw his arms over his head like some Olympic athlete who had done the impossible. He wanted to shout of his feats to the teeming masses of Kowloon.

Instead, the triad leader exercised great restraint, and gazed down upon his beloved chaos, silently proclaiming victory to the food mongers, the silk dealers, the whores, and all the smug bankers in their Hermès suits and five-thousand-dollar watches.

The filthy little peasant boy you all used to ignore or spit on? He's won. He's won, and will continue to win in the days ahead.

The Sons of Prophecy are all they're talking about on the news. The ambush in China. The bomb in India.

The missing diplomats. The SOP is everywhere, and the world trembles before us!

Look at the markets. The Shanghai Exchange opened sharply lower. So did Hong Kong and Singapore. But the bottom had completely fallen out of the Bombay Stock Exchange after the explosion. Its composite index lost eighteen percent of its value before the government stepped in and halted trading until the following Monday morning.

It was brilliant! Through intermediaries the Moon Dragon had shorted the composite indexes of every single one of those exchanges. By his reckoning he'd made somewhere in the neighborhood of eighty million dollars in the last few hours. When the European and U.S. markets opened, he'd make millions more.

I win! Long silently shouted at the swarming Kowloon streets below him. I own your fantasies. I can buy your desires.

You shake things up, and opportunity knocks. Isn't that the truth?

Look what was happening in the U.S. election. A week ago it was a close race. Now, according to the latest polls, Americans were growing increasingly scared that the Vice President would not be up to the job of fighting a terrorist organization like the SOP. After all, Vaught had been a member of the administration that had allowed the Sons of Prophecy to flourish without detection.

And we're not done yet, the Moon Dragon crowed silently. Not by a long shot. By the time we're done, they won't know where to turn or who to trust, blinded and paralyzed by their fear of the—

"Moon Dragon," Tuul said, breaking Long's reverie.

The triad leader looked over his shoulder at his body-guard, who was holding out a cell phone to him.

"Hello?" he said.

"Pretty darn impressive series of events, I wanted to tell you," drawled his southern friend. "The Chinese are already sending troops into Mongolia, just like you said they would."

"They're facing a new and audacious enemy," the Moon Dragon replied.

"They are indeed, thanks in no small part to you. How long do you figure until they change course?"

"Beijing? Soon than later."

"I think you're right. And when they do, they'll need cash to pay for it all."

"Lots of cash," Long agreed.

"And you'll be perfectly positioned to build them the machine to do it, and to profit mightily from it," his southern friend said in an admiring tone. "Well done, sir. Well played. You've gone beyond yourself, haven't you?"

The triad leader swelled with pride. Here was his victory parade.

"With your help, my friend," the Moon Dragon said. "I thank you."

"Ball's in my court now. They've got no idea what's coming."

Long considered that, agreed and said, "Not a chance."

"You'll let me know if I can be of service in the meantime?"

"Always," the triad leader said. "I'll be—"

The line went dead.

PART III

THE BRIGHTEST TOWERS

30

MONARCH AWOKE AT THE sound of snoring and for several moments had no idea where he was. Then he remembered the chopper that fished them off the cigarette boat and falling asleep on the ride into Kuala Lumpur. He'd told Barnett at the helipad that he needed at least two more hours rest to be effective. That was three hours ago.

He yawned, looked around the dim hotel room, looking for the source of the snoring, and saw a massive form under the sheets in the queen bed next to his, and an equally massive head facing the other way, sawing. Monarch smiled, picked up a pillow and threw it.

The pillow smacked off the snorer's head. John "Tats" Tatupu shot up right, head twisting all around. The Samoan-American with the King Tut beard looked at the clock, spotted Monarch, flopped back, and groaned,

"We just got in after forty hours of fucking travel, Robin. I just fell asleep."

"You should have come over on a Stealth," Monarch replied. "I was here in eight hours from D.C."

Tats flipped him the bird. "You always cruel like this? Hitting a man with a pillow when he's dead to the world?"

"You were snoring and that casaba melon on your shoulders was such a perfect target I couldn't resist."

Tats eyes were already closed. "Casaba melon's kind of small."

"Pumpkin then," Monarch said. "Or a mutant gourd."

"Good to see you, too."

"How's your mom?"

"On an oxygen line, but in her new place, and stable."

"Good to hear," Monarch said, and got out of bed.

Halfway to the bathroom he heard the big man snoring again. Monarch showered in cold water to fully wake himself. He dressed and snuck out of the bedroom into the main room of a suite. Chanel Chavez, a fit, attractive woman in her early thirties, sat before the ruins of a room service breakfast, looking completely rested.

Chavez grinned, set her coffee cup down, and got to her feet, saying, "How do you get us into the middle of these things?"

"A gift, a genetic thing," Monarch said, going to her, throwing his arms around her and giving her a hug and a kiss. "How come you look great and Tats looks like he got hit by Tats?"

"He can't sleep in those little seats, neither can Fowler," she said with a snort. "I can't stay awake."

"Where is Fowler?"

She gestured at the suite door, said, "Other side of the hallway."

"Your sister?"

Chavez sobered. "About as well as you can be when you've got two kids under four and the doctor tells you it's stage three already."

"If she's as tough as you, the cancer better just give up right now."

Chavez put her hands in her back pockets. "That's what I'm here for, Robin. I just wanted you to know."

"I'm not following," he said.

"The fee," she replied. "Ramona doesn't have insurance. And that kind of money will definitely help knock the bejesus out of the cancer."

"If we're successful," Monarch said.

"We're going to be successful, right?" she said, fixing him with a stare. "We're going to get Lawton and the money, I mean."

"We've got a strong lead and sixty-some-odd hours to follow it."

Gloria Barnett came out of a room on the other side of the suite, followed by Song Le, who looked much better than the last time he'd seen her.

"Any more on Mr. Tengku?" Monarch asked Barnett.

Barnett nodded, poured herself coffee, and gave him a bare-bones biography. Born on the southeast coast of Borneo, Ketu Tengku quit school at sixteen and was soon arrested in Jakarta for fencing stolen goods. He did two years in a juvenile facility there.

From that point on, Tengku appeared clean. He moved to Kuala Lumpur, built a successful import-export business, and invested in Malaysian real estate. Something of a recluse, he kept to his offices high in Petronas Tower Two and a heavily guarded house south of the city.

"He looks legitimate," she said.

"Of course he does," Monarch said. "That's why he's good. I know these kind of guys. Once a fence, always a fence. He's just good at hiding it."

"So what do we do?" Song Le asked. "Go ask if he's involved in the SOP?"

"Not a bad idea," Monarch said.

"I was joking," the Chinese agent said.

"I'm not," Monarch said. "It always worked for James Bond, right? Just march into the bad guy's lair and see if you can upset him. Direct approach. And it saves us time, which we are running short of. How far are these towers?"

"Six, or seven blocks," Barnett said. "But security's tight. I don't know if you could just go there and expect to talk to Tengku."

"So we'll get creative," Monarch said.

Rising nearly five hundred meters above the Malaysian capital, the twin Petronas Towers were once the tallest man-made structures in the world. Clad in stainless-steel skins, and ribbed with stainless-steel tubes, the gleaming skyscrapers boasted eighty-eight floors. At the forty-first floor, a glass and steel bridge connected the two buildings. Above that level, the skyscrapers got narrower and their silhouettes stepped back every ten to fifteen stories until they reached for the tropical sky with a ball and spire that looked like they belonged on a minaret or a Christmas tree.

As Monarch and Song Le crossed the plaza in front of the towers, he thought that they belonged in a Star Wars film.

"Test?" Barnett said, her voice coming over the tiny radio disguised as an in-the-canal hearing aide in Monarch's left ear.

"Perfect," Monarch replied, shifting the briefcase he carried.

A security guard opened the door to Petronas Tower One. Monarch and Song Le strode across the lobby, stopped at the counter, and said, "We're here about the floors."

The guard, who wore a badge that identified him as "Mr. Wari," looked confused, pressed his hands, and bowed slightly, said, "Certainly, Mr. . . ."

"Monarch. Robin Monarch. This is Song Le. We work for KBM Resurfacing out of Singapore."

"We're supposed to check the flooring for cracks in all public areas," Song Le went on, setting her briefcase on the counter and gesturing at the dark marble in the foyer.

"Seismic activity, they think," Monarch said, holding out his passport and giving the man a business card, and hoping the ink was dry.

Song Le did the same. The guard appeared more confused, said, "I am sorry, but the maintenance supervisor is not here. They've all—"

"You mean, Mr. Joyo the maintenance supervisor?" Monarch asked.

"Yes. Yes. But Mr. Joyo is gone for the day. I could try to find his—"

Song Le interrupted: "We were supposed to be here earlier, but our flight was delayed. If Mr. Joyo's gone, let's not bother him. It will take us at most an hour to inspect the floors, and then we may present our findings in person to Mr. Joyo in the morning, and let him feel that we were not wasting his valuable time today. Yes?"

After a momentary hesitation, the guard nodded, gestured at the floors behind them. "Go ahead."

"Could we start highest?" Monarch asked. "Forty-second story? Mr. Joyo was especially interested in the flooring of the footbridge."

The guard nodded to the security machines. "Put your briefcases through there. Elevators on your left. Stop at forty-two."

"We'll be done before closing," Monarch promised, shook the man's hand and set the briefcase on the conveyor belt.

He passed through a metal detector that whooped. Another guard ran a wand over him, pausing at his pen and his belt buckle.

"You're good," the guard said.

Monarch grabbed his briefcase and Song Le's as she endured the wand.

When the elevator doors closed and they began to rise, Monarch said, "Good call on the floors and the maintenance guy, Gloria."

"We aim to please," Barnett purred in his ear.

With a ding, the door opened. Monarch took an immediate right, heading down a long hallway toward the pedestrian bridge, where he stopped and looked up through the curved glass ceiling toward the upper reaches of Tower Two.

"Tengku's on seventy-four?" Song Le asked.

"Affirmative," Barnett said. "Offices on north side."

Monarch studied the face of the tower, searing the design into his memory before moving on. Boarding an elevator inside Tower Two, he pushed "71."

"But . . . ," Song Le began.

"Trust me," Monarch said.

When the elevator stopped and the door opened on the seventy-first floor, they faced the Malaysian offices of a U.S. law firm. He ignored it as well as doors that bore signs of a real estate venture and a global engineering firm, going instead to one marked "Fire Exit."

He pushed it open, finding the tower's internal staircase. They climbed three flights of stairs, checked the door at seventy-four and found it locked. Monarch had anticipated that possibility. From the briefcase he removed several large paper clips, straightened them, and in under a minute picked the lock.

"We could have just gotten out at his floor," Song Le whispered.

"Wouldn't have the same effect," Monarch muttered. "We come to his door real polite and ask for an audience, and we're meeting the fence on his terms. We break into his place, it's on our terms."

"You have a strange way of thinking," she said.

With that Monarch opened the door and stepped into the hallway of the seventy-fourth floor. To his right at the far end, he spotted a beefy Asian guy in a cheap business suit. He spotted Monarch immediately, reached in his jacket as if going for a weapon.

"Sir!" the guard yelled. "Ma'am! You are not allowed to—"

"We want to speak with Mr. Tengku," Monarch said evenly, walking right at him.

"Impossible," the guard snapped, and drew a semi-automatic pistol.

"Go tell him to make it possible, and now," Monarch said in a commanding tone. "Tell him we are foreign agents here about the missing U.S. Secretary of State and the Foreign Ministers of India—"

"And China," Song Le said.

The guard kept coming, and for a second, Monarch thought he had miscalculated, and this man was going to kill them first and ask questions later. But then the weight of what they'd just said hit the guard full force.

"You mean about those terrorist bastards?" he asked. "The SOP?"

"Exactly," Monarch said.

The guard shook his head. "You're in the wrong place, man. Mr. Tengku has nothing to do with that kind of nonsense."

"I'm sure, but the United States and China would like to hear him say so."

Tengku's guy hesitated, but then holstered the weapon, tugged a radio from his hip, turned and walked away muttering in Malay.

A few moments later, he said, "Mr. Tengku will see you."

Monarch nodded. "Thought he might."

The fence was a bitch of a man. Small, thin, and sallow, Ketu Tengku puffed on an electronic cigarette while looking through a jeweler's loupe at loose gemstones laid out on the desk in his office, a cavernous affair with fine oriental rugs, framed art, and glass cases that displayed various collections.

Two bodyguards, both bruisers, stood by, glaring at Monarch and Song Le.

Tengku did not bother to look up. "Who you say you work for?"

"President of the United States," Monarch said.

"The Premier of China," Song Le said.

The fence set down the loop, and sneered skeptically. "You got proof?"

Monarch shrugged, said, "You want to call the White House?"

"Or Beijing?" Song Le offered.

Tengku snickered bitterly, gestured around at the display cases, and the artwork. "What? You think I'm a stupid man? That I don't check authenticity of the things I buy and sell? The people I do business with? Tengku is a successful import-export man."

"And real estate investor?" Song Le asked.

"That's right," Tengku said, eyeing her more closely now.

"No offense, but you're a fence," Monarch said evenly.

"You deal in stolen goods. In fact, most of the stuff in here is probably hotter than lava. You just launder it into real estate holdings."

That infuriated the Indonesian, who spit back, "Who you think you are?"

His bodyguards took a step closer.

Monarch took a chair, said, "If you and your clowns don't back down and start answering questions, I *will* call the White House, and they *will* call Malaysian law enforcement officials, and *they will* make your life a living hell. You're an Indonesian national, am I right, Tengku? I can call you that, right?"

The fence toyed with his electronic cigarette, then sucked on it. Monarch saw the tip glow and then the water vapor escaping his lips when he sat back in his chair and said, "What you want to know?"

"The location of the diplomats would be good to start," Song Le said.

Tengku sneered. "You think I have ESP? How should I know that?"

"Because like most successful fences, you hear things," Monarch said.

"How you know so much about fences?"

"I'm a thief. Some of my best friends and worst enemies are fences."

That seemed to amuse Tengku. "A thief who works for the American president?"

"It's complicated," Monarch agreed. "But we have it on very good sources that you're the man to see for a good backroom arms deal, or when pirates need to broker a big haul like a load of Dutch electronics."

For the first time, Tengku smiled, almost laughed. "Who told you that?"

"Guy named Akrit Mahdi," Monarch said.

He thought about that. "No, never heard of that guy."

"He sure knew you," Song Le said.

"Then he delusional," the fence said, and took another puff. "I been audited by Malay government twice in past six years. Clean. And everything in this room? Bought at bargain. I simply a man who knows the value of things."

"What about a pirate named Ramelan?" Monarch asked. "An Indonesian."

In mid-drag, Tengku hesitated ever so shortly, just enough for the electronic coal to dim before he blew out vapor and said, "I hear rumors of him."

"What rumors?" Song Le demanded.

He shrugged. "A pirate no one sees. Calls himself 'Captain Ramelan.' Supposed to be complete crazy man."

"Where can we find him?" Monarch asked.

"No idea. *Really.* I never met him. I don't even know if he is real or person somebody makes up."

"All rumors are based on some fact," Monarch said. "Give me a fact."

The fence thought a moment, said, "It is fact that once a year, maybe twice, past six years, a group of pirates make spectacular hijackings in South China and Java Seas."

"Define 'spectacular'," Song Le said.

He set the electric cigarette down. "I read insurance reports. They have helicopters. Fast boats. Well armed. Very coordinated."

"Like militarily coordinated?"

"Yeah," Tengku said. "Appear, attack, disappear for long time, appear and attack. All big stuff. Electronics. Oil. That kind. And once, three years ago, Ramelan take ship bringing small arms, ammunition to Cambodia, attacked it in Gulf of Thailand."

From Monarch's perspective Cambodia was a long way from where the *Niamey* had been attacked, and even farther from where the oil tanker had been found. It wasn't like the old days when pirates could wander the seas at will. Modern pirates usually had a home base and home waters that they regularly plundered.

"The other hijackings," Monarch said, "Gulf of Thailand also?"

Tengku hesitated, but then shook his head. "All over. From Malacca Straits to East Java Sea, even north of Hong Kong in patrolled waters."

"So who's fencing Captain Ramelan?"

"Not me. Like I said, Tengku is honest businessman."

"With heavily armed bodyguards," Song Le observed.

He gave her an oily smile. "I honest, but paranoid."

Monarch said, "Okay. You've helped. Appreciate your cooperation."

"That it?" the fence said, sounding surprised.

Monarch glanced at Song Le who was studying Tengku implacably, and replied, "Unless you've got something you want to get off your chest?"

"No, no," the fence replied rather quickly, and stood to offer his hand. "Glad to help any thief who works for President. No good when diplomats kidnapped. No good when subways bombed. Better peaceful."

Monarch shook the fence's hand, finding it dry, and weak, and stared for a long moment into the man's eyes, finding them as skillfully blank as his own. As he turned away, he took one last look around the office, spotting a large air-conditioning vent above one of the display cases. The bodyguard who'd brought them to the office now led them to the elevators.

When the elevator door shut, Song Le said, "You believe him?"

"No," Monarch said.

"Why didn't you bring up the properties he owns, the cafés and the murdered family?"

"Because that's why I don't believe him, and I didn't want him to know we knew," Monarch said.

That confused her.

"Don't worry," he said. "I'm coming back tonight."

31

"**ARE YOU OUT OF** your mind?" Song Le asked.

Sixty-one hours before the threatened execution of Secretary Lawton and the foreign ministers, she and Monarch were thirteen hundred feet above the city on the observation deck of the KL Tower near the center of Kuala Lumpur.

Monarch lowered a pair of Leica binoculars he'd been using to get a strategic view of the Petronas Towers four miles distant. While he was studying the towers, he'd been explaining what he had in mind. At her question he lowered the binoculars and said, "I'm perfectly sane. I've done this kind of thing before. I've had training."

Incredulous, the Chinese agent looked at Barnett and Tatupu.

The big Samoan was wearing shorts, flip-flops, and a huge green Hawaiian shirt. He said, "It's how he stole Sadaam Hussein's battle plan before we attacked Iraq."

"There was a little more to it than that," Monarch said.

"But he did use the suit on that mission," Barnett confirmed. "The question is whether I can find one again on such short notice."

"And the other stuff I mentioned," Monarch reminded her.

"What time do you want to go?" Barnett said, looking pressured.

"Say, one A.M.?" Monarch replied.

"Seven hours," Barnett said in a doubtful tone. "The only thing you've got going for you is that Malaysia is a big place for deep cavers and other extreme sports creatures. But I'll need help."

"Whatever you want," Tatupu said. "Just tell us what to—"

A security guard came along to tell them that the observation deck was closing. Monarch took several pictures of the towers with his phone, and then followed the others to the elevator, where they were the final riders of the day. They went to a van parked out on the street and rode through the evening twilight back to the hotel. Barnett was typing furiously on her iPad, posting on several Malaysian caving and base-jumping forums.

"What can I do?" Song Le asked her. "I've got an iPad, too."

Barnett looked up, blinked, and said, "Find me a local supplier of industrial electromagnets."

The Chinese agent hesitated, and then started to work.

"There's our boy, right on time," Tatupu said, pulling the van over for Abbott Fowler, another member of Monarch's old team at the CIA.

In his late thirties, Fowler was like Monarch in that he possessed a face that fit in almost anywhere. He'd shaved his head, stained his already swarthy skin with henna, and wore a tunic, pants, and sandals.

"Get some round glasses, you could call yourself 'Gandhi,'" Tats said, and chuckled as he drove on.

"I'd have to lose a few pounds to pull that off," Fowler said, grinning.

Monarch said, "Well?"

Sobering, Fowler said, "Took a while to find, but it's doable."

"Single substation?" Monarch asked.

"Affirmative," Fowler replied. "Bang-bang and the curtain will come down."

"There's a backup generator system underground between the two towers," Barnett reminded them.

"That's fine," Monarch said. "The way I'm going in there'll be no alarms."

Song Le shook her head. "You don't know that. You don't even know what kind of system he has up there."

"I'm sure it's state of the art," Monarch replied. "But, like he told us, he understands the value of things, which means he knows how to cut corners to save a few dollars. Anyway, that's my hunch."

The van stopped again. Chavez got in wearing a sari and a headscarf.

"We good?" Monarch asked.

"I ran a laser on it," she replied. "Five hundred and fifty yards. Long as the wind stays down, we're okay."

A sudden clipping breeze brought raindrops that spattered off the windshield.

"Shit," Chavez said.

"Doesn't matter," Monarch said. "We're doing this."

They drove to the hotel, and set to work under Barnett's direction. She talked with the chopper pilot who'd gone to get Monarch that morning, and arranged for a new, shorter flight around 12:45 A.M. Song Le, meanwhile, located the Lift-on-Tech Magnetics Company of Kuala Lumpur. After several calls, she found the night manager and offered him a hefty bribe to sell her twenty-five industrial-grade electromagnets and four battery and rectifier systems.

While she was gone picking them up, Chavez helped Barnett hack into the computers of the architect who designed the Petronas Towers, and found a file containing three-dimensional representations of the skyscrapers. They pirated it, and then linked it to the GPS signal in Monarch's iPhone.

But by 9:30 P.M., however, they still hadn't gotten any response regarding the most critical elements in Monarch's plan.

"You might want to think about a plan B," Barnett told Monarch.

"You're a glass is half empty kind of gal, aren't you?" he replied.

"You've already used that line," she said smugly.

Five minutes later, Barnett got a message from a local cave explorer taking her up on her generous offer for a set of rubber strap-on knee pads, and a stout pair of leather gloves with strong wrist cinches. Two minutes after that, a local base-jumping fanatic contacted her, said he had exactly what she was looking for, and would rent it to her for two grand.

"It's highway robbery, but we've got no choice," Barnett said, dispatching Fowler with enough money to pay for it all.

Song Le returned with the electromagnets. They were round, roughly an inch in diameter, and a quarter of an inch thick. Each magnet featured thin wires to connect them to an energy source. She also brought quick-setting epoxy she'd gotten from the night manager, who said it would carry a full ton of weight.

The caver and the base jumper lived within thirty minutes of the hotel and Fowler got back fairly quickly. For the next hour, he and Tatupu used the epoxy to attach the electromagnets into the palms of the gloves, and onto the rubber knee pads.

Barnett and Chavez, meanwhile, fitted Monarch into the base-jumping suit. Made of cable-reinforced Kevlar parachute fabric, the suit was two-piece, black and silver, and featured soft wings like a flying squirrel's that hung down from the arms to the waist and between the legs of the suit from the crotch to ankle. People who liked to jump off cliffs had invented them in the mid-1990s. Monarch had experimented with the suits during HALO, or high-altitude low-opening, parachute training with the Special Forces. The suits allowed him to soar in almost any direction and slowed the speed of his descent. But once you landed they were awkward as hell.

Barnett cut up a hotel pillowcase, used it to sew a deep pouch onto the inner chest of the suit, and packed it with the other things Monarch had requested. Chavez used duct tape to attach four miniature 12v batteries to his outer forearms and thighs. Beside them she taped the rectifiers, small controls that connected the batteries to the electromagnets.

To test the system, they strapped Monarch into the knee pads and gloves and turned on the magnets. A fork Fowler held about three feet away flew through the air and stuck to his right knee pad. When Tatupu tried to pull if off, he couldn't until Chavez shut down the electricity.

"I still think this is insane," Song Le said.

"You know," Monarch said. "You keep talking like that and I'll starting thinking you care what happens to me."

She hardened instantly. "It's your life, Monarch. You do what you want."

"I always do," he said, before looking to the rest of his team. "I think we're good. Tats will take me to the heliport while the rest of you get in position."

It was twenty minutes after midnight and the west wind was blustery when Monarch bumped knuckles with Tatupu.

"Have a good flight. I'll have a cold one waiting for you when this is over," the big Samoan said.

"I look forward to that," Monarch said. He climbed into the helicopter. By the pilot's reckoning, there were fourteen miles from the Petronas Towers.

"Seven minutes out," said the pilot.

Monarch began zipping up the base-jumping suit and checking the straps on the gloves and knee pads.

"Four minutes."

Monarch pulled up the hood of the suit, careful not to disturb the radio in his ear, and clipped the microphone under the latex.

"Three minutes."

Tugging on the rock-climbing helmet Fowler had also picked up from the caver, he cinched it tight and put on a set of clear goggles courtesy of the base jumper.

"Two minutes," the pilot said. "We're at your altitude."

"Two minutes," Monarch repeated into the microphone. "You reading me?"

"Yes," Barnett said. "Everyone's in position."

Monarch checked his watch. He had fifty-four hours to find Secretary Lawton.

"One minute," the pilot said.

Crouching now in the open doorway ten thousand feet above Kuala Lumpur, Monarch looked through the thin wind-driven rain at the silvery Petronas Towers ahead and down, almost three miles away.

"Any sign of activity in that office?" he asked.

"Dark," Chavez said.

The helicopter hovered uneasily. The pilot said, "I think you're out of your mind, but you are go."

Monarch opened the helicopter door, set the heels of his gummy-soled shoes on the step and heaved himself forward and out of the bird. With the weight of the extra gear in the chest pouch, his torso tipped and he accelerated into a straight dive. Holding the position for a ten-count, he flung open his arms and legs. The wind caught the loose parachute fabric and stretched it taut, pulling him out of the dive, and pushing him sideways through space. He went with it, experimenting with his leg and arm angles until he was cutting across the wind and dropping, almost like someone bodysurfing a wave.

When Monarch fell below seven thousand feet, he realized he was going to overshoot the towers at this angle, and made his descent steeper. It was not what he had wanted to do. His goal had been to handle the glide well enough to approach the upper reaches of Petronas Tower Two at a shallow, almost stalling angle, which would allow him a better chance of snagging one of the tubular steel ribs that girdled the buildings without having to pull the parachute built into the base-jumping suit. Once deployed the parachute, which was silver, could attract attention, something he was trying to avoid at all costs. He splayed his arms and legs to slow his descent at two thousand feet.

Still too fast, he thought.

Monarch made a split-second decision and pulled the ripcord when he was five hundred feet above the spire of Tower One. He plunged another hundred feet into the gap between the two skyscrapers before he felt the chute open. Dangling now, pushed by the wind, and struggling with the toggle controls, he forced himself not to look down to see if people on the ground had spotted him.

Instead, Monarch threw his attention to those tubular steel ribs on the upper floors of Tower Two. Four seconds later he made one final adjustment of direction and slope before extending his feet. The gummy soles touched the top of one of those ribs and he threw his gloved left hand out at a stout steel post that connected the rib to the one above it. The magnets grabbed.

The rib, however, was wetter. Even in the climbing shoes, Monarch slipped. Wind caught the parachute and the fabric of the base-jumping suit, threatening to tear him off the side of the building. He did the only thing he could think of, kicking his feet out to the sides. He fell onto the tubular rib, straddling it like a horseman. The magnetic knee pads stuck to the steel. He grabbed the post with both hands and stuck there as well. He closed his eyes and breathed hard.

"Damn," Chavez said in his earbud. "You'd never see me doing that shit."

"Crazy, crazy man," said Song Le in Chinese. She was with Chavez on the roof of a building two blocks to the northeast of the towers, watching through binoculars and a spotting scope.

"You can see the chute," Tats reported from a roof southeast of the towers.

Monarch looked down, saw the silver parachute billowing in the wind.

"Fowler?" he gasped.

In response, he heard an immediate explosion somewhere behind him to the east, back beyond Tower One. The lights died in both skyscrapers and for blocks around.

"Well done," Monarch said.

"Wanted to make sure you were good before I flipped the switch," Fowler replied.

Monarch used his teeth to bite through the fabric, find the switches on his inner arm, and turn the magnets off. He released his right hand, unzipped the chest pouch and found the knife. He opened it with his teeth, and then reached up to his shoulders and cut at the cords holding him to the parachute. With each slice, he felt the wind's power over him ebb and then finally end as the parachute floated off into the darkness.

"Give me a minute," he said, now cutting off the fabric that hung between the arms and legs of the base-jumping suit. "Any idea what floor I'm on?"

"Eighty-two," said Barnett, still in the suite at the Shangri-La, monitoring his position on that 3-D model they'd stolen from the architect. "You have him, Chanel?"

"I do," she replied. "Right in my crosshairs."

"Good," Monarch said, feeling comforted by that fact. Chavez was a first-class rifleman, a graduate of and former instructor at the Marine Corps Sniper's School. She would cover him every step of the journey.

"How far off Tengku's offices am I?" he asked.

Song Le said, "They're two posts north of your position, maybe seventy, eighty feet, and down eight stories."

Monarch shut the knife, put it back in the pouch, hearing sirens below and behind him. Dim emergency lights suddenly showed through the glass in the windows to his right; the skyscrapers' auxiliary generator had kicked on. He was happy for the light; it gave him enough to see, but not enough to expose him to anyone casually looking up from below. Pausing several beats, he calibrated his position on the tower in his mind, some eighty feet above and eighty feet shy of the windows to the fence's office. He rehearsed the descent and lateral movements twice before starting.

The rain came harder as Monarch adjusted the knee pads until they faced inward to grip the rib. He flipped on the magnets, and marveled at the instant stability they afforded him. He forced himself to swing out of his straddle on the rib and around to clamp the knee pads on either side of the post, which fell away toward the next rib, some twenty feet below.

In quick motions, Monarch released pressure on his hands and inner thighs, and slid slowly for several feet before feeling a rivet and jerking to a stop so he could maneuver around it. It took him three minutes to reach the seventy-ninth floor. But by then, he had a handle on how best to manage the downward climb, and the process of turning the magnets on and off. Two minutes later his feet touched the rib at the seventy-sixth floor. And just over a minute passed before he reached the seventy-fourth floor.

Monarch straddled the rib there and rested a few moments, looking back and down at the flashing lights of police and fire vehicles heading toward the electronic substation Fowler had blown several blocks away.

In some ways he found moving horizontally on the ribs trickier than vertically on the posts. He shimmied forward, the knee pads gripping both sides of the curved steel tube as if they were the flanks of a horse. Every seven or eight feet, he encountered a bracket that connected the rib to the skyscraper, and Monarch was forced to make a contortionist's move to get around it without falling.

Still, four minutes after he began to move laterally, he sidled around a third steel post and heard Chavez say, "You're right there."

Monarch scooted across the bracket that fixed the rib and post to the tower's stainless-steel skin, up tight to the closest windowpane, a big plate of glass about eight feet by ten feet. For a moment he considered how best to cut the glass, but then happened to look up the metallic wall and saw a grated vent about three feet by two and a half feet.

"Hold on a second," he said. "We have a change in plans. Forget the glass, I've got access to the air-conditioning ducts."

"You'll fit?" Tatupu asked.

"I think so."

All business now, Monarch reached into the chest pouch for the heaviest thing he carried. His fingers closed around two canisters six inches long and two inches in diameter. They were duct-taped together and screwed into an adaptor that connected them to a thin gooseneck torch. He stuck the canisters between his thighs, scooted up tight to the tower's steel skin, turned the switch and felt the magnets engage. More stable now, he reached once again in the pouch and came up with a flint lighter.

"Going hot," he said.

"You're going to only get one crack at this," Barnett said.

"I'm good," Monarch said.

He twisted a knob on the bracket, heard the acetylene and oxygen hiss and spit out the torch mouth. He squeezed the striker. With a pop the gas caught and after a slight adjustment in flow burned like a searing hot scalpel. The torch cut through the eight bolt heads holding the grate in place like they were candle wax. He put pressure on the vent cover as he burned out the final bolt and held it there while he extinguished the torch and returned it to his chest pocket.

"We good?" he asked.

"So far," Song Le said.

Monarch tried to tug at the edge of the grate with his gloves on, but it wouldn't budge. He took off one glove, held it in his teeth, got his fingers into the vent and tried to get it moving. No go.

He got out the knife again, got the blade tip under the edge of the cover and levered it in more than an inch.

"Got you now," he muttered, and then twisted the blade.

To Monarch's surprise, whatever had been holding the grate in place suddenly gave way and the cover popped out at him. He caught the cover pinched between his left thigh and wrist. It was much heavier than he expected. He stuck the knife back in the chest sheath, then with his free right hand grabbed on to the vent cover where he'd cut away the final bolt. It was a brutal mistake.

Still searing hot, the steel edge blistered the skin of Monarch's bare palm. Instinctively he let go the cover. The heavy grate began to trip and fall, clanging down the side of the tower.

32

DUE TO A BOTCHED polio shot when he was four, Ibrahim Hafez walked with a crooked, ratchet gait and used a stout wooden cane for support. Now fifty-six, and more crippled than ever, Hafez hobbled from the sprawling hotel complex where he had spent the last few days lounging by the pool, and the last few nights eating, praying, and watching coverage of the Sons of Prophecy movement.

It was all Al Jazeera was talking about. CNN as well. A daring kidnapping. A brazen ambush. A masterful bombing.

Al-Qaeda? A movement of the past. The Muslim Brotherhood? Corrupt like Hezbollah. The Sons of Prophecy? The future of jihad! Striking at will around the world!

Thinking these empowering thoughts, Hafez limped south out of the small resort town, leaving the roads, avoiding the paths, and striking out across the stark desert landscape. Not once did he pity his lot in life. Indeed, he kept glancing at the moon that rose in the eastern sky, taking it as an omen of fortune, and giving thanks for this night, for this opportunity, for being chosen.

The Egyptian hitched and hobbled his legs toward the smell of brine. A ship horn sounded. Hafez came over a rise above the Gulf of Suez. He saw the running lights of a dozen or more cargo ships lined up out there in the deep channel, chugging northwest toward the canal, the Great Bitter Lake, Port Faud, and the Mediterranean Sea.

Hafez fought the urge to stand there and revel a moment in what he was about to do. Instead, he peered down at the rocky shoreline, seeing the shadows of men already at work. Three large black rubber rafts had been inflated. Two men in black wet suits were fitting powerful outboard motors to the rafts. Others were loading gear into them.

Hafez limped up to one man he recognized by his large silhouette. He knew him as Abu Ismailia, though he doubted that was the man's real name.

"I am here," he told the big man.

Abu Ismailia clapped him on his shoulder, murmured, "Behold the most important man on the most important night of his life. Are you prepared, brother?"

Hafez nodded. "I am."

"Then together, with Allah's blessing, we will actualize our dreams. Yes?"

Hafez wanted to weep for joy. "Thank you for this chance."

"Thank Allah. He made you. The perfect man for the job."

The perfect man, Hafez thought, grinning, and thinking about the hardships of his life, the long, long cruelty of his handicap. How many other men would have ever called him the perfect man?

"Get in," Abu Ismailia said.

Hafez looked back toward the rocky land of his childhood, and wondered if he would ever feel it again beneath his twisted legs and feet. If not, he decided, I will have left Sinai a better place, the world a better place. With help, he climbed into the raft and took the driver's seat.

The three rafts left the beach, taking separate routes out into the gulf. Hafez ran no running lights. He'd grown up on these waters, and navigating north by the moon and the stars as men had for thousands of years before radar and sonar and GPS. He passed three tankers and then a container ship. A second massive freighter loomed ahead of them about a mile shy of a horn of land that jutted off the west side of the gulf, south of the city of Suez. Hafez drove the raft in a wide loop well out in front of the container ship. He had a solid thousand-yard lead when they passed the horn of land and turned toward Suez, which glowed out there in the darkness.

Ahead of them several hundred meters, coming from the direction of the city, a speedboat was running with its lights ablaze. Hafez felt his stomach roil, and then called to Abu Ismailia, "There they are. Right on time."

"Take us to them," Abu Ismailia replied, and Hafez

saw men move to the bow of the raft and lay across the gunnels.

Hafez altered course, heading straight at the launch, and then cut his engines. He doubted the men on the speedboat would see the raft until they were almost on top of it. He was right. There was a shout of alarm, and then the launch's engines died and it came about twenty-five yards away. Two Egyptian soldiers were moving to the front of the launch, carrying rifles and spotlights. The men lying across the gunnels of Hafez's raft shot them both with silenced weapons. The driver of the launch tried to get to the wheel and the throttle, but they shot him, too. The last man in the boat threw his hands up, and began pleading for his life. Hafez brought the raft along side. Two men jumped aboard the launch and killed its lights. Then they helped Hafez get aboard.

The man kneeling on the deck of the launch, hands behind his head, recognized Hafez by his jerky movements. "Ibrahim?"

"Hello, Moustapha," Hafez said.

"What is this?" Moustapha asked in a nervous whine. "Have you gone mad? This can't be because of—"

Hafez swung his cane, smashing the man's head, driving him to the floor of the launch, where he writhed and moaned.

"Thirty years," Hafez seethed. "You took everything, Moustapha. What did you expect me to do? Just lie down like some crippled dog and accept that?"

Before he could answer, Abu Ismailia picked Moustapha up, threw him overboard. He bobbed to the surface, gasping twice before a silenced round sank him.

Hafez got behind the wheel of the launch, feeling no pity for the man who'd destroyed his life, and only partial satisfaction from his first moment of revenge.

Two of Abu Ismailia's men tore the uniforms off the dead soldiers and put them on. Then they dumped the bodies, and tied the raft off the rear of the launch. Hafez started the engines and headed south. The entire process had taken less than ten minutes.

The container ship was just coming into view around the point when the launch radio squawked, "Port of Tawfiq, this is *Rose of the South*."

Hafez grabbed up the microphone and answered, "*Rose of the South* this is Port of Tawfiq. We've got your pilot on approach. Kill your engines."

"Received and acknowledged."

Hafez sped them faster toward the massive container ship, which was lit up like a bazaar on a holiday night. They came in along the hull, and the arm of a deck crane swung off the side and lowered a large steel basket with rails. The men in uniform helped Hafez into the basket, and then followed. Abu Ismailia brought up the rear. Two men stayed with the launch.

The basket rose quickly on the winch. Abu Ismailia handed Hafez a heavy brown paper bag. The basket swung over the rail and settled on the deck. The man operating the boom leaned out of his control house and said, "Captain's on the bridge."

"Wait here for the signal," Abu Ismailia murmured.

Hafez felt like he was going to throw up, but the memory of Moustapha's just fate kept him under control as the men in the army uniforms climbed the exterior staircase to the bridge with Abu Ismailia in tow. The captain and crew working on the container ship would be expecting an Egyptian contingent to check their papers before a local pilot took over and navigated them expertly into the first lock of the canal. Hafez saw them enter the wheelhouse, and then caught violent movement in the shadows.

A moment later, one of the men in uniform came out on the catwalk and waved. Hafez limped up to the crane operator, stripping the brown bag from around his weapon, a small, black machine pistol. He pointed the gun at the man and said, "You'll do as you're told now, or you'll die. Understand?"

The operator threw up his hands, and said, "Anything you say, dude."

Nine minutes later, the last of Abu Ismailia's twelve men had come up on the basket and the crane was hoisting their rafts. They were all on the deck fourteen minutes after Hafez boarded.

"Now what?" the crane operator asked in a tremulous voice.

"Now you jump," Hafez said. "It's not a far swim."

"Jump?" the man cried. "I'll break my legs."

"Dealing with bad legs is better than death," Hafez said, and motioned for one of the other men to see the deckhand over the side.

He did not pause to watch, but limped and dragged up the metal staircase into the wheelhouse where Abu Ismailia and several of his men were moving the bodies of the captain and crew. Hafez did not pause for instructions. He knew exactly what to do. He climbed into the seat at the helm, felt instantly at home, and began punching in orders on the complex control panel. Deep inside the ship, the engines rumbled.

He grabbed the microphone, said in Arabic, "Port of Tawfiq, pilot Moustapha Farouk aboard *Rose of the South,* requests approach."

"Request granted *Rose of the South,*" a voice came back.

Hafez felt outside himself as he gave more orders to the control panel and swung the massive container ship out into deeper water and then northwest toward the gleaming port where a smaller ship was docked for repairs. To the right of those docks, Hafez could make out the narrows where the gulf squeezed toward the canal. Six hundred yards off the mouth of the canal and closing, the radio crackled with the voice of the harbormaster: "*Rose of the South,* cut your speed to two knots."

Instead, Hafez cut his speed to four knots.

At four hundred and fifty yards, the harbormaster started yelling at him to kill his engines. Instead, Hafez increased his speed to eight knots and spun the wheel hard to port before at last throttling back. The bow of the giant container ship swung lazily, slowly sideways. The harbormaster went crazy, screaming at him to throw his engines in reverse. Hafez calmly reached up and flipped the radio off.

He glanced over at Abu Ismailia and his men with a look of triumph, and said, "Brace yourself, my brothers. We're going to hit hard."

33

MONARCH WATCHED IN DISGUST as the steel grate that fell from his burned hand clanged and rang off the steel skin, posts, and ribs of Petronas Tower Two, falling all the way down, seventy-four stories before it struck cement with a sound like a church bell disintegrating.

"Oooh," Chavez moaned in his earpiece. "Nothing good about that."

"Nope," Tatupu said. "You already got security guards moving around the perimeter trying to figure out what that noise was."

"What noise?" asked Barnett, who was farthest away from the action.

"I dropped the vent cover," Monarch said through clenched teeth. The burning sensation in his palm was excruciating, and he was nauseated.

"You all right?" Song Le asked.

"Not exactly," Monarch replied, forcing the glove over the burn.

"You don't want it to get worse, I suggest you get into that duct ASAP," Chavez said. "There are guys with spotlights on the ground now."

Monarch saw the lights far, far below, moving quickly in his direction. Were the lights powerful enough to reach him so high up the side of the skyscraper? He wasn't waiting around to find out.

The wind gusted again, and with it came rain that pelted Monarch as he turned off the magnets and pushed his upper body into the duct with his hands leading. Wriggling forward, trying to get his hips over the lip, he reached in vain for a flange, anything that he could grab to pull himself completely inside.

"Those are powerful spots," Chavez said. "They're sweeping your side."

"Trying," Monarch gasped, straining his fingers forward in the darkness.

The magnet at the tip of his middle finger brushed an upright seam of steel. With one last gyration, he twisted his body forward just enough to lock three fingers on the seam and pull. His hips came over the lip of the vent, and in two pulls he was inside.

Light passed behind him. Static crackled in his earbud.

"We're getting interference," Monarch said into his mike. "Can't hear you."

Someone keyed their mike twice, letting him know they understood. Drained, shaky, and in pain, Monarch rested his head on the bottom of the duct, telling himself he needed to drink and to eat and to take care of the burn. Ordinarily he'd carry tubes of the energy paste favored by triathletes, but those had been one of the few things Barnett had been unable to find on short notice. And a first aid kit was one of the first things they decided to set aside for space and weight considerations.

Monarch closed his eyes, searching for that place in his mind that he sought in times of peril and pain, an almost reptilian location where his brain was cut off from everything but his objective. Reduced now, beyond the pain in his hand, and cut off from his team, he got up on his elbows, tugged off his left glove, and reached under his shirt, finding a tiny LED headlamp on an elastic band. He got it up on his forehead and switched it on. The duct was lit with a soft red glow.

Monarch began to slide and drag himself forward as if he were maneuvering through some deep tight cave passage. The magnets on the knee pads and gloves were now a hindrance because he had to pull hard each time to separate them from the floor of the duct. By the time Monarch was fifteen feet in he was drenched in sweat. But the vent that he'd seen in the fence's office earlier in the day was now right in front of his face.

For the second time, he got out the small torch and cut his way through the frame of the vent. Not wanting a second burn, he waited several minutes for the metal to cool and then cautiously pushed it forward. The moment he felt the sheet metal piece come free of the wall Monarch twisted into the hole he'd created and squirmed his head, arms, and chest out, busting off chunks of dry wall as he did. The air smelled of stale coffee as he peered around the empty office, seeing it much as it had been earlier in the day except for Tengku's desk, which had been cleaned off entirely. No computer there at all.

At first sweeping glance there did not seem to be any upgrades to the security system. He imagined for a moment that the only safeguards were at the entrance to the suite. But then he shook his head. This guy was a world-class fence, a dealer in high-quality stolen goods. There would be other aspects to the security system.

Shutting off the red lamp, he reached back with his burned hand and found the edge of the hole. He grabbed at the exposed dry wall, wrenching it this way and that until he smelled gypsum over the coffee odor. Gypsum has a Mohs hardness of two on a scale of ten, making the substance only a little less powdery than talc. When he felt he had enough of it, he poured the lot into his left hand, right on top of the dead magnets. He ground both hands together for several seconds, then lifted the gypsum dust to his lips and blew. The powder floated out into the office, revealing thin green lines, four of them crisscrossing the space.

"You read me?" he asked.

"Affirmative," Barnett said.

"I'm in, but he's got lasers in here, makes things a little trickier. Report?"

"The security guys with the lights are still looking for your grate," Tatupu replied as Monarch got free of the hole and crouched on top of the long display case that stretched toward the window. "But you're lucky, I think it must have bounced into the bushes there."

"And the police are still focusing on the blown power station," Song Le reported. "You have time."

Unlike many thieves who believed in quickness above all, when Monarch had time he took it. Haste, he'd learned the hard way, often led to mistakes. So he flipped back on the red headlamp, and lay belly down on top of the display case and carefully considering his next move. It seemed to reason that if the fence had lasers, he might have installed pressure sensors in the floors. The display cases had to be rigged as well.

Returning to the hole in the wall, he used the knife to scrape away a significant amount of gypsum that he again powdered in his hands. Instead of blowing it into the room, he pulled off his left glove and poured the batch in. Monarch slunk forward on his hands and knees then, ignoring the pain in his right palm, ignoring the way the leather irritated the burn whenever he put pressure on it. He could look out the window now, and see the flashing blue lights off toward the electrical substation. He saw a spotlight coming and ducked down until it had passed.

Tengku's big desk was no more than three feet away. Monarch studied it a moment, and took powder from the glove and blew it into the air. Again the four green lines appeared, bisecting the room. Monarch had near photographic memory, and for the next few moments he blew dust and took mental pictures of the laser lines, seeing them in relationship to the display cases and other pieces of furniture.

To his relief, the beams had been largely set to foil someone breaking in from the lobby and the elevator. Only one line diagonally crossed the window in back of Tengku's desk. Armed with that knowledge, Monarch tossed the glove containing the gypsum powder onto the desk. Rolling onto his left side, he tightened his core, pushed up hard on his left hand and then crisply swung his hips and legs forward out into space the way a gymnast might do when dismounting a pommel horse. As his legs swung out over the desk, Monarch pushed one final time, lost contact with the display case and dropped.

The desk made a cracking noise when he landed on it in a teetering crouch. He thought for one horrible second that his weight was too much and the desk was about to lose its legs. But it held and he soon regained his full balance.

From this new position and perspective, Monarch cast the soft red beam around the room clockwise once more. The cases on the opposite wall held Chinese vases, swords of various kinds, and a collection of crystals. Two of the cases on the wall closer to him displayed rare books, estate jewelry, and a collection of fine jade. As the light passed the nearest display case, he saw that it contained rare coins, most of them in clear sleeves and shown off like museum pieces, which they probably were. Oddly, tucked in the right rear corner of the case, he saw a cell phone.

He went to his hands and knees and then his belly on the desk. He reached over, found the desk drawers and gave them slight tugs. Locked. Not surprising.

Reaching out, he tried the credenza doors. Locked as well. He was confident they could be picked quickly, but first he shone the light under the desk and the credenza and spotted one of his prime targets: a cable running out from under a rug behind the desk to a blue box screwed into the wall.

"He's got data backup," Monarch said.

"Excellent," Barnett purred in his ear. "Hook up the parasite."

Monarch did just that, digging into the chest pouch for the "parasite," a small rectangular device about three inches long. It featured a two-inch cable, a Cat 6 connector, a high-speed bubble drive, a powerful processor, and a wireless transmitter. The second he attached the parasite Barnett would be able to remotely take control of the backup disk and copy it. He climbed off the desk staying well clear of the laser beam that bisected the window, eased back Tengku's chair, and slid under the credenza. He had the parasite attached and activated in under a minute.

"You getting a signal?" he asked.

"Loud and clear," Barnett replied. "Already attacking the password."

Monarch took a long breath and let it out slowly. He'd achieved the primary objective of this little foray. They'd have people back at Langley taking Tengku's files apart within the hour. If the fence had anything to do with the Sons of Prophecy, they'd all know soon enough.

In the meantime, he got up off the floor and sat in Tengku's chair. From his pants pocket, he got out a small pick set and quickly unlocked the center desk drawer. Instead of pulling it open, he got out a key card from the hotel. He slid the card back and forth along the top of the drawer, feeling for contact points. None.

Monarch tugged at the drawer. It came free.

To his surprise, the drawer was completely empty, save a square of black velvet and that jeweler's loupe he'd seen the fence using earlier in the day. Had he spooked Tengku into clearing out his—?

Lights blazed on. The door swung open. The fence and two armed guards stepped in, glaring at him. The guards trained pistols his way.

"Mr. Tengku, what a pleasant surprise," Monarch said, as if they'd had a chance encounter in a restaurant.

"Shit," Barnett said in Monarch's earbud. "Really?"

"Lights on in the office," Chavez confirmed.

"You need backup, Rogue?" Tatupu asked.

The fence's scowl turned to sour amusement as he entered the office. "I was warned about you. Lucky I have battery for office."

"That so?" Monarch said. "Warned by who?"

"Does not matter," the fence said, flipping one hand, and noticing the hole above the display case where the vent cover had been. "But they certain you return. I say it impossible to get in here, and yet, they right and here you are."

"And yet, here I am," Monarch agreed. "A man working on behalf of the President of the United States."

Tengku sniffed. "My perspective you look more like thief with big balls that are going to get shot. As far as I concerned, you an intruder. Nothing more."

"People know I'm here," Monarch said. "The Chinese agent and others."

For a second that threw the fence, but then he shrugged. "Does not change things. You are still an intruder. I am within my rights having you shot."

"And bring down the entire Malaysian law enforcement world on top of your head, looking into every nook and cranny of your life?"

The fence smiled. "I take my chances."

Chavez murmured in Monarch's earpiece. "If you can move him to the window, I think I can wake him up."

He made a clucking sound with his tongue, signaling that he would try.

"How about your chances with the world court?" Monarch asked. "Or a Guantánamo Bay tribunal?"

The fence snorted. "Like I say, I have nothing to hide. Well, nothing they ever find."

"Really?" Monarch said. "I think they'd love to know about the things we've discovered that tie you to the Sons of Prophecy."

"No ties," Tengku croaked.

"Several," Monarch said firmly. "You or your intermediaries own the two buildings that housed the Internet cafés where the SOP uploaded videos and Web site data. You also own the house where an entire young family linked to those video uploads was found shot to death the other day."

That seemed to unnerve Tengku, who said something harsh in a language Monarch did not understand. One of the guards thumbed off the safety on his pistol.

"Data transmission complete," Barnett said.

Monarch smiled, and said, "Tengku, you and I are not so different. We understand each other, the thief-fence relationship, I mean."

The fence said nothing.

"Here's the way I figure it," Monarch went on. "You did move a lot of guns sometime in the recent past, and I'm betting many of them were used in China and by the folks holding the diplomats. And you're involved in this propaganda machine the Sons of Prophecy have got going."

Tengku was cool, a good card player no doubt, but Monarch could tell in the subtle tensing of his torso that he'd come close to the truth, maybe not the whole thing, but definitely in the ballpark. The fence barked something at his guards. They both took a step toward Monarch, their weapons aimed.

"Can I show you *your* future before you have your apes shoot me?" Monarch asked, waving him over toward the window. "C'mon, you'll see it right down there." He pointed toward the ground.

"What is it?"

"Your future if you decide to shoot me," Monarch replied calmly. "C'mon. I'm offering you a free look into the crystal ball."

Tengku appeared torn, but like most men when offered enticing information in a mysterious way, he could not help himself. He said something to the guards and stayed well clear of Monarch as he sidled up to the window. He looked out toward the still blinking blue lights surrounding the electrical substation, and then down at the ground.

"I don't see anything," Tengku said.

In Monarch's earbud, Chavez said, "Target acquired."

"It's there," Monarch assured the fence. "In fact, at this very moment there are crosshairs aimed at your head from a sound-suppressed .338 Lapua sniper's rifle backed by one of the best shots in the world. If you flinch, you a dead man."

Tengku lost his poise then. Monarch saw the sickening look in the fence's eyes and knew the feeling.

"You're lying," Tengku said at last.

Glass about four inches above the fence's head exploded. The round ricocheted off the bulletproof glass of the nearest display case and smacked the rear wall.

Tengku trembled uncontrollably, and Monarch knew he had him.

"That was an intentional miss," Monarch said. "The next one won't be. Five hundred meters is a piece of cake for her. And the velocity of the Lapua is such that if you try to duck or turn, you'll be gone before you know it. So I suggest you stop shaking and don't move at all. I also suggest that you tell your men to drop their guns and let me out of here."

"Not a chance," the fence said, glaring out the window.

"If you die, maybe I die," Monarch replied. "But if I die, you now know you will definitely die, Mr. Tengku. What's it going to be?"

Silence, then, "How do I know your people won't shoot if I let you go?"

"You don't," Monarch said. "But how about this: Once

I'm clear, I'll call, let you know it's safe to blink again. And we'll call it good."

Monarch could tell the fence wasn't used to having the tables turned on him, he was used to being in control, and that he absolutely hated being outfoxed. But he was also a practical man, a survivor.

"Deal," Tengku said, and then barked at his guards.

They hesitated, but then set their pistols on the rug, and stepped back with their hands laced behind their heads.

"A wise decision," Monarch said, retrieving the parasite from the hard drive. He tucked it into the chest pouch, said, "Tell me the truth about Ramelan."

"I tell you the truth already," the fence said. "He's a ghost."

"I think he's very real and you know where he is."

Clenching his jaw, Tengku shook his head. "I don't."

"But you have a sense of where he is, how he can be contacted."

"I told you I never met him."

"Give me a country, somewhere to start," Monarch insisted. "Or I'll have her shoot off your ear, just for fun."

"That will be fun?" Chavez said in his earbud.

The fence struggled, said, "I heard he on Borneo."

"Big place Borneo," Monarch said. "What country. Brunei? Indonesia?"

Tengku stared him right in the eye. "I don't know."

"Okay," Monarch said agreeably. "One more thing and I'll be gone."

"You can't keep changing the terms of a deal!" the fence almost shouted.

"When the crosshairs are on you, you can feel it, almost like a tickle, am I right?"

Fuming now, Tengku said, "What else you want?"

"Key to the display cases," Monarch said. "I need a souvenir."

"What?" he replied, confused. "I thought . . ."

"The keys," Monarch said.

"Right pocket," Tengku snapped at last. "The small ones."

Monarch slipped up beside him and with the nimble fingers of a trained pickpocket plucked the key ring from his pocket.

"I'm interested in a coin," Monarch said.

"The key with the red marker," the fence said.

Monarch found it, unlocked the case, and slid back the bulletproof glass door. Instead of taking one or more of the rare coins, he grabbed the cell phone.

Tengku watched him over his shoulder and was clearly upset. "What—?"

"This will do," Monarch said. He walked over to one of the guards, plucked his security badge from his chest, picked up both pistols, stuffed them in his waistband and strolled out of the office as if he didn't have a care in the world.

When he reached the hallway, he heard Tengku shout something in that language they all spoke. He looked over his shoulder, saw a strong beam of light shining in the fence's office, and heard glass shattering.

"Missed him," Chavez said.

"Missed?" Monarch grunted, running now toward the elevators.

"A spot light hit the window and I couldn't see him for a second and—"

Monarch heard them coming. He reached the elevator and slapped the down button. He glanced back toward Tengku's offices, got in a shooting crouch. The elevator opened with a ding.

One of the fence's men appeared with a semiautomatic rifle. Monarch shot him in the thigh and leaped into the elevator just as the second bodyguard stepped out and opened fire. Monarch punched buttons for the thirty-ninth floor, the mezzanine, and the lobby. Rounds ricocheted off the door as it closed. The elevator plunged.

Monarch moved into the corner gasping, but careful to keep his face down; there had to be a camera somewhere in the car with him. As a former member of La Fraternidad de Ladrones, he'd been taught eighteen rules to guide his thieving. He thought he was beyond living by those rules now, but number five popped into his head: "Fit in."

He shed the last of the base-jumping suit in a matter of seconds, revealing a pair of dark pants and a workman's shirt. Carrying the remains of the suit and his tools under his left arm, he stepped calmly from the elevator when it opened on the thirty-ninth floor. He waited several moments, giving whoever was pursuing him time to absorb the stop at the thirty-ninth floor. He figured he had about a two-, maybe three-minute head start.

"I need a staircase," he said into his microphone.

A pause, then Barnett said, "Turn right and then right again."

Monarch was already moving. He stuffed the remains of the base-jumping suit and the tools he no longer had use for in a trashcan, and ran on. At the staircase door he heard the elevator sound in the distance. He slipped into the stairwell, and shut the door softly behind him. The tower's backup electrical system was working enough to softly light the red emergency bulbs on every floor. Instead of walking down, Monarch went up two flights, and exited into a dim hallway, contemplating his next move.

"Any kind of maintenance room on this floor?" he asked.

A pause then Barnett said, "Go right. Two hundred feet down the left wall."

Monarch spotted double industrial doors with a small sign in Malay.

"This it?"

"Affirmative.

Monarch picked the lock in twenty seconds. Glancing around inside, he saw a bucket and mop, and then shelves full of supplies and cleaning equipment. He grabbed several bundles of paper towels and dust rags and dropped them in the bucket. He took two cans of cleaning solvents and dropped those in as well.

"Bridge?" he asked.

"Reverse direction, take a left, you'll see the elevators and the bridge."

Monarch hurried back up the hallway, pushing the

mop and bucket before him. He peered around the corner, spotted the elevators, and then the span that linked
Petronas Tower Two to Tower One. With its glass walls
and arched glass ceiling, he knew he'd be exposed
while crossing the bridge. But he had no choice. This
was part of his exit strategy. Passing the elevators, he
noticed that one was stopped at the thirty-ninth floor,
one was dropping below the tenth floor, and another was
rising from the lobby. Monarch punched the up button
when that third elevator passed the thirty-fifth floor. He
reached around his back and felt for the pistols.

The elevator dinged and opened. Empty. Meaning
someone, perhaps Tengku, had called it from above.
Which was perfect. Monarch wheeled the mop and
bucket inside. Jamming his foot against the door, he
opened the two solvent cans and drained them on the
rags, paper towels, and mop. He got the mop and, using
the flint striker, lit the head into an inferno.

Stepping back out of the elevator, he speared the
flaming mop into the bucket. With a whoosh a plume
of fire rose. The door closed and the elevator began to
rise. Forcing himself to be patient, Monarch stood there
ten, twenty, and then thirty seconds as the elevator kept
going up past the sixtieth and then the seventy-fourth
floor where it abruptly halted.

He exploded into a sprint toward the bridge. Fire
alarms began to wail. There was no use trying to sneak
across now, and he accelerated, knowing he was exposed and wanting to make it for as short a time as possible. As he crossed, however, his attention kept darting
down and to the right toward the grand plaza in front of

the towers. Most of the lights there were still out, and he hadn't spotted anyone by the midpoint.

Ten yards from Tower One, Tatupu said, "Here comes the cavalry."

Monarch glanced again and saw police lights converging on the Petronas Towers from two directions, four, maybe five cars. The fire alarm could not have brought them so quickly. Had Tengku called the police? Or had someone heard the shooting from below?

He exited the bridge and slowed inside the hallway on the forty-first floor of Tower One, huffing for air, contemplating his next move. He could wait until the firemen responded and all eyes were on Tower Two, then take the elevator down to Tower One's lobby and try to bluff his way past the security guards and get out the front door. But he risked being detained and questioned by the police if he delayed that long.

Still, he opted to be patient, and said, "Tell me when you see the fire trucks."

"Lots of movement at the electrical substation," Fowler replied. "Two rigs heading your way."

"Chavez, alert me when they're in the plaza, and Gloria?"

"Rogue?"

"I'm going to need a way out of the basement of Tower One."

"Already working on it."

"Here comes the fire brigade," Chavez said.

Song Le said, "And the police. They're all moving toward Tower Two."

"Gloria?" Monarch said.

"There's a freight," she began in a harried voice. "No, that won't help . . ."

He caught the flash out of the corner of his right eye before he heard the muffled muzzle blast from far back out there on the bridge. The round slapped the trashcan right in front of Monarch.

"Son of a bitch—" he said, seizing one of the pistols from his waistband as a second shot zipped off the marble floor to his left.

Monarch instinctively shifted his profile, made it narrower and touched off three rounds left, center, and right before spinning and taking off in a series of cutting moves. Bullets skipped off the floor behind him. One caromed and slapped the top of his left trapezius muscle, shocking him, and he almost fell.

He kicked open the door to the stairwell, said, "I'm hit."

"How bad and where, Rogue?" Barnett came back instantly.

"Above the left clavicle, not bad, but I'm going to be leaving blood soon," he replied, already vaulting down the stairs, trying to ignore the burning sensation creeping down his left arm and up the side of his neck.

When Monarch hit the second landing, he kicked his shoes off into the void and went on in stocking feet, trying to land soft enough to hear the slap of shoes coming from above. Six floors down he heard a door open in the stairwell above him, and then the sound of someone following. Reaching the thirtieth floor, he pushed open the door and stepped into the hallway. Closing it to a crack, he aimed at the railing and waited.

Monarch felt the blood now, oozing from the wound and soaking his work shirt in the front and the back.

A man's voice. Close.

Shoes smacking. Closer.

A radio crackling. Closer still.

Monarch just kept aiming, and waiting in ambush.

"Rogue?" Barnett said.

He gave no reply, heard the shoes coming down the near stairs, wondering if he'd left a blood trail yet. A shadow moved and became a man's back at less than six feet. Monarch aimed lower, meaning to shoot the man through the side of one butt cheek, just enough to incapacitate him. He squeezed the trigger.

Click.

Tengku's second bodyguard heard the dry fire, spun, and started shooting. At the click, Monarch heaved himself to one side of the door, which burst open. The bodyguard stepped into the hallway, AR rifle leading.

With the butt of the pistol, Monarch chopped at the knuckles of the bodyguard's trigger hand, striking flesh and bone, and breaking both. The bodyguard howled in pain and let go of the rifle with the busted hand. But when Monarch stepped in to knock him cold, the bodyguard pivoted and swung the gun by its forestock. The butt end struck Monarch flush in the same sore ribs he'd injured jumping onto the *Niamey*. He felt the wind blow from him and swore he heard a crack. He stumbled, crashed into the wall, and dropped the jammed pistol.

The bodyguard swung the gun again, this time like a log splitter. The rifle butt struck Monarch right next to the wound to his trapezius, and he went to his knees, the pain like an electrical shock through his neck, shoulder, and arm. He almost blacked out, but then years of training and experience took over.

He rolled toward the bodyguard. The butt of the rifle just missed his ear and struck the floor. Monarch's heels came whipping over out of the roll and he kicked his adversary in the solar plexus.

"Uhhh," the bodyguard grunted and staggered backward.

Monarch came to his feet, left arm feeling useless. He kicked the man in the right kneecap, hearing his patella fracture. With another scream the bodyguard collapsed onto his side, still trying to hold the rifle with his one good hand.

Monarch stripped it away. "You boys should have quit while you were ahead."

The bodyguard glared at him. "You will never stop this. Nothing will stop this."

"You can tell that to the Malaysian authorities," Monarch said, and gave the man a crack to his head with the rifle butt. He'd be out for a good while.

After unloading and heaving the rifle down the hallway, he returned to the stairwell, hearing muffled sirens.

"Gloria?"

"Oh, thank God," Barnett said.

"Minor delay," he said. "How am I getting out of here now?"

"You won't like it."

Ten minutes later, Monarch was in a food service hallway on the second floor rear of Tower One. His neck

and left shoulder felt on fire. And he was definitely dripping blood behind him now, not a lot, but enough that
even a novice tracker could follow him.

"Almost there," Barnett said.

"Who's doing pickup?"

"Keep an eye out for a dashing Samoan."

Monarch smiled despite the pain.

"There, Rogue, on your left-hand side."

Monarch smelled something nasty, saw two steel
square hatchlike drawers set in the wall about waist high.
A lock held the lever shut. He stepped back several feet
and shot the lock off. He yanked open the doors, saw
nothing, but felt the tropical heat and then sniffed at the
putrid rotting garbage smell flooding up the chute.

"I'm probably gonna get sepsis," Monarch grumbled.

"You're going to get caught and arrested if you don't
move," Song Le said.

He gingerly lifted his left hand and dove into the
garbage chute. Monarch kept the edge of his burned
right hand against the side of the passage, and slid on
his belly down the steep greasy surface, feeling for the
end. The instant he lost contact with the metal, he ducked
his head and contracted his abdomen. The move caused
his chest and shoulders to rotate toward his knees as if
he were doing a flip off a springboard. He slammed into
reeking trash and slimy garbage, taking most of the impact on his upper back, the wind blown out of him a
second time in less than fifteen minutes.

"Nicely done," Barnett said. "Over the side now,
across an alley into the bushes. Tats will be waiting on
the road."

Monarch couldn't reply at first. He couldn't even move at first. Then he focused on the fact that he was bleeding and lying in garbage. He flashed on himself as a young man, seeing Sister Rachel for the first time, crouched over him in the slums, about to sink a needle into his chest. That was enough to rally him.

Moaning, he rolled over and started to crawl. He hit the side of the Dumpster, and struggled back to his feet. Spreading his feet for balance, he gritted his teeth and raised his hands and jumped. He caught the lip of the Dumpster, hoisted himself up, and got one leg over the side in a straddle. He gasped in pain, rocked the other leg over, and then let go. Dropping six feet, he landed hard on cement in a bay of some sort.

Turning, Monarch staggered out into a dark ally behind Tower One, hearing the sirens closer now, and men shouting somewhere to his left. The bank on the opposite side of the alleyway was covered in ivy and vines. He used them to crawl up into a dense grove of bamboo. Splinters of it stuck through his stockings into the bottoms of his feet.

Without warning, Monarch felt unbalanced, woozy. Seeing gathering spots before his eyes, he pitched forward, and knew only darkness.

34

FOR MANY HOURS MONARCH felt nothing, dreamed nothing, was nothing until a gentle tugging became someone gently shaking his shoulder.

"Robin, you need to wake up now."

Monarch opened his eyes to find Gloria Barnett looking very worried behind her reading glasses. Dull-headed, feeling his palm and traps throbbing with pain, he realized he'd been stripped down to a pair of athletic shorts and lay beneath fresh sheets. He looked at his burned hand, dressed with gauze and tape.

"Where am I?" he croaked.

"Back at the Shangrila," she said with relief.

He peered around the darkened hotel room, noticed razor seams of light shining through the drapes. "How did I—?"

"Tats found you passed out and got you out of there," Barnett said, checking a saline bag attached to an IV line inserted into the back of his good hand. "You were exhausted to begin with. But you were also badly dehydrated. The shock of being burned and shot just tipped the balance. Surprise, surprise, Robin Monarch is human after all."

He snorted softly said, "How much time did I lose?"

"Seven hours and change. We've got less than forty-five hours to find and rescue Secretary Lawton. And there have been two more attacks by the Sons of Prophecy."

"Two?" he said, sitting up. "Where?"

"Suez and Panama canals," she said, turning on his television to CNN.

The screen jumped to show the *Rose of the South* container ship slammed sideways across the mouth of the Suez Canal. A banner hung along the side of the ship. In Arabic and English, it read: SONS OF PROPHECY NOW!

The reporter said the ship was hijacked and rammed across the canal in the middle of the night. The attack in Panama occurred in broad daylight, with fourteen men storming an oil tanker in the locks at Pedro Miguel and hanging a similar banner. The SOP had issued another statement on its Web site, taking full credit for shutting down two of the world's most strategic shipping routes, and threatening to attack ships in the Gulf of Hormuz.

Shaking his head, Monarch said, "Who knows what's going through President Sand's noggin right about now?"

Barnett muted the television. "You'll get the chance to ask him in ten minutes."

"Wait, what?"

"Hopkins said the President wants to speak directly with you," she replied. "It's why I woke you up. Better put a shirt on. I'll get my iPad."

He struggled into a shirt, grunting at the soreness. When Barnett returned, he asked, "Has Washington been able to look at the files from Tengku's computer?"

"It was sent over hours ago."

"What about the phone?"

"It's there by your bed."

Monarch frowned, looked over, saw the iPhone she'd given him back in the Philippines. "No, the cell phone I took from Tengku's office, the one he had locked up."

"You didn't have anything like that with you," Barnett said.

"Are you kidding me?" Monarch groaned. "Send someone back to wherever Tats found me. It must have fallen from . . . damn it!"

"Calm down," Barnett replied. "I'll send—"

"Monarch? Is that you?"

They both startled at the voice, and looked at the iPad in Monarch's lap. Dr. Hopkins was sitting with President Sand in the White House Situation Room. The President looked concerned, said, "Is that an IV, Robin? Are you hurt?"

"It's just a precaution, Mr. President," Monarch said. "I had a small accident and got a little low on electrolytes."

Sand accepted that wearily, but then replied, "Ms. Barnett, might we have a word with Mr. Monarch in private."

She looked a bit flustered to be left out of things, but then nodded, mouthed "cell phone," and left the room, shutting the door behind her.

"Did you find anything in Tengku's files?" Monarch asked.

Dr. Hopkins pinched the bridge of his nose and the President shook his head.

"Nothing?" Monarch demanded incredulously.

The CIA director said, "We've had a team of twenty experts, forensic accountants and the like, working on the files, and they've found several transactions that could be arms dealings—money transfer and shipment records that fit that sort of pattern—but nothing definitive. We've checked every company named in the files. Most of them don't even exist."

"Sounds like he put me on to a second set of books, the legitimate business," Monarch said. "He's smart for a fence."

That only seemed to irritate Dr. Hopkins more. The President cleared his throat, "You've seen the news about the attacks on the canals?"

"I have," Monarch replied. "But just the barebones."

"We don't have much more than that," the CIA director said. "But it appears to us that what the Sons of Prophecy have done is recruit terrorists from all different movements and brought them together in a coordinated fashion."

"And we know that how?"

"One of the dead in China was a dissident. And the bombers in New Delhi seemed to have died in the attack. Their bodies were found and identified with fingerprints and DNA. They were cousins from the Hindu Kush who'd fought with the Taliban and were suspected of various terrorist acts in India."

The President said, "The point is that the SOP has proven itself willing and capable of large-scale attacks. We now believe that they will kill Secretary Lawton and the foreign ministers if their demands aren't met."

"Will you meet them?"

"No."

"Which means we're running out of time, Monarch," Dr. Hopkins said.

"Yes, sir. I know that, but—"

"No, I don't think you do," President Sand said sharply. "Today was one of the worst days in the history of Wall Street. The stock market reacted to the attacks by plunging so fast I had to order trading halted. Gold went through the roof. Oil prices are skyrocketing. People are clamoring for my head, and the Vice President's campaign is destroyed. Worse, you've lost the support of Bill Lawton, Monarch. He's siding with General Shipman and Elise Peck now, and has gone public with the fact that I hired a thief to find the Secretary of State."

"You pulling the plug?" Monarch asked, feeling sick to his stomach. He hated failure more than anything.

"It's been suggested more than once."

"Sir, with all due respect, we've still got almost forty-three hours. Don't pull us."

The President nodded. "I'm not pulling you, but we are sending another JSOC unit to join Six in Luzon, and two units each to Panama and Egypt."

That surprised Monarch. "You have the Egyptian's cooperation on that?"

"Both ships are Liberian registered, but U.S. owned," Hopkins replied. "We want updates every six hours, from here on out."

"Done, sir," Monarch promised. "In the meantime, start a search for an Indonesian pirate named Ramelan. And you should aim whatever satellites are available at the south and west coasts of Borneo."

Hopkins squinted. "Anywhere in particular?"

"Remote estuaries," Monarch replied.

Before either the President or the CIA director could respond to that, the connection was lost and the iPad screen went blank.

For a moment Monarch stared at the screen. All that risk to get into Tengku's office, and he'd come out with nothing? Worse still, the Secretary of State had less than two days now to—

A knock came at the door. Barnett returned carrying bandages and a garbage bag. "How'd it go?"

"We've still got the President and Hopkins on our side, but we've lost the support of Secretary Lawton's husband among others. Can you get me free of this IV?"

"What I'm here for," she replied, putting the garbage bag on a chair and coming to the bed. In less than two minutes, she had the needle out.

"Shower?"

She pointed at the garbage bag. "Put your arm and shoulder in up to your neck. I'll check the dressings when you're done."

He held up his burned hand. "We can do better than this, right? Something more functional?"

"If you don't mind scars."

"Can't help them sometimes," Monarch said getting to his feet. Moving gingerly, he grabbed the garbage bag. Every muscle in his body seemed to ache from the exertions of the previous evening. Heading toward the bathroom, he moved his arms and shoulders in a circular fashion and groaned at the fire that flared from the grazing gunshot wound.

But he had to get the area moving. He knew if he babied it, his shoulder and neck might stiffen up, rendering him useless. He could not afford to let that happen. Monarch turned the shower on hot. He shucked his shorts, ignored the garbage bag, and climbed in.

Biting into a washcloth, he moved the bad side of his neck and shoulder into the steaming water. It took everything in his power not to bellow in agony as he started lifting and lowering the shoulder and then rotating it front and back. Ten minutes later his range of motion had doubled though it was hardly normal.

He got out, dried, and pulled on the shorts. When he opened the bedroom door he found Tats on the couch, reading a copy of the *South China Morning Post*. Chavez was on a phone talking to her sister, who was undergoing chemo back in Houston. Barnett was hunched over her laptop computer. Fowler was drinking coffee, and watching coverage of the seized ships in the Panama and Suez canals.

As Monarch passed Tatupu, he patted his arm. "Thanks for the rescue."

The Samoan, in a remarkably good voice, sang, "Ain't no sunshine when I'm gone. Only darkness when I'm away."

"You should try out for *The Voice* or *Idol*," Monarch said. "I flat-out know they've never seen anyone like you up there."

"I may have to give that some serious thought," Tats replied.

Before Monarch could reply, Barnett came over looking very irritated that his bandages were wet. "Didn't I tell you to—?"

"The bag slipped," he said.

Unhappy, Barnett started digging through her medical kit and came up with gauze, scissors, and tape. "Sit," she said, pointing to a chair.

"You're that woman's bitch, Robin," Fowler said.

"Gladly," Monarch said. "What would we do without her?"

"Not a lot," Barnett said, removing the wet dressing.

He was about to ask where Song Le was when the suite door opened and shut. The Chinese agent entered looking tired but happy. She held out a cell phone.

"This what you were looking for?"

Monarch smiled. "Nice."

"It was just laying there in the dirt," she replied. "But I checked the history and the contacts. There's nothing. Zero. It was erased."

"Let me have a go at it," Barnett said. "Can you finish for me?"

Song Le hesitated, but then lobbed her the phone.

The Chinese agent took Barnett's place. Monarch said, "You know what you're doing?"

"Who do you think stitched you up?" Song Le asked.

The look on Monarch's face must have been good because Fowler chuckled, said, "Amazing what happens to a guy when he's out cold."

While Song Le redressed his wounds, he watched Barnett take the phone apart and remove the SIM card. She slid it into a port on her computer, and began typing.

A few minutes later, Song Le said, "There. That should give the area protection and some support."

Monarch moved the arm around. "Not bad. Got anything for muscle ache?"

Barnett never looked up from her screen when she said, "I had a portable ARP Wave flown in."

"Really?" he said, relieved. "That will do it."

An ARP Wave machine runs a DC current through injured or overworked muscles. Human bodies operate on a DC current, so the slight surge helps lengthen muscles, brings more blood to the area, and flushes out toxins, which speeds healing. Monarch had used the device before on injuries with excellent results.

"I'll put it together," Fowler offered. He got the machine, which was about the size of a hardcover book and twice as thick, with a digital display and leads that ran out to sticky pads that he placed around Monarch's shoulder and neck muscles.

Barnett looked over at Song Le, who had taken a seat at the other end of the couch. "What time did you find the phone?"

The Chinese agent shrugged. "Twenty-five, thirty minutes ago?"

Barnett nodded implacably. "It was password protected. When you tried to check the history it looks like you triggered an app that erased everything."

Monarch wanted to punch the wall with his burned hand. "We've got nothing?"

"I didn't say that," Barnett replied. "These scrubbing apps usually have a hidden trash bin. You just need to know where to look. This one was password protected, but you're not the only one proficient at breaking and entering, Robin."

"I've often said you are the best spy of us all," he said. "What have you got?"

Blushing, Barnett gestured at the laptop screen. "I haven't found the text memory yet, but there you go so far: lot of names, contact data, phone numbers, dates."

Fowler turned on the ARP Wave. Monarch felt light electrical prickling pass through his shoulder and all around the wound. It actually felt kind of good. Trailing the electrical leads behind him he crossed to Barnett and started studying the computer screen with great interest. The others crowded in around them. Monarch scanned the contact list, not recognizing any of the names or numbers in the first twenty. There appeared to be nearly five hundred contacts in all.

"Search Ramelan," he said.

Barnett entered the name and came up with "None Found."

"Can you sort the phone numbers to see the most recently dialed or received?" asked Song Le.

"Good idea," Barnett said and gave her computer the order.

The screen jumped. The first six calls were all to security at the Petronas Towers, and made shortly before Tengku left his offices the first time that day.

Then Monarch saw the seventh contact on the recently dialed list: "Temp Help." The call had taken place about an hour after he and Song Le had exited the fence's domain. The call lasted six minutes. His eyes drifted to the phone number.

"I can send this on to analysis stateside, Robin," Barnett offered. "They're much better equipped to run these all down in a hurry."

Staring at the "Temp Help" phone number, Monarch did not reply at first. He was feeding a growing sense of disbelief and outrage.

"Don't bother," he said at last. "Have our embassy alert the KL police that Tengku should be taken into custody on suspicion of multiple homicides as well as aiding and abetting the SOP terrorist group. And Gloria?"

"Robin?"

"We'll need another jet."

35

"STUPID GIRL!" MADAME LONG shouted. "What are you doing in there?"

Inside the Moon Dragon's office, Anna, the little Filipina maid, jumped back from the desk, terror-stricken, and holding a rag.

"Dusting, Madame," she said, bowing. "Cleaning."

"You were told never to come in here," the triad leader's wife retorted icily as she swept into the room, her silk robe lashing the wood floor.

"Yes, Madame," Anna said with a pronounced tremor in her voice. "But Mr. Long, he say dust and vacuum."

Madame Long tolerated her husband's secrets, but she could not abide anything going on in her house without her knowledge, even how and when it was cleaned. Giving off an air of utter disdain, she said, "The kitchen needs cleaning and there is ironing to be done before we leave for Lamma."

Relief flooded through Anna's face and she rushed around the back of the desk, eager to be out of the room and away from Madame Long's presence. As she passed, her employer said, "It's Saturday. You'll be taking the day off tomorrow?"

Anna slowed, her tiny body tightening, unwilling to look the woman's way. "Yes, Madame. It is maid's day off."

Madame Long said nothing for several beats, and then cruelly asked, "Do you remember our talk earlier this week? About your filthy animal habits?"

Anna looked at the ground, her hand traveling to her cleft palate, as she nodded almost imperceptibly. The Moon Dragon's wife smirked at her maid's humiliation, and said, "Good. My husband will be here before nine tomorrow to make sure you're clean and sober."

Looking defeated, Anna bowed again and left the room. Madame Long almost followed her, but realized that she rarely had access to her husband's sanctuary. Given his actions and emotions lately, the innuendo, the worry, and the odd questions he'd been asking of the I Ching, her curiosity was piqued. The triad leader's wife strolled around the room, noting trinkets and mementos from her husband's travels about Asia. Her attention swept past them to a framed photograph on the credenza behind his desk. The snapshot showed her dead son, Jin, and his wife, who held baby Lo-Lo in her arms.

Madame Long picked the picture up, and gazed in muted grief at the image of her only child, the wound of his loss still there all these years later. Then she glared at the image of the woman who had married Jin, who had taken him away, feeling old anger ignite, hating her dead son's wife so much she could not even use her name.

The wife had been responsible for her son's death. There was no doubt about that in Madame Long's mind, even now, and she moved the fingernail of her index finger to the glass above the wife's image and began to scratch at it, imagining that she was gouging the bitch's eyes out. Hearing a creak behind her, she set the picture down quickly, and turned, seeing her husband enter.

The Moon Dragon appeared suspicious at her presence.

"The girl was in here cleaning," his wife explained, moving toward him. "She said you asked her to do so."

"It had been a while," Long said.

Madame Long was disappointed. She had hoped to catch the maid at a lie, but said, "I was inspecting her work."

Distracted now, her husband nodded.

She stopped in front of him. "Do you wish to ask the Book something?"

That seemed to clear his thoughts. "I do," he said. "But later, before we go to the ferry. I have some work to take care of in the meantime."

Madame Long bowed to her husband, and left.

The Moon Dragon pressed the door shut behind him, and turned the deadbolt, thinking about the fence in Kuala Lumpur, and how many times he had tried to call him this morning. What had happened last night?

Had Tengku caught the thief? Killed him? Or had Monarch turned the tables on the fence, got him to talk?

That thought turned Long's stomach sour as he went to his desk. He pulled back his chair to sit down, deciding that, no, Tengku was many things, but a talker was not one of them. He noticed immediately that one of the desk drawers was open two inches. He always made sure it was closed. Had his wife been snooping? The Moon Dragon opened the drawer enough to see the pistol exactly as he'd left it after cleaning it the other day, along with a box of bullets that was *not* exactly as he'd left. Before he could consider this more fully, he felt his cell phone buzz, alerting him to a text.

Long got it out, read: "Try now. Video phone."

The fence.

Eager to find out what had happened, the Moon Dragon slammed shut the drawer, jiggled the mouse on his computer, and called up Skype. He found the handle "Estate Agent," and pressed dial. Long heard ringing before the shaky image of Ketu Tengku appeared on the screen. In the background he heard cars honking and people shouting. The fence seemed to be walking outside, holding his camera phone facing up at him.

"What happened?" demanded the triad leader.

Tengku hesitated and then in brief strokes described the events of the previous night. If the fence had been there in his office, not flickering on a computer screen, the Moon Dragon would not have bothered killing him in some subtle, ironic fashion like poisoned tea for a tea connoisseur. He would have throttled him with his bare hands.

"We gave you advance warning, and the thief still got in?" Long raged. "You had him seventy stories up and you let him escape?"

Though the camera jostled more, Tengku did not shrink at the tirade.

"Seventy-four stories, and he's devious," the fence replied tersely. "And he had help. Snipers. Sappers. A team of experts."

"What did he get?"

"Copy of hard drive and phone," Tengku replied, walking faster. "But don't worry. Only fiction on the hard drive, and the phone was programmed to erase if the password entered wrong. They've got nothing. Well, almost."

"What does that mean?" the Moon Dragon demanded.

"They found some real estate I own."

Long heard more honking coming from the fence's end. "Where are you?"

"On my way to airport," Tengku replied. "Life too hot in KL these days."

"Where are you going?" Long asked, sensing his tether was slipping.

"Somewhere no one finds me for a very long time," the fence replied. "I suggest you do same."

The Moon Dragon thought it through in a split second. "They've probably put out an alert on you. They'll catch you flying commercial. I'll send a private jet. Take you anywhere you want."

Tengku hesitated, and then said, "Yes, that helps."

"I will text you with arrangements," Long said. "In the meantime, post the last video and keep out of sight."

The fence looked like he wanted to argue, but nodded, and the feed went dead.

Fuming now, Long got to his feet wanting to throw something, anything. But he forced himself to control his emotions. But how could he? Tengku claimed that Monarch had gotten nothing, but if that was true, why was he on the run? And why had he told him to do the same? Had he been lying? Had the thief stolen something of value beyond some vague real estate connection, something traceable to his role in the plot?

A cell phone? He mentioned a cell phone. They were dangerous. That's why he almost always destroyed his burn phones after two or three uses. Did the one Monarch took have incriminating information on it? Whenever he had no answers to questions, the Moon Dragon got anxious, and sometimes violent. Indeed, part of him wanted to pull the gun from the drawer and pull the trigger again and again just to see things shatter. Instead, he did what he almost always did when the way ahead seemed dark and threatening.

Long found his wife watching Lo-Lo finish a bowl of pork dumplings and soup while the maid finished the last of the dishes.

"Are you ready to leave?" Madame Long asked.

"Soon."

"Are we going to Lamma?" Lo-Lo asked, excited. "Can we go fishing, Grandfather?"

The boy liked nothing more than to go down on the rocks below the island house and fish. He would do it for hours if the triad leader let him.

"We can go fishing," the Moon Dragon promised, and the boy clapped with joy. "But Grandmother has to help me with something first. Go get packed."

"You and I are staying until Monday morning," Madame Long told her grandson. "Two pairs of underwear. Two pairs of socks."

Lo-Lo looked to the maid. "Anna, can you help me pack?"

That greatly annoyed Madame Long, who snapped at the maid, "Just the necessary clothes, and his books."

The Filipina woman bowed, went to Lo-Lo, and took his hand, saying, "Anna makes sure you have your things now."

Long's wife glared after them as they left, but then turned her attention back to her husband. "You need me?" she asked.

"I do," he said.

While incense burned to heighten her sensitivity, six times the coins flew from Madame Long's hands and six times they spilled across the belly of the ancient sea turtle. She recorded and stacked the outcomes, and then translated the numbers into the trigrams K'un, or Earth, over Li, or Fire.

Long studied his wife while the pads of her long bony fingers slid across the yellowed turtle shell as if she were reading the carvings there like braille. He saw a painful quiver in her cheeks, and looked down to see that her searching had stopped.

"Hexagram thirty-six," she said in a tight whisper. " 'Ming I.' The Darkening of the Light, and the Wounding of the Bright."

In all his years of consulting the I Ching through his wife, the Moon Dragon could not remember a single time having this hexagram rise to foretell his fate.

"What does it mean?" he asked nervously.

" 'The sun has been swallowed by the earth,' " she recited. " 'A man of dark nature is in power and brings harm to the wise and able man.' "

Conflicting emotions pulsed through the triad leader. Was he the wise and able man? Or the man of dark nature?

"And the lines?" Long asked, referring to the position of the numbers that had yielded Hexagram thirty-six.

Madame Long swallowed, said, "Nine in the third place means 'Darkening of the light during the hunt in the south. Their great leader is captured.' "

The hunt in the south? Their great leader is captured?

The Moon Dragon was hunting Monarch in the south, wasn't he? But he felt more confused than ever. "Tell me."

" 'The strong, loyal man may meet the ringleader of disorder as if by accident, and seize him,' " she said, still reciting. " 'Thus victory is achieved.' "

Well, that was good, right? Long thought. But who was the strong loyal man and who was the ringleader of disorder?

"Nothing else?" he asked, and glanced down at the

paper where she'd recorded the numbers that yielded the hexagram. "What about six at the top?"

To his surprise, his wife turned away and would not meet his gaze. Then she said, " 'Not light but darkness. First he climbed up to heaven. Then he plunged into the depths of the earth.' "

Madame Long paused, and then looked sympathetically toward her husband, saying, "The I Ching is telling you to be very careful in the hours ahead. A climax of dark forces is coming your way."

Somber, the Moon Dragon stared several moments at the yellow belly of the sea turtle, wondering at the shell's strange and terrible dimensions. Though he felt it wanting to flame, he refused to allow fear to ignite in him. Instead he used the anxiety the Book of Changes had provoked to focus and to fight. He thanked his wife, who watched him with open worry on her face, and left.

Long crossed quickly through the house and out the front door, ignoring his grandson calling to him. Tuul was in the driveway polishing the hood of the Mercedes. His bodyguard quickly looked up the hill, where a sniper might hide, and then he came fast toward the triad leader.

"You should call me before exiting," Tuul said.

Long shut the door behind him so Lo-Lo would not hear, and said, "Take the jet to Kuala Lumpur, pick up the fence, and when you get out over the ocean, throw him out the door."

Part IV

LITTLE DRAGON SLAYER

36

NIGHT SWALLOWED BANGKOK. A monsoon rain pelted the tuk-tuk's windshield as the driver steered through gridlock traffic brought on by flooding streets. A two-cylinder motorcycle engine powered the little three-wheeled cab. It sputtered every time the driver hit the throttle or drove through too deep through a puddle.

"Hate these things," said Tatupu, who sat beside Monarch in the backseat, bent over so his giant head didn't bounce off the sharp flanges of the tuk-tuk's metal roof.

"We could have taken a regular cab," Song Le agreed, equally unhappy. The Chinese agent sat behind them on a bench barely sheltered from the rain.

"We'd still be on the other side of town," Monarch said, glancing over his shoulder to see that the tuk-tuk that held Fowler and Chavez was keeping pace. He looked down at his bandaged hand, moved his right shoulder around and wondered how much they could take.

Upon their arrival in the Thai capital, they had gone to the U.S. Embassy where they'd been supplied with weapons and body armor, and received a Skype briefing from Dr. Hopkins on the most up-to-date intelligence. The Sons of Prophecy had released another video, this one showing a brief clip of the three diplomats. Their wrists and ankles were tied to crude chairs. The Chinese and Indian foreign ministers looked haggard, hot, and filthy as they stared into the camera. But not Agnes Lawton. Though her face was dirty and swollen, the Secretary of State was still defiant, her head held high, her shoulders back. And she was blinking out the same message as before.

In his gut, Monarch believed her now more than ever. Along with the video, the terrorists had reiterated their demands for the release of all political prisoners and the ransom, which they now expected to be paid in gold.

"The drop will be over the South China Sea," the CIA director had told them.

"Thought you weren't paying," Monarch replied.

"We aren't," Dr. Hopkins said. "We're hoping to lure them into the open. You won't be a part of that plan, I'm afraid, Monarch. The President gave the assignment to the FBI and SEAL Team Six."

Monarch shrugged it off, said, "I'm confident we're on the right track."

"Let's all hope so," Dr. Hopkins said before bringing him abreast of further developments in the two canal zones.

Teams of U.S. commandos were gathered with local soldiers within striking distance of the two hijacked ships, and practicing assault scenarios.

"Zero hour?" Monarch asked.

"Not yet determined. The terrorists appear to be armed to the teeth and say they've booby-trapped the hulls. *Why* are you back in Thailand, exactly?"

"For the time being I'd like my activities and motives to remain secret," Monarch replied. "It will give you plausible deniability."

"Plausible deniability of what?"

Monarch disconnected the link to Washington.

Barnett made a clucking sound of disapproval, and said, "Hanging up on the CIA director? Plausible deniability?"

"I don't have time to explain," Monarch had said. "We've got to move."

They'd left Barnett behind at the embassy where she would provide real-time support. Armored up and wearing loose-fitting tropical shirts to cover their body armor Monarch, Song Le, Chavez, Tatupu, and Fowler left the embassy and went out into the third major storm of the week, hence the tuk-tuks.

In grimy water up to the hubs of the noisy little cab, they passed beneath Asoke subway station and the driver pulled over. While Tatupu resorted to contortions to get free of the vehicle, Monarch gave the driver a generous tip to hang around and wait.

Song Le took shelter under a tarp draped over one of the food vendors who crowd the sidewalks of central Bangkok. Fowler and Chavez pulled up. Hearing the pulse of disco music from down the block, and carrying a small knapsack, Monarch climbed out of the tuk-tuk with a mercenary agent foremost on his mind.

He'd seen Archie Latham's number associated with "Temp Help" on Tengku's phone. Monarch had been shocked and then bitterly angry. He'd known Latham almost fifteen years. They'd fought together in dire circumstances more than once and survived. Monarch had considered him more than a friend. He was a comrade in arms. Now, however, Latham had become not only a personal enemy of Monarch's, he was a public enemy of the United States, China, and India. As the rest of his team huddled beneath the tarp, awaiting his orders, he forced himself to sever the part of him that had once loved and admired the Australian.

Monarch pointed at Tats and Fowler, said, "Latham's never seen either of you. Up at the end of Soi Cowboy there's a bar called the Old Dutch. You'll slide in, get a beer, and show us the place on camera. If he's there, do not approach him. Latham is deceptive. Don't let that bad leg fool you; he's still deadly. And so is his bodyguard, a big black dude named Spooner."

"You?" Fowler asked.

"We're going to have a beer down the street, watch the show via remote until we know what we've got."

Tatupu bumped fists with Monarch, turned and walked south with Fowler tagging along. Monarch, Chavez, and Song Le waited until they'd disappeared into Soi Cowboy and then followed slowly. It was later than it had been during their visit two days before. The neon lights were all aglow making the red-light district look like a sex Disneyland. But an inch of filthy rain-water ran down the road. Working girls, desperate at the lack of customers, hooted to them from under the overhanging eaves that protected the outdoor drinking areas.

"Hey, c'mon sit down," they cried. "You bring your girlfriends! We show you all good time!"

"This is disturbing," Chavez muttered. "Some of them look underage."

"I think so, too," Song Le said.

"As I've said before, you hunt buffalo where buffalo live," Monarch said.

He glanced at Chavez, finding her no more impressed by that line than the Chinese agent had been. He led them into the Apache Beer Bar, where the girls regarded Song Le and Chavez with open hostility. They ordered beers, and waved off two girls who approached them while Monarch got an iPad from his knapsack and turned it on.

Plugging in a headset and microphone, he said, "Test."

"Got you," Tatupu said. "Almost there."

"I read you, too, Rogue," Barnett said.

"Tats, turn on your cameras once you get out of the rain."

"Roger that."

The screen soon filled with a feed from a tiny fiber optic camera clipped to Tatupu's breast pocket. An instant later, the screen split, showing Fowler's perspective as well. Both feeds revealed the outdoor seats at the Old Dutch Bar. They were all empty.

Song Le pointed at a table to the left of the door, said, "That's where the pervert was holding court before."

Monarch triggered the mike, said, "Go inside."

The feeds showed the two men stepping inside. Tatupu turned left, and Fowler right, giving Monarch opposing perspectives of the room and the bar itself. There were perhaps ten customers in the establishment along with six or seven girls.

"He's not there," Song Le grumbled. "This was a waste of time."

Monarch almost agreed, but then saw a young Thai woman come from the direction of the toilets. She plopped down in the lap of a small balding guy in a black shirt who had his back to Fowler's camera.

He studied the couple a second before breaking into a grin. "This wasn't a waste of time at all. Tats? Abbott? Take a seat. We'll be right along."

"What?" Chavez demanded as he stuffed the iPad back into the knapsack.

"Follow me. You'll learn a few things," Monarch said, threw cash on the bar, and went out into the rain.

Less than two minutes later, he opened the door to the Old Dutch Bar, spotting Fowler and Tatupu sitting at the bar, nursing cold beers. He didn't move toward them, instead angling toward the short bald guy playing kissy-face with the Thai girl, who was giggling and squirming in his lap.

She saw Monarch first and her smile evaporated.

"I don't think your husband would like to see you carrying on like that, Yuri," Monarch said to her, taking a seat, and looking to her benefactor. "And Sami, I know Latham would take offense at you groping his bride no matter how valuable you seem to have become to him."

Rafiq, the Lebanese forger, gaped a second at Monarch, then patted Yuri on the rear end and said, "We're just friends."

"Sure," Monarch said.

"No, really," Rafiq replied, and insistently pushed her off his lap.

Yuri scowled at Monarch, said, "You buzz-kill, you know?"

"Run along," Monarch replied. "Sami and I have business."

Yuri stood there a second, wanting to argue, but then stormed off, barely giving a glance to Chavez and Song Le, who'd taken seats behind and to either side of the forger.

Rafiq recovered enough to protest, "Robin, and I say this with all due respect to our prior relationship, I thought I made it clear that I did not wish to do business with you anymore after you destroyed my shop and life in Algiers."

"Yeah, you did," Monarch admitted sheepishly. "But I'm afraid you're going to have to deal with me for now. Where's Archie Latham?"

"What am I, his keeper?" the forger complained. "I have no idea. Latham comes and goes. Like the monsoon rains."

"Now you know that's not true," Monarch said with a knowing grin, and a pause. "You're not at all a brave man, Sami. Never been one to mix it up."

"Healthier that way," Rafiq said. "Safer, too. So what?"

"So, you know exactly where Latham is because if you didn't you wouldn't have had the balls to paw his wife's ass behind his back."

The forger said nothing.

Monarch hardened, leaned across the table. "I advise you to talk."

"Or what?"

"Or the two women behind you are going to handcuff you and take you to the Chinese Embassy, where you will be held accountable for your involvement in the kidnapping of the diplomats and the Sons of Prophecy conspiracy."

"What?" Rafiq cried, peering back at Chavez and Song Le before turning again. "Monarch, I swear, I had nothing to do with—"

"Latham does," Monarch said. "And he tried to have me killed because of it. Now where is he? Or are you going to go down as an accomplice?"

Song Le leaned over the forger's shoulder, said, "In case you did not know, under Chinese law, accomplices, even foreign accomplices to a major crime like kidnapping a state official, can be executed by firing squad."

Rafiq's fingers worried at the gold chain around his neck for a second, weighing the lesser of two evils, before replying, "Latham's in Pattaya. He and Spooner went down there to meet prospective clients early this afternoon, said they weren't coming back until Monday, Tuesday at the latest."

It made instant sense to Monarch. A coastal resort town seventy miles south of the Thai capital, Pattaya was the sex tourism capital of the world. It was also the favored retirement community for ex–Special Forces operators.

"Where's he going exactly?" Monarch demanded. "An address."

"I don't know where he lives. Ask his wife."

"I doubt she's been there, but Latham seems to do his best work in sleazy bars. Which one is his favorite down there?"

The forger knitted his brows, said, "I know roughly where it is, but I don't know the exact name of the place."

"No problem, Sami. You can take us there and show us."

"What? No."

"Wrong answer, old friend. Wrong answer."

Tatupu drove Rafiq's Land Rover with Monarch sitting beside him and Chavez and Fowler flanking the Lebanese forger in the backseat. Fighting torrential cloudbursts and flooding roads, the ninety-mile trip to Pattaya was tortuously slow. It took them two and a half hours to go fifty miles before the rains ebbed and they could pick up speed.

"We expecting a war?" Tats asked.

"I'm expecting one!" Rafiq shot back. "You're nuts to go after Archie."

"I'm trying to avoid it," Monarch replied. "Appeal to his better side."

"I didn't know he had one," Song Le said.

"So," Tatupu said, glancing at Monarch. "You never know, Robin, going into these kinds of situations, right?"

"And?"

"I need someone to look in on my mother if shit happens."

"Goes without saying," Fowler grunted.

"Absolutely," Chavez said. "And Robin, you know where my share goes if—"

"Where's this negative thinking coming from?" Monarch protested. "We go in, reason with the man, and we get things done the easy way."

"Latham will kill me if he figures out I fingered him for this," the forger complained as they finally drove into Pattaya, where night mist hung in the glow of streetlamps that turned gaudy and neon when they reached Beach Road.

"You didn't finger him, I did," Monarch remarked, his attention drawn to the crowds of tourists—men, women, and children—jamming the sidewalks on both sides of the street. "You're just giving us a guided tour of Latham's known hangouts."

"You don't understand what he's capable of," Rafiq insisted.

"No, Sami," Monarch said, his face going very hard. "Latham doesn't understand what we're capable of."

"Take a left up ahead," Fowler said. "One block west, then one south. The Marriott—it's the only place you'll get a parking place anywhere close to Walking Street."

Monarch looked over his shoulder, an eyebrow raised. Chavez leaned forward to look at Fowler. "What? You've been here?"

Amused, Fowler said, "An extended fact-finding mission back when I was young and impetuous."

Chavez shook her head. "I just don't understand guys."

The forger wove them through traffic to the Marriott entrance where they paid the valet to watch the car.

"Tell you what: I'll draw you a map," Rafiq offered. "I mean, what do you need me there for?"

"You're my good luck charm, Sami," Monarch said. "And I don't want to leave you to call Archie and warn him that we're here."

The forger looked insulted. "I would never do that."

"Right," Chavez said and pushed him ahead.

The night was hot and the air saturated. Wearing the Kevlar vest beneath his shirt, Monarch was quickly sweating. But to his surprise the heat and humidity found its way into his bruises, wounds and sores, and loosened them somehow, made them pliable, elastic.

The five of them walked back to Beach Road, and north again, stopping only once at a souvenir kiosk where Monarch bought a baseball cap that could be tugged down low over his eyes. Even a split second of confusion mattered when dealing with someone at lethal as Archie Latham. Sweltering in the body armor, they continued on toward a big neon sign that ran overhead from one sidewalk to the other, proclaiming that the area beyond was "Walking Street." Disco and electronic punk music pulsed and thudded as they passed under the sign into the largest sex tourism and party area on earth.

From the moment they entered, barkers called non-stop: "Welcome! Welcome! Come eat! Come drink. Find a girl! Find a ladyboy! Come upstairs for ping-pong show!"

Walking Street smelled of frying fish, cigarette smoke, urine, stale beer, and raging pheromones. Every time they walked past the open door to one of the go-go bars they were blasted by music that young girls danced to on stage while men twice their age sat around ogling them from below.

"It's like Soi Cowboy times twenty on the disturbing scale," Chavez said sourly.

"You ain't seen nothing yet," Tats replied. "Give it a couple of hours, and this place will really be going."

"You've been here, too?" Chavez demanded incredulously.

"Once upon a time," the Samoan said.

"You?" she asked Monarch.

"I'm as much a virgin here as you are," he replied, scanning the way ahead, seeing not only packs of furtive men in search of companionship, but couples and families of every color and language taking a tour of the carnal carnival and sexy sideshows. What was with that?

The deeper they went into the massive sex district, the denser the crowds became, and Monarch grew fearful that he just might stumble into Latham, or that the mercenary agent or Spooner would spot him before he could spot them. To make matters worse with this many people crammed into the streets he was growing

increasingly leery of what might happen if Latham put
up an armed resistance. Probably mass chaos, he thought.
Probably a stampede. Definitely collateral damage.
Definitely loss of life.

"We're getting close," the Lebanese forger shouted
over the pulsing music.

"How do you know?" Monarch demanded.

"I remember the stewardesses," Rafiq said.

Song Le and Chavez were already gaping at a group
of women dressed like 1950s stewardesses and trying
to lure men into a go-go bar called the Airplane.

"Where does Latham like to go?" Song Le asked
Rafiq. "In there? Airplane?"

The forger shook his head, said, "Up there on the
right. There's like twenty open-air beer bars that go all
the way out to the seawall. Archie will be in there somewhere."

Tatupu said, "I remember that place. No walls between the bars."

Chavez looked disgusted now.

"What?" the Samoan said. "What spec op hasn't been
here?"

"Me," Chavez shot back.

"And me," Monarch said.

"Your loss, the both of you," Fowler said.

"Take a walk, Tats," Monarch said. "You, too, Abbott.
You spot him, call."

The Samoan moved off, his massiveness causing the
crowds to part the way for him, as if he were Moses
splitting a sea. Monarch and the others moved back
against a wall opposite Airplane.

"It's going to take three showers to get this place off me," Chavez grumbled.

"And a very hot bath," Song Le agreed.

"It's not that bad," Rafiq said. "It's actually kind of healthy if you think about it."

"Quit while you're ahead," Chavez said, drawing a smile from the Chinese agent.

Monarch's head, meanwhile, kept pivoting, scanning the moving crowd. Had Tengku contacted Latham after he realized the cell phone was gone? Was he leading his people into a trap? Or had Latham already decided to run?

He felt his cell phone ring. He stuck a finger in his ear, and answered.

Tatupu said, "Got him."

"Tell me," Monarch said, closing his eyes.

"It's like Sami described it," Tatupu replied. "Big open space with a roof, like a hangar, and narrow U-shaped bars on both sides of a general walkway maybe one hundred yards long. Ends at a seawall."

"Where's Latham?"

"I spotted him leaving the john. Hard to miss with the limp. He's sitting way back in there, at the last bar on the right, his back to the seawall."

"How much support does he have?"

"Abbott's circling through on a look-see."

A smart move, Monarch thought. In addition to having a complex mind, Fowler was a fine actor. He rarely got noticed unless he wanted to be noticed. Monarch's cell phone buzzed again. It was Fowler.

He pushed send, said, "He have an army in there, Abbott?"

Fowler replied, "Can't tell the loyalists from the wannabes, Robin. But the whole place is crawling with military types, and there are definitely special ops studs in and around Latham's bar, six by my count, not including the bodyguard, like you said, big black dude. He's wearing body armor under a loose shirt like us."

"Smart guy that Spooner," Monarch said. "Where is he?"

"To Latham's left, up against the wall by the entrance to the men's toilet."

"Latham drinking?"

"Beer."

"Who's sitting to Latham's immediate left and right?"

"On his left there's a bar girl he seems cozy with. Right side: one of the special ops guys . . . wait . . . that boy's up."

"Latham?"

"No, the special ops guy. Another one is taking his place."

"Latham's running business as usual," Monarch said. "Interviews. Assignments. Contracts. All face to face."

"Looks that way."

Monarch considered the possibility that the mercenary agent was clueless to the fact that he had become a target of the investigation. It was plausible, the thief supposed, but he had to consider Latham fully informed and therefore completely unpredictable. It made things more complicated, and more unstable, but not impossible. The rough outline of plan began to form in his mind.

He said to Fowler, "Take a seat where you can keep tabs on Latham and the studs at his bar."

"Already there. Second to last bar on the opposite side of the walkway."

Monarch paused again, putting this together in a mental map, and then clicked send, said, "You still there?"

"Yes, indeedie," Tats grunted.

"If we can corner him against that seawall we might be able to take him down without a fight," Monarch said. "Go find a seat in the bar next to Latham's on his side of that walkway. Call when you see our boy heading to the toilet again."

"On my way," the Samoan promised.

He hung up, looked at Chavez, Song Le, and Rafiq, who said, "Can I go now?"

"When the fun's about to start? Not a chance, Sami."

Monarch pointed a finger at Chavez. "You play butch, move to the north side of that seawall, and wait for my call."

The ex-Marine sniper moved off without comment. Monarch looked at Song Le and Rafiq, said, "The three of us will go in together."

"In there with him and Spooner?" the Lebanese forger whined. "Are you out of your mind? I'm going to get killed."

"Not if you do what I tell you to do," Monarch replied, and then explained what he had in mind.

The Chinese agent said, "I can do that."

"I can't," Rafiq moaned.

Monarch hardened, said, "Would you rather I shoot you myself?"

"Right here?" the forger said glancing around at the masses moving up and down Walking Street. "You're a cautious man, Monarch. You wouldn't dare."

"But I would," Song Le said.

Resigned to his fate, Rafiq said, "Where do you want me?"

"Walking right up to Spooner," Monarch said.

"Spooner?" the forger groaned. "He's a psycho."

Before Monarch could respond his phone buzzed once more.

Tatupu said, "Latham's gone through two beers quick and looking a little anxious. Bladder must be starting to howl. I'd start moving this way if I were you."

"Will do," Monarch said, and looked at Song Le and Rafiq. "Hold on tight now. This could get a little bumpy before it's over."

Whenever he entered a tense, shifting situation, Monarch returned to basics. Pushing his way through the crowd, he ran the eighteen rules of the Brotherhood of Thieves through his head until he found one that seemed appropriate: Rule number thirteen: "Secrecy, deception, surprise, and guile will always beat strength and weapons."

Past the Airplane Go-Go, the wall of buildings gave way and Monarch could see out into a pavilion that was as crowded as the street.

"He's on his feet," Tatupu said.

Monarch started to move quicker now, staying tight

to the packs of revelers partying at the various bars. "Spooner?"

"Going into the can with him."

"Tats, move to Latham's bar now, opposite his seat," Monarch ordered, looked at the forger and the Chinese agent. "Get ahead of me. We'll be right behind you, Sami. And don't forget: make it sympathetic."

Rafiq looked ready to cry, but nodded and started to trudge through the crowd like he was going to the gallows. Song Le trailed him. Monarch brought up the rear about twenty-five yards back, the brim of the ball cap pulled low over his eyebrows. The forger slowed as he closed on Latham's bar. Tatupu was already settling onto a stool next to two bar girls who were playing some kind of drinking game.

He walked around Latham's side of the bar. Song Le trotted past Tatupu and the bar girls, heading into the women's toilet. Monarch threw a drunk stumble as he entered the bar area, staying slightly bent over so the liquor bottles on shelves down the middle of the U-shaped bar blocked the view of Latham's side. Monarch had no sooner thrown his arm around Tatupu's shoulders than the Samoan muttered, "Spooner exiting."

"Spooner!" Rafiq cried with a slur. "I found you! Where's Archie?"

"Sami?"

That was Latham's voice.

Monarch stayed put, not looking, still leaning over Tatupu as if he were telling him a joke. He said, "I need the seat to your right."

"Been looking for you everywhere," the forger went on loudly. "Wanted to party with my man, Archie!"

Latham thought that was funny and started to laugh. "Hell, I'll drink with an old friend whenever and however he shows up. Have a seat. Let's catch up."

Monarch didn't hear what Tats told the bar girls, but they looked suddenly horrified and moved off chattering. He took that as his cue to slide around the Samoan's broad back, and onto the now empty stool, directly across from Latham, whose attention was still focused on the forger.

Setting his iPhone on the bar, Monarch watched from under the brim of his ball cap until Latham had taken his stool and looked to the short dumpy woman who ran the bar, saying, "Two cold, Mama San."

Reaching below the bar into his pants' cargo pocket with his good left hand, Monarch drew out a Glock. He aimed at the bamboo curtain that wrapped the lower bar, then he pushed up his hat with his bandaged right hand and looked directly across at the mercenary agent and the Lebanese forger who sat beside him, terrified. Latham was as happily disheveled as ever, focusing on the tip of his cigarette as he thumbed a lighter. But Spooner spotted Monarch right way, and took a step in retreat, his right hand reaching around his back as if for a weapon.

"Don't," Monarch commanded loud enough to be heard over the music. "We've got two forties pointed at your boss's stomach."

Spooner froze, his eyes darting to Tatupu who stared at him like one of those monolithic statues on Easter Island.

Latham, meanwhile, had finally become aware of Monarch and started to laugh with delight. "Robin Monarch! Twice in one week? You old dog."

Grinning as if it were one of the very best moments of his life, the mercenary agent leaned forward across the bar, and said conspiratorially, "Oh, hell, I figured you might catch up with me sooner or later, especially after Tengku told me you took the phone, which is why the two lads to your left and the one to your right, and the three talents in the bar behind you are all prepped to blow your head off." He chuckled. "Isn't this great? A Mexican standoff in Thailand?"

Instead of looking around or over his shoulder, Monarch assumed that there were armed operators all around him, and played the concerned friend saying, "When exactly did you lose your mind, Archibald?"

Latham soured. "What are you, one of my ex-wives?"

"I figure it was when you were in that hospital in Melbourne, and they told you that your big-time run-and-gun days were a thing of the past."

"Robin Monarch, a psychologist now?" the mercenary agent snorted.

"Just trying to figure out how a stand-up guy went fruitcake, and joined forces with people interested in kidnapping the U.S. Secretary of State."

Latham shook his head. "You have too high an opinion of me, Robin. Me and Tengku were just good business. He's sent a lot of it my way. So nothing personal, and definitely nothing to do with Agnes Lawton and those others."

"Bullshit, Archie. You're in this up to your chin."

The mercenary agent accepted his beer from the Mama San, who looked concerned, as if she didn't understand the nuance of what was being said but got the undercurrent loud and clear.

Monarch's cell flashed. A text from Fowler: "Got the three behind you."

Latham raised his beer, said, "We're all entitled to our opinions mate. But the way this is going to work here is we're going to agree to disagree, eh? And me and the boys are going to walk out nice and clean along with our little betraying forger here."

"Archie," Rafiq began to plead.

"Shut the fuck up, Sami, if you please," Latham said, still looking at Monarch. "And you, Robin, and your impressive Maori warrior there are going to ease on out of here and go on about your business looking for those diplomats."

"I'm Samoan," Tats grunted.

"There you go," Latham replied, grinned, and sucked off his cigarette. "What a big sonofabitch you are? Isn't he, Spooner? Makes you look puny."

Monarch's cell phone flashed again. A text from Chavez: "Got duo to Tats's left."

"You're hardly in a position to dictate terms, Archie," Monarch said.

"Ditto, old buddy."

"Oh, but I *am* in a position to dictate terms," Monarch insisted. "I not only represent the full power and might of my client, the U.S. government, but I have men covering your men, and they will not hesitate to shoot."

For a heartbeat, Monarch saw uncertainty swim through Latham's face, but then the man's amused air returned in force. Smiling, he stubbed out the cigarette butt, shook another from his pack. He tried to light it, but could not raise a flame. Sighing, he set the cigarette in the ashtray, and then reached down on the counter for another lighter.

"I thought better of you, Robin," the mercenary agent said.

"Ditto, old buddy," Monarch replied.

"Heh, heh, touché," Latham said, raising the cigarette to his mouth and thumbed the lighter with his opposite hand. As he moved the flame to the tobacco, his eyes suddenly shot hard to his right, as if seeing something there that Monarch could not.

Latham sold the move so well that Monarch's attention darted there, too, only to see Sami Rafiq's abysmal expression.

When the thief looked back, the cigarette was lit. Latham was relaxing into that lazy default smile of his, setting down the lighter with his left hand and with his right flicking the glowing cigarette and a sparking cherry bomb right at Monarch's face.

37

MONARCH SLAMMED SHUT HIS eyes, and snapped his head and body backward just before the firework exploded eighteen inches away. Through his eyelids the flash was brilliant and blood red. The report rang his eardrums. And his skin felt peppered as he fell from the stool. His back, wounded shoulder, and head slammed against the cement floor.

He strained his eyes open, and for several choking breaths reality unfolded in excruciating slow motion. He was aware of women screaming and then gunshots all around him. Bullets chipped off the bar next to Tatupu and shattered liquor bottles beyond as the Samoan pivoted off his stool, and from the hip, shot the first of Latham's men in the chest.

The second operator had Tats dead to rights, aiming at the big man from less than ten yards. Another mercenary behind the Samoan raised his gun to shoot Tatupu in the back. Monarch tried to warn him.

But it was too late.

At Chavez's shot, the neck of the killer facing Tatupu ruptured and he dropped like a rag doll. But the shooter behind Tats got off a round before hunching up, and shuddering at the bullet Song Le sent through his spine. The shooter and the Samoan seemed to crumple at the same time.

"Tats!" Monarch gasped. Gunfire came in bursts amid the chaos erupting in the eighteen other bars between him and Walking Street. Adrenaline surged through him, and he rolled over and into a crouch, scuttling toward Tatupu, who'd fallen against the bar, holding his calf and gritting his teeth.

"How bad?" Monarch shouted over the gunfire.

"Leg's hit hard in the meat, maybe bone," he rasped. "Get Latham."

Hearing more shots toward the seawall, Monarch sprang up and looked for a target. He saw Spooner backing up with two pistols raised and aimed, one at Monarch, and the other at Chavez, who was taking cover behind an overturned table at the bar across the way.

Beyond Spooner, Latham was using Sami Rafiq as a human shield, dragging the weeping forger toward the seawall. Spooner shot with both pistols. Monarch felt the shockwave of a bullet rip past his head before he returned fire with a wild shot, and then another aimed away from Spooner's vest. He squeezed the trigger and shot Latham's right-hand man through the left butt cheek. A normal man might have buckled. But somewhere

Spooner had been trained to accept pain, taught to improvise, and change in an instant. He grunted, and tried to aim at Monarch once more.

Chavez fired twice. Her first round hit Spooner dead center of his body armor, knocking him into a stunned backward stagger. Her second round struck him in the exact same spot. Latham's bodyguard went down hard, slamming his head, and dropping his pistols on impact.

Monarch's attention shot to Latham, who'd reached the wall, his belly still tight to the back of the blubbering Lebanese forger, who was pleading to be let go.

"Oh, dear God, Archie, please, he forced me!" Rafiq cried.

"Give it up, Archie!" Monarch shouted, moving in an arc around the shambles of the bar, aiming at the mercenary agent, who now raised his stainless-steel cane beneath Rafiq's right arm, swinging the rubber tip of it back and forth. Chavez was out from behind the table, advancing on him from another angle.

"Not a chance," Latham laughed. "I'm going out in a blaze of—"

He swung the cane back toward Chavez. The rubber tip exploded outward, hurling buckshot that hit Chavez, blowing her pistol from her hands, and driving her to her knees. With a giddy expression Latham swung the cane back in Monarch's direction, causing him to dive to the ground. He landed on his left side, his better shooting hand pinned beneath him. Latham fired at him.

Buckshot zinged over Monarch's back and smacked against the low bamboo wall of the bar behind him. Hearing sirens for the first time, he lifted his head in time to see Latham hurl the forger and his cane away, and then pivot and throw his bad leg over the seawall. Monarch struggled to get his gun hand out from under his chest. Fowler shot from thirty yards behind Monarch, and hit the mercenary agent high and through the back of his good leg. Latham jerked, howled, tipped, and fell over into the night.

Lurching to his feet, Monarch sprinted past the forger, who was making frightened little whimpers as he belly-crawled away. Reaching the seawall, Monarch looked over, seeing that the water was no more than twenty-five feet below. Latham had already surfaced and though obviously hit was swimming toward a Sea-Doo conveniently moored and bobbing not a hundred feet from the pier stanchions.

Monarch climbed up on the wall and jumped. He hit the water, submerged ten feet, and then started to kick and pull his way forward. Above him, the lights from the bars shone down on the surface, letting him see shadows and movement.

When his lungs were at the point of bursting, he picked up Latham's shape as it struggled along the surface like a wounded seal. Kicking his way upward, Monarch breached with a gasp, finding himself right next to the Sea-Doo and Latham, who had almost dragged himself aboard. The upper right thigh of the mercenary agent's white linen pants was soaked in salt water and blood.

Latham saw Monarch and kicked at him with his crippled leg. Monarch twisted in the water, dodged it. Latham got hold of the Sea-Doo's handlebar and pulled himself up onto the saddle. The blood was everywhere now, enough to draw sharks.

Monarch lunged, grabbed hold of the ankle of Latham's wounded leg and yanked at it, causing the mercenary agent to scream and to fight for his grip.

"Stop Archie, or I'll have to kill you!" Monarch commanded.

In agony, Latham looked back at him with such intensity that Monarch thought sure he would fight on. But then the war went out of Archie Latham all at once. His shoulders lost tension. He grinned foolishly as he gestured at his thigh and said in a chuckle, "Feels like you already have killed me there, mate. That's femoral blood."

Then he pitched off the sled over into the water next to Monarch, who grabbed him by the collar and jerked his face up into the night air. He wanted to rip off a belt and tourniquet Latham's leg, but he could already tell he was fading.

"Who has Secretary Lawton, Archie?" Monarch shouted. "Where is she?"

The mercenary agent rolled his drooping eyes toward him, still amused, and said, "Who knows? Long as I was getting paid, I didn't care to know."

"Who paid you then?" Monarch said, seeing the man's cheeks start to sag.

Latham coughed. "You'd like to know, wouldn't you?"

Monarch wanted to choke him, but said, "Agnes Lawton doesn't deserve this."

Latham said nothing.

"You used to be a stand-up guy, Archie," Monarch said. "Now you've got no chance of redemption."

"Damned," Latham said in a whisper. "I am damned, Robin. Always have been."

"Who paid you?" Monarch asked. "C'mon, Archie. Take some of the weight off your soul."

Latham struggled and shuddered in pain before managing the barest of grins. Monarch thought he'd lost. But then, with his dying breaths, Latham said something Monarch would not forget as long as he lived.

"What the hell does that mean?" Monarch asked.

Before he could reply, the mercenary agent sagged and was no more.

Sirens were coming closer. Monarch could hear shouting and screams and crying now that the shooting had stopped. He looked back and up at the seawall in time to see Song Le jumping off it. She dropped twenty-five feet, splashed into the water, and quickly surfaced, swimming with powerful strokes toward Monarch and the corpse of Archie Latham.

"Rogue!"

Fowler was up there on the wall now.

"Stay with Tats and Chavez," Monarch called back. "Say nothing to any law enforcement official. Insist on contacting Barnett at the embassy. I will, too, once I get out of here and to a phone."

Before Fowler could answer, police blew whistles and men shouted behind him in Thai. Fowler jumped off the seawall, back toward the bars and out of sight.

Breathing hard, Song Le demanded, "What did Latham say?"

"I'll tell you once we get out of here," said Monarch.

He hesitated, assaulted by better memories of Archie Latham, but then pushed the mercenary agent's body aside. He started to swim south, away from the bar lights, toward the deep, dark shadows behind the Airplane Go-Go. He wondered about Tatupu and Chavez. A good part of him wanted to go back for them, but it would do him no good and would do Secretary Lawton no good were he to spend any more time in custody.

They made it to the shadows just in time. Flashlight beams played back there around Latham's corpse. Treading water, Monarch whispered, "Nice and slow until we're well back toward the Beach Road."

"How far?"

"Six, seven hundred yards?"

They breast stroked side by side, aware of the fading aftermath of the gun battle behind them, and the pulsing of techno music from the go-go bars on Walking Street that had not missed a beat despite the mayhem that had gone down at the last few minutes. As he swam, Monarch's thoughts alternated between concern for Tatupu and Chavez, and Latham's final words.

What the hell did it mean? Who or what was he talking about?

When they got close to the south end of Walking Street they could see the flashing red lights and heard the sirens of an ambulance leaving. Chavez? Tats? Spooner? Monarch tapped Song Le on the shoulder, pointed out into the Gulf of Thailand, and whispered in her ear. "We want to loop out and come in another couple of hundred yards down the beach."

Song Le nodded and started swimming out to sea. Monarch followed her in a lazy arc and fifteen minutes later he felt bottom and waded toward shore, seeing a bare-chested Thai man sitting up on the low sea wall by a gas lamp, watching them.

"Hey, man, you swim in your clothes?" he called and laughed.

"Hot out," Monarch said, moving past him, seeing that he sold coconuts.

Police cars raced by on the Beach Road, heading north toward Walking Street. Monarch stopped, went back, and said, "Two coconuts please."

The vendor used a machete to chop off the tops of the fresh coconuts and stick a straw in them. He paid the man twice his price, wished him well, and strolled off.

"What's this all about?" Song Le asked when he handed her one.

"Camouflage," Monarch replied. "Now we look like a couple of crazy tourists who went for a late-night swim, not fugitives from a shoot-out. And besides, coconut water's good for recovery."

They crossed Beach Road without incident, falling in with one mob of drunk pedestrians and then another and still a third until they'd reached the entrance to the Marriot Resort. To his surprise he saw Sami Rafiq climbing into his Range Rover in front of the valet station.

Monarch trotted up, pulled open the passenger side door and got in, saying, "You're helping me a great deal tonight, Sami."

"No!" the forger screamed. "Get out!"

"Now why would we ever do that?" Song Le asked from the backseat.

Rafiq looked wild-eyed at them. "Because you psychopaths almost got me killed ten times tonight."

"You dead?" Monarch asked.

The forger began to shake, and then to beg, "Please Monarch, no more. I just can't take anymore."

"Tell you what. Drive down the street, and give us the car."

"What? No. No!"

"Yes. Yes! And then you'll walk back and check into the Marriot and have a nice air-conditioned sleep on the U.S. government. I'll call and leave a message for you at the desk giving you the exact location of your car at the airport in Bangkok, and there will be an envelope with an exceptional amount of cash for your trouble. And you'll never see either of us ever again."

The Lebanese forger appeared on the verge of a nervous breakdown, but said, "You promise? Never, ever again?"

"Never," Monarch said, patting the poor man on the shoulder.

After a moment's hesitation, Rafiq nodded dully, put the car in gear, and drove out of the resort parking lot. Two blocks down the street, he pulled over, got out without another word, and slammed the door shut behind him. Monarch climbed over into the driver's seat. Song Le got into the passenger seat.

Glancing to his left, Monarch saw the forger standing like a zombie on the sidewalk. He rolled down the window, and said, "You should probably have a few drinks before you crash, Sami."

But Rafiq was still standing there shell-shocked the last time Monarch looked in the rearview mirror. Being in the middle of a firefight does that to some men.

"What did Latham tell you?" Song Le asked.

"Just a second," Monarch replied. "I've got to make sure my people are taken care of first." He gave her his iPhone and told her a phone number to call.

Annoyed at still being kept in the dark, the Chinese agent punched in the numbers, hit send, and then the speakerphone button.

Barnett answered. "Yes?"

"Gloria, it's Robin," Monarch said.

"Robin!" she cried. "Where are you? What is—?"

"Calm down," he said. "We found Latham in Pattaya and it got ugly. Six men are dead, including Latham. Tats and Chavez have been hit, but not fatal. Fowler's with them, and probably in custody by now. You'll want to get the embassy people working to spring them as soon as possible. You tell them that Latham was definitely involved with the Sons of Prophecy."

"Where are you?" she sputtered.

"Heading toward the Bangkok airport."

"Why? Where are you going now?"

"Hong Kong," Monarch said, glancing at Song Le before returning his attention to the road. "Before Latham died, I asked him who brought him into the conspiracy. He said, and I quote, " 'The Moon Dragon, old buddy. Fucking evil mystery of the Orient, Hong Kong.' "

Monarch heard a gasp, stared at the phone, but then realized it had come from Song Le, whose right hand had risen and now covered her mouth.

"What in God's name does that mean?" Barnett demanded.

Song Le was staring through the windshield as if she'd seen a ghost.

"I don't know," Monarch said, glancing over at the Chinese agent again. "But I think I'm about to find out."

He reached over, clicked off the phone, said, "That made sense to you? What Latham told me?"

Song Le's head came around slow and in disbelief. "The Moon Dragon? Hong Kong? That's what he said?"

"Well, not exactly," he replied, and then repeated Latham's dying words.

"It can't be . . . ," the Chinese agent said, pulling at her lip. "It's just not . . ."

"So you've heard of a Moon Dragon in Hong Kong?"

Song Le said nothing for several seconds before starting to talk in a shocked voice, "I know of one Moon Dragon in Hong Kong. He's powerful, extremely dangerous, and absolutely ruthless."

"Wait a second. That's his name? Moon Dragon?"

She nodded, said, "In Chinese he is Long Chan-Juan, Moon Dragon. He's the head of Shing-Tun, the most powerful triad in Hong Kong."

As the rain began to spatter the windshield again, he asked, "How do you know this guy?"

Song Le gazed at her lap, and said, "I don't know him really, never met him, I mean, but I have heard all about him and his wife."

"From who?" Monarch said.

"My husband, Jin," she said, tears appearing on her cheeks. "The Moon Dragon was his father."

Song Le's story came out in fits and starts as they made an agonizingly slow drive back to Bangkok airport over flooded roads that produced one traffic jam after another.

Song Le met Jin when she was twenty-one. She was a student in an English language class during officer training at the Ministry of State Security. Jin had been her instructor. Jin was unlike anyone Song Le had ever known. While she had been born and raised in parochial Chengdu in Sichuan province, the daughter of a teacher and track coach, Jin was from Hong Kong and possessed a worldview far larger than her own.

It was only after they'd fallen in love that Jin revealed his family's secrets, that his father was a criminal and his mother a fortuneteller and something of a tyrant. Jin said that his father had tried to convince him to join the family business, but he had refused, and left Hong Kong for the job in Beijing.

After asking Song Le to marry him and she had accepted, Jin went first to Chengdu to seek her father's blessing and then to Hong Kong in search of the same from his parents. Song Le's father had readily approved. But the Moon Dragon refused to see his son because Jin's mother had predicted a bad end to any union with a girl from the mainland.

"Jin should have listened to her," Song Le said hoarsely.

Instead they married and were blessed with a son.

When the baby was four months old, they decided to take him to meet Song Le's father. They traveled to Sichuan province by train from Beijing, a trip of several days. Jin rented them sleeping berths. In the middle of the night, Song Le was lying in her bunk, breastfeeding her son when she heard a screeching sound as if the steel wheels were protesting a long blemish in the rails.

"It all happened so fast, flashing, screeching, and noises like many claps of thunder one right after the other," Song Le said softly. "I held tight to my baby, screaming for Jin, before I was thrown through the air, and then nothing."

The Chinese agent sat there a long time after that, looking out through the windshield at the slapping wipers and the rain falling until Monarch finally asked, "What happened?"

"I woke up eight days later in a hospital in Chengdu," she said quietly. "My father was sitting by my bed and I knew right away from his face that . . ."

She sighed. "The train derailed. Twenty-three passenger cars jackknifed down a steep embankment. Fifty-seven people died, including my husband and baby boy. Their bodies had already been cremated by the time I woke up from the coma. A representative of Jin's father had taken half of my husband's ashes and half of the baby's. My father was given the rest."

Monarch felt sick at Song Le's loss. "I'm sorry. I can't imagine it."

Song Le nodded dully. "I could not either. My brain kept saying that it was impossible, and I just laid there

in the hospital and at my father's house, waiting to die
from sadness."

When Monarch asked what had prevented that she
told him that six weeks after the accident, a senior officer at MSS came to deliver official condolences and
to offer her a position as a field operative.

"He said my assignments would be investigative,
and dangerous, and that I might die on behalf of my
country," Song Le said. "I was already dead inside, so I
accepted his offer. As I said before, strange, isn't it, how
two doors close, and another door opens?"

Monarch flashed on himself as a teenager leaving
Sister Rachel's orphanage, on his way to Miami and
the army and everything that followed. They were approaching the airport at last. It was three A.M., twenty-
eight hours until the execution, when Monarch asked a
question that had bothered him during her entire story.

"So is it a coincidence that you were assigned to a
case that may involve your dead husband's father, or
something else?"

"I don't know."

"How were you assigned to this case?"

She thought about that, said, "My supervisor said
people higher up in MSS were pleased with my work
and specifically requested that I be the lead investiga-
tor into Minister Fung's kidnapping."

"Still doesn't explain it."

"I know," she said, hardening. "But I promise you
before this day ends I am going to figure it out."

38

SHIVERING, AGNES LAWTON HEARD the door to the thatched-roof hut creak open, and she roused, smelling something disgusting, and then opening her swollen eyes to see a blurry silhouette.

"Welcome you last day life," Captain Ramelan said. "Time meet Allah, be judged for you wicked ways."

The U.S. Secretary of State heard every word, knew their meaning, and realized that her clothes were soaked through and that she felt chilled despite the heat. She came wider-awake, noticing to her distress that the muscles in the back of her neck ached ever so sweetly, a sensation that traveled into the base of her skull and pulsed there, not quite a headache, and not entirely unpleasant. It was the third time she'd felt this odd throbbing in the past day and night.

The first time the comforting ague had come on slowly, and despite the whine of bugs all around her for the sixth night in a row she soon felt tired and content. Secretary Lawton had drifted into a deep sleep, one of the deepest she'd ever known, as if she were cradled in a cocoon and not laying on a bamboo floor in the jungle somewhere, tied at the wrists, shackled at the ankles, and held by a fanatic like Ramelan.

The captain inhabited the nightmares that seized her after that deepest of sleeps. In those dark dreams, Ramelan burned her at the stake, and she'd awoken hallucinating with a scorching fever that had eventually broken in a torrent of sweat followed by chills and chattering.

The second round had come on quicker, that wonderful ache, the deepest sleep, the nightmares, the fever, the sweat, and the shivering. Now that the cycle seemed to be starting up a third time, right on the heels of her last bout of sweat and shivers, she understood what was happening to her.

"I'm sick," she said to Captain Ramelan. "Malaria."

The terrorist shrugged. "Is will Allah's. The Indian, he have bad stomach. The Chinese weak heart. All will Allah's."

It was true. She'd heard Tarrant Wali vomiting during the night—the source of that stench no doubt—and she looked over now to see him curled up like a wounded dog, looking at her, and the Sons of Prophecy leader with sunken dark eyes. Fung sat against the wall in another corner, his skin a paler shade of gray.

How far they'd all fallen. How fast they'd all fallen.

"Please," she said, her tongue feeling twice its size. "Water."

Ramelan hesitated, but then picked up the jug. He brought it over to her and filled the tin cup she'd been given. The Secretary of State picked it up between her bound hands and drank it greedily, choking on the last gulp, and then holding it out for more.

Three times she emptied the cup and four times Ramelan filled it. Setting down a full cup beside her, aware of how weakened she'd become just since the night before, Secretary Lawson watched him take water to Fung and to Wali, the latter man almost unable to lift his head. She was overcome with sadness. These men had families. Did they have regrets like she did?

"Someone bring you food," Ramelan announced, breaking her from her melancholy thoughts. He turned to leave.

"My country won't pay you," she called after her captor.

He stopped in the open doorway, giving her a glimpse of other huts beyond, some of them up on stilts. He looked back over his shoulder at her and said, "We never think country pay."

With that he left, leaving Agnes Lawton to stare after him, feeling the sweet pounding at the base of her skull again, feeling the first inkling of that drugged sensation it seemed to provoke, and fighting to contain the fear of imminent death that now trickled through her.

39

MONARCH HEARD A BELL ring and groggily opened his eyes, finding Song Le asleep on his shoulder. He looked around blearily, recognizing the plush interior of the Gulfstream Barnett had arranged. He remembered the storms that had once again swept Bangkok, and how they'd shut down the airport for four excruciatingly long hours.

During the wait, he'd thought multiple times of contacting Dr. Hopkins or the President to have the triad leader Long Chan-Juan put under close surveillance pending their arrival. But he kept coming back to those words Secretary Lawton had blinked over during her second and third appearances as a captive on video.

No, he decided as the corporate jet banked over the casinos of Macau, and started its descent into Hong Kong. I am maintaining radio silence.

Monarch glanced at his watch, seeing he had less

than eighteen hours now. He was wondering what became of the fake gold drop when he heard the landing wheels unlock and rumble. Song Le stirred and sat up. She realized where she'd been sleeping and looked embarrassed.

"Don't worry," Monarch said. "I won't tell anyone you used a running dog imperialist for a pillow."

She couldn't help herself and smiled. Her hair was pushed to one side, revealing that long scar he'd seen before. He thought of what she'd been through, the loss of her husband and son, and wondered again about her connection to the Moon Dragon. What were the odds of that? If it was more than sheer happenstance, what was the motivation? And whose?

Light rain sheeted off the window as they dropped through iron-colored clouds. Wind pushed and buffeted the jet as it broke free, revealing dark water, dozens of forest- and mist-covered islands, and the vague outline of the skyscrapers of Hong Kong.

A thought occurred to him. What if Latham had been intentionally lying to him? Or what if he'd been so close to death he'd been out of his mind and—

They touched down hard on the runway and taxied to the private jet port. Clearing immigration, they picked up a duffel bag carrying the Kevlar vests and moved toward Customs, where Song Le said, "Wait here."

The Chinese agent went over to a man in a military uniform, who regarded her skeptically at first. She showed him identification and he did a complete about face in attitude. They disappeared through a door, and

Monarch took the opportunity to call Barnett. She answered on the first ring.

"Where are you?"

"Hong Kong, finally. How are Tats and Chavez?"

"Beat up, but stable," she said. "The Thais threw a shit-fit at the embassy over our demands they be released into U.S. care. But the ambassador intervened personally with the king and the prime minister, explained that all actions in Pattaya were taken in an effort to find and release Secretary Lawton and the foreign ministers."

"Where are they?"

"Tats and Chavez? On a hospital jet bound for Okinawa. They'll both require surgery. Fowler's here in the embassy, sleeping. Only other thing to tell you is that NSA came back on the rest of the numbers in Tengku's contact list. One of them is definitely out of Hong Kong. Where do you want me?"

"On call," Monarch said, seeing Song Le exit the Customs door. "Gotta go."

He clicked off, noticing that the Chinese agent carried a plastic duty-free bag.

"We're good," she said to him, and moved toward the exit.

"Doing some shopping?" he asked, falling in beside her.

"Some borrowing," she replied curtly. "Two QSZ-92s and six full clips."

"I didn't know you liked to shop," Monarch said.

The barest of smiles crossed her face before she said, "You didn't honestly think I was going to meet my father-in-law unarmed, did you?"

"I guess it wouldn't be the polite thing to do," Monarch said.

They passed through the doors of "Nothing to Declare" without incident. People were packed around the exit holding signs for various travelers. They each withdrew money from an ATM, went into a restroom, and put on the vests.

"Any idea about his address?" Monarch asked, as they headed toward the terminal exit.

"I know right where he lives."

"I thought you said you never met the man."

"I haven't. But I went there once a couple of years ago. Or up the street from where he lives anyway."

"You didn't knock? Ring the bell?"

"When it came right down to it, I realized that they had refused to acknowledge me when Jin was alive, so why would they want to know me when he was dead? I couldn't see the point of humiliating myself and left."

Outside the terminal, it was oppressively muggy. Cars honked. Buses sighed. People were smoking and yelling. They caught a cab. Song Le gave the man an address from memory, the intersection of two roads on the island of Hong Kong.

It took them nearly forty minutes to cross the bridges and small islands that lay between the airport, the Kowloon Peninsula, and Hong Kong. They took the Western Harbor Crossing. Ferries and boats crisscrossed brooding Victoria Harbor below them.

Reaching the island, they turned east on Connaught Road, eventually passing through the Central District of Hong Kong, a dense mélange of high-end fashion shops, banking towers, elevated walkways, and the hub of all public transportation, buses, subway lines, and the ferry docks. Monarch noticed bands of tiny Asian women talking, laughing, and carrying shopping bags. They seemed to be everywhere.

"Who are they?" he asked the cabdriver. "All those little women? They aren't Chinese."

"Filipinas and Indonesians," the taxi driver said in a dismissive tone. "Domestic help. It's Sunday. Maids day off."

"There are thousands of them," Monarch remarked.

"Tens of thousands," Song Le said disapprovingly. "Many families here hire them because they don't cost much. The Hong Kong people treat them like dogs. Some of them aren't much more than slaves."

"Maybe they deserve it," the taxi driver shot back. "Hundred years ago, it was the other way around, Chinese working in the Philippines for nothing."

"Still doesn't make it right," Song Le said. "You'd never see that on the mainland."

"Right," the taxi driver said sardonically. "Everybody's free on the mainland, that's why all of you want to come to Hong Kong."

Song Le looked ready to argue, but then let it drop. They drove the rest of the way in silence up a series of winding roads that climbed toward dozens of residential towers clinging to the steep mountain above Central. The driver finally slowed near the Altadena House on Barker Road.

"Don't pull in," Song Le said. "Just drop us up there at the curb."

"You want me to wait?" the driver asked after he'd complied.

"Not a bad idea," Monarch said, handing the man fifty Hong Kong dollars.

"I'll be right here as long as you want!" the driver promised.

After Monarch had exited the taxi he looked up at the large pink-faced apartment building, and said skeptically, "A big-time crime lord lives there?"

Song Le shook her head. She gestured toward the fence, said, "Be careful, last time I was here, there were armed guards patrolling."

Monarch slipped to the fence, and peered down through thick vegetation, seeing a steep slope that dropped to another road. On the opposite side of the lower road, with a breathtaking view of Kowloon, stood a large, pale-gray villa obscured by orchid trees.

A Chinese man in a rain jacket sat under the portico. If there were others Monarch didn't see them. Returning to Song Le, he said, "So what's the plan?"

"You're letting me decide?"

"Your country."

"Well, sort of," Song Le said, paused. "Why don't we march right up and ring his doorbell. I heard somewhere it always worked for James Bond."

Monarch tilted his head. Over the past few days she had begun to grow on him.

"Sure," he said. "Why not?"

"We have to go this way," she said, gesturing to their left. "The road goes on, then swings back around."

They skirted below the Altadena House apartment

complex, and as Song Le had said, Barker Road button-hooked. As they rounded the bend, a tiny Filipina woman rushed by them, and on up the hill, hurrying to be somewhere, raising her hand toward her lips, barely giving them a glance. But before she covered her mouth, Monarch saw not only that she had large beautiful eyes, but also that she had a slight cleft palate similar to one a friend back in Buenos Aires had. His friend used to shield his mouth with his hand all the time, too.

They had walked almost halfway to the Moon Dragon's villa, when Monarch stopped. "I don't like this."

"What?" Song Le said.

"Like you said, armed guards," he replied. "I'd like to know how many before we go charging in there."

He turned and started to trot back up the hill toward the bend in the road.

Song Le ran after him, calling, "Where are you going?"

"To find that little Filipina woman," Monarch said. "She has to be the Moon Dragon's maid."

Monarch rounded the curve, heading uphill, looking everywhere for the tiny woman who'd walked past them. She wasn't anywhere on Barker Road that he could see. Then he happened to look up toward the apartment complex and spotted her climbing into a taxi out front.

"She's up there!" he shouted back at Song Le, who struggled to catch up.

Monarch sprinted toward the cab waiting for them. The taxi carrying the maid was moving east and his was facing west. He tore open the back door, jumped in, and said, "Make a U-turn fast and follow the cab about to come out the exit to the apartment complex behind us."

The taxi driver frowned.

Monarch yelled, "Do it!"

The driver slammed the vehicle in gear and, with tires screeching, made a U-turn on the narrow road, barely missing the fence that overlooked the Moon Dragon's villa and almost running down Song Le, who managed to leap to the side at the last second. The taxi skidded to a stop as the cab carrying the maid left the apartment complex and headed east. Monarch threw open the door and the Chinese agent jumped in.

"Go!" Monarch shouted.

They sped after the maid's taxi, but the road was so serpentine that they lost it twice before reaching the intersection with the Peak Road.

"Which way?" the taxi driver demanded.

"There!" Monarch said, gesturing at the retreating taillights going downhill.

They cut across traffic, somehow managed not to cause an accident, and accelerated down the steep, wet windy road, fishtailing twice, but keeping the maid's cab just in sight. They followed when her taxi took a left onto the Wan Chai Gap Road and were closing ground when they reached Luard Street and headed toward Victoria Harbor. A bus got in their way crossing Hennessy Road and they were a full block back when her cab took a right onto Jaffe Street and disappeared from view. By the time they took the same right the maid's cab was just down the street from them, heading away. Monarch could see the driver, and no one else.

"Pull over," Monarch commanded.

"No," Song Le said. "She's getting—"

"She's out already," Monarch shot back. "She's right here somewhere."

Right here was a line of bars, Asian fast-food counters, and discos with unlit neon signs. There was a seedy quality to the street that practically screamed the wrong side of town. But which door had the maid gone through on the wrong side of town?

"I know where she is," the taxi driver announced.

Monarch looked at him in reappraisal, seeing that he was becoming valuable. "What's your name?"

"Kit," he said.

"Okay, where'd she go, Kit?"

"In there," he said smugly, pointing down the street at a tall, narrow, unlit neon sign that read "Poseidon Club Disco."

"It's three o'clock on a Sunday afternoon," Song Le said skeptically. "That place won't open for hours."

"Nah, nah," Kit said, wagging a finger. "The owner opens it in the afternoon of maid's day off. They like to party, come here to drink, dance, and pick up men."

Monarch threw another fifty at him, told him to wait, and climbed out. Song Le followed him. Music blasted out the door of the Poseidon.

"What are you going to say to her?" Song Le asked as they walked closer.

"Got to find her first," Monarch said, reaching the entryway to the nightclub where the dance tunes were making the whole building throb. He could hear women screaming and laughing down there.

"Did a little Filipina woman just come in here?" Monarch asked the two bouncers sitting on stools outside the club.

"Shit, man, there's five hundred of them down there," one of them said. "Give it an hour, they'll be seven hundred."

Song Le gestured to her upper lip, and the other bouncer got it. "Yeah, Little Lippy is down there."

Asshole, Monarch thought and moved to go down the stairs. But the first bouncer said, "Ten bucks Hong Kong entry fee."

He handed the man a twenty. The bouncer seemed mightily amused that Song Le was along for the ride. "You got a thing for little maids, too?" he asked.

She spat something back at him in slang Chinese that Monarch didn't catch, and then pushed by him, heading down a long flight of stairs toward the flashing lights and the pounding music. Monarch followed and stepped through the doorway after her into a whole other world.

Up one side and down the other, three deep in some places, tiny Filipina and Indonesian women crowded a smoky oval-shaped bar. Singing, toasting, laughing, crying, the maids partied the way Monarch had seen a lot of Special Forces operators blow off steam: with enough intensity and booze to numb terrible memories.

Here and there, towering over the maids, men of all ages and races save Chinese were buying the maids tequila shots, beers, and mixed drinks. Anything they wanted. In return, the little women crowded in around their benefactor, hugging him, and tickling him, and generally making him feel like the king of the world.

Monarch scanned the front room repeatedly. "I don't see her."

"Neither do I," Song Le said. "This is bizarre, by the way."

"Extremely," Monarch said, and moved toward the music through a gauntlet of tiny women who began to touch his arms and smile at him.

"Ladies," he said, not slowing. "You're making me blush."

Beyond the bar room, in a cavernous space fronted by a live band, the maids were really raving. Hundreds of them packed the floor from one end of the room to the other, dancing by themselves, with friends, or in gangs that attacked the men courageous enough to wade through the frenzied mosh pit of domestic help.

The band broke into a version of Labelle's "Lady Marmalade," and the maids went insane. Fists overhead the tiny ladies sang along like post-pillage pirates on a world-class bender. The colored lights turned to strobes, which only added to the disjointed energy exploding throughout the disco.

"We'll never find her in here!" Song Le shouted.

"You search over there, I'll go this way, and we'll meet back here in ten minutes."

Looking like a giantess among Lilliputians, the Chinese agent moved off. Through the strobe, Monarch could make out a sea of little women between him and a smaller bar in the back corner of the dance floor. He imagined himself Tatupu and set off like Moses hoping to part water.

Instead, the maids came at the thief in concentric waves, smiling and groping at him, singing—*Voulez-vous coucher avec moi, ce soir?*—and begging him to buy them drinks. He somehow made it all the way to the bar with his clothes on, and scanned the crowd, trying to spot a maid with a slight cleft palate. But it was low light, which made the job difficult, even when the strobe stopped, and the flashing reds, blues, and yellows returned.

When at last Monarch was satisfied he'd gotten a decent look at all the maids in this remote end of the club, he started back across the dance floor, heading toward the main bar. He'd almost made it when a whirlpool of little Filipina women swept him up. Before he knew what was happening he'd been spun, pushed, and drawn deeper into the mosh pit toward the stage and the band. One maid began to dry hump his leg. Others turned their rears to him and began bumping and grinding against him from every possible angle, all of them laughing and screaming with joy at his shocked reaction.

"Why are you such a macho man?" one maid yelled.

"Kiss me," another demanded.

Monarch honestly did not know what to do. Looking around wildly, he spotted Song Le waiting at the rendezvous point. The Chinese agent had seen what was happening to him, and was laughing, the first time he'd seen her do that since they'd met. He shrugged sheepishly, and threw up his hands.

"He's ours now!" one maid laughed maniacally. The others joined in, chanting, "He's ours now!"

"Really, really flattered, ladies," Monarch began. "But I've got to—"

He spotted her then, leaning against the wall toward Song Le and the main bar. The Moon Dragon's maid was watching what her colleagues were doing to him. She had a mixed drink in one hand, and was shielding her mouth with the other. He could tell right away that she was highly entertained by his current predicament.

He looked right at her, acted desperate, and yelled, "Help me!"

For a second, the triad leader's maid seemed not to believe he was talking to her. Then she did and her head and eyes dropped a moment, before rising to meet his gaze.

"Please!" he mouthed.

She cocked her head, hesitated, and then dropped her hand, revealing the cleft palate and a sober face, as if she thought he'd ignore her now.

Instead, Monarch grinned, and said again, "Help me!"

The Moon Dragon's maid finally smiled, and then held up her left hand and pointed to her ring finger. Confused at first, Monarch got it just as the song ended and the band broke over from disco into techno.

Looking down at the women rioting around him, he pointed to his own left hand and shouted, "I'm married, and I love my wife."

Faces fell all around him. The bumps and grinds petered out. The maid who'd been dry humping his leg stepped back, giving him space, and asked suspiciously, "Where's your ring?"

"I don't wear it when I'm working," he explained. "I'm sorry."

Sad now, the maids began to turn from him, looking for other prey.

Monarch took his chance and wove back through the crowd, trying to get to the Moon Dragon's maid. But she was gone.

He rushed toward the bar area. Song Le was waiting, said, "She just went by me."

Monarch said, "Let me handle this."

"You sure?"

"Very."

The Chinese agent nodded, and he went by her into the bar room, which was better lit. He spotted her just as a bartender set a drink in front of her. The Moon Dragon's maid saw him, smiled, looked down again, grabbed her drink and began to sip furiously from it as he approached. Monarch slid onto the stool beside the little woman and put his big hand on her shoulder. She looked over at him with an expression that was almost afraid to believe.

"Thanks for rescuing me," Monarch said.

The maid giggled, and said, "If they found out you were single they would have torn you apart."

"What's your name?"

She cowered slightly, and said, "Anna."

"Anyone ever tell you you've got very beautiful eyes, Anna?"

Instead of acting flattered, however, her eyes hardened

and she tapped her cleft. "You saying that because of this?"

"No," Monarch replied. "I'm saying it because it's true. And I don't particularly care about your lip. A good friend of mine had one, too."

Anna smiled at that. "True?"

He put his hand over her heart.

"What's your name?" she asked and started guzzling her drink.

"Robin."

She finished the drink and said, "Buy me one, Robin?"

"It's the least I can do. What'll you have?"

"Seven and seven?"

Monarch looked at the bartender. "One seven and seven and one Coke."

That seemed to throw the Moon Dragon's maid. "Coke?"

"I never drink when I'm working," Monarch explained.

That seemed to puzzle her, but she picked up her highball and began sipping it through the straw before asking, "I never seen you here before."

"Just got to town," Monarch said. "You work in Hong Kong?"

At the mention of her own work, Anna's face clouded, and she took another long sip of her drink. "Seven years," she said.

"Good family to work for?"

Anna stiffened, and said, "Some family good. Some not so good. The story of every maid in here."

"Why do it?"

The maid looked at him as if he were stupid, and replied, "For my family. Mother, father, sister, brother."

"So you're not married?"

"Once," she said. "You cannot be apart so long and not think another woman come into your husband's life."

"I'm sorry."

She shrugged, sipped hard, said, "I have a good life compared to many others."

Monarch sensed unfathomable dimensions to the Moon Dragon's maid, but decided to focus on the one that seemed to bother her most.

"You can have your lip fixed you know," he said. "Plastic surgeons."

She hardened again. "I thought you said you didn't care."

"I don't, but I think you do."

Anna glared at him a moment, and then looked away, saying, "Buy me another drink and go away, Robin."

"Hey," Monarch said softly. "It's not like that."

She stared hard into her lap, said, "I know about the operations. But they cost more money than I'll make in a lifetime, so I refuse to let myself think about them. They're fantasies to someone like me."

"It doesn't have to be a fantasy," Monarch said.

"Really?" she shot back. "Do you have a curfew, Robin?"

He blinked. "A curfew? Uh, no."

Anna looked back up at him, tears welling in her

eyes. "I do," she said. "I'm thirty-two years old, and I have to be back in my room at nine thirty on my only day off or I'll be fired and my family back home will fall apart. That's my life. That's why I can't let myself believe in dreams like plastic surgery."

Monarch thought of Sister Rachel, and wondered what she might say in a situation like this. And then it dawned on him.

"Start believing in that operation," he said.

She got angry, "I told you—"

"I'll pay for it," Monarch said. "All of it. And I'll give you enough money that you won't ever have to work as a maid again."

The maid turned her head slowly, looking dumb-founded, and then stony again. "You don't need to say things like that to sleep with me. Just buy me another drink."

"I don't want to sleep with you and you've had enough to drink," Monarch said. "And I am not kid-ding you. If you help me, I promise you I'll make sure your dreams come true."

Tears welled in her eyes. "You're lying. You're a cruel man."

He put his hand out, cradled her chin. "I'm not cruel. I'm one of the good guys. Help me and it all happens."

The confusion surfaced on her cheeks again before she said, "How can someone like me help someone like you?"

"Start by telling me about Long Chan-Juan," he replied.

At that Anna turned frightened. She drew back from him. "How do you know who I work for?"

"I saw you leave his house," Monarch replied. "I was one of the people you passed on Barker Road going to find your cab."

That upset her further. "You shouldn't want to know about Mr. Long."

"Why? Because you think he's a dangerous man?"

"I *know* he is a dangerous man," she retorted. "And he has many dangerous men who work for him."

"I've heard that," Monarch said. "Can I tell you a secret?"

She looked dubious, but nodded.

He leaned over and whispered, "I work for the President of the United States."

Anna hesitated and then pushed him away, laughed caustically, said, "Now I know you're lying. Just making this stuff up."

Monarch looked across the bar, spotted Song Le, and crooked a finger her way. The Chinese agent came around the bar. Anna looked uncertainly at her, and then puzzled, as if she'd seen Song Le somewhere before, and said, "Who are you?"

Song Le glanced at Monarch, who said, "Tell her who you work for."

"The Ministry of State Security in Beijing."

"Oh, sure," Anna said. "And Robin works for the President of the U.S."

"On a part-time basis, as I understand it," Song Le said, and smiled.

The maid's hand floated to her mouth. "You're serious?"

"We are," Monarch said. "Can you help us, Anna? There are people whose lives are at stake. Important people."

"How?"

Monarch and Song Le explained what they had in mind. Anna's face grew harder the longer they went along. "He could kill me," she said when they finished. "I know his wife would if he didn't."

"We're not going to let that happen," Monarch said. "Please."

Oblivious to the raucous party unfolding all around her, the Moon Dragon's maid peered off for a few moments into a place she'd never allowed herself to consider before.

At last she climbed off the bar stool, and said, "We better go right now before the alcohol wears off and I change my mind."

40

THIRTEEN HOURS AND FIFTEEN minutes until the threatened execution of the three diplomats, Monarch and Song Le once again stood on the upper Barker Road, watching Anna exit a taxi in front of the Moon Dragon's villa. The rain had finally stopped, and a breeze had picked up, rustling the leaves on the slope below them.

Anna walked to the guard in front, bowed to him as she passed. The guard was picking his teeth and barely looked her way. She was nothing to him.

But the Moon Dragon's maid had been very valuable to Monarch and Song Le already. She told them that there was usually a rotating contingent of six men guarding Long Chan-Juan's house, but Tuul, the most trusted of the triad leader's men, had been away since the day before.

The Moon Dragon was at his weekend retreat with his wife on Lamma Island, about an hour away by ferry.

He was not due back until nine that evening, his wife the following morning.

Anna went to a security pad by the front door, typed in a code, and entered, shutting the door behind her.

"How fast can you bring in MSS reinforcements?" Monarch asked Song Le.

"Twenty minutes," she said.

"Let's take a look around inside before we have them raid it."

Song Le agreed, and they made a quick plan.

They went in opposite directions. Monarch walked fast toward that hairpin in the road. But instead of following it around toward the villa, he entered the thick brush growing on the mountain. The breeze rustled thick wet leaves that dripped on him and muffled his movements down the slope. When he was at the same elevation as the Moon Dragon's house, he went straight at it, pausing every few steps to scan through the vegetation toward terraced gardens.

When Monarch was ten yards shy of the gardens, he spotted the second guard, smoking under an eave at the rear corner of the house, a good spot because he could watch two different sides of the home at one time. Anna said the third guard would be somewhere near the opposite back corner doing the same thing.

Monarch smeared black soil onto his face, then crouched, crawled forward, went belly flat. He reached out into one of the flower beds for handful of small landscaping stones. Retreating several yards, he studied the openings in the vegetation downslope, and spotted a shallow ditch used for garden run-off. He crawled to it, lay in the bottom of it, and gathered wet dead leaves that he used to cover his legs and upper torso.

With the pistol Song Le had given him in his left hand, Monarch used his right to toss the little rocks at the twisted trunk of a tree five feet below him and ten feet back toward the road. The whack, whack, crack noises alerted the guard, who stubbed his cigarette, drew his gun and moved through the garden toward the sounds.

When he was just shy of the vegetation, Monarch chanced one last movement, tossing the rest of the rocks at the tree trunk. There was a moment's hesitation before the guard came into the brush, pushing aside the soaking leaves, gun leading.

Monarch waited until the Moon Dragon's man was just past him before lashing out with his right foot and connecting just behind his knee. There was a crunching noise and the guard made a short painful cry before Monarch was up and onto him from behind. In one fluid motion he seized the wrist of the man's gun hand and arm-barred his throat. Arching backward to throw tension into both holds, he felt the guard struggle, try to call out, and then collapse, dropping his weapon in the mud. Monarch let the man's limp body fall into the ditch, picked up the pistol, and with the butt of it hit him hard at the base of his head.

He got the iPhone, texted to Song Le's cell: Okay.

Ten seconds later, she texted back: Done.

There was only the man at the front door left. Because he was visible from the street, they decided to gamble, leave him in place, and go in through a back door.

Twilight was falling when Monarch emerged from the brush with leaves and mud all over him. He rounded the corner and saw Song Le already at the door with Anna, who looked extremely nervous. She looked down at their shoes, saw the mud, and turned afraid.

"Leave them here," she said. "Or Madame Long will know."

They kicked off their shoes, and stepped into a storage room. Anna had told them that she had not heard her employer mention Secretary Lawton or the missing Chinese and Indian foreign ministers or the Sons of Prophecy. But she did say that the triad leader had seemed highly agitated lately, and spending much of his time locked inside a home office she was rarely allowed to clean.

"Take us to the office," Song Le said.

"It's always locked," Anna said, wringing her hands.

"I'll take care of that," Monarch said.

She seemed uncertain, but led them through the storage room into her pitifully small basement bedroom—a narrow bed, a small chest of drawers, and no windows—and up the stairs into the kitchen. They passed through and skirted a foyer dominated by a dramatic weeping wall fountain and polished slate floors. The air smelled of jasmine and sandalwood when they entered a large formal living area decorated with exquisite silk wallpaper, Oriental antiques, ancient vases, and rugs. The thief in Monarch was thoroughly intrigued by the collection of jade artifacts displayed in a glass case, but he did not linger to examine it.

"Seems good to be the Moon Dragon," he remarked

as Anna entered a short hallway, and stopped in front of a steel door protected with two deadbolts.

Monarch got out his pick set, leaned over to study them, and was surprised. "Shenzhen YLI," he said. "I've never dealt with this kind of lock before."

"They're part mechanical, part electronic," Song Le said. "Let me try."

"Have at it," Monarch said, handing her the kit.

The Chinese agent knelt in front of the door, and began working at the locks, saying, "The key activates the electronics, which controls the—"

There was a loud thunk as the first bolt threw. Twenty seconds later the second bolt was released and she pushed the door open.

"You've got mad skills," Monarch said.

"And a few more you don't know about."

Anna meanwhile was wringing her hands. "What do you want me to do?"

"Go have some tea," Song Le suggested.

"I'd rather have another drink of whiskey," the maid admitted.

"If you've got some don't mind us," Monarch said, moving into the office.

Song Le came in behind him and shut the door. "Where do we start?"

"I'll take the computers, you try the hard files," Monarch said, pulling the chair out from behind the desk. He looked at his muddy clothes, shrugged, and sat down. He grabbed one of the laptops.

As Song Le began to open up drawers and cabinets, he called Barnett at the U.S. Embassy in Bangkok. She answered on the first ring, and told him that Chavez came out of surgery with her fingers intact. Tats was still in the operating room.

Monarch explained his location and situation. "Any ideas?"

"You have the charger on your phone?" Barnett asked.

He said he did, and she told him to separate the USB cable from the plug, and use it to connect the phone to the Moon Dragon's computer.

"You're good to go," Monarch said when he'd finished.

"Start it up, and let me know when you're in," she said.

Monarch pressed the power button and heard the computer boot up. Several seconds into the process, Barnett's laptop took over and the screen began to flash. When it stopped flashing he'd be free to rummage around.

While he waited, he checked his watch. Ten minutes to seven. If the Moon Dragon was a man of his word they had roughly two hours until his arrival. Song Le, meanwhile, was engrossed in a thick file on her lap.

"Anything?"

She looked up, confused, said, "These are plans to open casinos on the mainland, Shanghai, Beijing, all over."

"I thought gambling was illegal on the mainland."

"It is," she said. "But the details . . . Long obviously believes there will be a change in policy, and soon. And if he does, he'll make many, many billions."

"Why would a guy about to make billions get involved in a terrorist movement?" Monarch asked.

"I don't know," Song Le said, setting the file aside, looking around. Her attention drifted to the credenza. She reached over and picked up a picture frame that was facedown on the top of the cabinetry. She turned it over and Monarch saw her free hand fly to her mouth to stifle a small gasp.

"What is it?" Monarch asked.

Her eyes glistening, Song Le sniffed, and showed Monarch a picture of herself holding a baby with a handsome young man's proud arm around her.

"That Jin?" Monarch asked softly.

"And my boy," she choked. "I threw my copy of this away years ago, couldn't bear to look at—"

The door jiggled, opened, and the Moon Dragon's maid looked in at them in complete terror. "He's here! The car just pulled in!"

"Shit," Monarch said. "The bodyguard with him, Tuul?"

Almost crying, Anna said, "No, but everybody else is."

The laptop stopped flashing. Monarch wanted Barnett to copy the entire hard drive before he made any more moves.

"Just go out there and act like nothing's happening," he told Anna. "Tell them you only just got home."

The maid hesitated. A door slammed somewhere in the house.

"Do it," Song Le urged, setting the picture of her family down.

Anna looked ready to dissolve, but nodded and scurried away. Song Le drew her pistol from the waistband of her pants, and moved toward the door.

Monarch leaned over to his phone and murmured, "Work your magic."

"On it," Barnett replied.

Monarch moved toward Song Le, who looked ready to throw the deadbolts. He heard muffled voices, and put his hand on the Chinese agent's back to stop her, and then ever so slowly moved her aside and cracked the door.

"Why are you home so early, girl?" demanded a woman somewhere out in the big living area.

There was a pause, and then Anna replied, "I not feeling so well, Madame. I came back just a few minutes ago."

"Have you been drinking?"

"No, Madame Long."

"You are a liar, I can smell it," Madame Long said with venom in her words. "And I'll bet you have the sweat and seed of a man on you. And what's this? There's mud on the floor and—"

"I don't feel good, Anna," came a young boy's voice, cutting her off.

Monarch looked at Song Le, seeing her equally puzzled. The maid had never mentioned a boy.

"He was complaining on the ferry of a stomachache," a man said. "But then again, he ate six sweet dumplings before we left Lamma."

"That's too much," Anna agreed.

"Get him changed into his pajamas and into bed,"

Madame Long said. "And then go clean yourself, and clean this floor!"

"Yes, Madame," the maid said meekly. "Come with Anna now."

"I don't want to go to bed yet," the boy complained.

"You can read your books then," Anna replied, her voice fading as she walked away. "Or play a computer game."

"She's drunk again," Madame Long announced in Cantonese. "She's been to that disco again and done who knows what else, and in the bushes and the mud no less."

"I don't care," said a man Monarch took to be the Moon Dragon.

"*You don't?*" Long's wife cried, as if insulted. "I warned her, and she defied me, and now I want that little animal gone from my house."

"Tomorrow," her husband insisted. "Right now, I need—"

"Yes, yes," Madame Long said testily. "The turtle. Is that all I am to you, husband? A tool? A means to an end?"

"No, my dear, not at all," the triad leader said, shifting back to English in a soothing tone. "You are many, many things to me. It's just that I very much need to have some better sense of the immediate future."

There was a silence before Madame Long said coldly, "As you wish."

Turtle? Monarch thought.

Listening to their retreating steps and a door on the far side of the living area open and shut, he glanced at

Song Le, who seemed preoccupied, and whispered, "I think we better talk to your father-in-law sooner rather than later."

The Chinese agent seemed to come up from some confusion, and focused on Monarch. She bobbed her head, and pulled out her phone, giving him a quizzical look. Monarch nodded. It was time to call in the cavalry. They would need backup soon. Song Le typed a text and sent it. Monarch drew the pistol she'd given him, and opened the door.

He went prowling down the hall to the edge of the big living area with Song Le hugging the wall opposite him. He paused, taking in everything, hearing Anna and the boy off somewhere, but not the Moon Dragon, and certainly not his shrew of a wife. When he was sure that was the case, Monarch danced straight across the room to the only closed door.

With his left hand he checked the knob and was relieved to feel it turn and give. He pushed the door inward, seeing mahogany flooring in a hallway that formed the entry into a large master suite. There was a bathroom directly in front of him, and an ornate bedroom to his left.

"What do you wish to know, husband?" said Madame Long, whose voice came to Monarch from his far right, beyond a walk-in closet, and a door that was ajar. He slipped toward it, heard the Moon Dragon say, "Ask the Book if I will fulfill my destiny."

With Song Le right behind him, Monarch pushed the door wider, saw the triad leader watching his wife throw three coins across the belly of an ancient sea turtle shell, and said, "Don't bother, Moon Dragon, I already know the answer to that question, and I'm afraid the news is not looking good for you at all."

Long Chan-Juan startled, saw Monarch and Song Le, and stood there dumbstruck for several seconds. His wife's reaction mutated rapidly from surprise and fear to utter loathing when she caught sight of Song Le.

"What are *you* doing in my house?" Madame Long hissed.

"So, you do know me," Song Le said in an equally harsh tone.

The Moon Dragon's wife looked wildly toward the door. "Get out. You have no right to be here. No right at—"

"I have every right," Song Le retorted. "I have been charged by the Ministry for State Security with finding Foreign Minister Fung. I go where I want to go. No closed doors. Not even yours."

Madame Long wasn't expecting that, and her jaw hung slightly open a moment before she stole a glance at her husband as if he were a stranger standing too close in a public space.

"She's lying," Long told her. "This has nothing to do with—"

"It has everything to do with it," Monarch said. "You are intimately involved in the Sons of Prophecy conspiracy. Archie Latham told us that you were the one who paid him to recruit mercenaries for the project. He gave us your name. And that fence in Kuala Lumpur, Tengku? His phone had records of a burn phone bouncing off the cell towers around this place. Way I

see it, you're going down on hundreds of counts of kidnapping, murder, and conspiracy in at least six different countries. Now tell us where the diplomats are
before we have you—"

"Grandma? Who's yelling?"

The little boy's voice startled them all.

He stepped into the door, wearing his pajamas, rub-
bing his eyes, and then seeing Monarch and Song Le.
He turned uncertain, and then spotted the guns they
held and became afraid.

"Go find Anna," the Moon Dragon's wife said desperately.

"No, Grandmother, I don't want Anna," the boy
said. "Who are these people? What's—?"

Her face ravaged by emotion, Song Le gasped,
"Lo-Lo?"

The boy shrank, took a step back from her.

"Lo-Lo," the Chinese agent said again, her gun lowering as she stared in disbelief, as if she were dreaming
an impossible, impossible dream.

Lo-Lo looked to his grandmother and grandfather.
"Who is she? How does she know my name?"

"She's nobody!" Madame Long shouted.

Song Le started to tremble, and then to weep, "Lo-
Lo, I am your—"

Monarch was so upended by this turn of events that
for a split second his focus wavered and he didn't see
the movement until it was too late. Tuul, the Moon
Dragon's bodyguard, was suddenly crouched in the
doorway, his weapon sweeping between Monarch and
Song Le.

"Drop the guns now, or die," Tuul barked.

At this angle, and at point-blank range, Monarch realized that he'd be dead if he so much as flinched. He let go the pistol. It fell on the carpet at his feet. Song Le did the same, but did not seem to care. She said, "Lo-Lo? I'm—"

"An insane person trying to hurt Grandfather and me," Madame Long shapped. "We're so sorry you had to see this, Lo-Lo. Tuul and Grandfather will take care of them."

"You wicked, wicked woman!" Song Le screeched and made to attack her.

The bodyguard proved blinding fast, moving three steps into the room, kicking Song Le's pistol away across the floor and hammering her hard high and between the shoulder blades with the butt of his gun. It blew the wind from her and she sprawled on the floor.

Monarch started to squat, reaching for his weapon, but Tuul swung around and got his pistol pointed at him so quickly that the thief froze once more.

"Back up to the wall and sit," Tuul said. "Both of you."

Coming up out of his crouch, Monarch could see no counterattack and did as he was told.

The Moon Dragon clapped, laughed, looking at his grandson and said, "You see, Lo-Lo? This is what happens to a thief when he tries to fight a man who can summon typhoons!"

Before Monarch could even try to make sense of that, Song Le moaned on the rug, said, "He's *my* son. "

"He's nothing of the sort," Madame Long snapped.

"He's our grandson," the triad leader said. "The future."

The Moon Dragon's wife called sharply, "Anna!"

The maid came into the room almost immediately, as if she'd been listening right outside the doorway, shaking from head to toe. Monarch could tell she was petrified that her employers might have figured her as an accomplice.

But Madame Long's command was simple. "Take Lo-Lo out of here. Now."

"Come, Lo-Lo," Anna said in a tremulous voice. "Anna reads you a—"

"No," the boy said, staring in confusion at Song Le, and then at his grandparents. "My mother is dead."

"I'm not dead," Song Le said, still lying there.

"I told you this woman is crazy," Madame Long said. "Now go!"

The maid took the boy's hand. Reluctantly he followed her out of the room, saying, "What is going to happen to the thieves, Anna? Are the police coming?"

"No one's coming," the Moon Dragon said to Monarch, walking over and picking up his pistol from the floor.

"You plan to kill a U.S. and a Chinese agent?" Monarch asked, looking for the effect it had on the triad leader's wife.

Long told his wife, "Don't worry. Tuul will take them to the authorities."

"No, he won't," Monarch told Madame Long. "And other people know we're here. No matter what he does with us, he won't get away with whatever it is he's really been up to. Not after kidnapping diplomats, blowing up a train station, and attacking ships in the canals."

Madame Long looked sharply at her husband.

"He's as insane as she is," he said dismissively, looked to Tuul. "Make sure our guests aren't going anywhere, then make arrangements to turn them over to the police."

The bodyguard got Song Le's weapon, tucked it in his belt, and left the room. The Moon Dragon kept Monarch's gun trained on them.

"So what's your connection to the Sons of Prophecy?" Monarch asked.

"I told you, I have none," the Moon Dragon replied coldly. "And I've never heard of this man, Latham. And these phone records? Cruel coincidence."

Song Le had come around enough to roll over on her side.

"Get over there with your friend," Madame Long sneered.

"But my son," the Chinese agent said, looking in a daze at her late husband's mother. "How could you—?"

"Take him for our own?" the triad leader's wife said archly. "After what you took from me? It was easy. You were in a coma, our son was dead, and the boy rightfully belonged to us. Even the authorities saw the justness of our claim. Mr. Long has many, many connections in Beijing. They saw to it."

Song Le looked ill, but said, "I loved your son. And Jin loved me."

"Liar," Madame Long sneered. "You seduced him. Distorted his—"

Tuul returned carrying his pistol and a roll of duct tape, and said, "On your stomachs, hands behind the backs of your heads."

Monarch did as told, but tried to tense his core like a spring in hopes of getting hold of the man and reversing the situation. But the bodyguard put his foot between Monarch's shoulder blades and mashed the tension out of him before expertly strapping his wrists to either side of his head. When he was done, he did the same to Song Le and stepped back, admiring his handiwork.

"The van?" the Moon Dragon asked.

"On its way from the dock," Tuul replied. "We'll deliver them directly to our friends at the Hong Kong Police Department."

The triad leader seemed to be enjoying things now. He set Monarch's pistol on the edge of the cradle that held the ancient turtle shell. He looked at his wife and said, "Should we consult the Book on their behalf?"

Madame Long seemed torn at the idea.

"Go ahead," the Moon Dragon urged. "You know the universe is with us."

Reluctantly, his wife picked up the three coins and tossed them across the shell the proscribed six times, recording each result on that pad of paper. When she'd finished transposing the numbers into trigrams and hexagrams, her fingers shook as they sought the markings carved on the turtle's belly.

"What is the pronouncement?" the Moon Dragon asked.

His wife said nothing for several moments, then swallowed and said, "Hexagram twenty-four, 'Fu,' or 'The Turning Point.'"

"What does that mean?" her husband demanded.

"'Thunder within the Earth . . . Things cannot be destroyed once and for all,'" Madame Long said, reciting from memory. "'When what is above is split apart, it returns below.'"

Monarch didn't completely understand what was happening. He grasped that Long's wife was a practitioner of the I Ching, but was oblivious to the nuance that seemed to have agitated her husband.

"The Book must be wrong," the Moon Dragon declared. "Things *can* be destroyed once and for all."

"Yes, they can!" Anna cried furiously. "Let them go! Now!"

The attention of everyone in the room swung to the tiny Filipina maid who stood in the doorway, both hands wrapped around a SIG Sauer pistol with a sound supression.

After the initial shock, Tuul started to laugh, and moved at her, saying, "Gimme that, Anna. Where'd you get that? You'll hurt your—"

The Moon Dragon's bodyguard was less than two feet from the maid when the gun went off, hitting him square in the chest. Rocked, dead on his feet, Tuul stayed upright for several beats, but then staggered back and fell to the rug.

"Stupid bitch of a girl!" Madame Long cried. "What have you done?"

Song Le, meanwhile, was struggling against the

duct tape, tearing it free of her head. Monarch started to do the same.

The Moon Dragon reached for Monarch's gun on the stand, but Anna yelled, "Don't, or I shoot again!"

The little Filipina woman looked crazy, but Long and his wife still seemed to think they had the upper hand.

"Do you think you can kill me, Anna?" the triad leader asked in an icy tone. "Do know who I am?"

"And me?" Madame Long demanded. "Is that what you want to do? Kill us for the life we've given you, your food, the roof over your head, money for your family."

Anna glared at Madame Long and screamed in rage, "No, I can't kill you for that. But I will *destroy* the both of you now and forever!"

The tiny maid swung the gun toward the Moon Dragon's wife, who backed up, saying, "You ungrateful little—What are you doing? You can't!"

Anna smiled, aimed just left of Madame Long and fired, and again, and again, and then four more times.

Eight bullets smashed into the seven-hundred-year-old sea turtle shell, so brittle and dry that large sections of it exploded into jagged shards that shattered into splinters and daggers against the hardwood floor.

41

ANNA KEPT PULLING AT the trigger long after the clip was empty and the action locked open.

Madame Long retreated during the shooting, her hands raised after being hit in the face and cut by flying needles of turtleshell. But now she dropped her hands, and blood trickled down her perfect porcelain skin as she gaped at the ruins of her life and legacy. The fortuneteller fell to her knees, landing on shell pieces that cut her skin, and she began to wail and to shriek at what had been taken from her.

The Moon Dragon stood a few feet in back of his wife, mouth and eyes slack and vacant, as if the chain that anchored him had been severed and he was a boat at the mercy of a typhoon wind.

Monarch's immediate focus was elsewhere. He was thinking that there were three loaded weapons still in the room: Song Le's in the waistband of the dead bodyguard, Tuul's own weapon two feet from his corpse, and his own pistol somewhere on the floor amid the wreckage of the sea turtle's shell.

He saw Song Le cutting at her bonds with a piece of shell, and was reaching for another piece when Madame Long's thoughts turned to vengeance. The triad leader's wife stopped her keening, and frantically crawled on bleeding hands and knees toward the base of the cradle.

"Anna!" Monarch yelled. "Watch—"

The Moon Dragon's wife came up with Monarch's pistol. Blood dripped from Madame Long's hands and down her shins when she stood. Sheer hatred burned in her eyes when she raised the gun and stalked toward her maid who stood there still glaring at her employer, weaponless now, but utterly defiant.

The bonds that held Song Le's wrists split. She dove toward the dead bodyguard's gun. Shreds of duct tape covered with hair hung off her wrists as she rolled and snatched up the weapon.

The two shots came one right after another.

Madame Long fired at Anna from fifteen feet away, and Song Le shot the Moon Dragon's wife from the floor from less than five. To Monarch's horror, the little Filipina maid spun on impact, crashed off the far wall, and crumpled. Madame Long was struck up under her rib cage so that she seemed to rise up like a dancer on point before collapsing onto the camphor-wood cradle that had held her family's prized possession for more than seven centuries.

"No!" the Moon Dragon shouted, coming out of

whatever curse had transfixed him, and he threw himself down by his dying wife. "No!"

Song Le was up on her feet now. She raced forward to get to the gun Madame Long had used to shoot Anna.

Monarch looked to the maid, who lay on her belly with a growing dark stain on her side. For a second he felt complete despair, but then saw her move.

"She's breathing!" he shouted, and then grabbed a piece of shell and started cutting at the tape that still bound his wrists. He got them free of his head. As he did he caught a flicker in the doorway, and saw the guard they'd left at the front door already aiming.

"Song—!"

The silenced shot hit the Chinese agent in the side, threw her off her feet. She smashed off the wall, fell, and lay deathly still. Monarch stared, unable to react, hearing the guard shout at the Moon Dragon as if from far away. In a matter of two seconds, Long went from disoriented by grief to infuriated past insanity. The triad leader dropped his wife's body, looked at Monarch, and screamed as he lurched to his feet, "Give me the gun! I'll kill them myself!"

The guard was taking in the carnage in the room, the bodies of Madame Long, Tuul, and Song Le. The triad leader snatched the weapon from the guard and came toward Monarch, saying, "I hate thieves. They're like mice or rats, or any kind of vermin. You have to wipe them out."

Monarch was suddenly certain he was about to die. He said, "Just tell me one thing before you pull that trigger."

"I don't owe you a thing," the Moon Dragon seethed.

"Where is she? Secretary Lawton?"

The triad leader seemed to be feeling some kind of sadistic pleasure when he pressed the silenced barrel to Monarch's temple, and whispered, "Karimata Straits. The jungles and mangrove swamps west of Pulau Sumadra. And now you can take that secret to your grave."

But then Lo-Lo began to sob, "No! No!"

The Moon Dragon looked over his shoulder at his grandson reeling into the small room, clutching something to his chest.

"Lo-Lo, get out of here!" Long shouted. "You shouldn't see your grandmother like—"

"No, Grandfather!" Lo-Lo screamed, showing him the framed photo Song Le had seen in his office. "You said my mother was dead!"

The triad leader looked more shocked by this than he'd been seeing the turtle shell shatter and his wife die. "Lo-Lo, you don't under—"

The boy threw the picture at him, ran past the corpse of his grandmother, and threw himself on his knees by Song Le's side, choking hysterically through his tears: "Please don't be dead. Please, Mother, don't be dead."

With the Moon Dragon and his bodyguard momentarily distracted by the boy, Monarch took his chance and kicked as hard as he could with both legs. The heels of his shoes connected hard with the Moon Dragon's right shin. He heard a solid snapping noise, and felt bone displace. The triad leader bellowed, buckled, and fell, pulling the trigger of his gun. The bullet blew a hole in the carpet next to Monarch's face.

The Moon Dragon landed writhing in agony, his lower leg offset at a gruesome angle. Monarch threw out his bound hands, ripped the gun from Long's fingers, flipped it, caught it, and shot the last bodyguard before he could take two steps.

Wiggling away from the wounded triad leader, Monarch got up on his knees, shaking from the adrenaline of the past few minutes. He used his teeth to rip his wrists free of the tape, and staggered to his feet. Anna's eyes were open, but glazed, and she was breathing hard.

Monarch went to her. "I'm going to get you to a hospital."

"Help Lo-Lo first," Anna said hoarsely. "Please?"

He turned and walked past the Moon Dragon, who was shivering uncontrollably, going into shock, as he watched his grandson crouch over his mother and pitifully stroke her back, still whimpering, "Please don't be dead. Please don't be—"

Monarch flashed on the image of his own mother dying, shot down in the streets, and felt the boy's sorrow as his own. He was reaching out to comfort him, when he saw Song Le's eyes flutter open and find her son.

"I'm not dead, Lo-Lo," she whispered. "I can't be."

The bullet had struck Song Le's Kevlar vest nine inches below her left armpit. The impact had thrown her sideways, smashed her head against the wall, and knocked her out. She had a nasty bump on her head, but was able to sit up within minutes.

Clutching Lo-Lo to her, Song Le glared in defiance and triumph at the Moon Dragon while agents from the Chinese Ministry of State Security poured into the house along with Hong Kong police officers and Fire Service emergency ambulance teams, all summoned by Song Le's text.

The Moon Dragon had lost a lot of blood from the compound fracture, and was incoherent from pain when the Chinese EAS techs tried to work on him before Anna.

Monarch interceded, said, "Tourniquet the asshole, and then leave him be. Help her first. The maid's the hero."

They hesitated, as if it was preposterous to treat a maid before a Chinese national, but then withered and complied under Monarch's glare. They went to Anna. She'd been shot through and through the left side of her abdomen. While one tech stemmed her blood flow, the other worked an IV into her hand, attached a bag of electrolytes, and a dose of morphine. Anna gave Monarch a pitiful look and passed out. He went with her to the ambulance, watched her loaded, and told the techs that the U.S. government would pay for the best care they could find in the city.

"St. John's Hospital," one said, and the other nodded.

They drove away with sirens wailing and lights flashing.

Only then did Monarch check his watch. It was 8:34 P.M. Hong Kong time. He had less than ten and a half hours to rescue Secretary Lawton. He punched in Barnett's number, and said, "Can you contact SEAL Team Six without going through Washington?"

"No," she said as if the question were ridiculous. "What's happened?"

"I know where Secretary Lawton is," he replied. "And I need all the help I can get."

"I'll have to tell Hopkins."

"Then do it, and tell him to tell no one else that we know where she is."

"Why?"

"Because of what she's been blinking in Morse code the last two times she's been on video," he said, and hung up.

Another pair of EAS techs came out the front door, wheeling the Moon Dragon handcuffed to the stretcher, and babbling deliriously about the I Ching and the fantasies that could be stolen in the streets of Kowloon. Monarch watched the triad leader loaded in the ambulance as well. He wondered what the MSS would find, and what exactly Long had hoped to achieve? There had to be more to the story, much more. He was certain of it, and also certain that the Chinese would use any means necessary to get the whole truth out of him.

Song Le came out of the house a few minutes later, walking slowly, helped by a Hong Kong police officer. Lo-Lo was holding tight to her hand, traumatized and bewildered like any six-year-old would be after the past hour.

"They want me to get checked for a head injury," Song Le said quietly.

"I've called in SEAL Team Six," he replied in a murmur. "Your father-in-law told me where the secretary and the foreign ministers are being held."

"Where?" she asked.

"Can't tell you," he said, saw her eyebrows narrow, and added. "I can take you there, and would without hesitation, but I suspect Long has too many allies in high places to let the location go up the line, even through you."

"So I go with you or leave here not knowing?"

"For a while anyway," he said.

She glanced down at her son, whose eyes were watering. "Don't go," Lo-Lo said. "Please, Mother, don't leave me."

Song Le looked at Monarch, and said, "You're on your own."

He smiled, and said, "I think you're going to be a great mom."

The Chinese agent hesitated before kissing him lightly on the cheek. She stepped back, her own cheeks burning, but said, "For what it's worth, I think you're a great thief." Then she and her son started toward a third ambulance just pulling in.

His phone rang.

"Six will be airborne within the hour," Barnett said. "Get to the Shek Kong Airfield. The Chinese have cleared an F-18 Super Hornet to land there and take you to join the SEALs aboard the U.S.S. *George Washington*."

"Where is it?"

"South China Sea. The President ordered the aircraft carrier there as a show of power the morning after Secretary Lawton was taken."

"Hopkins good with my request?"

"Upset that he can't tell the President, who he said has been depressed and removed for the past twenty-four hours. But he's keeping his lips tight."

"Anybody ever tell you you're the best?" he asked.

"What was she blinking? Secretary Lawton?"

Monarch told her.

"Jesus Christ," she whispered. "Who?"

"I don't know."

"Well, go save the day, will you? We'll figure it out later."

Monarch rode in an HKP patrol car to Shek Kong Airfield. Chinese soldiers at the gate were flustered to see their commanding officer come to meet Monarch and escort him inside. The F-18 landed at 9:47 P.M., nine hours and eight minutes until the scheduled execution of the diplomats.

"How far?" Monarch asked the navy pilot, climbing into the navigator's seat, and watching the odd sight of Chinese soldiers refueling a U.S. military jet.

"Twelve hundred and fourteen miles south southeast of here," the pilot replied. "She's sailing toward the Java Sea."

"What's your top speed?"

"Eleven hundred," he replied. "You'll be on deck in just over an hour."

"And Six?"

"They'll land just ahead of you."

Monarch nodded, tugged on the helmet, and placed the oxygen mask over his mouth. They roared off the tarmac at five minutes past ten. He drowsed as they climbed to cruising altitude, his subconscious mind chewing on slices of scenes from the past twenty-four hours.

Latham threw a cherry bomb at him. Tatupu fell, shot from behind. Chavez's hand was blasted by the mercenary agent's cane. Latham told him about the Moon Dragon as he died. Filipina maids mobbed him inside the Poseidon Club. The look on Song Le's face when she realized the little boy was her son. Anna shot Tuul and told Long and his wife that she was going to destroy them. The turtle shell exploded. The maid hit. Madame Long sprawled across the camphor-wood cradle. The pleasant sound of the Moon Dragon's lower leg snapping. Lo-Lo's whimpering before his mother opened her eyes. All these things came and went before his brain finally abandoned them all and plunged into darkness and sleep.

Monarch never heard the pilot calling to him an hour later, and awoke only when his chin cracked off his chest when the jet's tail hook caught the cable and screeched to a halt on the deck of the nuclear aircraft carrier. He looked around groggy and angry at being woken before remembering where he was and why. He was suddenly starving, and realized he hadn't eaten anything in almost fifteen hours.

The canopy rose. The tropical heat surrounded him. He shed the helmet and mask, thanked the pilot, and climbed down the ladder onto a deck that smelled of jet fuel.

"Robin fucking Monarch," said a voice behind him.

Still slightly out of it, he didn't recognize the voice at first. But he instantly knew by sight the lean, muscular, black guy with the short thick beard.

"Deon fucking Owens," Monarch said as if he'd only seen the SEAL the day before and not four years ago. "I didn't know you'd moved up to Six."

Owens said, "Yeah, well, we don't exactly advertise membership."

Monarch shook his hand, said, "Glad to know you're involved."

"Leading," the SEAL said. "I'm a commander now."

"Commander Owens, by all means," Monarch said. "I'm just here to help."

"Promise?"

"What are you trying to say?"

"You, my friend, have a reputation for going off on your own."

"I'm shocked that anyone would say such a thing about me."

Owens studied him a moment before saying, "I'm bringing you in despite a big part of me saying it's a bad idea."

"And here I thought I brought you guys into the game," Monarch said.

"That right? All by yourself?"

"I had some help."

Owens studied him again, then laughed and shook his head. "Let's go below. The rest of my team's waiting."

They went through a hatch and descended several flights of stairs before exiting into the cavernous hold where they kept jets not in use. Crossing through that vast space, Owens said, "There's a rumor about Archie Latham."

"He was in it up to his eyeballs," Monarch said.

"Was?"

"He passed on about this time last night."

"Jesus," Owens said. "Why would *he* be in with terrorists?"

"It's the root of all evil."

That seemed to make sense to the SEAL Team 6 leader, who said, "That's the problem when you go from doing this stuff for God and country to doing it simply for cash money. You lose perspective."

"And your soul unless the money goes somewhere noble."

They reached another hatch, went through it, down a short hall, and into a room used to brief and debrief pilots on their missions. Laid out like a classroom with small desks, the place was filled with hard men with easy dispositions wearing civilian clothes. Monarch knew none of them, and yet knew everything about them at a glance. They were all from different backgrounds, but they were people after his own heart: incredibly trained, but not robots, taught to plan, but also urged to improvise. To a man, they regarded him with suspicion.

"Gentlemen," Owens said, raising his voice. "This is Robin Monarch, handle 'Rogue.' He'll be joining us in the rescue mission."

The SEALs seemed highly displeased at the idea. Monarch didn't take it personally. Special Forces operators have to count on each other in times of tremendous stress. Owens picked up on it as well.

"I don't have time to bore you with a full list of his exploits, but he was part of a JSOC unit in the early days of Afghanistan, and single-handedly stole the Iraqi battle plan before we invaded. I'll deny ever saying it, but Robin's one of the best. I expect you to treat him the way you'd treat anyone assigned to Six."

The SEALs, who'd been uncertain about him, now nodded. One, a big guy with a scruffy red beard named Kyle Thomas said, "We hear you're a thief."

"You heard right," Monarch said.

"You're not going to pick my pocket, are you?"

"Depends on what's in your pocket," Monarch replied, and the place cracked up.

There was a knock at the door and Captain Harris Boone, a naval intelligence officer in his forties, came in, carrying a laptop. He was the only man wearing a uniform, and looked slightly flustered when he said, "We just got your drone data."

Captain Boone gave his laptop a command. Several infrared and thermal feeds came up on a screen on the wall. He speeded them up, saying, "We've flown four over the area in the last two hours. There's thick jungle canopy, but we think we've got them."

The intelligence officer gave his computer another order.

Up on the screen, one of the feeds enlarged, showing red, orange, and yellow heat images. Boone superimposed a map over the feed. Together they showed twenty metal or thatched-roof buildings, single story, many up on stilts on the north bank of the Pulau Indah River where it flowed through jungle and mangrove swamps toward the Karimata Straits of Indonesia, roughly two hundred and forty nautical miles from where the *Niamey* was attacked. There were a dozen thatched-roof structures on the opposite bank. The overall layout on both shores was chaotic, Monarch thought, built like a slum is built, one shack thrown up, and then another with no plan other than survival.

Boats were visible to either shore, some pulled up on the banks, others moored in the channel. But none of them was an oceangoer. Didn't mean anything, Monarch realized. They could have the big boats moored somewhere in deeper water. His attention cut back to the images on the screen.

Several campfires burned among the buildings. Two structures on the north shore and set back farthest from the river glowed with some large internal heat source. And if you looked closely at the thermal images you could make out various bodies lying in some of the buildings or moving around the water's edge.

"How long ago was this taken?" Monarch asked, his attention cruising all over the screen, taking it in, memorizing every detail.

"Twenty minutes ago," the intelligence officer replied.

Monarch walked to the screen and gestured in front of the building throwing off the most heat to a smaller structure that seemed to jut out over the river. Four people were in front of it. The shape of three others showed inside.

"Those are the diplomats," he said. "Got to be."

Commander Owens said, "Makes sense."

For the next two hours, until almost one A.M. in fact, they devised a plan of attack. Monarch found it remarkable to watch the SEALs work. Four members of the team immediately took the drone images, went out into the cavernous hold, and started laying out a reduced schematic of the tiny settlement using chalk on the floor.

At the same time, Owens moderated a strategic free-for-all, letting his men make suggestions about how best to enter and extract the Secretary of State. Monarch listened to it all in silence, synthesizing what he'd heard, and then said, "All these ideas are good, and solid execution might lead to a successful rescue."

"Might?" Owens said. "You saying you've got a better plan?"

"I just think that if you want to dramatically increase the odds of success in this situation, you gotta think a little less like a SEAL and more like an outlaw."

PART V

EXECUTION DAY

42

SIXTY-FIVE MINUTES BEFORE HER scheduled execution, Agnes Lawton roused weakly. She heard men shouting in a patois of local dialect and broken English. There was alarm in several of the voices, and she got the gist that many local members of the Sons of Prophecy had suddenly fled during the night.

"We do, then, without them," said a defiant voice she recognized as Ramelan's. "They want run? Let run. We no need them before, and we no need them now. We finish this. We mere prophecy real."

Then the door to the hut was flung opened, and Ramelan appeared carrying a machete and a flashlight, which he played on her and the Chinese and Indian diplomats behind her.

"Your countries leave you," he said. "They no take us serious. They no pay the ransom. They no let any prisoners go. So they give no choice. Allah waits you in one hour."

He paused and made a show of cradling the butt of the machete with one hand and resting the long wicked blade against his shoulder the way an infantryman might a rifle while marching on parade. Weak and sick as she was, Secretary Lawton would not give the man the satisfaction of showing him any fear or subordination.

"Water," she said. "Food."

"Please," Wali said.

"You need none now," Ramelan said sharply. "Who dies first?"

"I will go first," Agnes Lawton croaked before her colleagues could reply.

"Okay, you first," he said. He grinned icily at her and left.

Secretary Lawton lay in the dark, feeling her grossly swollen face, physically weaker than she thought possible. Four times the malaria had come and gone, and with each fever and sweating she'd felt more wrung out, more fragile.

But sapped as she was, her spirit and her mind remained strong and sharp. It was Sunday evening in the United States, thirty-six hours before the election polls opened. Could that be what this execution was really all about? Was it all part of the plot the NSA picked up on to throw the world into turmoil before the vote? Who would benefit if that happened? A great many people, Secretary Lawton supposed, powerful people who didn't like the current political winds. But would they follow this kind of insane strategy? The risks were mind-boggling. The logistics and secrecy were unimaginable.

On the other hand, what if the Sons of Prophecy were real? What if they were religious fanatics trying to make a name for their brand of zealotry? Would this execution draw recruits to their cause? The unanswered questions cascaded through her mind. Then, as suddenly as they had formed and overwhelmed her, the queries all faded to two: Am I ready to die? Am I strong enough to do this with dignity?

Secretary Lawton rolled over, caught a glimpse of the night sky softening toward dawn. She heard voices, birds calling, and other sounds of the last hour of her life.

"Secretary Lawton?" the Chinese foreign minister said weakly.

"I'm here, Mr. Fung," she managed.

"I wanted to say that it was an honor to have worked with you."

"I second that," Wali said. "You were brave. You are brave."

"We were and are all brave," Secretary Lawton said. "And it was indeed an honor, gentlemen. I for one will not give them the satisfaction of showing fear."

"Nor I," the Chinese foreign minister said.

"Never," Wali said.

Bugs buzzed and whined around her. As the water lapped against the piers beneath her, Secretary Lawton began to steel herself for death. She refused to wallow in the memory of the machete that Ramelan carried. Instead, she prayed, asking God to watch over her husband, her children, and her grandkids, and to give them comfort in the wake of what promised to be a gruesome passing. Then she prayed that her life had ultimately been one of deep purpose and meaning, and that her death would somehow serve a purpose and meaning beyond tragedy.

Halfway around the world, Ibrahim Hafiz, roused from sleep on a bunk aboard the massive container ship he'd crashed sideways across the mouth of the Suez Canal. The ship had suffered structural damage, not enough to sink her, but enough that with the tides she groaned, creaked, and moaned. The noise that brought Hafiz awake was different, however. It was the tread of Abu Ismailia and his men bearing heavy loads up the stairs.

He roused and checked his watch. One of his distant brothers in the Sons of Prophecy network would be striking another blow in less than an hour: the execution of three leaders of the Satan countries. He wanted to see them die. The ship's electrical and communications systems still worked. So did the engines. As a result, they'd been able to watch the effects of their noble act live on Al Jazeera and CNN.

Hafiz figured that was where Abu Ismailia and his men were going. He sat up, turned on the light, and dressed, thinking how blessed he was that the Sons of Prophecy had come calling two months after he was fired from the only job he'd ever loved. How generous God had been offering the opportunity to take revenge and in so doing strike a blow for religious freedom.

Hafiz left the bunkroom, sliding one leg and shuffling the other, over, and over, until he'd reached the ship's mess hall and galley. To his surprise, it was empty. The dining area was where they'd watched the news coverage the past few days, and he thought they would all be in there.

Hafiz climbed higher and found Abu Ismailia and his men sitting on the floor below the windows of the wheelhouse. Brilliant lights shone through the windows from spotlights the Egyptians had put up. The Sons of Prophecy fighters were dressed once again in the black wetsuits they'd worn during the takeover of the ship. There were also just as armed.

"What is happening?" Hafiz asked Abu Ismailia nervously. "Will they attack now? Is it time for our martyrdom?"

There'd been only one attempt to board the ship so far, and that had been within moments of the *Rose of the South* smashing across the mouth of the canal. Abu Ismailia and his men had opened fire on the Egyptian soldiers from above, driving them back. They then hung the Sons of Prophecy banner over the side and, since then, there'd been several attempts to make contact via radio, but little more. They'd heard, however, that U.S. Special Forces teams were in the area.

"It would make sense that they attack now," Abu Ismailia said, checking his watch. "They think we will be waiting for news of the executions, distracted."

Hafiz realized he was unlikely to live through the next few hours. But this was his fate, and he would gladly face death.

"What can I do?" he asked. "I can shoot a gun."

Abu Ismailia smiled, said, "When the time comes, brother."

Something big, something very big exploded not far from the ship. The spotlights flickered and died. Abu Ismailia and his men said nothing, didn't move.

"What do we do?" Hafiz asked desperately.

"We listen," Abu Ismailia said tersely.

Hafiz tried to listen, but his curiosity soon became anxiety. He had to know what was happening. The crippled ship's pilot got to his feet, peered out through the window.

"The lights," he said. "All the lights for kilometers are dark. The power station must have failed."

Sirens began to wail.

"The power station failed because we bombed it," Abu Ismailia said, as automatic gunfire sounded from the same direction as the huge explosion.

The SOP leader was on his feet and just a few feet from Hafiz now.

The other men were getting to their feet, grabbing gear.

"Why?" Hafiz said. "What is the—?"

A red laser cut the darkness of the wheelhouse, found the center of the crippled harbor pilot's forehead.

"It's time for us to leave, and time for you to go," Abu Ismailia said.

Before Hafiz could say a word, a silenced round blew through his skull, and ended his visions of vengeance and paradise.

Abu Ismailia squatted by Hafiz's body, and put the pistol in the dead pilot's hand, and a machine pistol on the floor beside him, saying, "If it wasn't for the gimp, we never would have pulled this off you know."

There were grunts of sad agreement, and then Abu Ismailia and his men left the bridge, and climbed down to the deck. Ignoring the creaks and groans the ship was making, they walked to the starboard side, which faced the entrance to the canal.

In the darkness they could hear people yelling, and flashlights playing about, and more gunfire. Sirens wailed from near and far now. Over by the repair docks, generators roared to life and already the sodium lamps there were glowing weakly. But it would be many hours if not days until power was fully restored to the area.

One by one, they jumped off the railing, falling more than ten stories before plunging into the warm, deep water. Abu Ismailia was the last to make the leap. He jumped as he'd been taught long ago, holding his nose, cradling his testicles, and pinning his ankles together.

Hitting at that speed sent a jolt up through his knees and hips, and he submerged a good ten feet before slowing and swimming back up.

When he breached the surface, he took a deep breath and whistled softly to his men. They answered one by one. Then they formed up in a group, and as a single unit began to swim up the canal toward the rendezvous point.

43

MONARCH SURFACED AMID VEGETATION and roots that over-hung the steep riverbank. He wore a black scuba mask and black combat-style clothes, gloves, a headset, a mesh utility vest that held a Glock 21, six full clips, two flash-bang grenades, two real grenades, and a nifty battle-hatchet about fourteen inches long. It seemed that the SEAL Team 6 boys all swore by the hatchets when things got sporty.

He was seventy yards downstream of the settlement where they believed Secretary Lawton was being held, seeing it for the first time in the low dawn light and the jungle fog, a loose village of wooden huts, some tin-roofed, others thatched, including several that jutted out over the water on bamboo piers. Cook fires burned on both banks of the river, throwing the scent of smoke and meat frying into the air. Music blared against a short-wave radio that trilled the news, some update about the crises in the Suez and Panama canals. Shallow draft dugout canoes with outboard motors were roped to posts set along the banks. Two bigger boats, sleek oceangoers that were not on the drone feed, now bobbed dead center of the river channel, bows facing downstream toward the sea. Someone was preparing an escape.

Commander Owens and the big red-bearded SEAL Kyle Thomas surfaced beside Monarch, wearing similar vests and carrying dry bags on their backs. They each took a quick look around.

"Like Kurtz's place in Cambodia," Owens whispered.

"As I remember it got napalmed at the end of the movie," Monarch replied.

"Like that idea," Thomas said.

Monarch checked his watch, said, "Change in plan. Take the big boats in the channel first. Set for oh-five-fifty."

Thomas nodded and slipped beneath the water.

The SEAL leader tapped Monarch's headset, whispered, "Use your comm. Saves lives and your hearing."

The headset, another favored SEAL device, was an Atlantic Dominator, which met IP67 waterproof standards and featured bone-conduction receivers, and detachable earbuds designed to buffer the sound of close-quarter gunfire. He turned it on.

Owens seemed to whisper inside Monarch's head: "I'll cover the bank as you go."

Monarch ducked under and swam in the murky water, right up against the reeds and the exposed mangrove roots. He grabbed the roots and used them to claw his way forward. He carried a black snorkel, but only stuck it up for a breath every ten yards or so. And he exhaled into the vegetation in a slow-steady stream so that any bubbles hitting the surface would be camouflaged from the bank.

He surfaced beneath one of the huts up on stilts over the river. The water there was surprisingly deep. His feet could not find bottom. The lashed bamboo floor was no more than two feet over his head. An outboard motor coughed and buzzed. Across the river, Monarch saw in the strengthening light two men loading nets into one of those dugout canoes.

Owens surfaced. Monarch gestured at one of the stilts supporting the hut overhead. The SEAL Team 6 leader treaded toward it. Monarch glanced at his watch. Seven minutes thirty seconds left. He needed to move on and fast.

Taking a deep breath, he ducked and swam as if many lives depended on it. He came up under the second hut, reached down to his lower vest, and came up with a small packet of plastic explosives attached to a tiny waterproof battery and timer. He strapped the device to one of the stilts with electrical tape.

Monarch swam on. The river got shallower, no more than three feet deep, and he realized that one of Ramelan's men might see him in the water and simply shoot him in the back. But he came up for air a fourth time without incident, immediately aware of the outboard motor revving and backfiring as it left the village and went downstream. He heard a boom in the distance, realized it was thunder. The water was barely waist deep here. Even with the overcast skies and the coming rain, daylight ruled. Now even someone across the river might spot him beneath the hut.

He checked his watch—6:55 A.M.

Five minutes left.

Monarch became aware of a generator running, and then footsteps as several men approached. A door creaked open in the hut above him. Chains moved across the floor before a man said, "The world will now see the true power of the Sons of Prophecy."

"I want to say good-bye to my family, Ramelan," said Secretary Lawton feebly. "You must grant me that."

"Get up, woman," the man said roughly. "We get nothing."

Three minutes forty. More footsteps overhead.

"You can't do this!" Fung shouted.

"Leave her!" Wali said. "I'll go in her place."

"She is first to go."

Footsteps. The door opened again. Cheers went up. There was obviously a crowd of Ramelan's followers gathered for Secretary Lawton's death walk. Men praised Allah for his greatness. Others screamed their anger at the United States, China and India, too.

Two minutes fifty. Monarch heard the crackle of transmissions through his cheek and jawbones as various SEAL operators muttered their positions on the move to surround the settlements on both sides of the river.

"This is Rogue," he said softly. "They're moving Lawton for execution right now. Override the timers."

"Switching to remote," Thompson replied. "Coming at you, Rogue."

Monarch wanted to attack the hut above him, but he knew he had to take cover. He crouched and protected his face just before a devastating explosion ripped through the gas tanks of one of the ocean-going boats moored at mid-channel, blowing it to smithereens. Debris flew in every direction, followed by a second boom and roar as the other seaworthy boat went up in flames.

Monarch tore the hatchet out and chopped at the bottom of the bamboo floor. Gunfire started from three hundred and sixty degrees. The black anodized head of the battle-ax was hand-forged, incredibly sharp, and brutally effective. It tore big gashes in the floor the way a utility knife might a cardboard box. With five blows he'd opened a hole big enough to muscle up and through. The Chinese and Indian diplomats were looking at him in total shock.

"Stay down and you'll be safe," he said in English and again in Chinese.

Monarch did not wait for a reply. He moved toward the door, seating the battle-hatchet in its sheath, and grabbing one of the real grenades and the Glock, while saying, "I have the ministers alive."

"Acknowledged," Owens said.

"Advancing in search of Lawton."

"I'm on your left flank."

Outside there was steady gunfire and the yelling of men trapped in chaos.

Monarch thrived in chaos. He yanked open the hut door, taking in the scene. Fifteen or twenty men were scattering, seeking to take cover or to pick up arms to defend the village from the assault. The three closest to him carried AKs. He shot the first one at eight feet, the second at twenty, and the third at thirty-five before any of them could return fire.

He hurled the grenade hard after the scattering men, and threw himself forward onto the ground. The explosion provoked more screaming. Monarch got to his feet and took off in a low, zigzag sprint toward the larger hut set back from the riverbank, the one that had been throwing so much heat when the drones flew overhead.

Out of the corner of his eye, Monarch saw Owens flanking him about forty yards to his left. The SEAL leader threw a second grenade, and they both crashed to the mud once more. The blast took down four more of Ramelan's men. But others had regrouped and returned fire as Monarch and Owens lurched to their feet. They started angling toward the cement block buildings where they believed Secretary Lawton had been taken.

If the Sons of Prophecy wanted to stream the diplomat's execution live on the Internet, they needed power, which meant they needed a generator. Monarch figured it was in one of those two buildings, and Lawton was in the other. Then he smelled diesel and knew the generator was in the smaller structure nearer to him, with the Secretary of State in the one closest to Owens.

The SEAL leader almost got there first. Then gunfire erupted behind him. Owens was hit, stumbled, fell forward, and behind an empty 55-gallon oilcan.

"I'm hit. Can't feel my right leg," he grunted. "Go."

Monarch was more an artist than craftsman now, single-minded in his purpose, willing to try anything to save Secretary Lawton. The heavy wooden door to the cement block structure was shut and had no handle, telling him it was barred in some manner from the inside. He didn't go near the door, but around the side of the cement block structure with the assault still raging all around him. Holstering the Glock, he freed one of the flash-bang grenades and the battle-ax.

That's when he heard Ramelan shouting inside. "They want me to let you go! But you foretold. We prophecy. I son of prophecy! Nothing stops me!"

"Big fire in the hole," a SEAL's voice said over the headset.

A massive explosion erupted on the other side of the river. It threw fire forty-feet in the air as the settlement's gasoline supplies blew. The blast waves hit Monarch and shook the building. He fell to one knee, noticed it was up on cinder blocks. Monarch saw opportunity and took it, pulling the pin on the flash-bang grenade, and bowling it deep beneath the structure.

He was running back the way he'd come when it went off. A searing metallic light flared out from below the building making a sound louder than a regular grenade, so powerful he felt the waves of it strike his ankles. Switching the ax to his left hand, he yanked out the pistol again. He rounded the side of the building into a full-on gun battle between the advancing SEALs and the last of the fanatics.

Monarch darted to the front door.

"Help!" he heard Agnes Lawton scream inside. "I'm here!"

Monarch swung the battle-ax where the door met the frame. Wood splintered at his first and second blows. On the third the hatchet blade broke through. Heaving his good shoulder against the door, he heard it crack before giving way.

He stormed into the shambles of a makeshift TV studio. Two cameras attached to tripods had crashed to the floor, which was littered with glass from the photographer's lights that had fallen and shattered when the flash-bang grenade went off. Secretary Lawton was strapped to a chair on the far side of the room, frightened, and trying to twist her head around to look for Ramelan.

The fanatic, obviously stunned by the explosion, was nevertheless staggering up behind her sporting a deranged look and a machete. Monarch drew and swung the gun on him, pulled the trigger, tried to kill him.

But nothing happened. The trigger didn't pull. The gun didn't go off. He looked at the Glock, and saw the action was jammed open. The spent casing and the loading bullet were slammed together. When had that happened? When did Glocks start jamming? He was frozen for less than a second, but it was long enough to see victory erupting in Ramelan's eyes.

Grinning and shaking in bliss, as if he saw prophecy materializing all around him, the fanatical pirate held the machete two-fisted as he reared back and cocked his entire body so that he might behead Agnes Lawton in a single, powerful cut. But before the pirate could begin his vicious swing, Monarch dropped the Glock, flipped the battle-ax to his right hand, and hurled the hatchet like a tomahawk.

Ramelan's machete made a savage arcing chop toward the nape of Lawton's neck. But five inches before it could bite skin and spine, the butt of the battle-ax's handle hit him in the face, knocked him off balance. The machete lost power, angle, and direction, but still struck a hard glancing blow against the side of the diplomat's head, causing it to whipsaw and sag, but not before it gashed open a wicked flap of bloody scalp and skin that drooped down over her ear.

The fanatic saw the wound, and reacted like a wolf to blood even as Monarch leaped to protect the secretary. Ramelan reared back to chop at her a second time, desperate to end his prophesized task.

Monarch was faster, stepping across Lawton's unmoving legs and throwing his arms around the sides of her head and toward the terrorist. His left fist pounded the inside of the pirate's inner right elbow. The strike there interrupted his swing before he could get his full weight behind it. His elbow bent. The machete slapped harmlessly against the side of Monarch's left forearm.

"No!" Ramelan roared, stepping back, seeking space and angle to chop at her and Monarch again.

But the instant Monarch felt the fanatic's muscles reversing course, he bowled Secretary Lawton over, and jumped across her and the chair, following the retreating energy, seeking to close space and angles of attack, doing what life and training had taught him to do in times of extreme violence.

Monarch threw an uppercut at Ramelan with the heel of his palm leading. It clipped the man's chin, causing his head to snap back, causing his weight to shift to his heels. And yet it wasn't a good enough strike to end the fight. Monarch went to unleash an overhand right, to hit the man hard on the bridge of his nose, but it seemed Ramelan was experienced in hand-to-hand combat as well. Though moving backward, Ramelan relaxed and turned his right hand and the machete in a spiral downward and inward. His left hand caught the back of the blade, turned it horizontal. With both hands he pushed the keen edge toward the oncoming blow.

Monarch stopped his knuckles an inch from the machete. Ramelan popped the blade at Monarch's face, missing, but putting him on the defensive. Now it was Monarch who was jumping backward, seeking to create space. His right calf caught up on the leg of Secretary Lawton's chair, and he stumbled in his retreat.

Ramelan's left hand let go the tip of the machete blade. He slashed back and down, just caressing Monarch's right cheek. Monarch felt the skin split and hot blood flow. The fanatic came back the other way with the next slash, this one upward and at a diagonal, as if he meant to cut him from the left hip to the right shoulder.

The machete sliced Monarch's clothes, but then struck and skittered across the Kevlar vest before it could reach vital organs. On instinct, Monarch made a half step to the side, coiled and exploded back at Ramelan.

The pirate tried that neat trick again, got the blade up, horizontal to meet any in-coming attack. Instead, Monarch feinted high before ducking his hands beneath Ramelan's and grabbing the man by the underside of his wrists.

The men grappled, each trying to push the machete toward the other. Monarch outweighed the Indonesian by at least fifty pounds, but Ramelan was surprisingly strong and fueled by some volcanic hatred. The fanatic kneed Monarch so hard in the right thigh that it felt electric. His quad went into spasm. His leg got wobbly.

Ramelan felt the sudden weakness, and kneed Monarch again in the same spot, numbing the leg before pressing in for the kill. Monarch stared into the fanatic's eyes, seeing how desperately Ramelan wanted to cut his throat.

"Not today," Monarch said through gritted teeth.

He rocked his weight to his good leg, and spun rearward. The countermove did not break Ramelan's grip on the machete, but it destroyed his balance, which allowed Monarch to haul him around and fling him back against the wall.

The pirate tried to fight back, tried to push the cutting edge toward Monarch once more. But the thief had clever tricks of his own. He let the blade come his way a fraction of an inch before he released the grips of his thumbs on Ramelan's wrists and clamped them instead against the back of his hands, about two inches below the ring fingers. Then he used every bit of his strength and physical cunning to twist and turn the fanatic's wrists and hands inward and down. That maneuver didn't break his grip either. But it didn't matter.

As Ramelan fought to prevent Monarch from continuing that twisting inward squeeze on his hands and wrists, he allowed his elbows to rise. The pirate tried to get off another knee strike, but when he did, he rose up on his tiptoes, and the machete blade completed its rotation. The keen edge was facing him now.

Ramelan went insane, kneeing Monarch in the thighs and hips again and again until the machete blade reached Ramelan's throat, cut through the skin and found cartilage. The kneeing stopped, but Ramelan continued to glare and spit at Monarch.

"You no end it," he said hoarsely. "I am prophesy. The serpent of moon's wife saw it."

"Then she must have seen me, too," Monarch said and threw his weight forward and heaved his arms sideways.

Five inches of honed machete blade passed through Ramelan's windpipe. The last nine inches went deeper, severing arteries, and neck muscle until it struck bone. The fanatic fell at Monarch's feet, his head flopping back off his spine.

Spattered everywhere with the terrorist's blood, gasping with relief and exhaustion, Monarch leaned against the wall for a long moment before pivoting to look at the Secretary of State.

Still tied by her wrists to the chair, Agnes Lawton was sprawled on her side on the floor, facedown, and unmoving.

Monarch gaped at Secretary Lawton, felt his stomach fall a thousand feet. After everything he'd done, after all the danger and lives taken he'd come machete close to saving her, but failed. She'd been right there in front of him and he'd failed. Failed. He sat down hard beside her, sick in his gut, and wanting to weep at the injustice of her dying at the hands of an insane bastard like—

He stopped, stared at her head. It was covered in blood from that brutal gash that had almost skinned off a palm-sized piece of her scalp and right ear. Sewing-needle sized little spurts of blood were still erupting from cut vessels.

Monarch's breath caught in his throat. He fumbled for the headset dislodged during his fight with Ramelan. He instantly heard the chatter of the SEALs, and realized the shooting had stopped.

"Owens, this is Rogue," Monarch shouted.

"Go, Rogue."

"I've got her! I need a medic. Now!"

Less than thirty seconds passed before Ryan Thomas, the big red-bearded SEAL, charged in.

"She's alive," Monarch said. "Breathing on her own. Pulse solid. But I didn't dare move her."

"Smart," Thomas said, rummaging through his dry pack for supplies. He glanced around the room. "You make a blood bath of things, don't you?"

"I could have used some fucking help."

"We were pinned down," said Owens, who came in, limping, aided by another SEAL. He'd been shot high through the flank of his right butt cheek. The shock had paralyzed his right leg for several minutes, but then his feeling had come back like a hot poker going through him. The fact that he was on his feet at all was a testament to the SEAL team leader's toughness.

But when Owens looked down on the Secretary of State and Thomas working on her wounds, he said, "Agnes Lawton, you are one tough old bird."

Monarch smiled and nodded his head. "Ornery. Feisty."

"I heard that!" Secretary Lawton in a weak, scolding whisper.

Monarch startled, looked down. Her eyes were open. She was looking up at him, said, "Feisty I'll take. But old and ornery?"

"Don't move, Madam Secretary," Thomas said. "You've got a nasty cut here I'm working on and you took a serious blow to the head."

"And who are you?" she said, unable to see him.

"Chief Petty Officer Kyle Thomas, SEAL Team Six," he replied as he gingerly daubed at the flayed wound with gauze drenched in antiseptic.

"And you?"

"Robin. Robin Monarch."

"SEAL Team Six?"

"No, I'm a freelance thief," he said.

Her expression turned puzzled. She repeated his name, and then said, "But you were a Ranger once. Didn't you steal—?"

"That was a long time ago," Monarch said, pleased that her mind seemed sharp. Perhaps she had taken enough of a blow to knock her out, but not enough to give her a full-on concussion.

"Madam Secretary, I'm Commander Deon Owens," Owens said, limping around where she could see him. "It's good to see you alive."

"It's good to be alive, Commander," she replied. "Can I have some water? Have you got Fung and Wali?"

"Both safe," Monarch said.

She sighed and nodded gratefully, closing her eyes a moment, and then opened them again. Beat up as she was, the woman possessed deep reservoirs of energy, Monarch thought. He was watching her get stronger by the minute.

"Secretary Lawton," Owens said. "Who do you want me to notify first?"

"My husband. My boys. My grandkids. The President. The whole world!" She began to weep. "I thought I was going to die. I've got a chance to be a better person now."

"Give me a second before we make any calls," Monarch said, crouching beside her. "Do you remember what you were blinking in Morse code when they were making the videos?"

She closed her eyes and nodded.

"We saw it," Monarch said. "And because of it I've kept my contact with Washington to a bare minimum."

"Okay."

Owens said, "Wait, run all this by me again. What were you blinking?"

Secretary Lawton told them.

Both SEALs, men used to facing extreme danger, dropped their chins and stared at her. "For real?" Commander Owens said.

She tried to get up, saying, "I had a long time to think here. It's the only explanation for—"

"Hold on there a second, Madam Secretary," Thomas said. He had lifted that nasty flap of skin back into place and was pressing it into place with gauze pads. "And please try not to move while I finish dressing this wound. You might have a cracked skull or spinal damage."

"I don't," she said.

"You don't know that."

"I do," she said, lifting her head and rotating it slightly. "See."

"That could have gone badly," Thomas said, displeased.

"It didn't," Secretary Lawton said. "Now please help me up. I can't abide talking to someone when I'm laying on the floor with blood all around me."

Thomas looked at Monarch. "Gimme a hand?"

Thomas held the flap of skin in place against Secretary Lawton's head and got his hands under her hips. Together he and Monarch lifted her. Owens set the chair upright, and they lowered her into it. She seemed to have a moment of vertigo, but it passed. Thomas began wrapping the scalp in place.

"So what are you saying?" Owens asked Secretary Lawton. "That you don't want me to tell anyone that we've got you?"

She looked pained, and hesitant at that idea.

Monarch said, "There are one or two people we could tell. But it might be better if most people back in Washington didn't know you made it, at least for a little while."

Secretary Lawton thought about that, said, "Let them think I'm dead?"

"Even better," Monarch said, smiling and gesturing to the bandage on her head. "You're brain dead."

44

FEELING BEAT UP AND wired, and looking worse, Monarch sat in a chair in the White House chief of staff's office, suffering a colossal sinus headache from the long supersonic flight. He was taking decongestants to fight it, and was sipping triple espressos to stay awake.

The President's chief of staff, Cynthia Blayless was sitting across her desk from him, looking mightily ticked off that Monarch would not answer any of her questions before he briefed the President.

"Well, then," Blayless said sharply. "Quitting cigarettes is the only way I could make this day worse, and I'm not that much of a masochist."

With that the chief of staff got up from behind her desk, took her purse, and went out onto the verandah where it was a beautiful autumn day with a brilliant blue sky at odds with the solemn tenor of the city. From his chair, Monarch could see lowered flags flying. He could also watch three television screens built into the walls of Blayless's office, tuned to Fox, MSNBC, and CNN.

The coverage depicted a nation in turmoil and mourning after news had leaked out of the White House suggesting that Secretary of State Agnes Lawton had been badly brain injured during a rescue attempt that managed to save the Indian and Chinese foreign ministers.

Internet users around the world who'd been monitoring the SOP Web site had seen Secretary Lawton in the execution chair, with Ramelan behind her wielding his machete. The world heard the explosions and the initial gunfire of the rescue attempt before the feed died. For hours no one knew what had happened, and people were still holding out hope for the Secretary of State's well-being.

That hope was dashed by word that while foreign ministers Fung and Wali were safe and recovering at a hospital in Singapore, Secretary Lawton was on life-support aboard a flying military hospital making its way back to Andrews Air Force Base. The President was meeting with his advisors, expected to make a statement around noon, and then proceeding to Andrews to meet the flight.

At the same time, China, India, Hong Kong, Thailand, Egypt, and Panama had hundreds of investigators combing for evidence to help them root out the Sons of Prophecy. After a bombing cut all power for miles around the mouth of the Suez Canal, Egyptian soldiers raided the container ship blocking the shipping lane.

They encountered no opposition and discovered four corpses aboard. All four men, including Ibrahim Hafiz, a canal pilot, were known religious radicals. Hafiz had been recently fired after attempting to recruit canal workers to jihad. It remained unclear whether Hafiz or the other men committed suicide, or were shot and left behind by forces unknown. In Panama, a similar dawn raid yielded similar results. There was no armed opposition, and the corpses of three known anarchists were found aboard.

"What is indisputable is that to date no member of the Sons of Prophecy has been taken alive," the FOX anchor intoned. "The terrorist organization remains for now in the shadows, a potent violent threat around the globe."

It wasn't true that no members had been taken alive, Monarch thought. Then again, he doubted the Chinese were making any kind of announcement regarding the Moon Dragon until they'd forced him to tell all.

He glanced at Blayless still out smoking on the colonnade, and then looked back to the news coverage. The Dow, the S&P, and the NASDAQ had gone limit down again. Trading on all three exchanges and the futures markets halted thirty-four minutes after the opening bell that Monday morning.

Politically, the election was being declared over before the voting even started. According to overnight sampling, seventy-five percent of the electorate held a negative view of how the Sand administration had handled the SOP crisis. The pundits were saying that the final nail had been surely hammered into the lid of Vice President Vaught's campaign coffin.

A knock on the door broke his attention. Dr. Hopkins looked in, nodded, and said: "The President will see you now, Robin."

The French doors opened and a strong warm breeze blew in, carrying the faint odor of tobacco smoke when the chief of staff came back in off the colonnade, popping a mint candy into her mouth, and saying, "Shall we?"

Monarch waited until she'd passed, then stood. He straightened his necktie and jacket, touched his bandaged hand, his bandaged face, his sore ribs and traps, and then followed her and the CIA director out into the hallway. A few steps away, Blayless knocked at a door, and opened it into the Oval Office.

Entering, Monarch scanned the room, seeing the same administrative officials who'd been present during his last visit. The President sat behind his desk. Drawn, sallow, and looking years older than the last time Monarch had seen him, Sand was hunched over and scribbling a memo. Shaken, Elise Peck, the national security advisor, had her arms crossed and resting on her thighs as she sat on the edge of the couch. Chairman of the Joint Chiefs Admiral Shipman stood by the mantel, holding a coffee cup and saucer, playing the stoic warrior, and tracking Monarch with a hard gaze.

In the near wingback chair, Vice President Vaught's posture suggested he was suffering ulcers or kidney stones. Monarch was surprised to see him here the day before the vote, but Vaught obviously believed his chances of being elected president were now next to nil.

Beside the Vice President, Bill Lawton, the Secretary of State's husband, looked off into the worst nightmare of his life. Homeland Security chief Ricky Lee Jameson was grimly entering from a door on the opposite side of the Oval Office. Behind him came a woman Monarch recognized as Attorney General Patricia Black, who was new to the situation as far as he knew.

President Sand got up from the Roosevelt desk looking like he hadn't slept in days. "Monarch," he said, shaking his hand. "I'm grateful for all you—"

"Grateful!" roared Lawton, whose face had turned beat red. "He failed. He said he'd get her back. He promised!"

"Bill," the President said sharply. "This man risked his life repeatedly to save your wife. I think we at least ought to hear his version of what happened."

Lawton chewed the air before nodding and hanging his head. "I'm sorry . . . Mr. Monarch. I was praying . . . It just wasn't supposed to turn out this way."

"It's all right, sir," Monarch said softly. "We're all praying for Agnes."

Everyone else in the room nodded.

"Robin," President Sand said. "The floor is yours."

All eyes turned coldly on him, and Monarch knew he had to be careful to describe the events as accurately as he could and let them draw their own conclusions. Quickly and succinctly, he began by describing the motorcycle attack soon after his arrival in the Philippines.

"How did they know to attack you?" Admiral Shipman asked.

"Good question," Monarch said. "And I don't have a good answer."

Instead, he went on to describe the search that he, Song Le, and Bashir, conducted aboard the *Niamey,* and how they'd been seized and taken to Saigon. He recounted the ambush assault in the Apocalypse Now Bar, and his trip to Bangkok to visit Archie Latham.

"I think Latham thought he was throwing me off course when he directed us toward the Malay pirate Mahdi," Monarch said. "But inadvertently it led us to Kuala Lumpur and Tengku, the Indonesian fence and arms dealer, which led us back around to Latham."

He described the mercenary agent's last words, and how Song Le had linked them to Long Chan-Juan, the Moon Dragon, a powerful triad leader and the father of her late husband.

"Wait," National Security Advisor Peck said, confused. "Was that a coincidence or something this triad guy wanted?"

"I honestly can't answer that yet either," Monarch replied. "But I know Song Le told me she's going to find out exactly how and why she was assigned to the case, and let us know. And I'm sure the Chinese are interrogating the Moon Dragon as we speak."

He described the assault on Ramelan's hideout, and his efforts to save Secretary Lawton. "Sir, I went straight to your wife," Monarch said to Bill Lawton. "She was bleeding profusely from a scalp wound, and . . . well . . ."

Tears welled in Lawton's eyes, and he hung his head again. "Was she at all awake? Did she know what was happening to her?"

"Before she was hit, she was awake, and knew what was happening," Monarch said. "She was fighting, and very brave."

Lawton nodded numbly, and then asked in a quavering voice: "Who was this Long in the greater scheme of things? Was he part of the Sons of Prophecy? Was he the leader? Or was he taking orders?"

"I'm sure we'll know more as the Chinese tell us more," Monarch said. "But my sense, for what it's worth, is that the Moon Dragon was integrally involved in the conspiracy, at least as far as events in Asia were concerned."

"Stop," Homeland Security director Jameson said, holding up his hand. "The triad leader. Is he Muslim?"

"No."

"Why would an Asian organized crime boss forge an alliance with an Islamic terrorist group, Islamic or otherwise?" National Security Advisor Peck asked.

"I don't think Long would have forged any kind of alliance with a known terrorist group," Monarch said, and then paused.

"What does that mean?" Vice President Vaught asked. "Be precise, man."

Monarch looked at Sand, and said, "I think there are better people to explain this part of it, Mr. President. With your permission?"

Sand nodded, and looked to Attorney General Black, who crossed to the doors to the White House's East Colonnade. She opened them. Flanked by Marines in dress blues, Gloria Barnett came in pushing a wheelchair. The figure in the chair was hunched over and attached to an IV line. But neither the black shawl she wore over her bandaged head nor the terrible swelling in her face could mask her identity.

Gasps went up all around the Oval Office.

"Agnes!" Bill Lawton cried, lurching to his feet and rushing to his wife's side. "My God, they said you were brain dead!"

"We did not say she was brain dead, Bill," the President said. "We suggested it."

Lawton looked up from his wife in confusion, and then as if he wanted to punch Sand in the nose. "What kind of cruel joke was that supposed to be? The flags . . . all of it?"

From the grumbling and nods Monarch saw, the other administration officials were not happy at being misled either.

Sounding weak and conflicted, Secretary Lawton patted her husband's hand before nodding to the others assembled, and saying, "A necessary deception, I'm afraid."

Before her husband could react, Secretary Lawton removed the shawl, revealing the thick white bandage wrapped about her head. "I look like Princess Leia, don't you think?" she asked, trying to diffuse the tension.

But instead the room erupted into questions and exclamations that were summed up by Vice President Vaught, who yelled, "What in God's name is going on here? I want answers. Now!"

The Secretary of State and President exchanged glances. He nodded.

Agnes Lawton said, "When Mr. Monarch described the tortuous course that brought him to the Moon

Dragon and to me, I had a similar reaction, that something didn't quite feel right."

Homeland Security director Jameson said, "What didn't feel right?"

Monarch said, "The idea that someone like this Moon Dragon, a lifelong criminal mastermind, would lend support to fanatical terrorists bent on wreaking havoc in a series of attacks all over the world."

National Security Advisor Peck complained, "But didn't you just tell us that this triad leader was integral to the Sons of Prophecy conspiracy?"

Before anyone could respond to that, Secretary Lawton said, "I heard my captors refer to the 'Serpent of the Moon,' and his wife who could see the future. So, yes, I think Long Chan-Juan was integral to the Sons of Prophecy conspiracy, but I have many reasons to suspect that using terror to provoke radical religious change in India, China, and the U.S. was not the goal of the attacks or my kidnapping."

"Exactly," Monarch said. "Think about it this way. What if there was no terror group? What if—?"

Vice President Vaught cried, "Jesus Christ, the Sons of Prophecy blew up a train station in Delhi, engaged and defeated PLA units in China, and halted all traffic in the two most important canals in the world. What else would you call their activities? And there were known terrorists found at every incident site."

The national security advisor chimed in, "And all recent chatter clearly indicates the SOP has sprung into being as an umbrella organization linking disparate terror cells and organizations into a global movement."

"Maybe," Secretary Lawton replied. "But remember that all the terrorists were found conveniently dead. Why? And the chatter the NSA's picking up now? What if it was all disinformation gone viral? What if it was designed to help the Moon Dragon create the image and fear of a global terrorist organization that he could use to shield his true purposes."

"Such as what?" General Shipman asked, sounding highly skeptical.

Secretary Lawton looked at Gloria Barnett, who up until now had been silently observing the meeting. "Gloria?"

"Yes, Madam Secretary," Barnett said, looking around confidently.

"Who is this woman?" Chief of Staff Blayless asked.

"Gloria Barnett, one of the smartest people I've met in years," Secretary Lawton said.

Monarch had to smile and he saw Barnett blush at the reaction of every other person present, all of whom no doubt thought themselves the smartest people the secretary had met in years.

"Goddamn it," Vice President Vaught said. "Give me one good reason why we ought not to think of this as terror, pure and simple?"

"Hundreds of billions of dollars," Barnett replied. "Song Le found files that clearly indicated that Long Chan-Juan was preparing a gigantic move into the gambling industry in mainland China, where today there are no legal casinos of any sort. All casino-style gambling in the region is currently restricted to the Special Administrative Region of Macau. But what if the Moon

Dragon's plot was to get the Chinese to change the law, and allow him to be the first and dominant force bringing gambling to the mainland?"

Monarch saw skeptical faces all around. So did Barnett, who pressed on with her argument, "The Chinese love gambling. It's in their DNA. They spend forty billion a year on it in Macau, and that's a very restricted area with all sorts of limits on currency importation from the mainland. Think of what would happen if billions of Chinese people could suddenly gamble legally. The potential profits would be absolutely stupefying. As I said, it would easily be hundreds of billions of dollars every year. The man who got in first would be among the richest people in the world, if not the richest."

"I'm hearing a lot of conjecture, and very few facts, Mr. President," Homeland Security director Jameson complained. "How in God's name do these attacks in any way shape or form lead to an opening up of China to gambling? Hard facts now."

"We can't give you hard facts right now, Ricky," Secretary Lawton said, holding up her hands before any more objections could arise. "But consider this scenario, and look at it from Beijing's perspective. There's suddenly a global terror organization brazen enough to not only bomb a subway station in Delhi, but to block the canals, kidnap the Chinese foreign minister, and ambush a PLA convoy on Chinese soil. What would Beijing's logical reaction be? I mean from a national security perspective."

There were several moments of silence before National Security Advisor Peck said, "They'd immediately increase military spending."

Admiral Shipman nodded in agreement. "They'd build up their army to protect their power in case of an open rebellion."

Pleased by their answers, Secretary Lawton said, "How big an increase?"

"Fifty percent," the chairman of the Joint Chiefs of Staff replied. "Maybe seventy-five."

"Exactly our thinking, Admiral," Barnett replied. "Now add to this mix the fact that despite Beijing's continual denials, there's undoubtedly a gigantic real estate bubble about to burst over there. That ghost city where the Sons of Prophecy attacked the PLA convoy and hundreds of others are proof of that. When the bubble pops, Beijing suddenly won't have the revenues to spend on a dramatic expansion of the Chinese military."

Barnett looked to Secretary Lawton, who said, "Unless they allow casino gambling on the mainland, with Beijing collecting a hefty percentage of the take. Suddenly, the Chinese army has as much money as it needs to stave off the threat of the Sons of Prophecy or any other group that might take the attack on the PLA in Mongolia as evidence of internal weakness."

Silence held the room for several moments before Vice President Vaught said, "But like Ricky said, where are the facts? Other than those files Monarch says the Chinese agent found in the triad leader's office, what links the Moon Dragon to gambling? I know he's an organized crime boss, but does he have any direct links?

And is he connected with enough people in Beijing to make this change happen any time soon?"

"I promise I'll come back to those questions, Ricky," the Secretary of State replied. "But before I answer them, there are three other strong reasons to believe that the SOP movement was nothing but a violent sham orchestrated by the Moon Dragon for his own ends. The first is that before I was taken to be executed, and before Monarch and SEAL Team Six arrived to save the day, I clearly heard Ramelan arguing because a dozen or more men who'd been part of the hijacking left during the night, and because someone told Ramelan to release me and the ministers, and to flee the area."

"But we saw it, Agnes," her husband said. "That man tried to kill you."

"Ramelan didn't like the order," she replied. "He was a fanatic, like the dead fanatics in Egypt, Panama, India, and China. I think he was supposed to be a showpiece, supporting the concept of the Sons of Prophecy. Who knows? Maybe someone was supposed to kill him and didn't, so he tried to carry through with the executions."

"Who was supposed to kill Ramelan?" Blayless asked in confusion.

Monarch said, "One of Latham's top-flight mercenaries, no doubt. We believe the mercenaries masterminded the attacks and the kidnappings in alliance with selected known radicals they could kill and leave behind to help create the illusion of a vast, highly organized, trained, and equipped terror group."

"Conjecture," Vice President Vaught said. "Flimsy."

"I don't think so, Ken," Secretary Lawton snapped.

"Not when you consider what we're saying in light of two other facts. Someone knew that we were meeting in total secrecy aboard the *Niamey*. Otherwise Ramelan would not have known where to find us. And someone also alerted people at Clark Air Base that Monarch was arriving."

"What are you saying?" Blayless said, looking unnerved.

"Exactly what Secretary Lawton was blinking to us in Morse code on those Sons of Prophecy videos," said Dr. Hopkins, moving toward her a few steps.

"Blinking in Morse code?" Admiral Shipman said, impressed. "What were you saying, Agnes?"

"Traitor in the White House," she replied.

There was a shocked silence in the room.

"Every one of us knew about Monarch except the attorney general," said Homeland Security director Jameson, nodding to Patricia Black, who had been silent the entire time.

"But none of us knew about your meeting on that ship, Agnes," Elise Peck said. "We were all shocked to learn you'd been taken."

"I'm sure you were," Secretary Lawton replied. "But we believe someone close to the President was in contact with the Moon Dragon nonetheless."

There was another long moment of silence before Vice President Vaught said, "Well, who the hell is it?"

"You'll be happy to know, Ken, that it was one of Senator Burkhardt's strongest supporters," the Secretary of State choked, and then looked miserable and grief-stricken as she sobbed. "It was my husband, Bill."

45

BILL LAWTON TOOK THE accusation as a slap to the face. Like a turtle that's been poked, his head retreated and he stepped up and back from his wife's wheelchair, his face twisting with shock, "What? What are you saying, Agnes?"

The Secretary of State stopped her sobbing, looked her husband in the eye, and said, "You were the only one who could have known I was to be on that ship. I don't know what you saw, or how. But you're the only one who also knew about Monarch."

Lawton's shock turned to earnest concern and he studied his wife of nearly thirty years. "You're accusing me based on that? How do you know that someone at State . . ." He looked at the President. "With all due respect, sir, I think my wife needs to be seen by a neurosurgeon. This is all—"

A door to the Oval Office opened. Fred Riggs, the

director of the FBI, entered solemnly. Lawton gaped at him, then looked incredulously at the President. "You can't be seri . . ." He gazed at his wife in disbelief, said, "Agnes? You know this isn't true. Why would I throw away thirty years of—?"

"Marriage?" she said. "Your life? My thinking is you decided that a bribe of a billion or whatever the Moon Dragon offered you was simply worth the risk. That's what makes it so crushing."

"What risk?" Lawton looked at everyone in the room as if he'd been thrust into a film devoid of logic. "I don't know what she's talking about. I didn't know about the ship until the President informed me. I have never met anyone called the Moon Dragon. You are listening to someone who almost had her head chopped off with a machete less than twenty-four hours ago. This is insane!"

"The Secretary of State is not insane, Mr. Lawton," said Attorney General Parker. "She showed us compelling evidence."

"Compelling?" Lawton snarled. "Of what? This is bullshit!"

The attorney general looked at Gloria Barnett and nodded. Barnett said, "I've spent the past ten hours going through the computer files we copied from the Moon Dragon's home office. He seemed to back up his drives there and from an office of an import/export company he owned in Kowloon. In those files, I was able to identify and track sixty different business entities that the Moon Dragon was involved with legally."

"Was my name there?" Lawton demanded.

"Well, no," Barnett said.

"Then this discussion is over," Lawton said, growing furious.

"One of those business entities was called Changes Ltd.," Barnett went on. "Changes is a Hong Kong company that made a quiet, but significant investment in the Xanadu Casino and Hotel, which recently opened in Macau. Another of the significant investors in the Xanadu was Proud Tower, a Nevada LLC, a shell corporation owned by another shell company, and several more. Ultimately, however, I figured out the companies belonged to Mr. Carson Richtel, the Vegas casino mogul. According to your wife, Mr. Lawton, you and Mr. Richtel have done quite a bit of business in the last ten years, isn't that right?"

"I have had the honor of helping Carson negotiate the labyrinth of the Washington bureaucracy, as I have with dozens of clients," Lawton said. "And nothing more."

He glared at his wife. "Agnes, I have zero knowledge of that Macau investment. Ask Richtel. He'll tell you the same thing."

"You're the only one who could have done this," she said again, sadly.

Lawton stood there a moment like a man Monarch had seen get kicked by a mule, head swaying from side to side before he threw up his hands and said, "Fine. I'm not saying another thing. I want to talk to my attorney. I'll see you all in court. And believe me, when I'm exonerated I will be suing each and every one of you, including you, Agnes, for this complete defamation of my character."

He walked toward FBI director Riggs, and said, "No need for handcuffs. And I'd appreciate it if I can have a cigarette before you take me wherever it is you're taking me."

Riggs shrugged, said, "Sure, Bill. That can be arranged."

They left without another word.

The President and many others in the room looked doubtful for the first time. "You're sure about this, Agnes?" Sand asked.

"As sure as a wife can be," she replied, breaking down again. "You'll find more evidence somewhere. And who knows what this Moon Dragon might tell us."

"I know why he did it," said Vice President Vaught, with vigor and awe in his voice, and suddenly looking like a new man. "Bill Lawton was one of Sandy Burkhardt's biggest fund-raisers, a paid consultant. He didn't do this for money. He was swinging the election his candidate's way! The strategy was ingenious. Cause a global crisis, pin it on the administration and so me, play it as proof of our inability to act. Lawton even got you, Mr. President, to let him on the inside of the crisis, where he could get up-to-the minute intelligence. Brilliant. And totally corrupt."

Vaught did not wait for a response, just headed for the same door Riggs and Lawton had exited through.

"Where are you going, Ken?" Sand demanded.

"To the White House briefing room," he said. "I've got a story to tell."

"You're not to talk about this until we can—" the President began.

"Fuck you, Bobby," Vaught said over his shoulder. "Try and stop me from saving my campaign with what I know and I will shout cover-up from the Truman balcony and cause the biggest constitutional crisis this country has ever seen."

He slammed the door behind him.

Chief of Staff Blayless said, "Sir? Secret Service?"

Sand threw up his hands, and shook his head. "All I can say is God help the country if that self-centered son of a bitch gets elected because of this."

"Mr. President?" Admiral Shipman said. "What do you want us to do?"

The President went back to his seat behind the Roosevelt desk, saying, "I want you to tell the truth when the time comes, Admiral. Exactly what happened, what was said, how I acted. All of you. Let history judge the entire affair."

"For the record, I think you'll turn out fine, Bobby," Secretary Lawton said. "You can't be judged for my husband's actions, whatever drove them. I suppose we'll find out soon enough."

The President turned to look at Monarch, who'd been a quiet observer the past few minutes. "The nation thanks you. I thank you."

Monarch smiled, accepting the praise, but then said, "I kept up my end of our contract."

Sand looked confused for several moments before saying, "Oh, yes, of course. What was it?"

"Fifteen million."

"You paid fifteen million dollars to get me back?" Lawton said, impressed.

"Worth every penny," the President said, then looked to his chief of staff and CIA director Hopkins. "We still have a slush fund for this kind of thing, don't we?"

"Several, sir," Hopkins said. "Wire or check?"

"Wire," Monarch said. "But right now, Mr. President, I need sleep a lot more than I do money."

"Of course," the President said, shaking his hand and then Barnett's.

Monarch and Barnett said good-bye to Secretary Lawton, who assured them that she would be fine and that the President had arranged for Marine One to take her to Bethesda Naval Hospital for a complete examination.

"I came in that way," Monarch said. "Very nice ride."

They left the White House with Dr. Hopkins, who led them through a series of hallways and staircases to a garage below the Old Executive Office Building. Bill Lawton was standing there outside a black car with FBI director Riggs and several men Monarch assumed were his agents. Lawton smoked and stared bullets at Monarch and Barnett as they passed.

Monarch stared right back, surprised when Lawton's face suddenly contorted. The Secretary of State's husband bent over double as if gut shot, dropping the cigarette and falling to the ground where he began to convulse violently.

In the mayhem that ensued, as they tried to keep Lawton alive, Monarch was baffled by this turn of events. But it wasn't until Lawton's body stopped quivering and died that he realized what was happening.

He turned to Dr. Hopkins, and said, "I'd be contacting the Chinese if I were you."

46

THE MOON DRAGON LAY in a bed surrounded by beeping monitors. He had no idea of the time or even the day. But he knew exactly where he was, and where he'd been since a government surgeon repaired his leg. He was in a cell/hospital room in the subbasement of a twenty-eight-story building on Lung Wui Road near Victoria Harbor.

The triad leader had driven and walked past the building hundreds if not thousands of time in the course of his life. Before reunification, it had been called the Prince of Wales Building. Today it was home to the Chinese People's Liberation Army garrison.

Drifting in and out of consciousness, his leg throbbing in pain, Long Chan-Juan wondered how long it would be until the PLA investigators came to talk. He wondered if he'd be sharp enough when they inevitably came to question him, whether he might be able to dope out what they knew and what they didn't, and then barter his way into some kind of leniency. He'd demanded a lawyer, but they'd ignored him, and called him a "traitor" before throwing him into this little black room.

Treason. Was there such a thing as leniency when you're guilty of betraying your country? The triad leader doubted it. Especially when the charge was coupled with his extensive organized crime activities, and the high number of lives lost across the spectrum of the plot. But then again, the Moon Dragon knew many things about the Sons of Prophecy, things that just might get him a shot at living out his days in a cushy prison cell rather than dying at the end of a hangman's rope, or shot by some firing squad, or left to expire in the dark like this.

The triad leader's thoughts arced painfully from questions of fate to stark images of reality. His wife lay dead on the shards of the turtle shell. Lo-Lo walked away from him. Though he felt shattered by his wife's death, and by the destruction of the shell, that last look he'd had of his grandson holding on to his mother's hand broke his heart. He'd loved the boy more than life itself and now Lo-Lo was gone. Forever.

The lights in the room blazed on. Throwing up his forearm to shield his eyes, Long Chan-Juan saw a man in a PLA uniform devoid of insignia and rank looking in at him sympathetically.

"We're moving you."

"Where?" the triad leader said. "I want to see an attorney. I have rights."

"Not in this building you don't," the man said simply.

He came around the back of the bed, kicked off some wheel locks, and began pushing the bed out of the room. "Where are we going?" the Moon Dragon demanded.

"A shower sound good?"

A shower sounded incredible. Maybe things were better than he thought. He said, "Can you give me anything for the pain?"

The man blinked, nodded, and reached into his pocket. Coming up with several capsules, he handed them to the Moon Dragon along with a warm bottle of water. He put them in his mouth and swallowed them down.

"What do I call you?" the triad leader asked, trying to look back at the man now pushing him down a hallway.

"My name is not important."

"Are you PLA? Or MSS?"

"Consider me your nurse," he said, directing Long's bed through a door into a locker room of sorts, with a gang shower at the far end.

Nurse? What did that mean? Maybe things really were looking up. Maybe they'd realized what he'd been up to: trying to shake China up so bad they'd open the mainland to gambling. Maybe that sounded like a good idea to Beijing after all, an unlimited budget for their army, and they want to make sure I'm okay.

The nurse got some plastic wrap and covered the cast around the Moon Dragon's lower leg, handed him crutches, and then helped him up. Long swooned a little.

"You okay to do this by yourself?"

The triad leader nodded. "Yes. I think so."

"Pull that cord when you're done," the nurse said. "And we'll try to get you some real food."

The nurse put towels and a clean hospital gown on a bench near the shower and left, saying, "There's no other way out of this room. I'll be outside."

The triad leader nodded, watched the nurse go out, and heard the lock thrown. As he stripped out of the hospital gown, he thought: a shower, real food, pain-killers, they think I have something big to tell them.

Long actually did have something big he could tell them. Having that kind of card in your back pocket is always the best policy. The Moon Dragon felt his confidence grow as he stepped into the ice cold shower. It was shocking and bracing and he felt renewed and reinvigorated when he at last climbed out, dried off, and put on the new gown.

He pulled the cord. The door opened. The nurse came, changed the sheets, and helped him back into the bed. They were moving again, but the triad leader was not curious about his destination. The drugs were starting to seal him off from pain and solid thinking. They rolled him into a very nice room with a gleaming wooden floor, white walls, and soft lighting. At the center of the room was a table with several plates of food under metal covers.

The nurse scooped him a plate of saffron rice, Peking duck, and several remarkably good dumplings filled with spicy pork and shrimp. Long was surprised. The garrison food was as good as any restaurant he knew of in Kowloon, or all of Hong Kong for that matter.

"Thank you," he said when the nurse came for the platter.

"Good, isn't it?"

"Remarkably good."

"Tea?"

"Please."

The nurse left the room carrying the dishes. The Moon Dragon felt pleasantly heavy in his stomach, and pleasantly heavy in his brain. His leg wasn't even on his mind as he flashed on his very young self, no more than six, Lo-Lo's age, when his family's desperation had been constant and he'd hung out the window of the squalid one-room apartment they lived in, looking down on the fantasy streets of Kowloon, promising that he'd steal every dream, that he'd own all of—

The door swung open, but it wasn't the nurse who carried the tea tray.

Song Le set the tray on the table, and walked up beside him. Her face was still bandaged in several places. There seemed to be no anger or malice in her when she said, "How are you, father-in-law?"

The Moon Dragon didn't know what to say, so he simply said, "I've been better."

"You're wondering why I am here?" she asked.

He nodded.

"Professional courtesy," she said. "I asked to speak with you before I left for Beijing."

He pondered that, said, "It was my wife. She hated

you, blamed you for Jin's death. She convinced me that taking Lo-Lo from you was the best thing for the boy."

Song Le placed a thin white bag of tea leaves in a pot and poured boiling water into it. "I must admit that you have raised him well, Long Chan-Juan," she said, and set the cover on the pot. "Lo-Lo is smart, polite, and he says he still loves you, and wonders if he'll ever see you again."

The Moon Dragon's eyes welled. He didn't know what to say. He hung his head rather than let her see the tears that dripped down his cheeks. "Tell him I love him, too, and I wish I could take him fishing on the rocks out on Lamma Island."

Song Le picked up the pot and poured tea into the two porcelain cups. She held out one to him. Long wiped away the tears with his sleeve, saw the cup, flashed on dark memories from his recent past and peered at it suspiciously.

"You think it's poisoned or something?" the Chinese agent said.

"The thought occurred to me."

"It's not."

He shrugged, made no move to take the cup. She drank from it, and then offered the other cup. He thought about it, shook his head. "I'm fine."

She drank from the second cup, gazed at him with a neutral expression, and said, "I'm trying to help you."

"Why would you help me?"

"It's my job. Are you ready to talk about the Sons of Prophecy? All of it?"

"What do I get in return?"

"A deal of some sort, I suppose."

He thought about that, resigned himself to his fate, and nodded. "I'd have to see the terms. But I think I know things that will be of great value to Beijing."

"We assumed that to be the case, that's why you're being treated so well," Song Le said, getting to her feet so she could look down at her father-in-law, who was watching her like a card player holding a winning hand.

"Very valuable," he said. "You'll understand the whole conspiracy."

"But that's the point, Long Chan-Juan. Forces far more powerful than you don't want me or anybody else to understand the whole thing. Ever."

The Moon Dragon's confidence cracked. "But . . . but I know things."

With little sympathy, she said, "And that's why you must die."

"No," he said too quickly. "I can—"

"It's too late," she said flatly. "That water you drank and those pain pills? They contained enough blood pressure medicine, narcotics and amphetamines to cause a heart attack or a stroke." She checked her watch. "It shouldn't be long. Another few minutes or so."

The triad leader felt his heart race. Was that real? Was it just a reaction to what she was saying?

"You're lying," he said. "You're trying to get me to talk and I said I'll talk."

She smiled icily, said, "You should have known your American friend likes to keep things tidy, no loose ends that might come back to haunt him."

"My American friend?" Long said, even as his face

flushed and then prickled and stung as if he'd been swimming and gotten into jellyfish.

His stomach turned leaden and upset, but his heart went from a trot, to a canter, and then on into full gallop. A sensation in his left arm began to spiral and radiate. Heart attack! he thought, and began to panic, and tried to reach for his chest, which felt ready to explode.

The Moon Dragon gazed up at his daughter-in-law, raised his right hand, and croaked, "Please, stop this. Help me. For Lo-Lo's sake."

"Never," Song Le said, and watched over him for the next few minutes, taking grim satisfaction as her late husband's father took his last breath and died.

47

MONARCH SAT IN A Dulles Airport bar, nursing a cold Sam Adams, and waiting to board a flight to San Diego where John Tatupu and Chanel Chavez were recovering from their wounds at Balboa Naval Hospital. He'd talked to both of them, and they'd assured him that they were sore, but fine, and that he didn't need to come, that the paycheck was what mattered. He ignored them and booked a flight.

Ordering a second beer, he watched the news, which pulsated with reporters tripping over themselves trying to explain all that had happened in the last twenty-eight hours. Vice President Vaught's impromptu speech to the nation yesterday revealed Bill Lawton's involvement in a bizarre plot to kidnap his own wife in order to swing the electorate to his candidate, Senator Burkhardt. Vaught charged corruption at the highest levels of his opponent's party. He accused the senator himself of "fomenting treason." And when word of Bill Lawton's death came, the Vice President charged Burkhardt with complicity in a homicidal cover-up.

The White House and Justice Department supported many of Vaught's claims. The news electrified the country, and swept across the political landscape with the power of a category five hurricane. Senator Burkhardt's supporters had immediately started howling "foul" and "slander." But the critical damage had been done.

Virtually every newscast Monarch had seen so far that day was predicting that Vice President Vaught had not only risen from the dead, it appeared he was about to win the election by a firm margin.

"You really *do* know how to shake things up," said Gloria Barnett, who slid onto a bar stool beside him.

"You're not so bad at it yourself," he said, smiling and tilting his beer bottle at her. "Fetching outfit by the way."

She looked down at a black pantsuit, heels, and a teal-colored blouse that set off her eyes. "I think I look like a big bright bird."

"Big, bright, beautiful bird," Monarch said. "Back to Chiang Mai?"

"After San Diego," she said. "Buenos Aires?"

"I probably won't get there for a couple of weeks," he said. "I'm going back to Hong Kong after San Diego, make sure Anna, the maid, is taken care of, and to arrange for an operation for her cleft palate."

"And to see Song Le?"

He shook his head. "She told me she's heading to

her father's house. He's evidently old and she wants him to see his grandson again. From Hong Kong, I'll head on to Delhi. I want to see the bombing site and find the Indian agent Bashir."

"Why?"

"Bash was good," he said. "Real good. I'm interested in recruiting him if need be. And the bombing site? I don't know really. If I could go to the ghost town in China I would, but I don't think I could get in there, even with Song Le's help. I just need to see it all for myself, to try to make sense of it all."

"Order me a lemon martini in the meantime. I've got to use the ladies' room."

Barnett slid off the stool and crossed out of the bar, looking indeed like a big, bright, wading bird. He ordered her drink, and another beer, and thought about Buenos Aires. He loved the city where he'd first learned his trade, from the slums to the fancy neighborhoods. It would be late spring, almost summer, by the time he got back. He would see old friends. There would be flowers blooming at the Hogar de Espera, the Refuge of Hope, Sister Rachel's orphanage in the foothills. He flashed on the good and decent face of Sister Rachel, imagining her shock and joy when he gave her this check, bigger than any before.

With the third beer, however, his brain suddenly sought grittier memories. There was Archie Latham as he died in the water off Pattaya. There was Ramelan's head almost cut off. He considered all the other men who'd died around him in the last ten days. Feeling suddenly heavy, morose, he thought: Face it, Monarch, you call yourself a thief, but sometimes you're nothing but an assassin.

He wondered whether giving most of the money he earned to Sister Rachel and helping people like Anna somehow balanced things out there in the universe, and in the eyes of God. He doubted it, and that bothered him. Though he would lie, cheat, steal, or kill to get his way, Monarch still thought of himself as a fairly noble person with remarkable skills out there trying to right wrongs and do good. But who was he kidding? Right?

Barnett slid back onto the stool, murmuring in his ear. "Dr. Hopkins just called. The Moon Dragon's dead. He had a heart attack while in PLA custody. And Lawton's cigarette? It had cyanide in it. Evidently Riggs is extremely embarrassed about the incident. He checked out the cigarette himself before letting Lawton light it."

That brought Monarch out of his funk. "So both committed suicide?"

"The Chinese are saying Long's heart attack was legit. He had a history of heart problems. High blood pressure. And the operation on his leg was tough."

A voice called their flight over the intercom. Pushing away the beer while Barnett guzzled her drink, he threw cash on the bar.

"I don't believe the heart attack story for a minute," Monarch said as they hurried toward the gate. "Someone's cleaning house."

"The SOP?"

"I don't know what that means, to tell you the truth. But I can't help feeling like there's some overlord or overlord group at work here, puppet masters pulling strings for reasons . . . ?"

"What?" she asked.

He didn't answer, staying silent until they'd taken their seats in first class.

"What were you thinking back there?" Barnett asked quietly.

Monarch shrugged. "I guess it really doesn't matter, does it? All these unanswered questions. Our job was simple: find and rescue Secretary Lawton. We did it. We got paid. Our job is done. I'm going on a vacation and a philanthropic spending spree. You're going to work on your energy and ride elephants. End of story."

"Well, we deserve it, Robin," Barnett said. "And sooner or later, with five countries investigating, they'll figure out who was behind the Sons of Prophecy."

"Maybe," Monarch replied, closing his eyes. "But I know for a fact that some secrets just stay buried."

48

AMID A SUBDUED CROWD of guests, Beauregard Arsenault watched the election returns on six different large screens hung about the ballroom of the plantation-style mansion he and his wife had so carefully and expensively restored outside New Orleans. A big man, with a big appetite for life, and affable boyish looks despite his fifty-nine years, Arsenault shrugged, and drained the last of the Maker's Mark bourbon from his glass.

"You don't seem that upset, Beau," his wife, Louisa, said, pulling his attention off the screens where ABC was already hinting that they would call the election soon after the West Coast polls closed. The anchors were trying to keep alive the possibility that Senator Burkhardt would survive to make it a real race, but given the reaction of the pundits who were backing the senator, it was all over, and they were just waiting for the fat lady to sing.

"Beau?"

Arsenault gazed at his beloved wife of thirty years, a dark-eyed beauty from Shreveport who looked twenty years younger than her real age and rather amazing in a tight gray dress despite bearing him five children and becoming a grandmother three times over. He sometimes wondered if Louisa had a portrait of herself in an attic somewhere that showed her real age.

"What can we do about it, sweet pie?" he asked, shrugging again. "Can't just shut the doors and pout when things don't go your way. We'll move on as we always have. We'll rebuild just like we did here after Katrina."

She sighed, looked around at the party. "Well then, we're hosting a wake."

"We'll make it an Irish one then," he said, trying to sound upbeat. "Tell the waiters to offer everyone another drink, and a free ride home if they've had—"

Arsenault stopped, feeling his cell phone buzz in his pocket. He pulled it out, looked at caller ID. "I've got to take this."

"Beau, really?"

"It's Agnes Lawton," he said. "What do you want me to do, ignore her?"

"No, no," she said, sympathetically. "Of course. Just don't do it in here."

Arsenault turned and answered the call on the fourth and last buzz. "Agnes," he said. "How can I be of service?"

"Beau?" she said.

"Hold on a second, won't you, until I can get somewhere quiet?"

"Sure," she said, and he thought he caught a choke in her voice.

Crossing a foyer outside the ballroom, Arsenault climbed a sweeping circular staircase to the second floor. He went into his office, shut the door, and sat in a favorite leather club chair.

"Agnes," he began. "I can't imagine what you're going through."

"I'm sorry, I just wanted to call and thank you, Beau. You and Louisa are among the few old friends who've contacted me to express their sympathy."

"What else could we do?" he replied. "Louisa and I would never turn our backs on someone who's been a dear friend for twenty-five years because of something she had no control over."

There was a quaver in the Secretary of State's voice, when she said, "Bill wasn't the man I knew, Beau. I just can't . . ."

"I can't either," Arsenault said with deep empathy. "I haven't slept a bit since I heard the news. Bill Lawton? Treason? It's unthinkable. And to put you in harm's way like that? I'm baffled."

"Do you know Carson Richtel?" she asked.

"I know who he is, but I've never had the pleasure," Arsenault said. "Then again, I don't do gambling. Never have."

"Did Bill ever mention him?"

"Richtel?" he replied. "Can't say that he did. Why?"

"It looks like Ritchel was the link to this organized crime figure in Hong Kong," she said. "The FBI is raiding Richtel's offices as we speak."

Arsenault said, "The world has lost its mind. What can Louisa and I do? Anything at all, Agnes. We are here for you."

There was a pause before the Secretary of State answered with raw emotion: "No matter what he did, Bill Lawton was my husband."

"Course he was."

"And the father of my boys."

"And the grandfather of how many?"

"Six now," she said, and he could tell she was crying. "The point is, I have to honor him no matter what he did."

"It's the right thing to do," Arsenault said.

"Would you, Beau, could you, speak at a private memorial service we're holding for him?"

"Agnes, it would be my great honor. When and where?"

"Next week sometime, once things have died down a little."

"Louisa and I will be there," he promised.

She wept for several moments, and then said, "Thank you, Beau. I knew you'd stand with us."

"Never a hesitation," he replied. "Do you have someone there with you?"

"I'm at Bethesda still," she said. "And the boys are here."

"Send them my condolences."

"I'll call once I know more details."

"Anytime," Arsenault said. "Day or night. You know that."

"Thank you, Beau."

"My great pleasure, Agnes," he said, and hung up.

Arsenault got a cigar from the humidor, went out the doors to a balcony. He lit the cigar, puffed on it, and leaned on the iron railing, looking out into the Louisiana night, listening to the muffled noise from the ballroom play against the hoot of owls and the cry of coyotes out there in the woods toward the swamp. He knew Louisa would soon come in search of him, or send someone, but he had just a few loose ends to wrap up. He got out a burn phone from another pocket and punched in a number he knew by heart.

"Riggs," the FBI director said.

"Beau."

Pause. "I thought we had an agreement."

"We did and do," Arsenault said. "I just wanted to commend you for so brilliantly dealing with our problem, and to tell you I am coming to Washington to eulogize Bill Lawton on Agnes's behalf next week."

There was a pause. "You are one cold sonofabitch."

"Seems it takes one to know one."

Riggs said, "Right." The line clicked dead.

"Papa Beau?" a reedy boy's voice said behind Arsenault. "Big Mama says you need to come downstairs and tend to your guests."

Arsenault turned to see his nine-year-old grandson, his oldest daughter's boy, wearing a jacket and a tie, tugged open at the collar. He grinned, opened his arms. "Little Beau, where you been hiding from your granddaddy?"

"I was with the others down on the dock," he said, hugging Arsenault back.

"Well, I know better than to keep Big Mama waiting," Arsenault said and kissed the boy on the cheek. He was about to follow him out when his burn phone rang. Phones, he decided, were the bane of his existence.

But when he checked the caller ID, he recognized the number. He answered, said, "Hold, please."

He looked at his grandson. "Go tell Big Mama, I'm almost done here. I promise."

"She's gonna be mad."

"I would expect so," he said, and winked at him.

The boy hesitated, then grinned and ran back into his grandfather's office. Arsenault waited until he heard the door slam before answering, "How can I be of service?"

"You can tell me we're done," said Song Le.

"Deal's a deal," Arsenault replied. "I told you, you just might be surprised if this thing turned out the way I thought it might."

She sounded murderous, when she asked, "How long did you know?"

"About your boy?" Arsenault said. "Thirteen, maybe fourteen months. I was actually hoping that if you did manage to find him, you might do me the favor of ending our mutual friend's life. And there we are. Foresight!"

"I never want to hear from you again," she said.

"Done," Arsenault said. "Go off and raise your boy to be a man his father would have been proud of. You've got enough money now. I think I've more than adequately compensated you for your services."

There was a pause before Song Le said, "How do I know you won't decide I am a loose end?"

"Because you're not," Arsenault replied. "If you talked about me, you'd be sealing your fate, and orphaning Lo-Lo. And you would never let that happen, now would you?"

"Good-bye then," she said, and hung up.

Arsenault dropped the cell phone on the floor of the balcony and crushed it with the heel of his hand-tooled cowboy boot. He'd get someone to clean up the mess in the morning. Stubbing out the cigar and returning to his office, Arsenault was thinking that, all tolled, and the election aside, it had been a brilliantly conceived and executed plan. A hugely profitable one as well.

Beau Arsenault was a brilliant investor and business mogul, with vast holdings in everything from shipping to railroads, steel, and oil. Two weeks ago, he'd been worth roughly six billion dollars.

He'd spent sixty-three million and change to fund the attacks in China, India, Panama, and Egypt. Using a wide variety of financial tools and third-party players, he'd placed massive bets in the weeks leading up to the attacks, knowing they would create chaos and fear in the markets, which in turn would profit anyone who'd had the foresight to act appropriately.

Appropriately? Except for the election, Arsenault thought he'd played the game to near perfection. He'd waited until this afternoon, until shortly before Wall Street closed, to unwind most of his short investments. He'd taken every bit of that money and rolled it back into a broad array of equities. If he was right, and he nearly almost always was, then his net worth would double at least, and possibly triple in the weeks ahead.

He smiled. Now that's how you did business. And who knew, if the Chinese did act the way the Moon Dragon believed they would, perhaps he'd invest in gambling for the first time.

For a moment, Beau Arsenault considered the ghost of Long Chan-Juan and his old chum, Bill Lawton, whom he'd known since their days at Yale. A lobbyist for years, Lawton had been a valuable contact in Washington, someone who'd performed many delicate tasks for Arsenault over the years. Lawton did that kind of thing for a lot of people. Three years before, during a trip to Macau with the gambling mogul Carson Richtel, Lawton met with investors in the Xanadu Casino, including the Moon Dragon, who had a shrewd take on the future of gambling in Asia. Richtel had dismissed the idea out of hand.

But Lawton had been intrigued by the analysis, and so had Arsenault, who had been growing increasingly concerned about the state of affairs in the world's three biggest economies. Hearing Long Chan-Juan's ideas, especially that a drop in the real estate market coupled with an internal rebellion would force mainland China to allow casino gambling in order to get revenues to build up the military.

The billionaire had played with the idea. It soon occurred to him that the appearance of a thing is often as powerful as the real thing. Why couldn't there be the appearance of a rebellion? It would create the same result. Out of that understanding came the realization that he could be in a position to profit gigantically if he had the audacity to shake things up, to make events seem larger and more threatening than they actually were.

Late one night two years before, and well into a bottle of Maker's Mark, he'd talked with Bill Lawton about his thinking, and his old friend had been supportive. In fact, it had been Lawton's idea to create the appearance of a terrorist organization at the heart of the plot.

"That's brilliant," Arsenault had said. "I'll give you a billion dollars if you're the front man, putting it together."

"Make it two," Lawton said, laughing it off.

"Two, then."

Lawton had set his glass down. "You're serious?"

"We're only here once. Why not roll the dice, and make the big play? Or do you want to live in your wife's shadow the rest of your days?"

The billionaire had known his old college friend had a chip on his shoulder about Agnes's success, and thought the jab might do the trick. It did.

"I'm in," Lawton said.

They met dozens of times in secret, refining the scope of the plot. Arsenault hired detectives to investigate the Moon Dragon. He learned in the process about Long's grandson, and Song Le and the way the boy had been taken and hidden from her. It made Arsenault despise Long Chan-Juan. A boy should be with his mother, after all. But he didn't have to admire a man to use him.

Lawton used his contacts in Beijing to track down Song Le, who'd established a reputation as one of the

Ministry of State Security's most valuable investigators. One night at a restaurant in Shanghai, Lawton used intermediaries to approach Song Le as she ate. They told her that they represented powerful men in China and the rest of the world, and these men wanted her to work for them.

She'd refused and denied she was even with the MSS, until the men suggested that her son might still be alive. When she'd demanded to know where, they'd told her someone would be in contact soon. Arsenault had called her anonymously on a burn phone three nights later, told her that he believed her son was alive, and that a time would come when he would need her. If she performed well, she'd be paid handsomely and given all the information he had on her not-so-dead son.

From that point on, as Arsenault continued to game and anticipate every possible counter action, he let Lawton do the heavy lifting. For a time the task seemed daunting, impossible. But then the Moon Dragon found Archie Latham, and from there on it had been largely a series of logistical challenges and payments from offshore accounts to accrue the necessary manpower and weaponry.

In September, Lawton told Arsenault about a secret meeting his wife was going to have with the Chinese and Indians aboard a ship shortly before the election. At first, Arsenault had thought it foolhardy to attempt something so radical. But when he learned that the diplomats were to meet aboard the *Niamey*—one of his own ships—he couldn't resist.

Arsenault and Lawton had listened to the radio traffic from the attack on the *Niamey* over an Internet link. Hearing the gunfire, Lawton had almost panicked, but Arsenault kept him cool until they got the word that Agnes Lawton and the others had been taken safely.

Getting Song Le involved after the attacks had required three phone calls from Lawton to a contact in Beijing who knew her superiors. Once activated, Arsenault had called Song Le, told her to keep him abreast of the investigation. She had, delivering reports to him from Vietnam, Malaysia, Thailand, and Hong Kong.

Through it all, except for Lawton, no one knew his identity. The Moon Dragon referred to him as his "friend." Latham had no idea who Beau Arsenault was. Neither did Tengku, the Indonesian fence. Not one of the fifty paid mercenaries who'd been part of the plot had a clue as to his existence. Even Song Le had been talking to a drawling voice in the void.

The only one who had known everything was Bill Lawton. Arsenault felt genuinely sad. Bill had been a great friend, a powerful ally, and a go-between of remarkable intelligence, creativity, and discretion. Arsenault mourned his old confidant. He really did. He would miss their plotting. But what would Bill have expected him to do? He had to have known.

Arsenault sat there in his office a long moment, thinking about Bill, and then putting him out of his mind. Life was for the living.

The billionaire knew he should go downstairs to commiserate with his guests about the election loss, but there was one thing still bothering him, something, or someone, he'd never anticipated in his wildest dreams.

Arsenault went to his computer and called up a growing file about Robin Monarch. He stared at a picture of the man when he was a Special Forces operator in Afghanistan. He dwelled on various details of Monarch's biography, the murder of his parents, his life in a slum gang, his strange route to the U.S. military, and his exploits there and with the CIA.

As a rule, the billionaire was scared of no man. He believed he was smarter than anyone on the planet, especially when it came to the big picture and how best to exploit it for his own ends.

But this thief, he thought, he could be a problem. Arsenault had nothing concrete to base the feeling on, but Monarch clearly made him nervous. He wondered for a moment whether he should make some calls, get Monarch taken care of before he somehow became a nuisance much less a threat.

A knock came at the door. Arsenault's grandson, Little Beau, entered again, and said, "Papa Beau, Big Mama says she's getting madder than a hornet's nest in a lightning storm, and you better put me to bed and get downstairs."

The billionaire grinned, shut off the computer, and scooped his grandson up his arms, saying, "Well, I guess I'd better then. There's nothing worse than a hornet's nest in a lightning storm."

"Big Mama is," Little Beau said, and his grandfather laughed and kissed him.

"Love you, Little Beau," Arsenault said.

"Love you, too, Papa Beau," the boy replied.

He rested his head on Arsenault's shoulder when his grandfather carried him to his room. As he tucked the boy under the covers, turned out the light, and shut the door, one part of Arsenault felt all warm inside. But the bigger part of him couldn't shake the sense that the thief was out there somewhere, curious, and sniffing about.

That dog won't hunt, Arsenault thought, and came to a quick decision. The world would be a much safer place without Robin Monarch in it.

He'd see to that in the morning.

Read on for an excerpt of the next thrilling
adventure of Robin Monarch—

THIEF

Coming this fall from Minotaur Books

THE THUNDERSTORMS BEGAN LATE that afternoon and continued on into the night, turning the streets to oozing mud in the slums.

Around nine-thirty that evening, the fourth wave swept over Villa Miserie, the worst slum in the city, and drummed down on the steel roof of a small medical clinic. Inside, a missionary and physician named Sister Rachel Diego del Mar had been up for nearly nineteen hours, and she felt woozy. Inez, the night nurse, sat in a rocker, a baby in her arms. Sister Rachel told the nurse that she was going to clean up and get some sleep.

"Yes, Sister," Inez said. "You sleep all night. I'll be right here."

After showering and changing into a fresh set of scrubs, she let down her long silver hair and tied it in a loose ponytail. Then she headed to her office at the rear of the clinic.

Then Sister Rachel heard a floorboard creak and twisted left. A big man with a goatee was already upon her. He wore a black stocking wool cap pulled down over his ears. There was a small camera mounted on a harness strapped to the cap. Before she could scream, he clamped a hand across her mouth and jabbed her in the neck with a syringe.

In seconds the room swam toward darkness.

But before she passed out, she heard him say, "Let's see if you can save Robin Monarch this time around."

Greenwich, Connecticut

This was the kind of job Robin Monarch loved. The stakes were high, but if he succeeded, the tycoon would be in no position to complain to anyone official.

The thief felt confident as he pulled the Rover up to the valet. He'd done his research. He knew his target, its location, and his method of entry. But in this sort of setting, with several hundred people mingling inside a grand home, things would be fluid. He was going to have to adapt.

Tossing the valet the keys with his gloved hands, he strode easily up the heated walkway, heading toward massive carved oak doors.

From beyond the doors came Christmas music, a beautiful woman's voice singing a soft jazzy rendition of "I Saw Three Ships Come Sailing In."

Before he could knock, the door opened and caught him in a blaze of yuletide light and good cheer. The doorman stood aside, and Monarch stepped inside a foyer that looked like a movie set, including an elevator with a burled walnut door, and a grand spiral staircase with a rail wrapped in fresh cedar ropes, flowing red bows, and pinpoint white lights that glinted like ice crystals falling on a bitter cold morning.

There were fifteen or so people in the foyer, all in evening wear and fine jewels, most of them moving toward a hallway and the ballroom.

"Can I get your name tag?" asked a woman in a light Irish accent.

Two young, pretty women, the Irish redhead and the other an Asian with frosted hair tips, were throwing him winning smiles, and sitting behind a table covered in badges adorned with sprigs of mistletoe.

Monarch tapped the hearing aid, gave her a quick glance at the forged invitation, and said, "Asa Johanson."

"You're the late add then?"

"Is that a bad thing?" Monarch said, affecting chagrin. "The late add?"

"Not at all. You are most welcome, Mr. Johanson. By the way, how do you know Mr. Arsenault?"

"Oh," he said, taking the badge from her. "Beau and I go way back. We used to ski together at Stowe. We ran into each other at a gallery I run in Soho and he insisted on having me out."

"Brilliant," she said. "He'll be thrilled to see you."

"Not as thrilled as I'll be to see him," Monarch replied, winked, and then moved aside as a new batch of the uber-rich arrived wearing enough mink, sable, and chinchilla to cause an emotional meltdown at PETA.

The ballroom ceiling was at least twenty-five feet high and made of embossed copper that picked up the soft light of several hundred electric candles and gas lamps that made the vast space glow as warmly as if the Ghost of Christmas Present were right there. Indeed, there was a strong Dickensian theme to the party. The ballroom had been decorated to resemble a snowy London street, complete with trompe l'oeil paintings of storefronts including Old Fezziwig's and Scrooge & Marley's counting house. And the servers moving food and drink among the guests were dressed for the nineteenth century with top hats and hook skirts.

The irony of a guy like Arsenault using *A Christmas Carol*, the story of a skinflint redeemed, was not lost on Monarch. Worth northward of fourteen billion dollars, Arsenault was utterly ruthless, a polished, and yet callous man who had never sported a callous in his entire life. The mogul rarely gave money to charity, braying often and publicly that fortitude and an enterprising spirit were all that anyone required. No one, in Arsenault's opinion, required a hand out or a hand up.

Arsenault was one of those guys who was born on third base. His father had been a successful oil wildcatter from Louisiana, and his mother came from an old money Connecticut family. Their combined wealth had topped thirty million dollars, which meant their son had spent his childhood moving between a plantation outside New Orleans, the estate in Greenwich, and beachfront cottages on Galveston Island and Nantucket. Beau had been educated at Phillips Exeter, Yale, and Tulane Law School.

When Arsenault was twenty-four, his parents died. Arsenault had left Tulane Law to take control of the family fortune, and in twenty-five years had expanded it exponentially to include everything from oil exploration and shipping to steel, pharmaceuticals, and government contracting. Along the way, he'd become a behind-the-scenes player in politics, spending lavishly in support of candidates who supported his causes.

Despite his stupefying wealth, the mogul liked to hoard physical cash in various currencies, as well as gold coins, jewelry, and bearer bonds as a way of keeping significant sums of undeclared income close at hand. That had gotten the thief thinking that the mogul's illicit stash might help Sister Rachel Diego Del Mar, a physician and missionary who rescued orphans from the slums of Buenos Aires.

So where did a mogul like Arsenault hide his loot?

Using construction plans as well as detailed digital blueprints, the thief was able to study the renovated mansion's layout, including an unlabeled space inside heavily reinforced concrete walls in the basement next to the wine cellar. This was what had brought him to the Christmas party with a forged invitation, a place on the guest list courtesy of the MIT hacker, and a need to grab that empty bourbon glass the mogul had been using.

Monarch snagged the cut-glass tumbler just as a waiter was about to bus it.

"Merry Christmas, Beau and Louisa!" the party crowd roared around the thief, raising their champagne. "And a profitable New Year!"

Arsenault took Louisa in his arms and they began to dance. Monarch glanced at his watch. It was seven-thirty on the dot.

Monarch stood a moment watching the mogul and his wife work the floor as if they were trying out for *Dancing with the Stars.*

With all eyes on the host and hostess, the thief got down to work.

Reaching up behind his left ear, Monarch turned on the hearing aid. Fitting his fingernail beneath the stem of the Patek-Phillip, he tugged it out about a sixteenth of an inch until he felt a click. Then he got hold of the pin that held the sprig of holly to his tux lapel and twisted it counterclockwise.

"Test," Monarch murmured, glancing over at the Arsenaults waltzing.

"Loud and clear," said Gloria Barnett. A tall, bookish, stoop-shouldered woman with wire-rimmed glasses and a shock of flame red hair, she was staying about ten miles away at the Delamar Greenwich Harbor, a discreet five-star hotel.

Monarch said, "Ready?

"Ready and waiting."

The room burst into applause as the mogul and his wife finished their dance and Monarch eased over by one of the Christmas trees set against the ballroom walls, pulled out the bourbon glass, checked it for prints, and found four sharp ones. Getting out the iPhone, Monarch used the macro lens to snap several close-up photos of the prints before setting the glass aside.

Monarch sent pictures, and said, "You should have them."

"Just in," she said. "Give me a few seconds."

"That's all we've got," he replied.

As more guests took to the dance floor, Monarch waited, wondering if the macro lens had picked up the fingerprints, wondering if his night was done, finished, right there, and right—

"We have a match," Barnett said. "It's number two. Repeat. Numeral 2. Index, right hand."

"Got it. Make your call."

"Here we go then," she replied. "Watch him."

Monarch slid out from beside that Christmas tree, and located the Arsenaults still on the dance floor. Arsenault had his hands overhead, cheering and clapping wildly, before Monarch saw the posture of his head change by several sharp degrees. The mogul began to reach into his tux pocket, but his wife's bejeweled hand shot out and stopped him.

Monarch could almost hear her as Louisa scolded her husband for trying to take a business call during the party. The tycoon nodded, acted chastened, and then kissed his wife before heading off, looking as if he were going to mingle with his non-dancing guests.

But Monarch knew better. Arsenault would check the caller ID on the phone once he was out of his wife's sight. It was his private phone, a number known only to a select few, and used rarely and for the most delicate of situations.

After wading through the crowd like a savvy politician, greeting and glad-handing every guest in his way, the mogul exited the ballroom into a broad hallway that ran back toward the foyer. He got out the cell phone. Monarch, watching from afar, saw Arsenault listen to the phone, and then jerk to a stop.

Knew that would get your attention, Monarch thought, suppressing a grin. Arsenault rushed past the thief, heading on a diagonal across the ballroom.

Who you going to for help, Big Beau? Monarch thought, scanning the crowd in front of the mogul, and then spotting his likely target.

With a rectangular build, military posture, and a short, tight haircut, the man had a bull's neck that looked garroted by his tux collar and tie. His name was Billy Saunders. A former Boston cop, FBI agent, and counter-terror specialist, Saunders was among the best security experts that money could buy.

Arsenault gestured Saunders aside and murmured something in his ear. Saunders went on high alert and asked several sharp questions. Saunders hesitated, then nodded and moved off quickly.

Saunders was soon back, with a woman in tow. Late forties, ash blonde, handsome rather than beautiful, and wearing a navy blue business suit, Meg Pratt exuded an air of competence. Pratt was Arsenault's personal attorney, a woman who had to know the closets where the mogul kept his skeletons. She and Saunders nodded at Arsenault as they hurried past him, heading for the only other way out of the ballroom.

"Fish on the hook," Monarch murmured into the small microphone in the boutonniere pin. "Saunders and Pratt too."

"I can be very convincing," Barnett said.

"Well done," Monarch replied, taking a glass of champagne off the tray of a waitress who was happening by.

Arsenault, meanwhile, watched his retreating attorney and security chief, and then pleasantly excused himself from a gaggle of stretched-skin women.

Trailing the tycoon and his aides out into a hallway, Monarch saw the trio pause near the far end of the passage before disappearing through a doorway.

"Looks like our instincts were spot on," Monarch murmured, heading for the nearest toilet. "They're going downstairs."

"Still the three?" Barnett asked.

"Unless there are guards down there," he said.

Fishing in his left pocket, Monarch came up with and put on ultra-sheer latex gloves. Then he got a pack of Rothman cigarettes from his breast pocket.

Carefully, he opened the box, revealing six cigarettes spaced neatly inside. Gaps between the cigarettes held four tiny darts. Three were fitted with miniscule blue fins. The fins of the other were tan. A tube cut and painted to mimic a cigarette was nestled beside them.

Monarch slid one blue dart into that stubby tube taped to his right wrist. The lone tan dart went into the tube on his left wrist. A second blue dart dropped snugly into the fake cigarette. Setting it down, he removed a small container of breath strips.

Opening it, four rectangular plastic strips came out. Finding number 2, which matched Arsenault's right index finger, he laid the print replica across the latex-covered pad of his index finger.

Someone knocked at the door.

"Be right out," he called in a slight slur.

Looking in the mirror, Monarch sagged the muscles of his face, and slid the glasses slightly down his nose while opening his eyes wide as if he were having trouble understanding his predicament. Then he pocketed the Rothman pack, turned his bow tie slightly askew, and snatched up the fake cigarette and the flute of champagne.

A bosomy blonde woman spilling out of a tight, shimmering dress looked at Monarch with a New Yorker's sense of disgusted superiority, and said, "Thought you'd died in there."

"Sorry," Monarch slurred and staggered slightly moving past her.

He proceeded to that door Arsenault and his handlers had gone through. He weaved down the hallway, acting like a man toying with the limits of alcohol consumption.

Abreast of the door, Monarch spotted the optical reading device set at handle height, slowed to a wobbly stop, and pivoted as if he'd realized he was heading in the wrong direction. The hallway behind him was empty except for two women waiting to use the powder room.

Taking a shaky step, Monarch reached out as if to catch his balance, and stabbed his index finger into the reader.

The door sagged.

"In," Monarch said, pushing it open.

"Godspeed, John Glenn," she whispered.

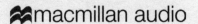